BRUTAL BILLIONAIRE

Hot Alphas. Smart Women. Sexy Stories.

BRUTAL BILLIONAIRE

New York Times Bestselling Author

LAURELIN PAIGE

Editing: Erica Edits

Cover photography: Chris Davis Studios

Cover model: Alex Cannon

Be sure to **sign up for my newsletter** where you'll receive **a FREE book every month** from bestselling authors, only available to my subscribers, as well as up-to-date information on my latest releases.

PRO TIP: Add laurelin@laurelinpaige.com to your contacts before signing up to be sure the list comes right to your inbox.

DID YOU KNOW...

This book is available in both paperback and audiobook editions at all major online retailers! Links are on my website.

If you'd like to order a signed paperback, my online store is open several times a year here.

This book may contain subjects that are sensitive to some readers.
Please visit www.laurelinpaige.com/brutal-billionaire for content warnings. May include spoilers.

I am an only child, but my mother came from a big family like the Sebastians. All those members can be confusing.

To help sort that out, you can find a family tree on my website.

For all those whose feminism leaves their body when a (fictional) alpha male pushes them to their knees and says, "Good girl."

CHAPTER ONE

BRYSTIN

Where the fuck are you? Are you trying to blow this?

I glance at the text, trying not to move too much since Zully is currently applying my eye shadow.

"Michael?" Zully asks with typical disdain. She's never liked Michael and has never made any attempt to hide it. She blames it on her Middle Eastern heritage, claiming that being mouthy is in her genes.

There's no point, but I defend him anyway. "He has his producer hat on."

"My boss ever talked to me like that, and I'd tell him to shove it where the sun doesn't shine, baby. Look up."

Looking up means I can't reply to the text. Anyway, I'm almost there, and I'd rather have Michael anxious than have smeared eyeliner. Thank God our Lyft driver isn't a thrill-seeker. Still, we've had more than a few stops and starts as we've crept along 52nd Street. "How are you even doing this in a car?"

"Very carefully." The speed of her words matches the carefulness of her hand as she lines one eye then the other. When she's done, she leans back, eye pencil propped in the air like it's a cigarette or a magic wand, and admires her work. "I really am brilliant."

My laugh is more giggle than usual. Must be nerves. "Not that you don't deserve the praise, but cocky much?"

"Yes, please." She waits a beat. "Oh, that wasn't an offer. I hear the word *cock* and my mind goes places." She pulls a pencil from the makeup kit spread across her lap. "Open up, sweetie."

I can't make any dirty comment in reply since now she's working on my lips. My phone buzzes again, another text from Michael, most likely.

"Touch your phone and die," Zully tells me. Just then, the driver slams on the brakes, and the pencil swerves. I can tell from Zully's wide brown eyes that the jolt caused a lining error. She glares at the back of the driver's head then takes a breath. "It's fine, it's fine." She uses her finger to blot at the skin above my mouth.

She pulls back to look at me again, her genie-style ponytail bobbing like she's about to grant a wish. "Actually, you look fantastic. I must be a god."

"Zully!"

"It helps that you're absolutely gorgeous, even without makeup, but you know that. You don't need to hear it. I do. I'm fragile."

She has one hell of an ego for being fragile, but I

suppose those two traits often go hand-in-hand. I squeeze her hand. "You don't know how much I appreciate this."

"I'd love for you to tell me, but we're here, and you're late." Zully reaches over me and opens my door before the car has stopped completely. "Fly, little bird!"

Sure that I have my phone and my purse, I'm giddy as I step out of the car, bolstered as I always am from my oldest friend's company.

"You're a knockout," Zully calls after me. "Everyone will be dying to get into your Simone Pérèles. Just remember to hire me as your face designer when you make it to the big time."

Of course the sidewalk in front of the Sebastian Center is busy as usual, and I'd be embarrassed about all the heads turning in my direction if I had the time.

But I don't. So I keep my chin up and ignore the looks and comments from strangers.

As I push my way toward the doors, I wonder briefly if this is how it will feel to be a celebrity. Because I *will* be one. Positive mindset, as Michael always says.

Inside, I skip the main elevators and hurry down the hallway toward the wing devoted to the media division of the Sebastian empire. This bank of elevators is only for employees, which technically I'm not, but since I'm an anchor at one of the Sebastians' local news networks, I'm on the list tonight.

"Brystin Shaw," I say to the security guard when he asks for my name.

While he enters it into his iPad for confirmation, I look around to get my bearings. There's a trio wrapped in conversation a few feet away, dressed in cocktail attire, suggesting they might also be headed up to the ceremony. There's also a man in a tux, his head down as he types something into his phone. I seem to be the only one trying to get on the elevator, which means I'm *really* late. Everyone else is probably already upstairs and seated.

Michael's so going to kill me.

I catch my reflection in one of the steel panels. At least I look good. A dark lip, smoky eye, my blonde hair pulled up with a few wisps curling at my shoulders. Zully really is a magician.

"News 9 in Jersey?" The guard draws my attention back to him.

"That's me."

"Got you. Head on up to sixty-three."

I scurry past him and into the waiting elevator and hit the button for the sixty-third floor. The doors begin to shut, and I let out a sigh of relief.

But then an arm shoots through the opening, and the doors part once again. It's the man in the tuxedo. As is typical for many women when put in a small space with a man they don't know, I scoot toward the back corner, lower my head, and try not to make eye contact.

He doesn't even acknowledge me, which is helpful.

When the doors are shut, and we're on our way, though, I sneak a peek in his direction.

And the breath is knocked from my lungs.

Holy shit, holy shit.

My phone still in my hand, I unlock the screensaver and pull up Zully's name in the text app.

Holy shit! It's him! In the elevator!

I follow the message up with a covert snapshot of the man who is none other than Holt Sebastian, the CEO of Sebastian News Corp. The man I'm supposed to be charming the pants off tonight in hopes that he'll notice me and one day give me my own show.

I study the photo I took while I wait for the messages to go through—stupid weak elevator signal. As the youngest CEO of SNC, Holt has more than his fair share of media attention. And because I aspire to work for him—like in this very building, not for one of his lowly network stations that no one ever watches anymore—I have done plenty of internet stalking. I already knew he was wicked attractive, but damn. Even at the weird profile angle my camera caught, his jawline is a work of art. I can't imagine looking at him straight on. My ovaries won't be able to take it.

I zoom in on his face and realize his mouth is upturned into a smirk. Did he know I was taking his picture?

Before I can get too panicked about it, the elevator halts abruptly.

I look up at the indicator to see where we've stopped. Instead of saying a number, the panel is blinking a bright red ER.

"Are you fucking kidding me?" I imagine the letters stand for error, but I feel like it should mean emergency, because this is truly a disaster. Michael is going to go ballistic.

Though, if he knew who I'm stuck with, he might feel differently.

Speaking of Holt, if he's concerned, he doesn't show it. He pulls his phone out from his inside jacket pocket and types something. "Dinner is worth missing." He doesn't look up from his phone. When he's finished his message, he puts his phone back. Either he has better cell service than I do, or he's not concerned whether or not the message goes through.

I hadn't planned on eating anyway. No way am I messing up Zully's makeup job. "I'm more concerned about missing the actual ceremony."

Holt turns to face me, crossing his arms over his chest and leaning his back against the steel wall. "I don't imagine it will start without me."

No other explanation. As if I'm supposed to know who he is, which I do, but still. It's awfully presumptuous.

Or *that's* what it's like to be a celebrity.

"At the very most," he continues, "you'll miss the local awards."

My stomach drops. "I'm receiving one of those local awards." I turn to mirror him, sighing as I press my back into the wall behind me. I don't know if I'm more disappointed about potentially missing my moment in the sun or about Holt Sebastian not knowing who I am.

But why would he know who I am?

SNC has hundreds of stations across the country. Holt can't know everyone who works for him. Even ones that are here tonight to be honored for excellence.

He studies me a second, and I wonder if I was wrong, if he'll recognize me now. But his gaze looks more predatory than perceptive, and all he says is, "Whoops."

Again, what did I expect? These events are probably everyday for him. He was born at the top of the ladder. He doesn't know what it's like to have to start from the bottom, what an achievement it is to even get up one rung.

It occurs to me that this might be a perfect opportunity to introduce myself. That was the goal for the night, after all —make him get to know me. Make him *remember* me.

But what if that's too forward? Too eager? I'll get the chance to meet him later.

Or I will if I don't miss the fucking ceremony. "Should we hit the emergency button?"

"Hm?"

"Do you think we should hit the emergency button?"

He's staring at me intently, so I know he heard me, but it seems to take him a second before he comprehends my words. "Oh. I was too busy thinking about how tempting the zipper is on your dress."

Heat runs from my decolletage to my cheeks. Truthfully, it was the point of this outfit. A Dolce & Gabbana splurge that Michael picked out, the dress is a modern reinterpretation of a classic black sheath dress, with a double slider zipper that runs all the way from my cleavage to the bottom hem and another one that matches in the back. It means I can make the neckline—and the backline—as low as I'd like. Michael had suggested I go low enough to not be able to wear a bra. He said men would be thinking about unzipping me all night.

I didn't go quite as low as Michael had wanted, but apparently the dress has still done the trick.

I guess that's something to be happy about.

I might be if I can get over my shock. The dress was supposed to be sensual so he'd remember me. I didn't expect him to come on to me. I'm a stranger to him. A stranger except that he knows that I work for his company.

Who would have the audacity to say something so forward?

Oh. That's right. He's a Sebastian.

"I suppose with your name, you don't have to worry about Cancel Culture." And I suppose that was probably a thought better left in my head instead of spoken aloud.

He seems as surprised by my comment as I am. His brows raise, and his jaw flexes as though he's considering. His shock gives me the opportunity to really look at him, and I was right—face-to-face, he's devastating. His cheekbones are cut high, but not too sharp. A closely trimmed beard darkens his jaw, preventing him from looking too pretty, which he might otherwise. Especially since his skin is flawless. No makeup or photoshopping needed.

And those eyes.

They're deep set under a severe brow line, but not so deep that his forehead overtakes his features. The color is unreal—a blue-gray that I wasn't sure existed in nature. In fact, I'm not sure they aren't contacts, and I almost take a step toward him to see before remembering that he's Holt fucking Sebastian, and I'm practically a no one who needs to mind herself.

"I guess I didn't realize what I'd said was inappropriate." By now, his expression has become more sly than mystified—most likely because I've been staring at him like a fangirl for the last thirty seconds—and of course he didn't realize he was inappropriate. Privilege with a capital P. I mean, he *is* practically American royalty.

With that in mind, I should probably backpedal on the accusation. "I'm sure I took—"

He cuts me off. "If I'm going to be canceled anyway, I might as well say what I was really thinking."

I shouldn't ask. I should not ask. "What were you really thinking?"

He pushes off the wall and steps toward me. Two strides is all it takes before he's right in front of me, practically caging me in. So close I can smell his wood and musk and citrus scent. "I was really thinking, I wonder if we'll be stuck in here long enough for me to unzip her and find out what's underneath."

His eyes flick down to my cleavage. This close, he has a good view. "Or what's *not* underneath."

Holy. Fuck.

This is what it's like to be a celebrity. Not just the kind of confidence he exudes, but also the reaction it draws from me. I should be appalled—and a little bit, I am. I should feel threatened—and that I am, for sure.

But the tremor of my pulse is not from fear—it's from excitement.

Ridiculous, I know. I don't have time to examine it closely because just then, the elevator jolts into movement.

"I guess not." Holt is still very much invading my personal space. His teeth graze his bottom lip. "Shame."

It's only seconds before we reach the sixty-third floor. The doors open, and Holt steps out, abandoning me without a glance back, as if we hadn't been stuck alone in an elevator together. As if he hadn't said what he'd said. Done what he'd done.

What even was that?

I blink as I step out after him, trying to get my bearings.

"Thanks for the rescue," I hear Holt say to another

sharply dressed man who seemed to be waiting for our arrival.

So he was able to text for help. Was he just messing with me to fill time?

"There you are!" Of course Michael is waiting at the elevators. He's probably been here all night, freaking out every time a car arrived without me in it. "Was that—?" He darts his eyes in Holt's direction. "Did you ride up together?" He can barely contain his excitement. "Did you get to talk to him?"

I'm still reeling from the him in question. My gaze follows as Holt rushes off with the other man, presumably heading to his designated spot for the occasion.

"Brystin?"

I force my attention back to Michael.

"Never mind." He ushers me into the event space. "You can tell me later. You're just in time. They're about to start. You look stunning, by the way. Well worth the wait."

I'm grateful he lets the subject go. I'm not sure what I'd say, or what he'd say in response. Or what he'd do to Holt in my defense.

One thing is certain, though—I have to change my entire approach where a promotion is concerned. Because at this rate, Holt Sebastian will eat me alive.

CHAPTER **TWO**

BRYSTIN

"Smile on," Michael whispers. "VIP headed in our direction."

If I wasn't so giddy from the excitement and champagne, I might be annoyed. First, I haven't dropped my smile once in three hours—my aching cheeks can attest to the fact—and second, it seems that everyone who has spoken to us during the after party has been a VIP. I feel like I'm in a receiving line. One executive after another has passed by with congratulations and nice-to-meet-yous. Every part of my body is exhausted.

But when I glance at the group walking our way, I see why Michael nudged me, and any hint of irritation dissipates. "Oh my God, it's Samuel Sebastian!" I barely have time to put my professional face back on before he's upon us.

"Brystin Shaw." Samuel extends his hand toward me.

"Pleasure to meet you. Congratulations on the award. Well deserved."

I imagine that the chair of Sebastian News Corp has probably been thoroughly prepped. There have been too many awards given tonight, too many mentions of outstanding work in journalism for me to feel like he might be able to single me out without the help. Still, I'm thrilled to hear my name come out of his lips. In many ways, it's a dream come true.

Hopefully, I'll make a good enough impression that he won't need the prep next time we're face-to-face. "The pleasure is mine, Mr. Sebastian. It's an honor just to be in the same room with so many notable people in the industry, yourself being at the top of the list. I'm really a tremendous fan."

He dismisses the compliment with a wave of his hand. "Samuel, please. My father doesn't even go by Mr. Sebastian."

I laugh politely and plan to introduce Michael, but that also turns out to be unnecessary. "Michael Endlich. It's been a while. You're producing *New Jersey Now*? I should have guessed. Your hand shows in the work."

I'm jealous as the two slip into easy banter and I'm sidelined, but I remind myself that Michael's been in the industry much longer than I have. He's closer to Samuel's age than mine, though he doesn't look it. Where Samuel looks like a grandpa, Michael's graying hair is distinguished. He's as trim and fit as a man half his age and appallingly attractive. The kind of attractive that gets better with every passing year, much to my envy. If he hadn't been at my side all night, I have no doubt he would have had the women swarming.

Men too, for that matter.

Add his charisma and business sense, and no wonder he's maintained meaningful connections. It's exactly the reason I've tied myself to him—Michael is the kind of man who goes places. I'm lucky he's chosen to take me with him.

Still, I'm looking forward to a time when I'm not the extra wheel in these conversations.

Fortunately, I'm not forgotten for long.

"I'd like you both to meet my nephew, Scott." Samuel gestures to the man at his side. "He's relatively new over here. Officially his title is VP of Public Integrity, but that's just a fancy way to say he's in charge of PR."

I do that ridiculous thing of downplaying my skills/highlighting my weaknesses because I'm a woman and that has been ingrained in my sex since birth. "Oh, dear. I hope you're not here to scold me about my Instagram account."

"Not that kind of PR," Scott assures me.

"More like he makes certain we don't look like assholes," Samuel says.

Another round of polite laughter, during which I'm racking my brain for something witty or intelligent to say. I'm usually faster on my feet, but it's been a night, and I'm not as quick as I want to be.

Always to my rescue, Michael chimes in before the second of silence becomes awkward. "I have to say, Samuel, the reporting that SNC did on the King-Kincaid financial scandal was next level. Would love to have been in on that. Talk about public integrity."

I kick myself for not thinking of that talking point myself. It's been the biggest story that Sebastian News Corp has had in a decade. Easy fruit, and I missed it.

"That was all my son," Samuel says. "When I appointed him CEO last year, I told him he had to come out of the gate swinging, and he sure did. Though, I have to say"—I'm surprised when he shifts his body to include me—"that piece you did on college entrance requirements was particularly innovative."

I imagine Scott is silently scoring Samuel points for turning the conversation back to the subject of my award. The whole intent of this night is to honor local news anchors, an obvious PR move in itself. Make sure that the little guys feel like we're part of the bigger company so that we'll keep getting eyeballs on programs that bear the SNC logo.

It might be all publicity, but it's working. I do feel special.

"Especially for a local team," another voice pipes in. "The piece did a good job of packaging fluff into something resembling news."

And there goes my dignity.

Michael puts a comforting hand on my back as we all turn to acknowledge the newest member of the party. While I'm sure he's a Sebastian, he's not one that I recognize, and Michael doesn't seem to either. He has an intensity about him that threatens a shudder through my body, and while the feeling is very different from what I felt in the elevator with Holt, I'm sure this man is just as brutal.

Samuel also seems to be repelled as his previous warmth evaporates instantly. "Don't mind Hunter," he says, tightly. "He doesn't work for SNC, so his opinion doesn't matter."

The flash in Hunter's eyes says there's a lot of baggage between the two of them. Scott's twitching jaw confirms it. I smile awkwardly, and even Michael doesn't seem to know how to handle the uneasy situation.

Then I feel it. A very bold, very male presence at my side. The kind of presence that dominates any space it's given, and I know without looking that it's Holt. Suddenly, I feel cowed in a very different way. I can't move my eyes in his direction, afraid of what my expression will say if I meet his gaze. It's like we have a secret, which of course we don't, and I'm scared I'll give it away. Scared it will consume me.

"What Hunter fails to recognize," Holt says, and I feel the cadence of his words in a pulse point on my inner thighs, "as he has repeatedly in the past, is what exactly makes a worthy and compelling news piece."

"Holt," Scott warns.

Hunter takes the opportunity to lash back. "And you've proven you know better?"

"We don't need to do this here." Samuel shifts his body, trying to leave Hunter out.

But Holt puts a hand up, demanding attention. "No, Dad. This is relevant. We're here to recognize the work of these journalists for a reason. The particular piece you mentioned came out of a heightened public distrust of the college entrance process, and while it was set off by a celebrity scandal, Brystin used that fodder to pull viewers into a segment that revealed the depth of brokenness in a corrupt system. That's real news, Hunter. Everyone here would agree.

"But the more intriguing aspect of *New Jersey Now* and Brystin's reporting is her ability to not only maintain but, *build* viewership in a daily roundtable show that tackles sociopolitical topics that don't often make the headlines. Without using comedy or sensationalism, which we all know is near impossible these days. Brystin's segments on homelessness and infrastructure were two of my favorites, though I could give you a list of at least a dozen, whereas I highly doubt my cousin could tell you a single thing about any of the anchors honored tonight nor the shows that they host."

Since I'm avidly not looking at Holt, I don't miss the flare of Hunter's nostrils. "Cousin?" He lets out a gruff laugh. "I see."

"Do you? Because I can make it clearer."

From the reactions around me, I have the distinct impression that Holt gives his cousin the bird.

"Not here," Samuel says again.

At the same time, Scott claps a hand on Hunter's back. "I have something I've been meaning to run by you, cuz. Got a minute to discuss?"

It's clearly a tactic to draw Hunter away, but he goes willingly, and there's a collective sigh of relief.

From everyone except for me, anyway.

Because Holt is still here, and his presence feels like stars underneath my skin, tingling along various points of my body.

Then, with his cousin out of the way, he angles himself

toward me, and now I *have* to look up. Have to look *at* him. He ensnares my gaze instantly, and my heart does some weird flip thing in my chest that I swear it hasn't done since I was seventeen.

"We didn't get a chance to meet formally," he says, as he takes my hand in his. It's a business shake, but also not. Another secret, the way he runs his thumb along my skin. The way I feel it, like it's fingers trailing down my neck. "Holt Sebastian."

"Brystin Shaw." Though, clearly he knows.

He *knows*, and at that thought, my heart flips again.

Did he know in the elevator or has he put two and two together since? Either way, he is familiar with my work. Or he's asked about it. Either way, he now definitely knows who I am.

Which was tonight's goal. So why am I as terrified as I am thrilled?

"You had a chance to meet already?" Samuel seems back to the jovial mood he'd been in before Hunter arrived on the scene.

"We shared an elevator." Holt doesn't mention that we'd briefly gotten stuck, and that feels relevant somehow. Yet another secret.

His words from earlier rush through my head, bringing heat to my face. *I wonder if we'll be stuck in here long enough for me to unzip her and find out what's underneath.*

I feel like I have to say something. "He commented on my dress."

God, I'm an idiot.

His mouth upturns slightly, and it's only now that I

realize he's still holding my hand. "I did. It's a very lovely dress."

"Quite," Samuel agrees, really looking at me for the first time.

"That dress." Michael *tsks*, reminding me of his presence. Reminding me who picked it out, who paid for it.

I drop Holt's hand and put it on Michael's shoulder. "Have you met Michael Endlich, my producer?"

"And her husband."

When he offers a hand to Holt, he wraps his free arm around me, with an air of possessiveness. It's odd coming from him. He was the one who decided we didn't need to wear rings. I'm usually the one who's grabbing for his hand, eager to show people he's mine.

Whether it's out of jealousy or out of a husbandly duty to protect his wife around someone who is so obviously a predator, I'm grateful for the gesture.

Strangely, though, I felt more protected by Holt's defense of my work than by this indication of ownership.

If Holt is surprised by the discovery that I'm married, he doesn't show it. "You did some freelance at SNC in the past, didn't you, Michael? My father has mentioned he'd love to have you back."

"I have," Samuel agrees. "Perhaps you'll think about working with us on something again."

I can practically feel Michael vibrating, and for a horrific moment, I wonder if he's going to forget that we're a team and bail on me.

But of course he doesn't. "I'd love to. But we're a package deal these days."

"Ah, well…of course. Makes sense." Samuel is already

writing us off. It's always the men they want. The women are just extra weight. I feel unnecessarily guilty, and have to clench my jaw so that I don't say something stupid and set Michael free to discuss opportunities without me.

But maybe that's the way to get me in. Let Michael pave a road first.

Before I can make an impulsive decision on the matter, Holt speaks. "Hold on, Dad. Do you have something in mind, Michael?"

"I do."

His words momentarily negate the late nights sitting at the kitchen table, hours and hours of brainstorming together.

But then he fixes it. "*We* do, actually. Brystin and I. We'd love to discuss it with you sometime."

And this is it. Our moment. The reason we wed in the first place, always hoping to get here. Our entire marriage is built on our shared ambition, on the notion that we'll go further together than alone.

Right now, we see if that notion pays off.

Holt takes a beat, as though considering. The whole time, he's looking at Michael, but I feel his eyes like they're still raking down my body the way they did in the elevator.

It's overwhelming, and I move tighter into Michael's embrace, as though he'll shield me.

"I'm having people over to my country house next weekend," Holt says finally. "A creative retreat, so to say. I'd love for you to join."

Samuel nods in approval. "Great idea."

Holt's invitation isn't directed at me, and even though I hear Zully in my head, telling me to stand up for myself and work my way in, I keep my mouth shut and let Michael accept.

But then Holt's eyes are back on me for real. The intensity of his attention feels like a spotlight, and I feel both lit up and unprepared. "That's enough time to get a substitute for the show?" he asks.

"Oh, me? You want me there, too?" I sound like an idiot, which is nothing compared to how I feel.

"I took the package deal to mean the two of you?"

Something about the question is challenging. Makes me wonder if he's asking something else, something I don't know how to answer. Something I very much want to answer correctly.

"Yes, more than enough time." Michael jumps in because he's *not* an idiot and not affected by blue-gray spotlight eyes.

"Good. I'll send a car Friday morning." He turns to his father, dismissing us with the physical shift of his body. "Have you met the Camdens yet? I'll introduce you."

And then they're gone.

"He likes you." Michael watches after them.

I don't know what's worse. That he's right? Or that I like it?

I KICK my shoes off as soon as we walk into our apartment. With my feet free, my exhaustion no longer overwhelms my excitement, and now I feel like I'm walking on air.

"He had to know who you were in the elevator." Michael's buzzing almost as much as I am. "Those segments he mentioned were not part of the recognition clip they showed."

"He sure didn't seem like it. Maybe someone just brought him up to speed later." I throw my purse down on the entry table and take my phone with me. In the kitchen, I grab a banana and climb up one of the barstools.

Michael follows after me. "He was too familiar with your work. He knew you."

I look up from peeling the fruit. "Maybe?" If Holt did know who I was, it changes the moment in the elevator. He wouldn't have said those words to someone he knew worked for one of his stations, would he?

I suppose it's just as crazy if he'd said it to me thinking I was a stranger.

Not crazy—offensive. Offensive was definitely the word I was clinging to, even if my insides didn't feel the same.

"Point is," Michael begins.

But I jump in, knowing exactly where he's going. "Point is, we're in."

"We're in." He grins. Then pumps the air in a very un-Michael gesture. "Fuck yeah!"

I laugh and pick up my phone to check the text that just arrived.

He did not say that to you!

Of course, I told Zully the details of what happened in the elevator. There are husbands and there are besties. Anyone who doesn't know the difference hasn't had both.

He did!

I can't decide if that's rapey or hot. Tell me it was hot.

I think it was, in actuality, rapey, but I answer from my gut. Or lower than my gut, rather.

It was wet-my-panties hot.

My breath stutters thinking about it, and I have that stupid girl, boy-crazy stomach flutter going on again.

I told you I was brilliant.

"Is that Zully? Is she taking the credit?" Michael grabs a beer from the fridge. He's high class professionally, drinking sophisticated liquors, but at home, he's much more laid back. "This wasn't her. It was all you."

"And you," I say as I type another message to Zully.

I think it was the dress.

Michael speaks at the same time. "It was the dress."

I look up at him, recognizing that heat layered in his tone. It doesn't ignite the same fire as a shocking come-on from a rich, hot, powerful man, but we've been together awhile. The way he looks at me is familiar. Comfortable.

And it still does the job.

Particularly when added to the excitement of the evening.

I squeeze my thighs together, enjoying the tingle

between them. "You look good tonight. In your fancy tuxedo. You know I love seeing you all snazzy."

His eyes are dark and he gives me a lazy grin. But then he gets serious. "The dress gets attention, but it doesn't keep it. We do good work, Brystin. That's what's getting us in the door. You earned this. We earned this. We deserve this."

My eyes get a little misty thinking of all the hard work we've put in to get here.

I turn back to my phone, trying to mitigate the overwhelm of emotion, and take a bite of my banana. I'd been too nervous to eat, and now I'm starving so I scarf it down while reading Zully's last series of texts.

> You're the one who put that dress on. I know you. Be careful, girl.

Having a friend know me that well is both the best and the worst. Zully still thinks of me as the twenty-five-year-old girl who fell head over heels for a man twenty years her senior, a man who vehemently doesn't believe in love. It's true. I was that girl.

But Michael does believe in partnerships and politics, and when he proposed marriage, I knew full well the arrangement didn't include love.

I'm thirty-three now. I'm not that girl anymore.

Not interested in defending myself, I put my phone down, and give Michael the same heat he'd given me as I take a bite of my fruit.

"Pretty suggestive over there eating that banana." He comes around the counter, puts his beer down, and wraps his arms around me from behind. "Should we celebrate in the bedroom?"

In *my* bedroom, he means, because we never have sex in his room. Despite our open marriage arrangement, I don't love seeing the evidence of other women in my home.

I do love seeing him in my bedroom, though, which Zully contends is proof that I'm still into him more than I should be.

Honestly, it's proof that I enjoy having sex with my husband. Is that a crime?

His hand slides down the neckline of my dress to caress my breast, and I let out a soft moan. I arch my back and give him my mouth, which he takes urgently. I can feel him hard at my backside, and considering how arousing this entire evening has been, I could easily see us not making it to the bed.

But when he starts to undress me, I urge him to my room. The blinds are already drawn, and while Michael has a body that's meant to be seen, I prefer the dark, tonight. In the dark, I can embrace all the excitement from the evening. In the dark, I can imagine a different hand unzipping my dress. A different mouth breathing hot on my neck.

A different cock slipping inside my pussy, and when I come, it's blue-gray eyes watching me as I shatter into nothing.

CHAPTER **THREE**

BRYSTIN

Without moving my eyes from the car window, I reach over and nudge Michael awake. "You gotta see this."

He makes a noise that sounds like he's stretching then clears his throat. "Are we here?"

"I think so," I whisper, even though the partition is up in the limo, and I don't think the driver can hear us. "We just stopped at an entrance."

After a moment, the iron gate parts as it swings open, and the car starts driving again. Michael undoes his belt buckle and scoots close so he's looking over my shoulder. "Are those cherry blossom trees?"

"Yeah. Pretty sure they are." It was what I'd wanted him to see. They're in full bloom, lining both sides of the long drive. It's been a long time since I've seen anything so beautiful.

"Lucky timing. Another week, and we might have missed it."

It's been a week since my encounter with Holt in the elevator, and every day that passes, I feel more and more that I must have made the situation up to be more in my mind than it really was. The exhilaration from being invited to possibly move to the next level in our careers has surpassed whatever I felt near the CEO, anyway. Then today, the two-and-a-half-hour luxury ride to Greenwich and the arrival at what looks to be a gorgeous estate has lifted any last remnants of unease I've had about this weekend's meeting.

A couple of minutes later, the limo is parking in front of a massive house that I can only describe as a mansion. I'm too excited to wait for the driver to open my door, and I jump out as soon as it unlocks.

"Holy fuck." The mansion is even bigger when not framed by the window of the limo. While I've seen some big houses in my time, never anything like this. "It's got to be twenty thousand square feet."

"More, maybe." Michael climbs out behind me. "And to think—this is only a weekend house."

I make a gesture with my hand that indicates jerking off because this building is the very definition of pompous.

Before the driver can catch sight of my action, Michael grabs my hand, but he laughs when he does. "I thought this was the lifestyle you wanted one day."

I shrug. "I want the career that can afford this kind of lifestyle."

He looks at me with an eyebrow raised. We both know that this level of opulence is not likely reachable, even if everything goes perfect on my path from here on out. Anderson Cooper and Sean Hannity are probably the only two news personalities who might come close. The closest female, Diane Sawyer, is worth less than half of either of the top men. Needless to say, I'd settle for much less.

"Okay," I amend, "I want the career that gets invited to this kind of lifestyle on a regular basis."

He shifts my hand so that our fingers are interlaced. "The first was better. Dream big, sweet girl. You never know what's possible."

I glow in his direction. Michael has always been generous with his faith in me. It was probably why I fell so hard for him, because he had so much passion about my abilities, about my potential, about who I could be. I thought it had to be love. It sure felt like love. What else could blind someone to all my imperfections?

I've since learned the stars in his eyes are about his dreams coming true, not necessarily mine. He's honest about it, at least. I'm the one clinging to the idea it might be something else someday.

No, that's not right. I *was* clinging. Not anymore.

"Mr. and Mrs. Endlich." I've been so wrapped up in admiring the estate that I'm only now noticing the woman in a pin-striped blouse and fitted trousers.

"She's Ms. Shaw," Michael says.

"My apologies. I'll get that fixed. I'm Carol, the house manager here. I'd like to welcome you both to Adeline."

"Adeline?"

"It's the name of the estate," Michael informs me, show-off that he is.

"That's right, Mr. Endlich. Named after Irving Sebastian's late wife."

"Samuel's father?" I ask, trying to make sure I have all the VIPs straight. And now I wonder if the estate actually belongs to him rather than Holt.

"Yes. Though it was Holt Sebastian who named the place when he purchased it. In honor of his grandmother." Well, that answered that. "He's very glad to have you here this weekend. I trust your journey has been excellent so far?"

"It's been amazing," I say as a man in a waistcoat and tie collects the luggage that the limo driver has deposited on the drive. "Oh, thank you."

I look to Michael to see if we should give a tip. He hasn't reached for his wallet, and I trust him to know what to do in these situations better than I do.

Carol steps out of the way so that the man can go past her. "Glad to hear it. Alejandro will take your bags to your room. Would you like to go there first and freshen up, or would you like me to orient you to the grounds?"

I look at Michael who is still holding my hand.

"Up to you." He thinks my stare was meant to be a question about the tour. Really, I was trying to determine his feelings about sharing a room. He's not an all-night-in-my-lover's-bed type of guy.

I try not to make anything of the fact that he doesn't seem bothered. "Orientation first, I guess."

We follow her through the front door only to find there is another door on the other side of the foyer. It's outside the second door that she types in a code in a panel on the wall before leading us into the actual house.

As to be expected, the insides of the mansion are as grand as the outside. More so, even. There's a spiral staircase and a crystal chandelier that extends from the ceiling on the upper floor into the great room. Floor-to-ceiling windows that overlook the extensive acreage line the far wall. The furniture is modern, but everywhere I look, there are touches of opulence. Crystal door handles, gold-plated mirrors, intricate trim work.

Though Michael is more experienced in the world than I am, he seems just as entranced. "The flooring looks like copper," I whisper to him.

"I think it *is* copper," he says.

Damn, I mouth. He squeezes my hand in reply.

"Library is in the east wing." Carol points down a hallway. "As well as the gym, the game room, and the movie theater. Kitchen is in the west wing, but you shouldn't need anything from there directly. If you're hungry, pick up any house phone and dial 2. Same with drinks, though there is a bar in the library and another here, off of the dining room." She points to each thing as she talks about them.

"There's an actual movie room?" I don't mean to sound as awed as I do, but I am that awed.

"And a gym," Michael teases, knowing I have no interest.

"Well, you know where I'll be," I tease back.

"The library." He lets go of my hand to playfully slap my ass.

Stop, I mouth, feeling my face heat.

If Carol sees the interaction, she doesn't acknowledge it. She continues on with her orientation, taking us to the windows, I think at first, to let us see how beautiful the view is. It turns out the choice was more practical. "The seating out here on the patio is available to all and can be accessed via the door at the other side of the room. The pool is to the left." She points. "Pool house beyond. There are showers there as well as a sauna. It's all coed, so be mindful of that."

I glance at Michael, but he's still looking out the windows.

"The outdoor kitchen is past the pool house. Lunch will be served there in about an hour. Buffet style, so no need to dress up or be on time. On the other side of the house we have the tennis courts and beyond that the stables. There are rackets in the storage room on the edge of the court. Sheva is there with the horses until the evening, if you'd like to ride, but I recommend going in the morning. The grounds are prettiest then and the horses fresh."

"A ride tomorrow might be nice, Michael."

He toggles his head back and forth noncommittally. "Or perhaps a game of tennis."

He's tried to teach me and knows I'm a lost cause. "You're on your own there."

"I'm sure there's plenty else for you to do without me." He drifts away from me to get closer to the window, craning his head in the direction of the pool.

I follow his gaze and see there are people over there. We're not near enough to make out any faces, but there are definitely women. Shapely women in bikinis.

"You've noticed we have other guests." Carol seems to think that's what Michael's interested in.

I know better.

"Looks like most of them are at the pool, and you're

more than welcome to join them. We're very casual today. No formal gatherings other than dinner."

"Is Holt around?" I don't know why Michael's gawking makes me think of him, but it does.

Michael turns back to me at the mention of the CEO's name.

"I'm afraid he hasn't made it back from the city yet. But he has asked me to be your host and make sure this weekend is enjoyable to you in every way."

I'm not sure why I'm disappointed. Or why I'm suddenly worried that this weekend isn't about talking possibilities or that "creative retreat" might mean something different to Holt Sebastian than it does to me.

Michael doesn't seem to be deflated. He puts his arm at the small of my back. "Should we get to our room and freshen up for lunch? I for one would love to hit that pool."

The pool or the women at the pool? Sometimes I forget that the distinction shouldn't be my concern.

It's forced, but I smile up at him and nod.

I LOOK up from the book I'm reading to find yet another woman entering the swimming area. Several have come and gone all afternoon. Men too, but I'm not comparing my body to them. It's because of all the beautiful women—women that have to still be in their twenties—that I chose the fish from the buffet instead of the pasta.

I haven't recognized anyone so far, but at least one looks like he's a Sebastian, and Michael has pointed out several industry people. He introduced me to a few at lunch, but no one has interested him enough to draw him away from sunbathing with his iPad. Other than his dip in the pool earlier, he's stayed by my side.

Doesn't mean I haven't caught him looking. Of course, I've been looking too, but I assume my looks are for different reasons than his.

When this newest woman strips off her robe, I realize she's actually closer to Michael's age than mine. Then I realize I know her. "Oh my God, that's Jessa Jones."

Michael lowers his head to look over his sunglasses. "I haven't seen her in years. She looks great."

I swivel my head to stare at him incredulously. "You never told me you knew Jessa Jones." She's the biggest female personality on SNC. He knows what a career crush I have on her. That woman is serious goals.

"I'm sure I have." No, he hasn't. "I don't *know her* know her. We've met once or twice. In passing."

That means he fucked her. I hope it was a long time ago, but I decide not to press him about it in case it wasn't.

As if he senses I'm feeling vulnerable, he reaches over and casually strokes my bare thigh. "You should go talk to her."

Out of the blue? No way. "What would I even say?"

"I can introduce you."

Open marriage or not, I find it uncomfortable to be with him and a woman I know he's slept with. "No. That's okay."

He stares at me like he thinks I'm being ridiculous, but when he speaks, his tone is encouraging rather than chastising. "This weekend is about mingling with other people in the business. You aren't some fangirl approaching her on the street. Be assertive. Talk to her."

I know he's right, but I can't get myself to move from my chair. I've assumed all the women in bikinis were here just to be eye candy, but it occurs to me now that they might all be like me—local journalists hoping to get their own show. I put on my smallest bathing suit today too. Are we all trying to use our feminine wiles to get our brains noticed? I suddenly feel silly and small.

Michael senses my reluctance if not my reasoning behind it. "It's only our first day here. There will be other opportunities. If it doesn't feel like the right time, wait until dinner or breakfast tomorrow."

He's being understanding, and that makes me feel guilty for being insecure. "No. I'll talk to her now. I just need a few minutes to practice what I should say in my head."

He laughs at me. "You speak off the cuff every afternoon on television with more than half a million viewers a week, but you have to practice how to say *it's nice to meet you*."

"Because, obviously, I can't just say nice to meet you. It has to be witty and charming and smart. Definitely smart." I'm flustered thinking about all the ways I can embarrass myself.

He leans over from his chair and kisses my shoulder. "Whatever you say, sweet girl." His gaze slides across the pool landing briefly on a particularly buxom redhead before continuing to a group of men we spoke to earlier. "I should put my money where my mouth is." He stands up. "I'm going to catch up with Joe and Arman. I believe that's Steele Sebastian they're talking to."

I try to remember the family tree. Holt's little brother. "Samuel's youngest?"

"His youngest son, anyway. I heard he's working in development. Might be nice to have his ear."

"Okay." My focus is back on Jessa. Back to thinking what my best approach should be. But when Michael stands up, I think to add, "Good luck, honey."

Then I lift up my book and pretend to read it while getting up the nerve to speak to my idol.

"Excuse me, I don't mean to interrupt."

Rarely, but on occasion, procrastination works in my favor. When I shade my eyes from the sun, it's Jessa Jones standing there, asking for my attention.

"Hi. Hi!" I scramble to sit up, flinging my book on the ground as I do. "I'm sorry."

She apologizes at the same time, bending over to grab my copy of *The Witching Hour* for me. "I didn't mean to startle you."

She hands it over to me, my place lost. Annoying, but who cares? It's Jessa fucking Jones. "No, it's fine. I just…hi. No bother. Really."

See? I didn't have this planned, and so I'm fumbling.

"You seemed really caught up in your book, but I couldn't help myself. I had to come over and meet the woman that finally snagged Michael Endlich." She glances down at my bare finger, and suddenly seems horrified. "You are the wife, aren't you?"

There's nothing to do but laugh. "Yes. I'm the wife."

"Phew. I thought I stepped in it for a minute." She sits down on the edge of the lounge chair next to me. "Well, let me tell you, girl, if you didn't know, you are the envy of many a woman."

"I'm aware."

"He worked on the show that filmed after me—when was that? Ten years ago, now, at least. He might not even remember. God, that hint of German in his accent. Is there anything sexier? Unf." She puts her hand to her chest, swooning.

"Tell me about it." Strangely, it's not weird to have someone salivate over my husband. It's a nice change from all the bitchy stares I usually get from women wondering how I landed someone like him.

"Everyone I knew in the studio had a plan to get a ring on his finger. The general consensus in the end was that he was never going to settle down. So congrats to you."

"I'm not sure that he's settled down. And neither of us wear rings, so the general consensus was not really wrong. But there was a ceremony, and I do have a certificate that says we're legally wed." I glance in his direction and notice that, although he is indeed talking to Joe and Arman, the busty redhead has also joined them. "If that counts for anything."

Quickly, I move my eyes back to Jessa, but it's too late. She's already tracked my gaze. "It counts. Trust me, it counts more than you think."

Not sure that's true, but I'm not unloading my petty doubts on the goddess of SNC. "You know—I can't believe I'm admitting this—I was trying to get the nerve up to come over and introduce myself. I'm sure you get this all the time, but I'm really a big fan of your work."

She waves her hand at me. "Oh, please. I'm so

approachable." After a beat, she laughs, and I join in with her. "Fine, maybe I'm not. But these are supposed to be mixers. Honestly, until I saw you with Michael, I thought you were one of the bunnies."

"Bunnies?"

"The 'Bastian Bunnies? That's what we call them." She nods toward the redhead who has shifted so her focus is on Michael. "It seems like there are always a handful of them here when I visit, none of them the same as the girls here the time before. They're basically Sebastian groupies, though I don't know that any of them have ever read anything related to the news. I don't even know if they know that's what SNC is."

She looks back at me. "Sorry. That was catty, and I don't like to be someone who demeans other women. My point was that I was happy to realize that you were not just a bunny."

I appreciate both her cattiness and her apology for it. "Nope. Not a bunny. Just a wife."

"No, not just a wife. Am I wrong, or aren't you in the biz? I thought that's what I'd heard."

"Oh, geez." I'm suddenly shy. "It's a small show. *New Jersey Now*. I feel like I'm telling a Broadway star about my little high school production."

"Stop. We all have to start somewhere. How old are you? Barely thirty?"

"Thirty-three."

"And you already pulled an invite to a development weekend. Is the team pulling you over to SNC for something?"

Not wanting to put the horse before the cart, I shrug.

"I'd gotten the impression we'd talk about it, but I don't know."

"Who invited you? Samuel? Richard? Steele?"

"Holt."

"Ah." There's a lot of subtext in that single syllable, and though I can't decipher it, I can tell the tone of it.

"I shouldn't get my hopes up. I get it." I thought I was being reasonable with my expectations, but disappointment sinks in my stomach like a heavy stone.

"No, no, I'm not saying that at all." Jessa stretches out on the lounge chair, keeping her body turned to the side to face me. "Look, I came on when Samuel was in charge. Samuel was…I'm not going to make him out to be a hero. It's a man's world, we both know that. But he'd keep his eyes above the neckline when he talked to you, and he based his pay on viewership rather than gender—sometimes there isn't much difference between the two. But he was consistent. He played by the rules—rotten rules, but he didn't deviate. With him, you knew what to expect."

"And with Holt…?"

She shakes her head, unsure. "He's only been in the position for a year now, so really too soon to say."

"Soon enough for you to have an opinion, it seems."

She grins as though she's been caught. "The King-Kincaid scandal was a big win for him. But that wasn't his journalists who brought that to the station—it was Holt himself. With an anonymous source, to boot. It all checked out in the end, but where did he get the info? He's in the billionaire club, so he has connections, but the billionaire club generally protects their own. Exposing one of the brothers is…"

"Against the rules," I finish for her.

"Right."

I consider the new details of this story. As an outsider, I'd assumed the info had come from one of the reporters who broke the story. Jessa is presenting it as a minus about the CEO. I'm not so sure. "Maybe he really cares about the truth."

She seems dubious. "I think he cares about the scandal. Either way, he's a disrupter, and that means he's unpredictable. And unpredictable means I have no idea what Holt plans to do with you."

Once again, my gaze turns toward Michael. It's no surprise he's getting cozy with a hot young bunny, and I have to wonder…is unpredictable really such a bad thing?

HOLT STILL HASN'T ARRIVED when I retire to my bedroom for the night.

I spent the rest of the afternoon at Jessa's side. We joined Michael, Joe, and Arman for dinner. The bunnies, it seemed, weren't invited to the dining table. But after the meal, Michael disappeared for "man time," which I was sure was a euphemism, and so I spent the rest of the evening checking out the library.

After I've washed my face and changed into my sleep shorts and a tank, I climb into the queen size bed with my book and try not to wonder where Michael's spending the night. The clock on the nightstand says a quarter to midnight, when my door opens.

"Hey, sweet girl. In bed already?"

I hate myself for being glad that Michael's here. "I didn't think I'd see you tonight."

He cocks his head and looks at me like I'm being silly. "Where else would I sleep?" he asks, toeing off his shoes and unbuttoning his shirt.

In the redheaded bunny's room. "I don't know."

He pauses his undressing and frowns down at me. "Brystin." It's his soft voice. The one he uses when he's being sweet or when he wants to win me over.

My eyes sting, so I turn them back to my book.

He stretches out on the bed and places his hand on top of my thigh, over the covers. "Hey. I'm here with you, Brystin."

I shake my head, disgusted for feeling emotional. He hates it when I'm jealous. "I wasn't sure."

"Be sure. Hey. Look at me." He waits for me to do as he says. "We're here for us. Okay?"

"Right. Okay." I run my hand through his floppy hair. "I wasn't being…" I don't know how to finish that because of course I was being whatever the word is that follows it. "I was just…"

He takes pity on me. "I stayed out too late. I'm here now." He crawls closer so he can cup my face and kiss me. It's so easy to get lost in his kisses. They're almost manipulative the way they make me forget what I was thinking.

It's not too long before his hand trails down my neck, under my tank to squeeze my breast.

"Michael," I moan, but I pull away. "People might hear us."

"Let them." He resumes the kiss and travels his hand

lower, slipping it down my shorts to rub me the way he knows I like it.

"Michael." I push him away. Gently, but definitively.

"Really?" He's frustrated, and it almost makes me change my mind.

Almost.

"If people overhear you fucking, you get clapped on the back. If they overhear me, I get called a slut and suddenly I'm a woman who isn't smart enough to tell the news." It's true, but more true is that I don't know if he's come to me from someone else's bed, and I'm not in the mood to compartmentalize that tonight.

"You could be quiet." But he seems to know he's already lost the battle.

"I'm terrible at being quiet." Also true.

Reluctantly, he draws away. "I understand. I'm going to jump in the shower then."

"Okay. What time are you planning to get up?" I reach for my phone to set an alarm and realize it's not here. "I think I left my cell in the library."

"Want me to go look?"

"No." I consider getting it tomorrow, but then it will be dead, and I hate being without a charged phone. "I know exactly where I left it. I'll be right back."

The hallway is dark, but the library is easy to find since it's the last room. It's a two-story booklover's dream room. There's a fireplace and desk on the first floor with bookcases lining the walls. The second floor opens to below in the middle, but another row of shelves line the entire perimeter except for a few windows with window seats. It's definitely my favorite place I've discovered on the estate so far.

At the end of the hall, I push quietly through one of the glass doors, and don't even have to turn on a light because the shelves are lit and I can see my phone right where I expected it to be. I grab it quickly, planning to dart right back out.

But then I hear voices below, and when I recognize one of them as Holt, I freeze.

"I wanted to be here, believe me," he says. "Everyone get here okay?"

"Seems so."

I step carefully toward the railing and peer over the side and realize it's Steele that's with him, his younger brother. I met him briefly at dinner, but I didn't talk with him enough to know him from voice alone.

"Nothing interesting happened without you." Steele delivers a glass with deep red colored liquid to his brother who is standing at the desk.

Holt takes it, downing half of it in one swallow. "Thank you. I needed that."

"What the fuck kept you? The board meeting couldn't have taken that long."

"Wanna bet?" Holt takes another sip of his drink then sinks down in the chair. "Numbers from the last quarter came in this morning."

"Oh. That bad?"

I know I shouldn't be here for this conversation. I'm curious by nature, but it's not just journalistic inquisitiveness that keeps me glued to my place. It's this man. This strong, intimidating creature who, in this moment that he thinks is privately shared with family, looks vulnerable and raw.

"Dad wasn't unhappy." Holt lets out a slow breath. "But he's only one person, and the numbers weren't bulletproof. Certain members of the board—I'm sure you don't need names—poked holes at them for hours."

"Fuck. They have to be on Uncle Reynard's payroll. You know that."

"Can't prove it."

Steele sits on the edge of the desk. "So where did it end up? Are you out?"

Holt shakes his head and takes another sip of his drink. "No, I'm not out. Yet."

"You have a plan, right? You have to have a plan."

Holt lets out an almost laugh. "Working on it."

I swear I don't make a sound, but something seems to alert him to my presence because, just then, his gaze lifts and smacks into mine. His eyes drink me in, and I'm paralyzed. A deer caught in the sightline of a hunter's pointed gun.

"Believe me." Though he seems to still be speaking to his brother, I'm dead certain he's talking to me. "I'm working on it."

I don't know if it's a threat or a promise, but it's bold enough to stir me from my immobility. I push off from the railing and slip out the door, scampering back to the safety of my husband and my room.

CHAPTER **FOUR**

BRYSTIN

I put my hand over my eyes to shield the sun and look as far to my right as I can see. Nothing but trees and grassland. Same thing to my left. And behind me. The one direction I know not to go is straight. There's a giant pond a hundred feet or so in front of me, and I definitely haven't seen that yet today.

Everything within view is beautiful.

Problem is, none of it is familiar.

With a sigh, I pull my phone out of my pocket and do the thing I've been procrastinating for the last half hour—text Michael.

I think I'm lost.

I watch my screen. Fortunately, the signal is good out here, and my text seems to have gone through, but it hasn't been read.

And why would Michael read it? He opted to play tennis this morning with Joe, and Michael is a vicious competitor who removes all distractions when he's in a game. I can't remember a time he's taken his cell with him to play anything.

To make matters worse, I'm pretty sure the dark clouds heading my direction are the kind that bring rain.

Fuck.

This is what I get for choosing exercise over joining Jessa in the theater room with the group that wanted to watch a not-yet-released movie from that asshole director that I can't stand.

I do one more shield of the eyes and turn in each direction, looking for anything at all to hint that the house is near. This time when I turn back to the pond, I see a horse and rider trotting by.

I'm about to signal when I suddenly have a bad feeling. Like, what if I've wandered off the Adeline estate? What if the rider is someone who will be angry I'm on his property?

Worse, what if it's someone from the house, and I'll have to admit I'm lost?

Worst yet, what if it's Holt?

At that thought, I crouch down, hoping I won't be seen over the long grass. I crawl like this to the nearest tree and then slowly stand and brace my back against the trunk. I hold this pose for what feels like a lifetime, my heart thundering in my chest.

Finally, I peek around toward the pond. No horse and rider there.

Because they're right behind me when I turn around.

I practically jump out of my skin. "Oh my God."

"Startle you?" The throaty rumble of Holt's voice makes my pulse double.

Of course it's Holt. Of fucking course.

"Startle is an understatement. You scared the fuck out of me. How did you even approach so quietly? Are you a ninja?"

His lips curve up on one side. "I'm intrigued by what it means to scare the fuck out of you. Does that mean you are no longer capable of fucks?"

I'm suddenly back in that elevator, face-to-face with a man who has no boundaries. A man who clearly wants to invade mine.

Without consciously doing so, I take a step back. "Just a phrase. Um. Never mind it."

Meanwhile, I'm trying very much to never mind the look of his hard thighs in tight riding pants as they cling to both sides of the horse's back. Less successfully, I'm trying to never mind the pierce of his eyes as they sweep along my curves and scour every inch of my bare legs.

I really should have worn jeans instead of shorts.

"If you insist, Ms. Shaw. And in answer to the question —Knight is trained to hunt for sport. He knows how to approach prey without being heard."

The suggestion that I am prey sends a not exactly unpleasant shiver down my spine. "Oh. Right."

He nods. "I generally understand why a fox or a hare tries to disappear from sight. Would you like to share the reason you were hiding?"

"I wasn't hiding," I lie. "I was…" I'm not fast enough on my feet for this shit. Channeling Michael, I throw back my shoulders and attempt to redirect the narrative. "Funny story. This morning, I'd actually considered taking one of the horses out, but then I was afraid I would go too far out and get lost. So I decided to take a walk instead. And I still got lost."

He smirks, well aware that I've avoided answering his question. "Quite a walk. You're almost three miles out from the house."

"Three…miles? Wow…" But he's moved Knight closer, and I'm really wowing at those thighs again. If I met him like this, with no prior knowledge of the extent of his wealth and power, I'd know by the way he commands this horse.

He doesn't laugh, but his expression says he's clearly amused. "I'm sure the long walk had as much to do with taking the fuck out of you as anything else."

I run a hand over my hair, several strands having come loose from my ponytail, and try to think of something clever to say in return. Which is impossible for a myriad of reasons I can't examine on the spot, not the least of which, I think it might be dangerous to think too hard about fucks and Holt. And strong thighs. And things that are hard.

"I don't know what to say to that," I blurt out instead. Honest. Too honest since now he knows how easily he trips me up.

To be fair, I'm sure he knew anyway.

This time he laughs. "Touché."

Seriously, why am I such a mess every time he's near me? I need to never be alone with the man. "Good thing you're here now. If you could point me in the direction of…" I pause because he's getting off Knight.

Oh God. If he offers to walk back with me, I'll literally die. "What are you doing?"

"I'm getting off my horse." Once he's on the ground, he leads Knight in my direction, closing the distance between us. It wasn't that big of a distance to begin with, and I'm starting to feel both claustrophobic and thrilled.

"I promise I can walk back by myself. I just need to be shown the way. No need to..." And now he's right beside me, smelling like horse and musk and that damn sandalwood.

"Say hello to Knight, Brystin."

"Oh, you're introducing me to your horse." Okay. I can get with that. "Hello, Knight. Nice to meet you." I stroke down the animal's nose, black like the rest of his body. What else would Holt Sebastian ride but a black horse? It's so on brand, I could have predicted it.

"Yes, I'm introducing you to my horse. You should never, never get on an animal without at least an introduction."

My stomach flips as I remember that first meeting. He'd come onto me without an exchange of names, and before I can stop myself, I challenge him on the fact. "*You* always get an introduction?"

Again, that smirk. "You should know something about me—I don't always do what I should."

I'm kind of the teacher's pet kind of girl. Good, on the whole. A rule follower. But I'm fairly attractive, and I've been propositioned by my share of rogues over the years.

Not once have I ever been so tempted to be bad.

No, forget that. Forget him. Focus on what matters.

My career is important, and flirting with the man who

can make the biggest impact on my future is not a bad idea —it's the worst.

And then it dawns on me what else he said. "Wait. I'm not getting on your horse."

"Do you hear that, Knight? You're coming on too strong for the lady."

I don't know what to do with Holt's attempts to be cute, other than ignore them. "I can't. What will you do? I'm not leaving you to walk three miles."

He looks at me like I've said something insane. "I'm not suggesting I walk three miles."

"Good."

"I'm riding the horse along with you."

"Oh, no. No. That's. I'll just." I make the mistake of picturing it—me sitting behind him, my arms around his middle, my face pressed against his back—and I feel my face flush. "Which way to the house?"

He studies me before answering. "That way." He jerks his head to the left. "But I doubt you'll make it before that storm."

As if on cue—because obviously even the heavens answer to Sebastian command—thunder rumbles in the distance.

Well, shit.

"Come on, Brystin. It's a long walk, but it's a short ride. Hop up." Without warning, his hands come down on my waist, directing me where to stand, and even through the thin layer of my tank and the thickness of his leather gloves, I feel heat. The kind of heat that happens low in the belly. The kind of heat that leads to trouble.

Yeah, this is a real bad idea.

But considering how I have no good excuse, it's also a bad idea to refuse. Just for different reasons.

"Okay. Sure." He helps me put my foot into the stirrup, and I try not to think about the way his hands linger on my ass when he helps push me up to the saddle. Instantly, my shorts are riding up my butt crack. "I should have worn jeans."

The comment only draws Holt's attention to my legs, but he misinterprets my reasoning. "I'm sure I'll keep you warm."

"That wasn't. I meant." Do I really want to explain what's happening with my panties? It doesn't help that now I have goosebumps sprouting down my skin. From the attention, not the cold. "Okay."

I'm burning from embarrassment, but yeah, okay.

And then Holt climbs on the horse—not in front of me, but behind me. On a saddle meant for one. "Oh."

"It will be a tight fit." His body practically encases me. His arms come around my center, his thighs hug my hips, and since I'm sure he intended the double entendre, my mind is so completely in the gutter. "But we'll make it work."

Make it work means that I'm pretty much sitting on him. I try to adjust, moving myself forward so that my weight is on my thighs, but he pulls me back against him. "You're good like this," he says. His words are hot at my ear, and he was right—if I was cold before, I'm definitely not now.

"Are you sure? You can't be comfortable." I squirm, trying to somehow make more room.

"Brystin. I'm good." His voice is even deeper than usual. "Trust me."

Then I feel it.

I feel exactly how *good* he is. How blessed he is, anyway, because I'm pretty damn positive that the bulge against my ass has grown. A lot.

All that money and power and God thought Holt Sebastian also needed a big dick.

Life is officially not fair.

With a *tsk,* Holt starts Knight toward the house at a fast walk, and I try not to breathe, afraid any movement will encourage the party in Holt's pants. It's a short ride. He hasn't technically tried anything. All I'm doing is sitting close. Really close. If that makes a rich man happy enough to give me a shot at national television, I can live with that.

Right?

Except then he wants to talk as well. "You told me why you chose a walk over horse riding. You weren't up for tennis?"

He doesn't mention Michael, but I hear the subtextual ask. "It's not my sport, if I'm honest."

"Perhaps you need a less vicious opponent."

I'm not sure if Holt has actually witnessed Michael's game or if he's guessing. "I'm sure you're not volunteering."

He chuckles, his chest rumbling against my backside with the sound. "You don't think I'd be a good match?"

I answer honestly. "I imagine you obliterate anyone who steps up against you in anything."

"Fair assessment." A beat goes by. "I was actually suggesting my sister Adly. She'll be around in the morning, if you want to play."

"Thank you, I'll consider it." I won't, but it was decent

of him to offer. Though I suspect the conversation was an attempt at feeling something out about my relationship with Michael rather than an honest inquiry about tennis.

Or maybe that's some bizarre bit of wishful thinking.

"You weren't interested in the movie?"

"*Gatsby in Manhattan*? No. Definitely, definitely no." I don't bother to hide my disdain for the Rudy Winter film. "You couldn't pay me to watch it. Or I suppose you could, but only if I get to deliver a brutally honest criticism afterward."

"Not a fan of Winter?"

"God, no." This is good—talking about something I'm passionate about is a good distraction from what's happening beneath me. "I mean, he's a creative genius. He hires the best, or at least, brings out the talent in the people he works with, but every single film he directs is decidedly problematic. His female characters are always young bimbos. The romantic heroes are always twenty-plus years older than the women."

Realizing that description could be used to describe my relationship with Michael, I hurry to share other issues. "I don't think he's ever passed the Bechdel test. He's a slut shamer while his male leads are unabashedly promiscuous. He frequently reduces female worth to how often they're willing to forgive the shit men who use and abuse them over and over and over again. Don't even get me started on how he behaves on set. The work itself is some of the most blatant displays of misogyny in present Hollywood, and I'll never understand how it continues to get rewarded and awarded every single Oscar season. It's disgusting."

Holt is silent when I've finished my rant, and it occurs

to me that there is probably a reason why he has an early copy of a yet to be released film. "I'm sorry. He's probably your best friend or your uncle or something."

"You assume because you have the same criticism about me?"

"No! No. No. Sorry. No." I let out an awkward laugh. "I meant because you have a copy. I figure you have to know someone."

"I do know someone. Lots of someones." I feel his breath along my neck, and I have to try hard not to shiver in front of him. "In this case, I know the president of the distributor. They send me everything early. I have no formal acquaintance with Rudy Winter."

"Thank God. I apologize for almost calling you a misogynist."

"No worries," he says. But his tone has a hint of mockery. It's a tone I've encountered in my work, and I'm sure he's holding something back.

The fun part is figuring out what.

"Let me guess, you don't think misogyny is a problem in our culture, do you, Holt Sebastian?" Fuck, the guy was probably one of those men who believed in reverse sexism too.

"Hatred of women? Sure. Sometimes." A conveniently vague answer.

"But you don't think that it's as big of an issue as many of those angry feminists seem to make it out to be."

"You're putting words in my mouth, Ms. Shaw. Aren't journalists taught to refrain from leading?"

I know I should watch my words with Holt, but the

inference that I'm doing my job wrong makes me defensive. "I'm sorry. I didn't know this was a job interview."

"Everything's a job interview, Brystin. Everything."

I had known that in my gut.

With the validation of the fact, I feel like I've been given permission to be assertive, and for once, I have a quick comeback. "Then I take back the apology. I'm an opinion reporter with investigative elements. I'll lead whenever I think it will get me to the honest answer."

I can practically hear the smirk behind me. "And what answer are you looking for, exactly?"

I can't turn and face him the way I'd like, but I turn my head toward my shoulder. "What else explains the system? Women statistically don't get hired for the same jobs men get hired for. They don't get paid the same. They don't get elected to office. They don't receive an equal education, and please don't try to tell me that men are just better than women. Scientifically, that's been proven untrue."

"The system is set up for men, yes. I won't deny that."

I nearly let out a sigh of relief. It's comforting to know my superior isn't an unreasonable idiot.

Then he goes on. "But I don't think it's because of hatred of women."

"Not a hatred of women? Then what else is it?"

"Self-interest."

Thunder claps through the sky, closer this time, and Holt picks up Knight's pace to a trot. It's harder to talk now, but I'm determined to continue the conversation. I need the distraction more than ever now that the horse's clip has Holt's erection bouncing against my ass. "Self-interest? Please explain."

"Once upon a time, physical strength mattered and men took power. We evolved. Women can care for themselves, better than a lot of men can, but the system was already in place. Working to change it takes energy. We don't bother because it's easier for our sex to let things stay the way they are."

Even though he can't see my reaction, I scowl. "In other words, you are putting yourself above others. Above an entire sex. I think it still qualifies as prejudice."

"I don't hate women." The evidence of such is thick and hard between us. "There are plenty of things I love about them."

"Boobs, ass, and lips?"

"For your information, it's a woman's brain that gets my cock hard first."

I'm too surprised, considering our current predicament, to stop myself from asking, "Always?"

His mouth is so close to my ear, I swear he's about to kiss it. "Always, Brystin."

Always.

The next crack of thunder splits the sky open, and the drops begin to fall. "Almost there," he says, though I still can't see the house. "We'll run the rest."

I feel his leg shift as he uses his heel to set Knight into a gallop. It's two minutes in pouring rain, two minutes with my skin wet and my shirt clinging so tightly that I'm sure my nipples are clearly visible. Two minutes of being held by a warm, protective arm. Two minutes of my heart pounding so hard I could have been the one running. Two minutes wondering what he's doing to me, why he's doing it, what it means.

Terrified that whatever this is will stop.

It's the longest two minutes of my life, and they go by in a blink.

I'm sure the horses aren't usually taken across the pristine back lawn, but Holt delivers me directly to the back patio.

He helps me off the horse without getting off himself, my shirt riding up under his grip, and God, I'm wishing it was his fingers on my skin instead of his gloves. Wishing there was more to this...whatever it was.

On the ground, I blink up at him, drops sticking to my eyelashes. I know I should say something, thank him for the ride. But all I can do is stare at him, with lips parted, heart in my throat.

He stares back for heavy seconds. "I'll see to Knight." Holt gallops toward the stables.

When I hear the door open behind me, I know it's Michael before I turn around. "Get in here, sweet girl. You're drenched."

We must have been seen approaching, because Carol has sent for towels, and Michael wraps one around me as soon as I walk in the door. "What were you doing out there?"

He's not alone in the great room, but I'm glad that there's not a huge crowd witnessing my arrival. Joe and Jessa and a couple with names I've forgotten.

"I got lost," I announce, feeling like I need to make it clear that we hadn't been out on a ride together. Not on purpose. "He rescued me."

"I bet he did." Joe's comment is under his breath but loud enough for me to hear.

"We should get you changed." Michael steers me toward the stairs.

I can feel the judgment of the others, sure they're putting me in the category of *sleeps her way to the top,* a category I very much detest, though I'm sure some would argue that my marriage is why I first earned the label.

But it's not worth trying to say anything. The more I protest, the worse it will look, so I let Michael direct me until we hit the bottom step. Then it occurs to me that this is his fault. He should have been the one to rescue me.

"I texted you."

"I just got it. But the rain was already pouring. Carol was about to send out someone to search." It doesn't feel like enough.

I glance back at the others, laughing in the great room. Laughing about me? "I'm gossip fodder."

Michael dismisses the notion. "Fuck them. How was the interaction with Holt?"

For a second, I think he knows. Knows about Holt. Knows we have a secret. I don't even know what our secret is, but I feel called out.

Then I realize I'm probably being paranoid. "He rescued me," I say again, because everything else doesn't feel right to repeat.

"Damsel in distress. That could work. A lot of men are into that."

It takes me a second to understand that Michael is talking about our potential show. I was lost in the pouring rain, and his first thought is whether or not my rescue works in his favor?

Suddenly pissed, I start up the stairs, ready to be away

from him. I only make it a couple of steps before I turn back toward him. "Why were you first into me, Michael?"

He hasn't moved, one foot on the bottom stair, his hand on the rail. "What kind of question is that?"

It's out-of-the-blue, I know, but I think it's a valid question. "What made you want to be with me? What first attracted you?"

"Besides the fact that you give the best head known to man?"

I roll my eyes. "What got your pants down in the first place?"

"I don't know a straight man alive who wouldn't drop trou for lips like yours."

"Michael, I'm serious." I realize he might very well be serious too. He supports my talent and believes I'll go far, but the beginning was very possibly all about the physical. Aren't most relationships?

I've asked now, though. So I stand for the answer.

He sighs. "Honestly, Brystin?" He climbs the few stairs so there isn't any distance between us before he continues. "There are a multitude of reasons that I'm attracted to you. You know that. We wouldn't have this partnership otherwise. But the *first* thing that I liked about you? The *very* first? It was how much you liked me.

"Now let's get you upstairs and warm."

I nod as he passes by me. Nod like I want to be upstairs and warm. Nod like his answer was what I had expected instead of the answer that sheds light on everything I've been trying not to see.

CHAPTER
FIVE
BRYSTIN

A member of the staff is waiting for us when we come downstairs for dinner.

"Mr. and Mrs. Shaw, you'll be dining on the veranda tonight."

"Mr. *Endlich* and Ms. Shaw," Michael corrects, less irritated than I expect him to be. Usually people are trying to pin me with *his* last name. I don't generally mind, but it is sort of satisfying to see the shoe on the opposite foot.

The server looks down at her iPad. "I see. I apologize for that, Mr. Endlich. If you'll come with me."

Michael takes my hand as we follow her down the hallway, turning in the opposite direction of the dining room where I can hear the sounds of others gathered, and through the conservatory toward a glass door leading to a private patio.

"Do you think we're in trouble?" I whisper-ask Michael.

"I'm betting the opposite. Do you need me to run up and get your shawl?"

The rain stopped in the early afternoon, but the temperature is still cool outside. Since I'd expected to be inside tonight, I'd chosen a dress with bare shoulders. "The shawl doesn't match. I'll tough it out."

As soon as we're outside, I see it won't be a problem. Along with a small dining table, there are several outside warmers, all turned on full blast. The air smells like new grass and fresh rain, and piano music is playing softly from outdoor speakers. When I look up, the sky is clear now, and the stars are visible.

Letting go of Michael's hand, I move to the table and finger the petals of the rose bouquet centerpiece. "It's a very romantic setup."

I notice there are plate settings for three at the same time Michael does. "Perhaps we're being courted."

Just then, another door opens, and Holt walks out. My stomach flips at the sight of him. He's dressed in a designer suit, minus the tie, and the hair that had been clean and natural this morning has now been styled. It's impossible to ignore how attractive he is, even standing beside the man I've always thought was the most beautiful man on earth.

The tingle in my lower regions is telling me I may have been wrong on that account.

Out of some strange sense of guilt or loyalty, I reach again for Michael's hand.

"Ah, you're here," Holt says. "I hope you haven't been waiting long."

"Just arrived," Michael says.

"Excellent. I'm told dinner is ready for service. Shall we sit?"

My husband looks at me, excitement in his eyes. *This is it*, they say. *This is the beginning*.

I feel it too, that thrill at being closer to my dreams than ever before. It's a very similar feeling to being aroused, which explains my reaction to Holt. Not just tonight, but every time I've seen him. It was simply excitement about the possibilities he delivers.

Buoyed by this realization, I gift him with one of my most genuine smiles. "We'd love to."

Dinner proceeds much like a first date. Our conversations are easy and without weight. The beauty of the night is thoroughly discussed, as well as the estate and the best parts of visiting in each season. Holt shares an anecdote about the wine. Michael recalls the first time he met Holt's father, Samuel. Once prompted, I complain about my time at NYU versus working on my master's at Emerson. No one mentions *New Jersey Now*. No one approaches the topic of a show at SNC.

Meanwhile, Holt treats us to a five-star meal with a much fancier menu and presentation than dinner last night. A french onion soup, followed by a salad with Asian pears and candied walnuts drizzled in honey vinaigrette. The main entree of balsamic glazed lamb chops makes me a fan of a meat I've never really loved. All paired with a Bordeaux wine that Holt chose himself for the occasion.

By the time dessert arrives, I swear I've already consumed ten pounds of food. "Thank God it's berries so I don't have to be a good girl and turn it down."

Michael puts his hand up to the side of his mouth, as though he's telling a secret. "She wouldn't turn it down."

"I would too!"

"Okay, she might. But then she'd steal half of mine."

The truth is that I'm very disciplined with what I eat—television requires it—and I don't necessarily like pretending otherwise, but I understand Michael's merely attempting to be entertaining so I not only concede but go one further. "Honestly, I'd steal the whole thing."

Under the table, Michael squeezes my thigh, validation that we're on the same page. We're after the same thing. We're a team.

Holt sits back in his chair, an after-dinner liquor in one hand, and waves a finger at the two of us with the other. "Tell me about this. How did you meet? How long have you two been together?"

They're fairly mundane questions, ones that we've been asked many times before, and yet something about the way Holt asks makes them feel oddly personal and I'm reluctant to answer.

Michael steps up to the plate when I hesitate. "Married for two years last December. Together for a year before that."

"A *year* before that?" I'm not surprised by his answer, but he's wrong.

"Almost two."

"Almost *six*."

Michael frowns. "That didn't count."

"It counted to me." I'd been head over heels, though. To him, I'd been a lowly weekend morning news reporter with a massive crush. It took six months before I finally cornered him at a holiday party and convinced him to take me home.

After that, I was a hot coworker he fucked on occasion. Like lots of naive girls, I clung to the notion that one day he'd wake up and realize he was taking me for granted. Realize he wanted more as much as I did.

I know exactly the day that he did realize he wanted more. Not the same kind of more as I'd imagined, but more nonetheless. The day that he counts as the beginning for us. I'd just been promoted to daily news coverage when I'd been tasked with covering the local school board elections. I ended up going over and beyond, and had even asked Michael to help me to get the segment perfect before turning it in. It was a good piece, and he knew it. He looked at me differently after that. Maybe he knew I had the potential to be something. Maybe he could finally see where we could fit together. He asked me out on a real date the very next day.

I wonder how Michael remembers it as he holds my stare. Eventually, he says to Holt, "She was young. *Too* young for me. For several years, I didn't think we could be anything serious."

"What changed your mind?" Holt asks.

I turn toward Michael, putting the pressure on him to say something good. But all he does is shrug. "After a while, she became impossible to ignore."

I make a show of rolling my eyes. "'Impossible to ignore.'" I laugh. "You, on the other hand, were just impossible." It's my turn to address Holt directly. "We'd been casual for four years. Four years that count. Then we were on set more together, and we kind of realized we worked.

We started officially dating. A year after that he got me on his new show, which was, of course, *New Jersey Now*, and a year after that we tied the knot."

At city hall on December thirtieth, in time to get the tax break for the year.

Holt glances down at my bare ring finger, and while I usually let people have their opinions on the matter, I suddenly feel defensive about it. "I'm not a big fan of jewelry." I rub the empty spot with my thumb. A terrible lie considering how I'm always wearing earrings and necklaces.

I could correct the statement, say I just mean rings, but I'm over the subject, and instead reach for my wine.

"A fortune to spend to declare to the world something that is really very personal." Michael takes my free hand in his, lacing our fingers together on the table where Holt can see them. "She kept her maiden name, too. Not just on air. A very modern woman."

"Modern marriage all around." I smile at him, but it feels forced.

Holt seems to study us, as he's seemed to study our every reaction throughout the meal. Probably, I'm being paranoid.

After a beat, he says, "And now here you are. Poised to be a power couple."

"'A power couple.'" Michael raises his liquor glass. "From your mouth to God's ears."

Holt smiles at him in a way that can only be called devilish. "Haven't you heard, Michael? God answers to Sebastians."

It's a cocky statement, one that would have me saying

oh, please if it were uttered out of any other man's lips. When Holt declares it, it feels somehow modest.

More importantly, the topic has been broached, and I'm sure the only natural segue from here is into discussions of what Michael and I could bring to SNC.

Holt surprises me when, instead of continuing the conversation, he stands. "Would you care to join me for after-dinner drinks in the game room? I'm not sure if you've discovered it yet. It's off the library."

He directs the library comment to me, and I know he's reminding me he saw me there last night. It feels like being scolded. Like I was somewhere I shouldn't have been, even though the library was never pointed out as off-limits. I suppose it wasn't where I was that was forbidden, but the conversation I'd listened in on. I'd known it was private, and yet I'd stayed.

Is that why we're still not talking about careers? Am I being punished?

Definitely still being paranoid.

"Love to," Michael answers for us, and soon we find ourselves leaving the veranda and heading inside.

The game room, it turns out, consists of a mahjong/card table, a shuffleboard, darts, and a pool table, as well as an antique pinball machine.

"We're uneven in numbers. We could do cards or darts to be inclusive, but I have to say, I'm really in the mood for a nice round of pool. Do either of you play?" Holt looks at Michael.

Pool is actually a game where my husband and I are evenly matched. But I understand what this is, the same way I understand why game rooms exist more often in rich men's houses than women's. This is a male honor thing, a chance for Michael and Holt to whip out their dicks and measure.

Michael knows it too, and is already going for the pool stick when I say, "I'll watch and cheer on."

"But who will you cheer on?" Holt stares at me, unabashedly. In a way that most men wouldn't dare to stare in front of that woman's husband.

The question is undeniably a challenge, and I'm wary of making the wrong choice. One is my husband. One is a king. In a king's house, you should always cheer on the king.

But somehow I know that Holt doesn't want flattery for the sake of flattery. "Whoever's winning," I say.

"Good answer," Holt says. The right answer, I'm sure from his tone.

The first game goes quickly. Michael plays poorly, on purpose. He misses shots I know he could make drunk. But he plays competitively enough to make it look close when Holt wins. I happily cheer on every sunk ball, no matter who shoots it in.

The second game is much the same, except that now Holt invites conversation to the match. "If you were given a time slot at SNC, what would you imagine you'd do with it?"

As producer, Michael is usually the one of us who pitches, but as he's concentrating on the balls, I jump in. "Much like *New Jersey Now* but on an international level. Spending time each night in different states across the U.S., giving national attention to local issues, and not just the issues that affect federal politics. I don't think viewers realize how common some city level concerns are, whether you live in New York City or Portland or Atlanta. Likewise, I don't think some viewers realize how national policies can affect communities so differently.

"In a time when the nation is looking for unity, it's exactly the show that should be produced."

Holt takes his turn, asking his next question as he lines up his shot. "Same format? A team of regular anchors?" He makes the shot then lines up the next.

"No. Just one."

Holt hits the ball then stands to deliver his full attention to me. "Just you?"

I hope I'm imagining the condescension in his expression. "Yes."

"Brystin is why *New Jersey Now* works," Michael clarifies, eager to sell me "right."

"Do you believe that?" Holt asks me, ignoring Michael.

"Yes." I answer boldly. I know I should say more, speak up for my chance. Convince him to give me this shot.

But I can hear my heart pounding in my chest, and my hands feel clammy, and all I can think about is how much Holt sees when he's staring at me like that. How I think he can see everything. How I think he knows more from his eyes than from any words I could give him.

"You're a local reporter, in a small state, with a small following, considering what larger states see in viewership. You think there isn't another person with more experience who should do the job?"

"You need more women-helmed shows," Michael says. "That's a fact. Your demographics are begging for it."

"It's your turn." Holt barely gives him a glance before

he's back to me. "Jessa Jones, for example. She's here this weekend because she's bored. She wants something more challenging. This sounds like a perfect project for her."

She's my idol, a woman who would own any show she helmed. And I know how this business works. I know the reality of how people get promoted. I'm not at the level to be asking for my own show yet. Our best hope is for Michael, a man with experience, to be asked to produce and for me to come on as one of the off-air reporters. That's the realistic path.

But I have a fire in my belly, and this is *my* show. My idea as much as Michael's. It was made for me.

And I have the benefit of what I overheard last night. "Jessa Jones will draw viewers, no matter what show she's anchoring. But she's already earned her audience. She earned it with Samuel in charge, and so any project she's on will succeed because of him. I would have to work to earn mine, and that's what *you* need. Someone who comes in fresh so that any success will be attributed to Holt Sebastian. If you want more of the same, sure. Go with someone more experienced. If you want to make your name, if you want people to know you're more than just Samuel Sebastian's son, then you make me a star. *We* make me a star, and you'll get all the credit."

Holt's expression is guarded, and I can't read his reaction. Behind him, Michael looks equally unsure, and I'm abruptly struck with doubt. My bravado is gone, and I hate myself for having spoken up at all. I should have left it to Michael to sell me. He knows how to talk me up better than anyone I know.

After what feels like a lifetime, Holt turns so he can see

both of us. "You make a good case. More for the position I'm in rather than for yourself, but a good case all the same. It's still a gamble." He glances down at the pool table. The game is even at the moment, each of them having sunk two balls. "Tell you what. We play out this game. Michael wins, we can negotiate a show. I win, I go with the tried and true."

He gives that fucking devil's grin again. That grin that says he knows he has all the power. That we're just entertainment. That things that would make a real difference in our lives are as trivial to him as a game of fucking pool.

I hate him.

I hadn't known until just now, but I'm sure. I *hate* him. He plays the good host and makes my girly parts tingle when he eats me up with his eyes and flaunts his ability to make things happen, but I hate him. Part of me wants to tell him to fuck off. Wants to pack up my things and leave with Michael tonight.

But the thing I hate most is that the other part of me, the bigger part of me, wants to stay. Wants to win. Wants him to give me this chance. I'll even get on my knees and thank him. Every day of my life, if that's what he wants.

Michael doesn't hesitate. "Sure. It's on." He doesn't hold back any longer. He sinks three balls in a row.

Though Holt won the first game, he truly did seem the poorer player. Seems he was holding out as well, because he also sinks three balls. Then he sinks a fourth. He misses on the fifth, and the turn goes back to Michael.

I no longer cheer for either of them. I sit quietly, my stomach in knots, my hands clasped in prayer position at my lips. *Please,* I say to the universe. *Please, please, please.*

Back and forth it goes, until all that's left is the eight ball.

And it's Michael's turn. One shot is all there is between us and our dream future.

He lines it up, he shoots. The black ball goes in the pocket…

…immediately followed by the white ball.

It's the quickest switch from elation to disappointment I've ever felt. One second I'm flying, and the next, I'm smashed against the rocks.

Michael feels worse than I do. I see it in his posture. This was his responsibility, and he fucked it up. That's what he's telling himself.

Once the shock wears off, I wonder if I'll blame him too.

"White ball in the pocket means you lose." Holt states what we already know. He can't be oblivious to the tension. I'm even tempted to say he enjoys it.

Michael clears his throat. "Good game," he says sullenly.

"Oh, don't be so hard on yourself." Holt claps a hand on his back, as though they're buds. He looks from Michael to me. Back to Michael. Back to me, lingering this time. "You know what? I can't do this to you. It was such a close shot, and so much riding on it. I'm going to give you another shot."

My stupid heart gets excited again. At just the chance. Like a fucking lottery addict who loses every day and yet still perks up when they get a new set of numbers.

"I don't know if I can take the pressure of another game." Michael eyes me. If he's asking me to take his place in the challenge, I might be sick. Actually, I'm sick already.

Holt laughs. "Nor could I. Pool is done for the night. Let's do this the old-fashioned way—over bourbon in my study, aka the library. It's right next door."

"All right," Michael says tentatively. Then more sure. "We'd like that."

"Oh, just you, I meant. I don't generally negotiate directly with the talent when they're unknown. And call me old-fashioned, but the library has always been the men's room in the evenings. We'll hammer everything out, and you can consult with your wife afterward." He turns to me. "I'm sure you understand, Brystin."

I can't imagine the look he sees on my face. Probably one of abject horror and disgust. Disgust because he's playing his misogyny card hard, doubling down after our conversation this morning. I have no doubt. Out of spite, perhaps. Because he can.

Horror because I absolutely don't trust Holt Sebastian. Not one bit. I don't believe this pretense of good intentions, and I'm terrified of whatever game he's going to try to play next.

Just because he can.

CHAPTER SIX

BRYSTIN

By midnight, Michael still hasn't returned to the room.

I've been a mess trying to pass the time. I showered. Changed into pajamas. Tried to read and failed. Texted about the evening with Zully, who found a way to blame Michael for everything. Cried for a while about how degrading the whole experience has been, and then put light makeup on my clean face to hide my puffy eyes.

I'm considering putting on a robe and going to look for him when the door finally opens. I practically jump on him. "Well?"

He runs his hand through his hair, assessing me in silence.

I feel like punching him. "Don't just stand there. What happened? Tell me!"

"I'm…I'm trying to figure out where to start."

Usually, I like hearing things from the beginning, but

I'm too miserable and anxious. "Did we get it? That's all I want to know."

He's serious, and I'm nervous. He's always serious, but not *this* serious. Slowly, he begins to nod his head.

"Oh my God! Are you kidding me? Oh my God!" I know what time it is, and I'm trying my best to keep my voice down, but I've never been good with containing excitement.

He shushes me with a smile and puts his hands on my shoulders to settle me down. "Hold on, hold on. There are…" He takes a breath. "It was a negotiation. There are stipulations."

I somber, understanding setting in. "We got the show, but I'm not the anchor."

"I didn't say that."

"I know. You've barely said anything. I feel like I'm pulling at an anchor to get the words out of your mouth."

"So stop pulling. Give me a minute. Why don't you sit down."

"I don't think I can." I think I'm too twitchy to stay still. I'm disappointed about not being an anchor, but I'd always known that was a lofty goal. Fucking Holt was the one who made me think for a few minutes tonight that it was actually within reach. I swear he must get off on yo-yoing people around.

But okay, I have work to do. This is a damn good place to start, and I can't be down about that.

Michael does not share my enthusiasm. He doesn't seem exactly unhappy, but he's wary. He picks my earlier discarded clothing off the armchair and sets them on top of the dresser, clearing me a spot to sit. "Just try, will you?"

"Okay, okay." I perch on the edge of the chair, my knee bouncing. "I'm sitting."

"So you're right, in a way—he agreed to give us the show. A few minor tweaks to what you've proposed, but all-in-all the same vision."

I can't stop nodding. "Good, good. That's really good. You producing?"

"Me producing. He has some other people already lined up that he'd like to pair us up with. All names I know. A good team."

He pauses, and I pounce. "And who does he want to anchor?"

"He hasn't decided yet. But you're not out of the running."

My heart is already beating so fast, but it kicks up another notch. "Really? Are you kidding me?" I can't help it —I burst out of the chair and hug him. "I still have a shot, Michael! And we got the show!"

He hugs me back, though somewhat reluctantly. "We got the show."

"We got the fucking show." I pull back to look at his face. "What does he need me to do? How can I prove myself? Recommendations? A resumé portfolio? Does he need me to audition?"

His smile fades. "He wants you to…go to his room."

"Right now? Okay. I'll change." I push away, headed for the closet. "I thought he didn't negotiate with talent. That asshole. Or should I say assHolt." I laugh at my own joke. "Does he want me to beg? On my knees, probably."

Then it hits me.

Like an idiot, it takes almost a full minute. I still, letting go of the dress I'd been about to grab. Slowly, I turn to face my husband. "He wants me to come to his room. Right now. After midnight. By myself."

Michael gives the subtlest of nods.

"He doesn't want to negotiate. He wants to fuck me." I put my hands up to my face, afraid that I might cry again.

Except I'm too mad to cry.

It's easiest to turn my anger on Michael, since he's here. "He wants to fuck me. And you said…? You said…what? You told him I'd come? You told that asshole I'd come?"

"No!" He spoke too loudly, and his voice is lower when he continues. "I didn't tell him you'd do it."

"Did you tell him I absolutely would not do it?"

He looks taken aback. "I told him I would ask."

"You didn't tell him, 'Fuck no, that's my wife, and no job is worth selling her out'?" My voice cracks. Maybe I'm too mad *not* to cry.

"Brystin, come on." He takes a step toward me, but I put a hand out to stop him from getting closer. "Jesus fucking Christ, that's not us. That's not our arrangement."

"Right. Not our arrangement." A stupid tear leaks down my cheek.

He turns his back on me in frustration, then spins back toward me. "We said, 'Anything it takes.' That's what we said. We pledged that to each other. 'Anything it takes to get there.' So I got your segment nominated for the award. I got you in that building, which got us here. I played his fucking douchebag game tonight."

"A fucking messed-up game of pool is not the same as letting him inside my cunt."

"I know. Believe me, I know, and if our positions were

reversed, there'd be no fucking way I'd let him in my ass." He raises a sharp finger. "But I'll tell you what, Brystin. If he asked me to suck him off, I'd think about it."

"So you're saying that I should—"

He cuts me off. "So I'm saying it's not my decision to make for you." Again, his voice has gotten loud, and he takes a beat, calming down.

I let his words sink in.

Then I sink onto the bed, one foot underneath me.

He sits next to me. "I didn't know what to say. You might have been pissed if I'd spoken for you. I didn't know how much you wanted it, and I thought you should have the chance to decide for yourself."

He reaches out to touch me, but backs off when I flinch. I'm furious with him. Furious. But really, I'm furious at Holt. Because Michael got what he wanted, he got his show. He could have refused to let Holt turn me into a whore, and then what? Then my chance would definitely be shot. Possibly forever.

And if Michael felt deeply enough to protect me anyway, it might have been worth giving up my dream.

I suppose I'm most furious at myself. For still wanting Michael to love me like that. For still expecting that he might surprise me.

"I'm sorry," he says, and I know from the weight in his tone that he means it.

"I know you are. This isn't on you. I was asking a lot."

"Stop it." He shifts so he's facing me. "You're asking for what you're worth. It might not be the usual timeline, but you're too good to follow those rules. You deserve this show. This belongs to you."

I usually appreciate his support. He knows it's my love language, and his words have done a lot to bond us over the years.

Right now, though, it all feels hollow. "It doesn't belong to me, Michael. It belongs to him."

He reaches out to stroke my hair, and I let him. "But it still could be yours too."

"You think I should go?" I peer over at him, a tear on the edge of my eyelash in my peripheral vision. "You think I should do it."

"I want you on the show. Of course I do. But do I want you to do this?" He sighs. "You could go to him on your terms. Just to talk."

I turn my head away from him and bite back a harsh laugh. Just like a man to not understand how vulnerable a woman can be in the presence of a man like Holt. In his bedroom. Alone.

The worst part of it is that I don't think any of those things sound so bad until it's framed as the price of my dream job.

Again, I put my hands over my face. "I don't know. I don't know what to do."

"You don't have to do anything, sweet girl." He runs his hand down my back. "And if it means anything, I don't want you to do anything that you don't want to do."

"Great. Thanks."

"I mean…" He withdraws his hand, and I know he's thinking carefully about his words. Trying not to hurt me more, I'm sure. "I mean that I don't want you to do anything with him that you don't want to do, but what happens with you and other men is none of my business."

Like what happens with him and other women isn't my business.

Open marriage. Open relationship before that. We've never been monogamous.

Rather, he's never been monogamous. The open relationship was important to him. The way no rings was important to him. And me keeping my maiden name. It was all the price for owning a part of Michael Endlich. I never argued with any of it, but multiple partners wasn't for me. Except for a few guys I slept with in the beginning, before we were officially together, I've only been with Michael. I've only always wanted to be with Michael.

And I understand that's the foundation that Michael is drawing on when he says that this is entirely my choice. But fuck him for the wording.

"In other words, as long as I'm okay being a whore, you're okay with it too. Got it." I stand up, no longer able to be next to him.

"Brystin."

I don't care that he's frustrated. His feelings are the least of my concerns right now. "Look, Michael. I get what you're saying. This has nothing to do with you. This is all about me. You're just the messenger. I get it."

I head into the bathroom to look at myself in the mirror. Not too horrible. Visine will help. I dig through Michael's toiletry bag to find a bottle. I put a drop in each eye, and when I look in the mirror again, he's standing in the doorway behind me.

"I'm sorry."

"You said that already."

"I feel like I should say it again."

"So now you have." I grab a tissue and dab at the tears from the drops.

Michael leans against the frame. "You sound like you're angry with me."

He wants me to say something to make him feel better. Wants me to take any guilt off his shoulders, but I can't. "Because I get it, Michael, but I hate you a little bit right now."

"Hate *me*? Why?"

I toss the tissue in the trash and turn around to face him. "For being the messenger. For being a man. For having it easy." For not being my knight riding in on a white horse.

Or even a black horse.

I would have ridden away with him into the sunset.

"I understand." He doesn't, but he knows well enough not to argue. "What are you going to do? What do you want me to do?"

"I don't know, okay?" I brush past him, into the bedroom to retrieve my phone. "I need to think. And I need you to leave."

"Leave?"

"Leave this room. I don't care where you go. I just can't have you here right now."

For a minute, I think he's going to stand his ground. Tell me I'm being unreasonable. This isn't his fault. But he must recognize how upset I am in the end. "I'll go join Joe in the hot tub then."

If Joe's there this late at night, there are probably 'Bastian Bunnies there too.

And I don't care. Not my business.

At least he makes the pretense of grabbing a pair of swim trunks before heading for the door.

When he's opened the door, I suddenly feel guilty about tossing him out. "Give me an hour."

"Okay. Text me if you need anything." Then he's gone.

I open my texting app, not to message him, but to message Zully.

Would you fuck someone to get a job?

Depends on how good the job is. And how hot the guy is.

Dream job. Really hot guy.

My phone rings in my hand. Zully's face appears on the caller ID. "Are you thinking of fucking Holt Sebastian?" she asks when I answer.

I perch on the side of the bed, trying to decide how much I want to say. The clock is ticking, though, and I don't think I have the energy to replay everything that just happened. "I think I might be considering it. Is that bad?" It feels really bad.

"Two questions—would you fuck him if there wasn't a job on the line?"

"If I wasn't married?"

She groans. She's always trying to get me to take advantage of my open arrangement with Michael.

I ignore her. "If I wasn't married, then…probably, yes." It's the first time I've admitted it, even to myself. But there's an attraction with Holt, and if I were available, then yes. I could very easily see myself in his bed.

"Real hard for me not to say go for it just from that, but there's a second question—are you hoping that it will make Michael jealous?"

I blink, refusing to get teary again. "I know it won't make Michael jealous," I say.

"I'm not exactly sure that's true," she says, to my surprise. "But the point is that you're not thinking about doing this for the wrong reasons."

"I'm only thinking about the job. And I really want the job." Especially now that I'm pissed at Michael. I hate the idea that he's going to walk out of this with more than I have. I'm sure I won't feel that way tomorrow, but right now I feel it hard.

"Okay, another question—if you do this and you don't get the job, will you regret it?"

Honestly, I don't know. Maybe I could have one steamy night with the man and let it be just that.

But then I think about what I know of Holt. How he played with us all evening. He probably thought of it as foreplay, and even after he got in my pants, I'm not sure he wouldn't withdraw his offer.

"Your hesitation is answer enough," Zully says. "Much as I hate to advise you not to fuck a rich, hot asshole, I know you. You'll feel guilty, and you won't ever be satisfied if this is how you get your show. Which is stupid, if you ask me. Doesn't matter how you get your place. Matters what you do with it, but you're a good girl, and you think you have to do things the right way, and somehow I love you despite that."

I laugh. "I'm not *that* good."

"Sure. Whatever you say. But let me make sure you

know that whatever you do with the rich boy, I have no problem with it. In case that needed saying."

"You won't think I'm a whore?"

"Definitely not."

Actually, it makes me feel better. Even though she's right—I can't sleep with Holt and feel good about myself. Not while I believe in my commitment to Michael, however one-sided it might be. Not when it's in exchange for something I should have earned without getting on my back.

And realizing that makes me pissed again. This time my anger is directed where it should be—at Holt. For playing with people's emotions like he does without consequence. For putting me and Michael in this impossible position. For thinking he can have anything he wants because of his last name.

My anger gives me momentum. I throw my phone down on the bed, shed my PJs, and find something quick and easy to put on—a simple wrap dress that I planned to wear on the ride home.

Then I gloss my lips and throw on some flats. Holt wants me to come to his room? Then I'll come to his room. I want to see his face when he hears the word I'm sure he rarely ever hears—no.

CHAPTER **SEVEN**

BRYSTIN

I'm in the hallway before realizing I don't know exactly where Holt's room is. With a vague impression that it's somewhere on the first floor, I head downstairs.

To my surprise, there's a member of the staff waiting for me, one I haven't met yet, most likely because he's on the night shift. "Ms. Shaw, if you'll follow me." He walks without asking where I'm going or who I'm looking for.

Which means he already knows.

I have half a mind to turn around and forget the whole thing. The egotistical nerve of Holt Sebastian, to be so sure that I'd jump at his command, that he had someone waiting to escort me to him. It would serve him right to find out he's wrong.

But I'm also self-centered, it seems, because it's more important to me to see his face when I tell him no than to let him be pissed that I didn't show up.

Also, I'm not about to get his staff in trouble for my actions. I wonder about my escort as I follow him down the hall to the right wing of the house. He seems to be older than me, younger than Michael. What has he seen in his time with Holt? How many women has he taken to his employer's room in the middle of the night? How often did those women have a partner or spouse somewhere else in the house?

I want to tell this man—a man who hasn't even shared with me his name—that it's not what he thinks. I'm not like them. I'm not the kind of woman who will trade sex for status.

I don't know what keeps my mouth shut, but I don't speak up, and eventually we're at Holt's room. The staff member knocks on Holt's door for me, then throws it open when Holt says, "It's open."

I take a step in, but while the door is still ajar behind me, I blurt out loudly, "I'm only here to talk."

The words are out before I've even located Holt in the massive suite. When I do, he's closer than I'd expected, pouring a bottle of wine at his mini bar, his back to me. He's made himself comfortable since dinner. His jacket is gone and his dress shirt is untucked. He's barefoot, which feels strangely personal, and makes my lower belly tingle in a way I find disturbing.

He waits until the door clicks shut before he speaks, but he doesn't turn. "If that was for the staff, you don't have to worry about them. I only hire people who have proven they can be discreet."

It's amazing how the guy can prove himself to be even more of an asshole than I thought he was. "That wasn't for

—" Well, it sort of was. "That was for you. I'm telling you. I'm only here to—"

But then Holt turns around, and his shirt isn't just untucked—it's unbuttoned. And holy shit, that man has abs. Like rows of them. The six-pack kind. Eight-pack, actually.

"Whoa." Damn, I really need a filter.

"You're only here to…whoa?" His lip curls at one side in amusement.

I don't know what pisses me off more—his amusement or his abs. Either way, the curse slips from my lips without thinking. "Fuck you."

"I'd love that." He winks. "But first, how about some wine?"

My face is instantly hot, and I put my hands up in the air, as if I can stop what's happening. As if Holt can be stopped at all. "No. No. Definitely no. I came here to talk. I came here to tell you that you can't just summon women to your room, dangling their future above them like a predator. And you trying to romanticize it with wine and dim lighting and whatever this is playing—"

"Sibelius," he says, patiently.

"Sibelius, thank you. It's very nice, by the way. But it doesn't erase the fact that you are using your power to try to coerce me into fucking you, and it's not happening. Not, not happening."

"Not not? Is that a double negative?" He extends a glass out toward me, despite my speech.

"It was for emphasis." And because I could actually really use a drink right now, I take the glass and down half. "Thank you."

"It's a Vieux Château Certa. Two thousand five."

"That means nothing to me." Admittedly, it really does taste good.

"An exceptional year for Bordeaux because of the dry winter—"

Honestly, Holt is unnervingly charming, and at dinner I learned that I'm kind of fascinated with most everything he says. Despite that, somehow, I remember myself, and cut him off. "Stop. I'm not here to learn about fucking wine."

"You're here to talk. I'm talking."

"Oh my God. That's not what I want to talk about."

"What is it you do want to talk about, Brystin?" He leans against the bar, and the tilt of his hip opens his shirt up farther, and *unf*. The man really has impressive abs.

I force my gaze away from his perfect washboard and realize that of course he's caught me ogling. His lip twitches, and I can tell he's trying not to laugh.

Refusing to let him throw me completely off task, I focus on my point. "I want to talk about all that I've already said. Were you listening?"

"Very carefully."

"And you have nothing to say for yourself?"

"I have much to say. It's late, so I keep the lights down. I often play music when I'm alone in my rooms—classical is my favorite in the evenings. It's beautiful, and I like beautiful things. The wine is also something I quite enjoy. I poured you a glass as well because I'm a good host. Let's see…then you mentioned something about me being a predator and that I couldn't summon women to my room. But you're here, aren't you? So it seems that I…can."

He must sense that I'm about to blow because he

sweeps his hand in the air, as if to erase the words he's just said. "I think perhaps the most important thing you said was that I was trying to use my power to coerce you into my bed—"

"I said fucking. Romanticizing again." I take another sip of my wine, though, because I'm starting to feel a little unbalanced. Ironically, it's probably the wine's fault.

"'Coerce you into fucking.' That's right. Where exactly did that notion come from?"

Now I definitely feel unsure. "Uh. Michael said…" I try to remember his exact words. "That you would give me the anchor spot on a show if I came to your room."

Holt nods, not in agreement, but like *I see*. "Actually, what I said was that I couldn't give a job like that to someone so green. I suggested that if you truly were interested, that I'd need to spend more time getting to know you."

"Huh." I can't decide if he's trying to convince me he meant something different than he most obviously means or not.

Or if he might actually never have meant it the way Michael perceived it.

"You were right when you came in here, Brystin. We should talk." He takes my near empty glass from my hand and turns to refill it. "Why don't you make yourself comfortable? I'll be right over to join you."

He nods toward the seating area, and though I'm pretty sure that no good can come of me staying any longer, I'm also hung up on that teeny tiny possibility that I might still get the job from just a conversation.

So against my better judgment, I say okay and head

further into the suite, taking the opportunity to soak up the surroundings. It's really more like an apartment than a suite. There's a living room set and a fireplace and bookshelves and walls with fine art and the bar has a full size fridge and microwave. There's a door to my right that seems to lead to a bathroom and a door at the back of the room that probably belongs to the bedroom. It's open, but the lights are off beyond it, and I find that strangely comforting.

The furniture is manly but modern, all in deep earth tone colors. I sit on the couch, assuming he'll sit in the armchair across from me, but when he crosses to hand me my drink, he sits next to me, twisting so that one leg is bent, and he's facing me.

No, he definitely meant what Michael thought he'd meant.

I don't drink anything from my wineglass before setting it down on the coffee table. "Look, you're gaslighting me." I put a finger up to stop him from interrupting, which I can tell he badly wants to do. "Don't try to tell me that 'get to know me' isn't some kind of euphemism."

He laughs, the sound low in his chest, but not ominous. "Like in the biblical sense?" He considers as he takes a sip of wine. "I mean…" He opens his free hand to the air, as if to say, possibly.

"Yeah, yeah, see?" I shift so I'm facing him as well. "You don't want to say it outright, but the implication is plain as day. If I want this job, I have to fuck you."

"That's not—"

I cut him off. "Yes or no, you'll give me this job if I don't?"

"Let's be clear about the situation, okay?" He throws an arm over the back of the sofa. "I have a full schedule of shows. I don't need a new one. I'm not even in charge of programming. That's taken care of by people much further down the chain of command. But I obviously have the ability to make things happen, if I want, and I'm very inspired by this concept you and Michael have brought to the table. I want this show. I want Michael to produce. I want you to be part of it.

"But let's not for one minute pretend that hiring you to be the anchor is not a big ask. I'd be foolish for doing it. You're thirty-three. You're without national news network credentials. You're untested. You haven't earned it. There are a dozen anchors who already work in my studio that deserve the promotion. I'd have to defend myself to the board. I'll piss off my VP of programming, not to mention the flack I'll get from my staff. Particularly women who are two decades older who have worked for SNC for their whole careers."

They're hard words, but they're honest. And I need to hear them. "I understand. I'm not ready."

"I didn't say that, Brystin. I said I'd be foolish to hire you. It would be a risk, and I'm asking you why I should take a risk like that on you?"

For a second, I think he's asking me to sell myself again.

But then I realize he's just explaining why I'm here. In his room. Why he feels justified in wanting what he wants.

And now I'm confused.

"It's transactional," he says. He leans over and puts his glass next to my glass, and when he sits up again, his knee touches mine.

Instead of immediately moving away, I glance down at the point of contact. His body is hot against mine, even through the material of his pants, and I suddenly feel warm everywhere. Especially between my legs. Is this really so bad? Would *more* really be so awful?

"Transactional," he repeats, and now I've hesitated too long, and I have to let my knee stay where it is, pressed against his. "I have something you want. You have something I want. And I'd venture to say that I have far more at risk than you do."

I squint at him, ready to protest, but he intervenes. "I'm not saying that what you have isn't worth a lot. More, probably. To you. I'm just letting you know where I'm coming from."

He's good. Really good. But I recognize it for what it is. "You're a master manipulator, Mr. Sebastian."

He groans but he follows it up with a lazy smile. "I'm laying out facts, Ms. Shaw. That's all."

"You've done this before, I bet."

"Traded one thing for something else? Yes. I have."

"With women."

"Never given a woman a contract who hasn't earned the promotion, if that's what you're suggesting."

Like I said, he's good. Blatantly putting me in my place. Flexing his power.

As if he can read my thoughts, he defends himself. "I'm not threatening to blacklist you from the industry. I'm not saying I won't hire you as a team reporter. I'm not taking away your livelihood or thwarting your career track. It's transactional." He grows serious. "I think you're already used to transactional relationships."

It's not the first time that he's tried to see inside my marriage. He's not wrong, but it's all guessing. No way did Michael tell him the basis of our partnership, and like hell will I give him the satisfaction of knowing he's right.

But I am honest in my reply. "I married my husband because I loved him."

He studies me for a beat. "Ah, I see."

"Oh, fuck you, you don't see anything." I reach for my wine, letting the movement take my knee away from his. Missing the touch immediately.

I take a swallow of my wine, hoping it will replace his warmth, but it does nothing. No, touching him *isn't* that bad. More wouldn't be awful. It might even be nice.

Or maybe I'm remembering how much Michael hurt me by sending me here, and as Zully suggested, that would be a bad reason to let anything happen with Holt. "Let's not talk about Michael," I say. I put my glass back on the table, and this time, it's me who lets my knee rest against his when I sit back up.

"His name is gone from my lips. This is about you, anyway." Funny how he echoes Michael's sentiment. "No one else. Well, you and me, I suppose."

I hate the way he's paired us together like that. Made us a unit. It's what he's done since that first moment in the elevator when he made our interaction feel like a secret.

And I'm just as bad because I know what he's doing, and I still like it.

Which makes me hate us both. "What this is about is sex work." I'm trying to control the narrative. "It's prostitution."

"Is that how you define the relationship of women with sugar daddies? Or sugar mommas?"

No because that starts to be very near to the terms of my marriage. Transactional, as Holt suggested. "It's not the same."

"I beg to disagree, but fine."

"A woman dating a man for his money isn't forced into the situation. She chooses it."

"I'm not forcing you into anything, Brystin."

I'm determined to define the difference. "She isn't opposed to earning her lifestyle by lying on her back. I want to earn my career on merit."

"No one gets to where you want to go without some exchange of favors along the way. But if it makes you more comfortable, I'll be sure to never directly say your contract is contingent on it."

And now he's said exactly that without saying it. Clever. *Fuck.*

I hate this. I hate everything about this. I hate his reasonable presentation. I hate his devil smile. I hate the touch of his knee and the scent of his cologne and the way he makes my pussy clench. I hate how much I want this job.

I hate that he's asking me to choose it. To choose him.

It would be so much easier if he would force me, and I hate that I could ever have a thought as vile as that.

I shake my head then lean over to grab my glass and take three large gulps. "Favors?" I don't look back at him. "Is that what we're calling it?"

"What I'm interested in, I would very much consider favors."

"Favors. Plural." We haven't defined anything, and I'm

all of a sudden aware that I might still have something to negotiate. Like Michael said, there's a big difference between penetration and a blow job.

"A leading anchor spot, Brystin. It will change the rest of your life."

"How do you know I wouldn't change the rest of your life?" I turn back to him, an eyebrow raised.

A grin plays on his lips. "I guess I want the chance to find out." He holds my gaze, and for whatever reason, I'm all of a sudden remembering what he'd said earlier today, on the horse. How he'd said that he's attracted to brains before beauty, and I wonder if this isn't exactly what I wanted—for someone in a position of power to notice that I have something to offer. I wonder if this is what that looks like.

I wonder if he's hard right now.

"What favors are you willing to give me?" he asks quietly when the silence between us has stretched taut. "For me to take a risk?"

It's ridiculous how much I want him to kiss me right now. And I'd accused him of romanticizing this.

I force my eyes away from him so I can think. So I can spell out what I'd be willing to give. "I don't like pain," I say, slowly, because I'm making this list up as I go. "Nothing gross. Um." I pause to reword, not wanting to shame any kink he might be into. "I'm not into shit or urine or vomit or anything too outside of the mainstream. And if you're expecting me to be some kind of Dominatrix, that's not happening."

"All that sounds reasonable."

I'm bolstered by the ability to put my wants on the table

and having them be acknowledged and heard. *Transactional.* Just like he said. It makes me brave enough to say my biggest term yet. "And no intercourse."

"No intercourse?" He chews the word as he says it.

I sit back, giving him my full attention. If I'm going to be strong enough to make this demand, I should do it to his face. "No intercourse," I repeat. "I don't want to cheat on my husband."

"Even though your husband—?"

I cut him off. "It's my rule." Partly, it's an excuse to keep some control, to not give this man too much.

To be honest, I wish that was all it was. Lord knows I shouldn't care if Michael doesn't, but stupidly, I do.

Holt mulls it over, and for a long stretch of seconds, I think I might have pushed my luck.

Then, without saying anything, he stands up and reaches his hand out to mine. Unsure, but curious, I slide my palm in his. Goosebumps scatter down my arms, and I shiver as he leads me away from the couch.

To the bedroom?

But we only take a few steps before he stops. He positions me then, like I'm a doll, smoothing my hair behind one ear, pulling it forward on one side. He studies me. Looks at the light above me. Nudges me back an inch. Studies me again.

Smiles slightly.

He trails his palms down the length of my arms, positioning them with a bend, my hands splayed at my hips. Then he moves his grip to my waist, and I'm mesmerized by how bold his touch is. He's not asking for permission. He's commanding me with his fingers and his hands, and my breath gets caught, thinking about how bold his touch could be in other places. Places that are begging for his attention.

"You're a work of art, Brystin." His thumbs graze my ribs, below my breasts. Too far below. "Outside and in. Beautiful." He fingers the sash of my belt. "And I really like beautiful things."

One tug, and my dress falls open.

Oh, we're doing this.

I didn't bother with a bra, so the fabric parts to reveal steepled nipples and a black lace thong that leaves little to the imagination. Heat pours through my veins like liquid fire as he pushes the dress off my shoulders. It catches on my elbows.

"Don't move." Without moving his eyes from mine, he walks backward until he reaches the armchair. He sits, casually spreading his legs.

At the sound of a zipper opening, my attention flies past those gorgeous abs to the bulge in his crotch. Big bulge. Bigger than it had felt pressed against my back on the horse.

"Eyes on mine," he orders, and without hesitation, I do as he commands, locking my gaze to his. Out of the corner of my vision, I see him reach toward the end table next to him. I hear a drawer open. Hear him fumbling around before I hear the sound of a bottle cap. Hear the squirt of liquid into his hand.

Then I hear the very distinct sound of his palm rubbing rhythmically over his flesh.

The next several minutes go by this way—me posed and nearly naked, him with his shirt open and cock out. I see the movement of his hand in the periphery, can very clearly tell what he's doing, but I can't actually *see* it.

And, God, I want to.

I'm dying to study his anatomy. Touch him. Put him in my mouth. At the very least, I want a good glance at the scepter he carries between his thighs. It's torture to be denied even one peek.

Each second that passes, it becomes harder to keep my eyes pinned on his, but I do. Because he does too. He's barely looked at my body, if he has at all. Hasn't noticed how my nipples are painfully erect. Hasn't seen the wet spot that I'm sure is on the front of my panties. But I can tell he's very aroused, his breathing coming faster, almost as fast as mine.

It's about the power, I realize.

He's turned on by how much power he has over me. How he's been able to get a woman—someone he barely knows—to shed her clothes and stand before him in his room while he jacks off. It has to be intoxicating.

I might be disgusted if I weren't so turned on too.

And beyond the degradation, beyond the sex part of it all, is the actual eye contact. It's overwhelming. I read a study once, about how strangers could develop passionate feelings for each other with just two minutes of prolonged eye contact, and holy shit. I don't know that what I'm feeling would be considered passionate, but it's certainly intense. It feels like I'm being cut through and splayed open. It feels like I'm being dissected and discovered and *known*, and when Holt's hand movement becomes jerky and his face contorts, and a ragged moan slips past his lips, I swear I'm about to come too.

He cleans up quickly, and by the time he breaks eye contact, and I'm free to look where I want, he's put himself away. Without saying a word, he crosses to the sink at the bar and washes his hands.

"I'll take care of giving notice to your station." He avoids my eyes now as purposefully as he pinned them a minute before. "I'll get the ball rolling first thing Monday morning."

I'm still standing with my dress peeled open, not sure yet if I'm supposed to move. Wishing he'd look at me like he had. Or that he'd touch me. And weirdly, I feel like I might cry if he doesn't.

I get my hopes up when he starts in my direction, but he passes by without looking up, headed somewhere behind me.

"And Brystin."

It's a relief to hear him say my name. To acknowledge I'm human, and I'm still here. Eagerly, I turn to find him standing in the doorway to his bedroom.

"Make yourself available. When I call, you come." Finally—finally—he trails his eyes down my bare breasts, but it's a quick glance, and seems to have no impact on him. "You can go. Errol can show you back to your room if you're lost."

He disappears into his bedroom, shutting his door behind him.

It's the harshest dismissal I've ever been given. As quick as I can, before I do something stupid like start sobbing or follow after him into his room, I refasten my dress and start for the door. I make it three steps before going back to the coffee table and pouring back the rest of my wine in a single chug.

As Holt had suggested, the man who'd brought me to his room is waiting for me in the hall. Errol, I suppose, is his name. I shake my head when he looks at me. "I know where I'm going."

Going straight to the top of America's most famous, that's where. It feels good to remind myself that, and so I say it over and over as I climb the stairs to my bedroom. I intersperse the mantra with a lot of cursing, all of it directed at Holt. Calling him an asshole. A fucknugget. A flea on the bottom of a pile of dog shit.

I'm so in my head when I walk in, I've forgotten all about Michael. He's waiting, awake and still dressed, and if I had to guess, he's been pacing.

He pounces as soon as he sees me. "Thank God. I've been sick about…worrying. What happened? Are you all right? Tell me you're all right." He wraps his arms around me, and I shudder, not wanting to be touched.

Not wanting to be touched by *him*.

I push out of his arms. "I need space." It's tripping with me as much as it's got to be tripping with him. I rarely deny his affection, and I don't know if it's about what happened with him earlier or what happened with Holt, but I desperately need to be alone.

Probably worried by my unusual behavior, his tone gets sharp. "Did he hurt you? If he hurt you—" He cuts himself off, though I'd kind of like to know how he'd finish that statement.

He'd…what? He hadn't thought it his place to protect me

before something happened, and now he's ready to defend my honor? Ready to slug Holt in the nuts? Ready to dump all thoughts of his career and take me off into the sunset?

Yeah. No.

And I don't care enough to be in his presence to press him on it.

"I'm—" I stop myself before saying *fine*. He doesn't deserve to have his conscience cleared that easily, and it's kind of validating to see him worried. Instead, I say, "Look, I don't want to talk about it. Please. Can we just not talk about it?"

"Okay," he says reluctantly. "If that's what you want."

"It's what I need."

He surveys me, and I know he's looking for hints of something that will give away what my words won't. Signs of a struggle. Signs of rape.

I wrap my arms around myself, more uncomfortable with his stare than I had been with Holt's heavy-lidded gaze. "I'm—" Again, I have to stop myself from saying *fine*. "I'm going to take a shower." I brush past him, turning back to give him the one piece of information that he does need to know. "He'll get everything rolling on Monday."

Without waiting for his response, I escape into the bathroom, locking the door behind me. I strip quickly, turn on the shower, and get in before the water's warmed up.

Then I brace an arm against the tile wall and barely have to touch my clit before I come.

CHAPTER EIGHT

BRYSTIN

The next morning, I'm sitting on the chair by the window in our room, buckling my sandal when Michael walks in, dressed in his running outfit and covered in sweat. I can't decide if I'm glad he's back or disappointed. On the one hand, I didn't have to face another interrogation about Holt when I woke up to an empty bed.

On the other hand, I hadn't been looking forward to venturing downstairs on my own.

This is probably better, I decide. It's not like I can hide from my husband forever. "Good run?" I ask.

He nods. "Beautiful property. I could get used to the scenery. I'd hoped to get back before you woke up." He's staring at me, hoping I'll fill in the blanks about last night. When I don't say anything, he wisely changes tactics. "Have you been down for breakfast yet?"

"Just about to. I'm in desperate need of coffee."

"Wait a few minutes for me to shower and change, and I'll go with you."

I agree, and he peels off his clothes, leaving them in a pile before disappearing into the bathroom. Normally, I'd take the opportunity to ogle over his lean runner's body. Even at fifty-three, the man has zero fat.

But it's been less than eight hours since I saw Holt's washboard abs, and now I might be ruined for life.

Thinking about the ripples on his torso makes me think about the rest of last night, and I'm glad Michael's gone so he doesn't ask about the heat in my face. The heat in my entire body.

Wishing the room had a balcony, I peer behind the curtain to check how hard the window is to open and start to grin when I see Jessa Jones standing in the driveway by a luxury sports car. I abandon both the grin and the task of opening the window when I see Holt is standing with her.

Not wanting to be caught spying on him a second time, I pull back enough to not be seen, but I linger on watching for another few seconds. While I can't hear what they're saying, there is obvious tension in Jessa's body. From the animated way she's moving around, I would swear she's telling him off.

I could be projecting.

Holt appears to listen to her with his full attention. If she is telling him off, he seems unaffected by it. He even gives her a slight wave when she gets in the car and peels out of the driveway. So yeah, I'm probably wrong about the conversation. Besides, he's her boss. I doubt she'd lay into a superior like that, never mind the badass she is.

A badass that drives a Porsche Boxster. Once again, that woman is goals.

I go still when, after her car can no longer be seen, Holt turns back toward the house, but my wariness is in vain. He never looks up.

I remind myself I shouldn't be disappointed by that, and, dropping the curtain, I pick up my phone instead. I'd woken to two texts. I'd opened Michael's telling me he was out for a run and left Zully's unread so I click on it now.

Did you bang the hottie?

I did not. But I think I got the job.

A paragraph of celebratory emojis follows, and my grin returns. *We got the job.* I haven't had time to really let that set in. *We got the fucking job.* Whatever that was with Holt, it was fine. I'm fine. And it was nothing compared to what I'm getting in return.

If he keeps his bargain, that is.

I send another text telling Zully that I'll fill her in when I know more. By the time I finish typing, another text has arrived, this one from an unknown number.

Can't seem to keep your eyes off of me now, can you?

My pulse picks up and a shiver rolls down my spine. I open the curtain again, but Holt's gone. This has to be from him, right? I can't decide if it makes me feel worse or better if it's not him.

And am I supposed to respond?

Michael walks out of the bathroom with a towel wrapped around his waist. He drops the towel to put on a pair of briefs. "What's that look for?"

Whatever my expression had been, it changed at his question. I try to remember how my features felt so I can determine what they'd been saying, and I can't. "What kind of look was it?" I ask.

"Good. Happy."

There's a ball in my throat at the realization. Holt texted me, and I was happy. What the fuck's with that?

Thinking quickly, I give Michael another response, one that will invariably open the door to the questions I'm trying to avoid. "We got the job."

He pauses midway through pulling up his jeans. Then he smiles. "We got the job." He finishes putting on his pants. "We really did? Both of us? He's giving you the spot?"

I stand up from the chair, slipping my cell into the pocket of my romper. "He says he'll get it started tomorrow. So…yes. I think so."

He pulls on a clean T-shirt and puts his hands on his hips, studying me.

"Don't," I tell him.

"Don't what?"

"I told you last night, I don't want to talk about it."

"Ever? I thought you just meant last night."

"I mean ever." When he gives me a worrying scowl, I put a hand up in protest. "I just want to focus forward. We've worked our asses off to be here. We deserve to be here. And now we are."

I'm not sure if I'm trying to convince him or myself, but

it does the trick to distract him from whatever happened between me and Holt last night.

Tugging me into his arms, Michael wraps me into a giant bear hug. He leans in to kiss my lips, but I turn slightly, and it lands next to my mouth. "Congratulations." He's unfazed by the dismissal of his kiss. "I knew you could do it."

I stiffen in his arms, unsure why his confidence in me is so off-putting. Perhaps because it feels like it's confidence rooted in my ability to use sex to promote myself rather than confidence in my journalistic abilities. I know that's not true, that he's always believed in my talent, but right now I wish *he'd* tell *me* that we deserve to be here. That I earned it before we even stepped foot on Adeline's grounds.

Apparently, he's not completely unaware of what's going on in my head. "You sure you're okay?"

I force a smile. "Just really need that coffee."

A few minutes later, we're downstairs and seated outside at one of the round dining tables that have been set out around the patio for breakfast. A staff member comes by and takes our drink order, as though we're at a restaurant.

I order my coffee.

"Add a mimosa for her and get one of each as well for me." He's not the type to order for me, and I raise a brow.

Just then Holt walks out of the house and onto the far end of the patio, and though he's talking to one of his staff, he's looking right at us.

Somehow I manage to concentrate on Michael while he's talking.

"We're celebrating, sweet girl. We have to have mimosas." He takes my hand in his, setting it on the table, and I'm surprised by how much I appreciate the gesture. Not because he's showing he's with me or because he's declaring he's happy about the job, though both are probably true, but because it feels like a blatant display of ownership. A claim on me. Hours too late, but a claim nonetheless.

The best part of it? How Holt's eyes blaze.

I can see the fire in his gaze from several tables away, and it makes my stomach flip and my heart skip, and then my brain screams at me, because no way am I into that man being jealous. I don't care how he feels. I don't care how he makes me feel. I care that he gives me this job. That's all. *That is all.*

Except it isn't all, because I can't tear my eyes away from Holt, no matter whose hand mine is laced with.

I don't even notice Michael gesturing for Holt to join us until Holt has walked back inside and the servant he was speaking to has approached us. "Is there something you need, Mr. Endlich?"

Michael shakes his head. "I was trying to get Holt's attention."

"I'm sorry, but Mr. Sebastian is going to be out the rest of the day. He said he regrets that he wasn't able to see you off personally, but he'll reach out to you this week to follow up on the business you have with him."

"Huh. Sorry to hear that." Michael doesn't sound that sorry. "Appreciate the update. Thank you."

"You're welcome, and those mimosas are just about here."

It's too late, and he's definitely gone, but I withdraw my hand from Michael's, in case that's the cause of Holt's need to disappear. Not that I'm disappointed that he's gone or anything.

And when immediately my phone vibrates with a text in my pocket, I don't have to look to know it's Holt. In a weird need for a sense of power balance that I'll never actually obtain, I ignore it.

After a toast with the mimosas and a full cup of coffee, I'm ready for food. Michael has already gone inside and come back with a plate full of healthy protein in the form of a veggie egg white omelet and turkey bacon.

"Did they have any yogurt?" I try to decide what I'm in the mood for before getting up.

"I didn't notice," Michael says. "There were some awfully tempting homemade banana muffins though."

"My greatest weakness," I groan.

"I have faith in you." He waits until I stand up before adding, "But if your willpower fails, bring back one for me too."

Laughing, I turn to go inside, less nervous about walking around without Michael now that I know Holt isn't here. Yesterday, I'd skipped breakfast all together, having left for my walk after my coffee, so today it takes me a bit of exploring to discover the buffet set up in a sunroom off of the kitchen. There are a few round tables in here as well, for people not wanting to eat outdoors, I suppose, and several guests have chosen to do so. Most are people I've seen already as well as a few 'Bastian Bunnies and a couple faces that aren't familiar.

What I'm really into at the moment, though, is the glorious display of food.

There are twelve feet of hot plates with eggs, oatmeal, sausage, bacon, and potatoes, as well as several bowls of fruit, boxes of single serving cereals, various pastries, and finally, yogurt. There's also a window to the kitchen where people can "order" eggs cooked to specification.

I grab a bowl and start mixing some granola and berries with yogurt then drizzle the concoction with honey. I've spotted the banana muffins and am about to grab one to split with Michael, when I overhear a woman talking at a round table behind me.

"Have you seen Jessa today? Should I talk to her? Would that make things better or worse?"

Meaning to be helpful rather than nosy, I turn to the woman to share what I know. "Jessa Jones has already left."

The woman frowns and exchanges a glance with the man with her, who, now that I'm looking, I realize is Steele Sebastian.

"I didn't know." He looks at me. "You're sure she's gone?"

I'm a little less keen on being helpful knowing that I'm addressing a Sebastian, but I have to roll with what I started. "I saw her get in her car and drive off. My bedroom faces the driveway. Maybe she's coming back?"

The woman addresses Steele. "He probably pissed her off, didn't he?" The way she speaks with him is familiar, but something about their interaction doesn't feel exactly intimate. "I'm gonna fucking ream him when I see him."

The conversation definitely doesn't involve me, and I

know how to take a cue, but I'm also highly interested in anyone who would dare threaten to ream Holt Sebastian.

Of course, I'm only guessing that's who she's talking about, but it did seem like Jessa was yelling at him, and because I'm in the mood to "tell" on Holt, I offer what I know. "She was with Holt before she got in her car," I say. "Seemed like they might have been arguing."

"Great," Steele says, sarcastically. The woman throws her head back in frustration.

"I knew inviting her this weekend was a bad idea. Once he gets something in his—"

"She asked to come," Steele interrupts.

"I, for one, was really glad to have the chance to talk with her." I don't even know why I'm still talking. "So not a totally bad idea."

Both of them turn their heads toward me, gazing at me strangely, as though they'd forgotten I was there.

Then the woman's expression shifts into recognition, and she points a finger at me. "You're *her*."

"I'm *her*? Who? What?" There's no way she can think I'm Jessa Jones, but there isn't any other *her* we've been talking about.

"Bristol Shaw," she clarifies.

"Brystin," Steele and I correct at the same time.

"That's right, Brystin Shaw. Sorry. I'm terrible with names. Half the time I say Jessa's last name is James, and I've known her practically my whole life." She waves her hand to dismiss what she's just said. "Point is, I've seen your work. That New Jersey show, right? *New Jersey Now* or something?"

"Yeah, yeah. That's it."

"Ad," Steele says, and it sounds sort of like a warning.

The woman either doesn't get it or decides not to heed it. "I'm Adly." She doesn't bother to try to shake my hand, thankfully, since I'm carrying both a bowl and a muffin. "Adly Sebastian."

"Sebastian," I say at the same time she does, because there probably aren't that many Adlys hanging out at Holt's house. This one is definitely his sister, which explains the familiarity she has with Steele, since he's also her brother. "So good to meet you."

"Nah, whatever. I'm boring. But you aren't boring. I watched several of your episodes."

She seems about to say more but Steele interrupts her. "I'm going to…" He stands and gestures with his head, as though he's asking her to come with him.

"Fine. Go look for him. If she's gone, it's too late now."

"Adly…" Another prompt for her to get up and leave. I barely know the man, and I even understand that he's trying to get her to stop talking to me.

Obviously, that makes me more interested in the conversation.

"I'm not playing his game, Steele. I can talk to who I want to talk to, so stay or go, your choice, but I can tell a woman I think her work is fantastic if I feel like it."

Instantly, I like her.

Steele lets out a sigh. "Yep. Do whatever you want. I don't care. Not my problem."

I watch after him as he walks away before turning back to Adly. "This entire interaction is very fascinating."

Adly laughs. "I know, I know. We're annoying. Steele is in talent development and thinks everything should be Top

Secret All the Time. I'm doing my time in HR—because my dad's an asshole and thinks that's where the girls belong—and I've found plain old authenticity and transparency to be the best tactics in dealing with anyone remotely human.

"All that to say, Holt had me watch a bunch of your episodes. He wanted my opinion, or so he said, but I'm pretty sure he'd already made up his mind. As well he should have. You're a star. Anyone who says they can't see it is bullshitting you. But you're here, so you already know it. Only one reason you get an invitation to Adeline. Welcome to the big leagues."

I manage to thank her without sounding like an idiot. Without sounding like I'm distracted. Without letting on that my brain is unraveling the meaning of everything she's saying.

Then I politely extract myself from her company, grabbing a second banana muffin since I'm no longer in the mood to share, and then slip out of the sunroom.

I take the hallway toward the living room instead of going directly out to the patio, so that I can lean against the wall and try to catch my breath.

Only one reason you get an invitation to Adeline.

He'd already made up his mind.

He was going to give me the job anyway.

Fucking Holt Sebastian ordered me to negotiate in his room, and he was going to give me the job anyway.

CHAPTER
NINE
HOLT

Hunter has issued another threat to the board, my top female star is mad at me, and my father is breathing down my neck about my plan for invigorating the network, and all I can think about is Brystin fucking Shaw.

Closing my eyes, I bring to mind what she looked like with her dress pulled down, tits jutted out, nipples at attention. I barely got a look at her body because my eyes were glued to hers, but I remember everything that I saw in that quick glance.

Specifically, I remember that I want to see more. And I definitely want to do more than see.

It's driving me out of my mind.

I set my wineglass down on the patio ledge—a 2005 Bodegas Roda Cirsion that would usually distract me from anything but its exquisite taste—and open my phone to read the last text message I sent her for the millionth time today.

It seems I can't keep my eyes off you either.

I sent it twelve hours ago, and it still says it's unread.

Fucking Brystin. What part of *make yourself available* did she not understand?

"Did you really have it out with Jessa Jones in the middle of your driveway?"

I look up to find my sister staring at me with accusation in her eyes.

I pocket my phone as I glance over my shoulder at the door to my bedroom. My private patio is accessible from the garden, if you know where to look—which Adly does—so there is absolutely no reason she should be coming here through my suite. "How did you get in my room?"

She makes a face like I'm being ridiculous. "Errol knows me, you idiot."

"That doesn't explain why he'd let you in." Obviously, I'm going to have to do some staff management.

"He let me in because *he knows me*. Also, it's fucking freezing out here." She moves to the outdoor fireplace and flicks the switch on.

"Good thing I wasn't beating my meat." And it's actually a warm night for April, if you ask me.

"God, Holt. Why are you so disgusting?" She returns and plops herself on a chair facing the fire. Then she reaches for my wineglass, managing to grab it before I can stop her. She takes a swallow and makes a face.

"I could have told you that you wouldn't like it."

She waves her hand to say *no problem*. As if she's the one being put out here. "So are you going to tell me about Jessa or not?"

I don't give a fuck about Jessa so pulling my mind from where it wants to be is extra difficult. "There's not much to tell."

"That doesn't work with me. Besides, there were witnesses."

"What witnesses? What did you hear?" I'm pretty sure I know exactly which witness she's talking about, though I'm not sure how the fuck Brystin ended up saying anything to Adly about what she saw from her window.

Brystin. Now I'm itching to pull my phone out again and check to see if she's responded.

"I don't share my sources."

"Not even with me?"

"You didn't share your sources when you got the scoop on King-Kincaid. I think it's only fair to play the same."

"That Shaw girl told her." Steele appears at the bedroom door. "This one was all over her telling her how much you loved her work, welcoming her to the team. You need to talk to your sister about non-disclosure."

"Fuck you, Steele. I'll remember you're a tattler."

I don't really care what Adly told Brystin. I care about my privacy. "Is Errol asleep out there or something?" I ask. Errol is usually really good about keeping people out of my wing, but maybe that's because my family rarely comes looking for me.

Which begs another question—"What are you both still doing here? It's after ten p.m. on a Sunday."

"I'm working virtually tomorrow," Adly says.

"Joe's still here and we're meeting in the morning to discuss programming changes." Steele lights up a hand-rolled cigarette and takes a puff before going on. "What are you still doing here? Expected you to be back in the city by now."

"I missed the last train. I'll go in the morning." I'm suddenly wondering if that's why my siblings are sneaking into my room—because they don't expect me to be here. "Does Errol always let you in here when I'm gone?"

"Stop harping on Errol." Steele exhales, and now I know that he's not smoking tobacco. "I told him I had pressing shit to discuss with you. He understands I wouldn't say that lightly."

I'm dubious. "Okay, then. What pressing shit?"

Steele nods to Adly. "I'm with her. We want to know about Jessa. Did you fuck that up?"

"No, I did not fuck it up." I reach over to swipe the joint out of his hand. If I have to listen to this shit, I'm going to need to be buzzed. Since Adly still hasn't surrendered my wine, I'll have to settle for this.

Of course, Steele takes the joint back after I get one hit. "She left and has refused to answer any of my calls. Sure seems like you fucked it up."

Adly scowls. "Why are *you* even calling her? This should be an HR issue at this point. Calling her should be my job."

"And have you called her?" Steele challenges.

Adly's hesitation is an answer in itself. "I was waiting until the workweek."

He laughs. "Sure."

She tries again. "I was waiting to hear Holt's side of the story."

Now both pairs of eyes are on me. "I don't know what you want to hear from me. I'm not giving in to hostile demands. That is not the precedent I'm setting up at SNC."

"Hostile?" Adly rolls her eyes. "Jessa Jones is a strong woman, but her *requests* were reasonable."

"They didn't fit into my vision." That's not exactly true, but Jessa has a timeline that doesn't agree with my own. She'll have to go on the backburner for now, star female anchor or not.

And I'm not getting into any of that with these assholes.

"Let me guess—your vision is Brystin Shaw." Steele's been completely supportive about my plans for Brystin before tonight, but his subtext says he's more skeptical than he previously let on.

That's the problem with my younger brother. He likes to play the winning side. If he suddenly thinks my ideas might lose, then he'll jump ship and support Hunter instead.

A good reason not to tell him everything.

"Oh…Holt." My sister is about to scold me, and I'm really going to need my drink back if she continues. "I love her. I really do. I was as enamored with her when you showed me those clips as you were."

Doubtful, but okay. This isn't bad.

"And I totally think you need to give her a shot. But if you expect her to be your whole plan…"

Steele snaps and points at our sister. "Exactly that. She is not going to move ratings."

"She's a long-term investment. A way to move the needle five years from now, which is important."

"And who even knows if she has the right stuff for that."

"I think she has the right stuff. She's got what it takes."

"To replace Jessa?"

"To build with Jessa."

"Not if Jessa isn't part of Holt's vision." Steele stares at me.

Adly sets down my wineglass and stares at me with him.

I swipe it before she can pick it up again and take a nice size gulp. "I know what I'm doing."

"Do you really?" Steele laughs again, and I wonder if he's already high. "Do you have a plan for how to explain your vision to Hunter?"

"Forget about Hunter," Adly says. "How are you going to tell Dad?"

I take my time responding. It's not that I'm not concerned. It's not just my half-brother and my father that have to be convinced. The whole department is going to question my decision.

It doesn't help that the president of programming is Hunter's best friend. I don't have to mention him because Adly brings him up on her own. "Axle is going to have a field day. He'll probably give her the midnight time slot."

"Fuck Axle Morgan. I should fire that shithead." I should have fired him the day I took the job of CEO.

Adly reminds me why I can't do that. "The board wouldn't like it."

"You'd piss off Hunter, and he's already on your ass."

Steele doesn't add that our half-brother thinks he can do a better job than I can, but that's what it comes down to. That Hunter wants my position. That Hunter thinks he should have been given the job. Never mind that we share a mother, not a father, and it was Dad that I replaced when I took the CEO position. The sole reason he has any opinion about it is because he's on the board.

And the only reason he's on the board is because *his* father put him there.

And once we start talking about Hunter's father, then we're opening doors to a whole bunch of other baggage that the three of us would rather forget exists.

"Maybe firing Axle is exactly what he should do," Adly says. "Show the board Holt isn't willing to be their puppet."

"You just hate Ax."

She grins. "They aren't mutually exclusive. I could just as easily like him and still think it's a marvelous idea to have him out of our business. You're creative. Help me come up with an uncontestable reason to boot him."

"Help you think of a reason to ax Ax?" Steele can't keep from laughing, and now I'm certain he's high.

The thing is, high or not, he *is* creative. And Adly's smart. I should use this opportunity to pick their brains and help me come up with a solid plan to make a bigger name for myself at SNC. That's everything I want—everything I've always wanted—to surpass the achievements of my father. To be the CEO that is most remembered for shaking things up. Like Steve Jobs. Like Elon Musk. Like Walt Disney and Henry Ford.

The scandal I broke with King-Kincaid got me a leg up

—thank you, Donovan Kincaid, for getting me what I needed for that—but the news from that is already dying down. I need an impressive second act. I need a story that will be sustainable. I need to turn SNC on its head. Need something that will get viewership up, send it through the roof, and keep it there for a long time.

Am I fucked in the brain for thinking I can do just that with Brystin Shaw?

Adly and Steele would give good advice if I let them all the way in. Hard advice, probably, but good advice.

Good advice doesn't always mean the best advice.

I let my siblings banter about my options and pull out my phone again. I'm not exactly obsessed. More, I'm fascinated. Besides my extended family and Axle Morgan, very few people try to test me. I'm the kind of person that says jump and people are soaring off buildings to their death without blinking an eye.

But not Brystin Shaw. She laid down her own rules. She told me no to fucking. She ignored my text for twelve fucking hours.

Except when I open the chat thread, my message now shows as read and three dots say she is currently typing. I watch until the text comes up on my screen.

> This kind of talk is really inappropriate, Mr. Sebastian, and I'm not beyond bringing it up with HR.

Shit, Adly would love that.

But more importantly, is Brystin goddamned serious right now?

I stand up, wine in one hand, phone in the other. "How

about you two work it all out for me? When you're done, you can see yourselves to bed via another route."

"Good night, asshole," Steele says as I open the door.

"You're welcome in advance." Adly's words are the last thing I hear before shutting the door behind me.

I lock it to be sure I don't see them again tonight.

Once I'm safely in the privacy of my bedroom, I set my wineglass down, pull up FaceTime on my phone, and dial the number I entered into my contacts earlier this weekend.

I shouldn't be surprised when Brystin doesn't answer.

I send another text.

I'm calling you. Pick up.

She replies quickly.

Who is this? I don't have this number programmed in my phone.

She knows who it is. She addressed me as Mr. Sebastian in her text a few minutes ago. She's toying with me, and I'm so unused to it that it intrigues me.

I sit on my bed and lean against the headboard while I think of my reply.

I'm not sure you want to play games with your potential career.

This time she answers when I call. "Me playing games? What about you with your 'if you win at pool then I'll give you a show'? 'If you come to my bedroom, I'll give you a show.' You were always planning to give us a show. Admit it. I didn't have to negotiate anything."

She's kind of adorable when she's feisty like this. Or maybe what I like is this casual look of hers that I haven't really seen. I glimpsed it when she was in my library that night in her skimpy pjs. And again when I found her lost and flustered on the grounds. But usually she's put together and professional, like she's ready to walk on camera any minute.

She was even like that in my room last night, with her dress open, and her skin bared.

Now, her hair is up in a casual twist. Several stray wisps frame her face. She's makeup less and wearing another tank top. No bra. I can see the outline of her tits through the fabric.

"Were your nipples erect before I called or was that just for me?"

Instantly, she throws her arm across her chest. "That's exactly the kind of talk that is inappropriate. And how did you get my number?"

"I own your place of employment, Brystin. It shouldn't be that big of a mystery." I shift so that my legs are stretched out in front of me. "The bigger mystery is why you seem to have gone back on our deal, less than twenty-four hours after we've made it."

Sighing, she plops down on the edge of what appears to be a bed. "This is exactly what I was trying to explain, if you were listening. You were going to give me the show anyway. I didn't need to agree to your deal."

"Ah, but you did agree to the deal."

"And now I have more information."

This new information must have come from Adly. I'm still not concerned. Honestly, I should thank Adly for spilling because this whole arrangement just got a lot more fun. "New information or not, the deal stands."

"Not if I don't say it stands."

"Then I retract my offer. Glad to know this was the situation before I put things in motion tomorrow."

She hesitates. Her lips wrinkle when she's working something out, and I'm oddly attracted to it. "Are you really retracting the offer? See, I don't think you really are. You're just playing another game. You want me to think you're retracting the offer so I'll do whatever you want."

"It's possible." I let that hang. "It's also possible that I might lose interest in this whole idea by morning. I've heard a lot of great pitches this weekend. You weren't my only guest at Adeline."

There's that wrinkle again. She's confused. Doesn't know how to play her next card.

I decide to help her out. "Some advice, Brystin. It doesn't matter what I would have given you. This is what we settled on. You can't go back and offer less after you've put the offer in. Now I know what you're willing to pay, and you'd better believe I'm going to make you pay it. I'm sorry you didn't come out with the advantage."

"You're kind of a dick," she says.

I grin because of course I'm a dick. It's enchanting that she dares to say it to my face. I almost want to ask her to say it again.

But then I notice the pillows behind her in various shades of pink. "Are you in your bedroom?"

"Yes." She sounds wary, as she should be.

"Show me."

It takes her a second to decide to do it, but then the view

on my screen swings from one side of the room to the other. It's a quick sweep, but I've seen what I wanted to see. Twinkly lights, a lace canopy, feminine nightstands with girly lamps and accessories. "You have separate bedrooms." I know I'm right.

I'm not sure why it feels like a victory, but it does.

"No, we don't," she says too quickly. "Why would you say that?"

"There's no way a man would sleep in that bedroom."

"Not you, maybe. But Michael is comfortable with his sexuality."

I shake my head. "He's not that comfortable. You sleep in separate rooms."

I wonder if he's fucked her in that bed. It's not something I usually care about. I'm casual with my sex, and I don't expect the women I'm with to be any more loyal than I am to them.

But here I am wondering if he's fucked her in that bed, and I want to punch my hand through the wall at the probability that he has.

"Okay, fine. We have separate bedrooms," she admits. "Lots of married couples have separate bedrooms."

"He wouldn't if he truly loved you." Cruel, and quite possibly untrue, but I want to wound her.

It does the trick. Her jaw goes tense. "Like I've said before, you don't know anything about my marriage."

"You're right," I concede. I regret hurting her. Not because I care about her feelings, exactly, but because now she's guarded and buttoned up. "I don't know what I'm talking about."

The admission loosens her up. And surprises her. "Thank you. I appreciate that."

"Is your door locked? Will he come in?"

She's sitting on the bed again and glances in front of her, presumably to the door. "He won't come in," she says. "He's already asleep."

"Poor guy. The weekend away must have worn grandpa out."

She smothers a laugh. "Stop it. He's not that old."

"Sorry. I meant Daddy. Ten o'clock is when my dad goes to bed too."

This time her laugh escapes. "You're a dick."

"So you've said." Both times she's said the word, my dick has reacted. I'm fully hard now, and it's my dick that's steering the conversation. "Take off those shorts. I didn't get to see your cunt last night."

"Uh…no thank you."

"I bet it's a pretty cunt."

"I bet you'd love to find out, but not happening."

I make a show of letting out an exaggerated breath. "Are we back to disputing whether or not we've entered into an agreement? You're smart enough to understand how business works. Don't try to tell me that you aren't."

"You're right. I am smart enough to understand business. And no, I'm not disputing our agreement anymore." She's stoic, but I can tell she's honestly accepted our terms. "However, I have already proved that I will uphold my end of the bargain. You have not."

Whoa. She's bold.

Why am I suddenly even harder?

"What exactly are you asking for, Brystin?"

"Evidence that you plan to do as you say. You could string me along for God knows how long, promising me a job, never delivering. Meanwhile, you have every which way with me—"

"Not every which way," I remind her. "There were terms you laid out pretty adamantly."

"Not every which way, no." I'm sure it's my imagination that she seems regretful. Or I've misinterpreted the wistfulness in her tone. "But the point remains—I've shown good faith. Now you show me yours."

"If you're asking for me to take my cock out for you—"

She cuts me off. "Show me you mean what you've offered. I need evidence."

My brain speeds ahead, trying to figure out if I can have a contract drawn up tonight. I'd drive myself to New Jersey right now to have her sign it if she'd let me put my mouth on her. I'm as eager to taste her pussy as I am to open my 2005 bottle of Domaine de la Romanée-Conti.

Fortunately, another part of my brain knows to put on the brakes. There's no rush. I'm giving her this show, and she'll have plenty of opportunities to thank me for it.

"If you need evidence, then fine. I'll get you evidence. But I'm telling you now, Brystin—when I call, you answer. When I text, you respond. When I say show me your cunt, you show me your cunt. Plenty of projects get killed in the making. I can end things as easily as I start them. Are we clear?"

I swear her cheeks are flushed when she nods her head. "We're clear," she says breathily.

"Good. I'll get back to you soon." I hang up before she can say anything. Hang up and then toss my phone aside so

I can pull my cock out of my pants and rub myself to the fastest orgasm of my life. With nothing but spit on my hand, that's how worked up I am.

When I'm able to think straight again, I replay our conversation.

Then I laugh.

"Evidence?" I say to the empty room. She wants me to prove myself with some fucking evidence?

That girl has some nerve.

She's going to be my biggest star.

Either that, or she'll be my downfall. At least it will be fun trying to figure out which it is.

CHAPTER
TEN
BRYSTIN

Zully looks up from the nail she just painted. "And you haven't heard from him since?"

"Not a peep." I try not to sound disappointed about Holt's lack of communication. It's been six days since he called me over FaceTime. I should be relieved.

I wonder if Zully can tell that I'm not.

The benefit of having a best friend who professionally does personal cosmetic services means that we have a standing Saturday brunch appointment where she paints my nails and tweezes my eyebrows while we eat carb-heavy delivery food and catch up on our lives. She's been here for over an hour, and all we've talked about is Holt.

I've been honest and forthcoming about most of what's happened between us, including the terms of the arrangement he proposed, but I haven't included all of the ways Holt makes me feel. Mainly because it's confusing. And a little bit embarrassing.

A whole lot embarrassing, and I can't explain why, even to myself.

"But he's for sure giving you a show?"

"Michael's been in the city all week almost every day in meetings with the SNC programming department. He's there again today, even. They're still negotiating details, but he assures me it's happening, and that I'm still currently the headliner."

She must hear the doubt in my voice. "You don't believe it?"

"I don't know." I shake my pinky finger where the coating has smeared to get her attention. Then I think more about her question as she fixes it. "It's funny—if Holt had offered us the show that night, I would believe it was a done deal. I know that's not how the business works. Lots of projects get killed in planning, but I would have believed it because I wanted to believe it so badly."

"You still want it badly. I know you do."

"I do. Maybe even more than before. But now I feel like I haven't earned it yet." I realize how backward it sounds, and yet there's no other way to say it.

Zully stops painting, her nail brush suspended in midair so she can give me a severe look of disbelief and disappointment. "And you think spreading your legs is how you earn it?"

"I told you I said no to—"

"No penetration. I heard you. But it's all the same. It's sex. It's a man valuing you for your body and not your mind. You get that, right?"

Her words make sense.

Still, I remember Holt fully aroused on his horse and what he said. *It's a woman's brain that gets my cock hard first.*

When I don't answer right away, she repeats herself. "You get that…right?"

"I do. I get it." I slide my fingers under the drying lamp when she moves to my other hand. "I get it, but I think that's oversimplifying."

Her mouth gapes when she glances at me this time. "Oversimplifying? What the fuck, Bryst. He wants you to perform sexual favors in exchange for a contract. How can it be any more complicated than that?"

"It just is." It's not enough of an answer, so I scramble to give her more. "You wanted me to sleep with him, at first, remember?"

"Because I want you to get laid by someone other than that dirtbag husband of yours. Not because I wanted you to enter into a deal with a devil."

"You're being dramatic."

"Am I?"

"Barely anything has happened between us, so yes. I haven't had to do anything uncomfortable at all."

"You shouldn't have to do anything uncomfortable at all." She finishes the coating and puts the brush back in the bottle while I change out which hand is under the lamp. "Look, when I suggested you sleep with him, I wanted it for *you*. For your sexual desires to be met. This is all about *him*. Then add that he's requiring this from you in exchange for you getting a job that you deserve—"

"—but I don't. I haven't put in my time."

"Bullshit. That's him gaslighting you. Sure, it usually takes longer to get a deal like this, but sometimes it doesn't.

If you're good enough to be considered, then it doesn't matter how much time you've put in."

I feel my lips turn down. I lower my head so she can't see my thoughts in my expression. This was what was embarrassing about explaining my feelings. Because everything she says is right and true and accurate, and yet I feel like something else is happening between me and Holt. Maybe he hasn't given me sexual pleasure, but I've given it to myself. Every night this week, in fact. That's how much of a turn-on the whole situation has been for me.

It's why I'm practically aching for him to reach out again. Not because I want to know what he's doing to get me the job but because I want him to flirt with me again. Want him to ask me to undress. Want to see him get worked up over our intense connection. Want to watch him explode.

I don't know how to express that without sounding like I'm a brainwashed girl with a crush.

Zully knows me well enough to get some of that without me saying anything at all. "I just don't want to see another Michael situation," she says, softly.

My head lifts sharply. "Holt is nothing like Michael."

"He's not?" She pauses, letting me see the picture she sees. When it's clear that I don't, she continues. "A man in a powerful position gives you attention, and you turn it into something more."

My eyes suddenly sting. I shake my head, refusing to let the hard words affect me. "I see how it sounds the same, but it's not. I promise. I'm not in love with Holt."

"Not yet."

I ignore her comment. "I know what we are and that

this is all transactional. I knew it from the very beginning, which was not the case with Michael. My eyes are open."

She still looks skeptical.

"If I'd known from the beginning that Michael only wanted us to be a partnership of convenience, I would probably have still agreed, Zully. I know you think I'm looking in the wrong places for true love, but the truth is that I'm not looking for true love at all. My career is my true love. There is very little I won't give to get where I want to be."

Her features soften, and she lets out a breath of air. "I hear you. I just think you're wrong."

My jaw tightens, but I try to remain reasonable. "About which part?"

"About your career being your true love. I think you've convinced yourself that it's what will make you happy because you're too scared to put your heart out on the line. Afraid someone will break it the way Michael did."

Again, my eyes prick. "Even if that were true, I'm committed to him now. This is the life I've chosen." The lamp timer goes off, and I pull my hand out and offer it to Zully to check.

"One more round each hand and you should be dry," she says.

I slip my left hand under again, still thinking about what she's said about my heart and not putting myself out there. "Also, I'm confused by what you want from me. Are you saying I should put my heart on the line for Holt?"

"No. No, I'm not." She considers for a moment. "I'm saying a few separate things, I guess. In my dream version of your life, you would get the job at SNC, and fine, get it by exchanging favors, if you're good with that. But you'd also leave that fuckhat of a husband of yours, and you'd find a man who loves every part of you so much that you can stop compartmentalizing and give him all of you. Not just the sexy parts. Not just the good-at-your-job parts. The whole package. Someone who loves you like I do."

Now I want to cry for different reasons. "Well, you're fucked up in the head, so that's unlikely. But for what it's worth, I love you too."

"Ew. You're being squishy."

"You started it," I say with a laugh. "Seriously, though—you could do a YouTube show where you do a makeover for them while giving them therapy." She says she loves that her job is low pressure and lots of variety, but she's often wondering if she should try to do something more ambitious. Having her own shop has never appealed to her, and I get that. Having a show though…

"Make them up just to have them cry it off?"

"Okay, maybe the idea needs finessing. But you should think about it." My phone starts to ring, and I glance down at the ID. "Oh my God. It's him."

"Michael? Oh. Holt."

I nod. Butterflies take off in my stomach, and my brain goes blank. Like, what should I do? And why am I torn between wanting to hear his voice and wanting to run into my bedroom and put my head under the covers?

"Are you going to answer it?" As much as she's harped about him this morning, Zully sounds as excited about his call as I am.

Shook into action, I scramble to pick up the phone and

push accept, ignoring her warning to, "Be careful of your nails!"

"Um, hi. Hi. Hello. Hi." Great. I've suddenly forgotten how to use the English language. "What's up?"

Zully covers her mouth, but I can still hear her laughing. I glare at her and take the phone with me to pace the living room.

"Get ready to go into the City. I'm on my way to pick you up." Laid back and flirty Holt from Sunday night is gone. This Holt is all business.

"You're...what?" I'm an hour outside Manhattan. It makes no sense. He should have had me meet him somewhere or sent a car. "You're in a car?"

"Yes. In a car. Driving. On my way. To you." He sounds irritated, and something about his tone makes me pretty sure he's actually driving, not being driven.

I want to ask about that, but the other bit of info he landed on me is more pressing. "Get ready for what?" I look back at Zully, my eyes wide as I mouth, *he's on his way here.*

She mouths, *what*? I don't know if she's echoing my sentiment or if she didn't understand what I said. Either way, my attention is on the voice coming through the phone.

"It doesn't matter what for. Dress to impress."

I blink, trying to decide if I want to be irritating or not. A glance at Zully, and my decision is made. I don't want her thinking I'm being taken advantage of. Irritating it is. "Dress to impress can mean a lot of different things. It would really help to know where we're going."

"Like I said, it doesn't matter where we're going. It matters what I want you to look like."

Something about that statement makes me feel warm. From the look Zully gives me, I'm sure she sees it on my face.

I turn away, ignoring her. "Okay, well, like formal? Or like for a job interview?"

"Something like what you wore in the elevator." He sounds annoyed and impatient, but the fact that he said the elevator and not the award show gives him away. Lets me know what direction his thoughts are going.

It sends *my* thoughts in that direction, anyway. "Something tempting?"

"Something classy." He's brusque, as if our arrangement is the last thing on his mind.

My back stiffens, and when I turn once more toward Zully, she has a disapproving look in her eyes.

What? I mouth.

"Stand up for yourself," she whispers.

In other words, be more irritating. "How long will this take? What if I already have other plans?"

"Don't do that." Even more annoyed.

"Don't do what?"

"Don't pretend like we didn't get this hashed out. I'm giving my Saturday up for you. When I ask you to be somewhere, you drop everything to be there. Any other woman up for an anchor job at SNC would do the same."

I start to say something when he adds, "Even if they weren't willing to take their clothes off."

My face heats, thinking about what I've already let him

do. Zully might be right in some ways. I've set a precedent with him that I can't unset now.

But he's right too—if I want this job, I need to cooperate. Within reason. "Fine. I'll be ready. How long do I have?"

"I'm about to turn onto the 287."

Fuck. That's max twenty minutes away. Fifteen minutes, knowing my luck. I start toward my bedroom, waving Zully to follow along with me. "That doesn't give me much time."

"Then you better stop talking and—" I don't hear what else he says because I hang up on him.

I throw my phone on the bed and immediately start shedding my clothes. "I don't have time for a shower. Can you do something with this hair?"

"We'll do a knot." Zully passes me to flip through the dresses. "What look are we going for?"

"Something like what I wore to the award show." I don't need to look at the contents of my closet to know I don't have anything up to that level. It's why Michael had splurged for me to buy the zipper dress.

"You could do your black." She holds up the generic dress I wear to almost everything. It looks good on me, but it's not impressive.

"It's forgettable." I already know what the best choice is. "I'll wear the zipper dress again. It's all I have that fits the bill."

"I'll start pulling out your makeup. Meet you in the bathroom."

Exactly fifteen minutes later, I'm sitting on the toilet, dressed, and my hair up while Zully puts the finishing touches on the quickest makeup job ever. Suddenly, she pauses. "Is that your phone buzzing?"

I strain to listen, but she's already heading toward the bedroom. A handful of seconds later, she returns with my cell. "Three texts and four missed calls. All from him."

My stomach drops as I quickly read through the texts. The first two came back-to-back.

> You hung up on me?

> No one hangs up on me.

The third came only a moment ago.

> I'm turning down your block.

The most recent missed call came right after that. I hit redial and scramble to find my shoes, preparing an apology when he answers. "I'm not happy," he says, forgoing any greeting.

"I'm sorry. I was—"

"You can defend yourself on the ride into the city. I'm circling the block until you get down here." This time *he* hangs up on *me*.

Zully seems to have heard him because she doesn't ask questions. "Grab your purse. I'll get the hairspray and lipstick and we can finish putting you together in the elevator."

Five minutes later, we're standing on the sidewalk when the most gorgeous Bentley Continental GT pulls up, in front of the fire hydrant, no less, because of course Holt gives no fucks about the law.

And when I say gorgeous, I mean gorgeous.

It's totally a sports car, but a super luxury version, all speed and money.

Needless to say, it's very Holt Sebastian.

"Holy fuck," Zully whispers, as the tinted driver side window rolls down to reveal a sunglass-wearing Holt behind the wheel. "Hot."

"The car or the man?"

"Yes."

At least she understands my dilemma. I'm not even into cars, but I might even fantasize about this later tonight.

Right now though, he's looking at me expectantly. Probably wanting me to circle around and get in the passenger seat, but my friend is standing by me. "Holt, this is Zul—"

He cuts me off. "What are you wearing?"

I look down at the dress, as if it will be something other than what I know I put on. "You said something like—"

"*Like* is the keyword. You can't wear the same thing. Isn't that a rule you women made?" He's terse, and I can feel Zully at my side, itching to stand up for me.

I put my hand on her arm to stop her before she says anything that will do damage. Besides, I need to prove to her I can handle myself with Holt. "I don't have anything else that's this caliber," I explain. "If I'd had more time, I could have purchased something, but even then, it probably wouldn't have been this nice."

"You're saying you don't possess the wardrobe for the job you want."

"Because I also don't possess the salary of the job I want. Funny how that works."

A car honks, and I look up to see if it's a cop. It's not, thankfully.

Holt doesn't even look. Doesn't seem to care if he's holding up traffic or not. He does check his watch, though, and frowns. "We'll have to skip the luncheon. It will be tight. Let's go."

I turn to say something to Zully, but he won't even afford me the courtesy of telling her goodbye. "We're running late, Brystin. Get in."

Sorry, I mouth to her, as I circle around to the passenger side. She does the universal gesture for *call me* then waves.

I give her the universal gesture for *pray for me*. Then I slide into his car, and hope I'm not a willing lamb off to slaughter.

CHAPTER ELEVEN

BRYSTIN

As soon as my passenger door is shut, Holt pulls away. "Seat belt," he says, as though I'm not already scrambling to buckle in.

I try very hard not to blow.

Unfortunately, I'm not successful. "All right, assHolt. I know that we have an arrangement, but that doesn't give you permission to be a complete and ut—"

He puts his hand up to silence me. For some reason, I obey him.

Then he pushes a button on the steering wheel. "Call Adly."

I cross my arms over myself and wait while the phone rings, frustrated at being cut off. Pissed at submitting to his every command. Infuriated by the man's mere existence.

Still my silly brain finds room for concern and I hope this was how he sent the texts he sent me—using voice technology. I hate to think of him typing them out on his phone while he was driving.

Actually, I take that back. I don't care.

I mean, of course I don't want him to get in an accident, but mostly because that would be an obstacle on the pathway to getting our contract signed. No other reason.

Besides, he's fine. He made it to my apartment and is now using our time together to try to talk to someone else.

Argh!

Adly answers on the fourth ring, her voice filling the car. "If you're calling to tell me you're going to be late, I don't want to hear it."

"I'm going to be late."

She groans. "This happens once a year, Holt. You could make an effort for one flipping day a—"

He interrupts her, which is validating since it seems to be a him issue in general, and not just something he does to me. "I don't have the energy for this right now, Ad. And that was secondary information. Not the reason why I was calling."

"That makes more sense. You're usually late without the courtesy of informing me beforehand."

I stifle a laugh, knowing that I should probably try not to listen in on this personal call. On the other hand, if he wanted privacy, he could have called before I got in the car.

He glances at me, seeming unamused by my amusement. "I need you to get me in with your friend that owns the boutique."

"Mirabelle?" She sounds surprised. "You know she's a Pierce. Or was before she got married."

"And?"

"And Dad and most of our uncles will never do business with anyone related to a Pierce."

"I'm not Dad, and like you, I don't give a fuck about the family's petty rivalries. Call her and let her know I'm coming."

I can feel her desire to argue in her hesitation. The momentary silence also lets me hear the background more thoroughly. The clinking of dishes and muffled chatter sounds like she's at a restaurant or luncheon. A luncheon that Holt is supposed to be at? A luncheon he seems to think I should be at as well.

Finally, she sighs. "Okay, I'll call her. When do you want to see her?"

"Now."

"Now?"

He checks his watch. "In about forty-five minutes, if you want me to be precise. And I'll need a valet. It's an emergency."

I want to shrivel up into the passenger seat, realizing I'm what he's calling an emergency.

No, I take it back. I don't want to shrivel. I want to stab him in the thigh. I look damn good in a damn good dress. So I've worn it before. It's not like anyone will know. And what a stupid gender-centric rule anyway. He's probably worn his outfit plenty of times, and no one has called him an emergency.

"Why? What kind of emergency?"

"I'm bringing someone. She's not dressed"—he glances at me—"appropriately."

"You're bringing someone?" She sounds surprised but

elated. I guess this means he doesn't usually bring a plus-one.

For some reason, that makes my stomach flip.

"It's business," he says quickly.

"Oh." Her happiness deflates, which is probably why mine does as well. Some sort of sympathetic reaction. "If it means you will get your ass here so that I don't have to suffer this occasion alone, then I'll call her. But you have to try not to be a dick to her. I actually like Mira."

I peer sideways at him as they talk. It's the first I've truly looked at him since getting into the car. Along with his aviator sunglasses, I now see that although he isn't wearing a bow tie, he's in a tux. The satin lapel gives him away. And man, he can wear a tux. Even seated, I can tell that the sleeves of his jacket were made to hug his body.

Lucky jacket.

But that wasn't why I was noticing his outfit. I was deducing the dress requirement. Wherever we're going, the event isn't quite black tie or he'd have a bow tie. Same requirements for the award show, which means my dress shouldn't be a problem.

Unless, of course, there are a lot of people at this event who saw me wearing this dress less than a month ago. In which case —gender-centric rules being what they are—I need to change.

I refuse to feel guilty about it. Based on his sister's comment about this happening annually, he should have had plenty of time to give me a heads-up.

It's almost hard to be mad at him considering how good he looks, but I promise to make a valiant effort.

Except I'm still evaluating the attractiveness of his

profile when I realize that the phone call has ended, and Holt is looking at me as though he's asked me a question.

"Sorry. What was that?"

"I said, you can go on with what you were saying." His tone is short and clipped, and I wonder why he's even bothered to pick up the thread of whatever it was I was saying before he cut me off.

"I forget." Since he'd obviously rather not talk at all, why should I put any effort into conversation?

Unfortunately, he doesn't let it drop there. "I believe you were about to give me a piece of your mind."

Oh, yeah.

Just like that, my irritation sparks anew. "I was allowed to say so little before I was so rudely interrupted, I can't imagine how you worked even that much out."

"You called me an assHolt." His lip seems to twitch, trying not to smile, perhaps. "Can't say I've heard that one before."

"Probably because you don't let people talk long enough to say what they're truly feeling. I assure you it's not because no one's thought of it before."

He turns his head to stare at me long enough that I start to get nervous about his driving.

When he finally puts his eyes back on the road, he's definitely smiling. "I like you, Brystin Shaw. Remind me I said that when you start to get on my nerves."

I stare wide-eyed at him then shake my head. "What will you remind me of when you start to get on my nerves? Because, spoiler, it's already happening."

He laughs, and my pussy spasms. As though the sound

of his laughter is a vibrator pressed against my clit. What the fuck's with that?

"I suppose I'll remind you that you wanted what only I can give you. And that what I can give you is worth me being on your nerves."

For half a second, I forget that he's talking about my career. That what he means to give me is something much more base and primal in nature.

But then he says, "I think you'll find the show will be worth it," and I remember that it's my gift to him that's base and primal, and that he's the one that wants sex from me.

"It's a transaction." It's for myself, but I say it out loud.

"Exactly. A transaction."

A transaction in which I have offered him various forms of sex. My outfit shouldn't matter if that's all today is about. Obviously, it's about something else. Just when I'm about to ask questions, the car alerts an incoming text from Adly.

Mira's expecting you.

"Excellent." Holt changes his destination on the GPS to her boutique.

"Where are we going? Our final destination, I mean."

"An art show."

"An art show?" That was not what I'd been expecting at all. "Why an art show?"

"Because that's where I want you to be." He glances sideways at me. "Don't worry about it. You'll get to keep your clothes on. Mostly."

"Mostly?"

This time when he glances at me, he looks at the dress. "I'm sure you surmised we're getting you out of that—what was the term we were using? *Tempting* number. But you'll have something else to wear instead."

"Something more *appropriate,*" I say, enunciating the word he'd used with Adly. "Less tempting, I'm guessing."

He's silent for a grip of seconds. "I doubt you could ever be less tempting, Ms. Shaw."

I take a deep breath, telling myself to let the subject go, but I can't. "I don't know what to do with that statement, Mr. Sebastian."

He's stoic when he replies. "That makes two of us."

We ride in silence for several minutes, my head in a fog, thoughts flying in and out of my mind without fully showing their shape. My body, however, is buzzing everywhere. Like I've had too much caffeine or someone slipped me an Adderall. It's not a mind/body balance that I enjoy, and so I struggle to find something to hold on to.

Out of the blue, a question arises. "How did you even know I was home?"

"Hm?" The low vibration in his throat does odd things to my already sensitive girl parts.

"You were already on your way when you called me. It's Saturday. I could have been anywhere. How did you know I was home?"

"Michael told me."

My husband's name skates over me like a ghost. Haunting me though he's alive and well and still very much my spouse. I hate thinking about him when I'm sitting next to Holt, but I hate even more the feeling that Michael is somehow orchestrating all of this. As though he's the one who decided what I'd give to Holt and the cost. A glorified pimp for a high price call girl.

"Michael," I repeat, trying to detach myself from the two syllables.

"Yes, Michael. Your producer?" Funny how he leaves out the more meaningful relationship tie. "I saw him yesterday. And the day before. Pretty much every day this week. He's a little tedious in large amounts, but I'm sure I don't have to tell you that. He's been keeping you apprised of the contract negotiations, hasn't he?"

"Uh, for the most part." What I'm really thinking is how glad I am that he kept talking so I didn't have to defend Michael when he called him tedious. I've never felt that way about Michael, but having to say so now would feel weird. "Any snags?"

"All standard procedure," Holt assures me. "Your lawyer will make sure your stipulations are met before you sign. Mostly, we're debating the scope of marketing and airtime and when we'll go live. Logistics. Nothing worth talking about at this point."

"Our agreement isn't mentioned at all?" My tone is sarcastic, but I'm honestly not sure there isn't a side contract being worked up alongside the other one.

"No. But it stands. I take verbal agreements as seriously as anything on paper. Were you worried I'd forgotten?"

"Worried? No. No." I sound too defensive to my own ears. "I just didn't think attending art shows was what you had in mind when we made this arrangement. Unless you think I'm going to be posing." I'm suddenly horrified by all the sexual things he could have me do that I didn't exclude originally. "I should add nothing in public and no group anything to my stipulations."

"It's too late for stipulations. I said I wanted to spend time with you, and that means however I want to spend that time. If I want you to attend an event with me in public, then you will."

"I meant…" I don't know how to phrase what I mean.

"Go ahead, Brystin. Say it."

He's trying to rile me up on purpose, and even though I know that, I feel sufficiently riled. "I meant the sexual part of our arrangement. That is still one of the terms. Right?" I hate that I sound like I'm asking out of hope.

"Ah, yes. Yes, still very much a term, but you need not fear. That part of our arrangement is very much private. I'm not a man who likes to share his toys."

I shiver at the way he refers to me as his, and my pussy spasms again at him equating me with his playthings. There's obviously something wrong with me in the head.

I hug myself tighter so he won't see that my nipples are rock hard.

"But in case you're worried that the sexual terms of our arrangement are being neglected, you're welcome to blow me while we drive."

I swing my head in his direction, anxious to see how serious he, is and find him unreadable. It wouldn't be the first time I've given road head, and honestly, I'm not really scared that's what he wants from me. I'm more scared that I might like it.

Then I remember I'd offered a clause the last time we spoke. "I told you—I'm waiting for evidence."

"Something to look forward to then."

And goddammit. Now I'm also looking forward to sucking off the man who shouldn't deserve my lips on his cock.

A beat passes. "I drove all the way to Edison, New Jersey for you. That isn't evidence?"

"No. That's called insanity." But I spend the rest of the drive thinking about those words—*for you*—and wondering exactly what he thinks I need him to prove.

I'M STILL MULLING it over half an hour later when we pull in front of a shop in Greenwich Village with the name Mirabelle's on the window. It's not the kind of place that usually has a valet, but as soon as we're parked, a woman who was waiting on the sidewalk approaches us and says she'll deal with Holt's car.

Without any concern for his mega expensive automobile, he hands over his keys.

"Are you sure you're going to see your car again?" I ask when it's just the two of us standing on the sidewalk.

"I hope so. I'll have to pay my driver double if I call him in on his day off."

Whatever he pays his driver, it isn't as much as that car is worth, but if Holt isn't worried, I'll try not to be as well.

While I'm thinking about money… "You know I can't afford this place."

He scoffs. "As if I wouldn't be buying."

"Just making sure."

The door in front of us, which has a keypad and a bell rather than a knob, opens as if on cue, and a brunette woman with a pixie haircut greets us when we step inside. "You're Holt? Nice to finally meet you. I've heard a lot about you, all of which you probably don't want me repeating. I'm Mira, by the way. I see Jesi has taken care of your car."

Holt glances at me as if to say, *see?*

While Mirabelle's is a posh fashion boutique that requires an appointment, I'm positive this kind of white glove treatment only belongs to those with a billionaire status.

Must be freaking nice.

The bubbly shop owner continues, barely taking a breath. "Adly said you had some sort of emergency, and that you're in a rush, and she gave me the details about the event, so let's get to it right away. I have a room ready and waiting." Finally she addresses me directly. "And you are—"

"The emergency." I reach out my hand while she laughs. "Brystin Shaw."

"Oh, I like the name!"

"I was just thinking how much I like *your* name."

"We're very original."

"I suppose it's probably our parents who deserve the credit, but I'm happy to take it for myself."

"All right." Holt interrupts our banter. "Time crunch. Remember?"

I want to remind him that his sister told him he had to be nice to her friend, but Mirabelle is a professional, and she's already moving us along. "I went ahead and pulled some things already if you'd like to take a look."

She's leading me to a rack at the center of the store, but

Holt once again interrupts. "Brystin, go to the dressing room and get undressed. I'll pick something for you."

I don't even consider agreeing. "No, no, no. I need to do the picking."

His eyes widen slightly, as if he's appalled that I would defy him. "We really don't have time to discuss this."

"Which is why you should let me get to looking at—"

"Which is why you need to go to the dressing room and start undressing."

I straighten my spine. "Look, I know this seems like an easy task, but it's not. I have a brand to live up to. There are certain do's and don'ts when you're in a position like—"

"Brystin." His voice is sharp and irrefutable. "I'm choosing the dress. Go to the dressing room and wait for me. Now."

As though these kinds of arguments happen every day in front of her, Mirabelle smiles cheerfully. "I'll show you where it is. Right this way."

Begrudgingly, I follow her.

"Not my business, but want to make sure you're all right," she asks as soon as we're out of Holt's sight. "If you need me to get help, I'll step in. I know it can seem like men with money get away with everything, but I know my way around them."

"Thank you. That's very kind. But he's fine. He's an ass, but he's not going to hurt me." At least, I don't think he will. "And this isn't what you think it is. He's my boss. That's all."

"Oh, okay." She doesn't sound exactly like she believes me, but she does seem reassured. "Then is there anything particular you'd like me to direct him toward?"

I jump on the offer. "Yes. Please. Nothing slutty. Nothing that implies bimbo. I need to look smart, but not frumpy. Sharp. Notable. Cleavage is good, but nothing that makes you think of a Playboy bunny."

"Got it. I'll see what I can do."

She leaves me alone in the dressing room, and I try to be optimistic as I strip out of my zipper dress, but I don't succeed. Michael and Zully are the only two people I would trust to shop for me, and even Michael at times tries to put me in clothes with too much leg. It's not that I don't have the body for it—being on TV requires strict awareness of my figure—but rather it's that I have to prove I have a mind as well. It's the obstacle women in my field run into over and over again. *Be pretty, but if you're too pretty, people will think you're dumb.*

Actually, that's probably the obstacle women face everywhere, not just in journalism.

Point being, I carefully choose my event wardrobes, and to be honest, I'm doubtful we'll find anything suitable in such a short time frame. Me being relegated to the dressing room will only make the process take longer.

I'm undressed when there's a knock on the door. A short rap that sounds more masculine than feminine, and I know it's Holt before he speaks. "Open up. I have a dress for you."

One dress?

I hold up my zipper dress to cover me—as if he hasn't seen me near naked—prepared to argue with whatever outfit he's brought me and open the door. Wordlessly, he sticks his arm in just far enough to hang a dress on the hook.

I'm not sure where he goes after that because my eyes are on the dress.

The gorgeous, breathtaking dress.

Not something I would have chosen for myself in a million years, but it might work. There's no price tag, which means it's super expensive, and I wouldn't have chosen it for that reason alone.

But oh my God, it's to die for.

I shut the door and quickly put it on, eager to see if I'm as enamored with it on my body as I am with it on the hanger.

I'm surprised as shit when I like it even more.

It's somehow both simple and stunning, a basic white sheath skirt that goes all the way to the floor with gold bands of ornamentation and a matching gold bodice. Though it's low cut, and requires I go braless, it holds my breasts well, letting nothing spill out. I can't wear panties either. Not with how tight it is around my hips. The gold bands are delicate needlework, and my skin can be seen through them, but it's classy rather than slutty, and all the needlework in the bodice is layered with a material that matches my skin.

I'm still staring in the mirror, still gaping, when Mirabelle arrives—apparently, I left the door slightly ajar. She drops some gold shoes on the floor and moves to zip me up, then peers at my image with me. The dress fits me like a glove, like it was made for me. Not just the tailoring, but the design itself. I look somehow sultry and wise. Like a goddess.

"It's perfection," she says.

"Thank you. I was scared he'd pick out something terrible, and this is…I don't know what to say. I see why you have the reputation you do."

"Well, thanks, but this was all Holt."

I turn to face her. "No way."

"He flipped through the dresses I'd picked, barely looking at them, then went off to search on his own. This is what he came up with. Your size and everything. He even picked out the shoes."

"He got lucky." This wasn't luck. I'm not sure what this was, honestly. A man with a good eye for fashion, probably.

It feels like something else. Like a man with a good eye for me.

"You'd better hurry and show him," Mira nudges. "He's waiting."

Quickly, I put the shoes on, then start toward the front of the store, suddenly nervous. Not because I don't think he'll like it, but because I know he will. Because I know now what he thinks of my potential. That he sees me as a stunning siren. That he sees how beautiful I can be without compromising my values.

Funny that this is the same guy who has extracted sexual favors in exchange for my dream job.

With my head held high, I step out from the back hallway and hold my breath, waiting for his approval.

He's typing into his phone, so it takes him a few seconds to notice me. When his head lifts, I notice his eyes flash with something dangerous before he masks his expression. "Come here," he says, and without question, I walk over, stopping when I'm only a couple of feet away.

He nods as he walks around me, inspecting me from all angles. When he's in front of me again, his brow furrows.

"We'll take it, right?"

He considers.

"Holt?" I glance behind me where Mira is watching the whole interaction. When I look back at Holt, his furrow is gone, and his eyes are dark.

"Kneel down."

"Uh…what?"

"I said, *kneel down*."

"Kneel down? Like…" I know exactly what the like is without him filling in the blank. He's looking forward. He's thinking about my mouth on his cock, and knowing that's what's on his mind makes liquid trickle between my thighs.

My cheeks flush with understanding.

Then I have to make a decision. The dress is awfully tight. I can probably manage if I'm careful, but why should I try? Why, when it's clearly meant as an act to demean me? Why should I dress in an outfit that makes me look and feel powerful, and then submit myself to the likes of Holt Sebastian?

I can't answer any of those questions.

And still, something draws me to my knees. In the middle of Mirabelle's boutique with the shop owner looking on, I kneel in front of him and look up at him. Without thinking to do so, my tongue flicks across my lower lip, and even though my eyes are caught on his, I know his pants are suddenly on the verge of tenting.

"We'll take it," he says softly. He holds his hand out to help me up. "*This* is your brand, Brystin Shaw."

I'm not sure he means me in the dress or me in the dress kneeling in front of him. Whichever it is, I know he's right.

CHAPTER **TWELVE**

BRYSTIN

I stare at the sign outside the gallery as we walk past. *Adeline Sebastian Showroom*. "I didn't realize there was a museum at the Sebastian Center."

The center is quite encompassing in both size and range of attractions. I also hadn't realized there was a valet and parking garage until Holt drove through the entrance. Probably because it's not open to the public, but still, it was a surprise.

Holt doesn't address my comment, seemingly too busy guiding me past security. There's a line for the show's event that we bypass with a nod to the woman on duty. Holt's hand is on the small of my back, directing me where to go, and while there is much to process sensorily in this moment, it's only the hot touch of his fingers on my bare skin that registers in my brain.

Once we're inside, and his hand drops, I feel instantly cold.

Wrapping my arms around myself, I take in my surroundings while Holt collects a brochure. The gallery is box shaped, and consists of several floors. A grand staircase, modern in design with sharp angles, is the focal point —an art piece in its own right. I glance up and count four levels. At the very top, a balcony extends, and the small group of black-tie individuals overlooking the mass below seem not unlike royalty gazing over their people.

"Ready for this year's showcase artist?" Holt holds up the pamphlet to read the title out loud. "*Lonely World by Anita Sendari*." He flips through the pages. "Apparently, the show is all photographic images of empty spaces. Spaces that are usually occupied. Feels unoriginal, doesn't it?" He lets out a bored sigh and tosses the brochure in a recycling bin. "Let's get this over with."

Again, his hand settles on my back, and he leads me toward the nearest display. The sound of the crowd muffles around me, and again, his touch and the thud of my racing heartbeat in my ears are at the forefront of my awareness.

I force myself to find logical talking points and settle on the most obvious one. "What exactly are we doing here?"

Holt doesn't answer until we're standing in front of a large black and white photo of an empty sports arena littered with garbage and confetti and streams from pompoms. "We're looking at images of our lonely world. Keep up, Brystin. This particular piece looks very much like my parents' house after Adly's high school graduation. Partied out, is what I'd call it."

I offer a different term. "Trashed."

"Good one." He guides me to the next photo—a black and white of an empty playground. "Again, unoriginal."

"Uh-huh." A woman next to us turns her head sharply in our direction, apparently not impressed with Holt's critique. I lower my voice when I rephrase my question. "But why are we here?"

"It's my grandmother's birthday. She's passed, but she was an art lover so once a year, Grandpa Irving flies in from whatever retirement home he's currently living in, to celebrate her special day with a new show by an up-and-coming female artist and a formal luncheon—which we were, unfortunately, too late to attend." He directs me to the next piece of work—an image from an empty hospital after what seems to be a fire or bombing of some sort. "I'll tell you what, though—Grandma Addy loved supporting women in the arts, but this is not at all the kind of display she would have been into. Too cold and dark. She preferred colorful modern pieces. Jackson Pollack and Liz Barber."

He moves us to another image, but I'm more interested in his unusual candor and the still unanswered heart of my question than the art. "Grandma Addy's birthday. Art show by a woman she would have disliked. But why am *I* here?"

"Because I asked you to be here."

"You *told* me to be here, if we're being precise. And I can't figure out exactly why."

His eyes still focused on the exhibition, he gives yet another sigh. "Because I'm required to be here, Brystin. As I'm required to be every year, and it's so boring and dull that I decided it would be more entertaining to have you come along."

This time when he tries to move me forward, I don't budge.

"What?" he asks, his tone bordering on irritation.

"You bought me a dress and made all that fuss just so that I could come here and…what? Be your distraction?"

"That sounds like a fair summation."

I stare hard at him for several seconds. "Do you not have any friends?"

He laughs. "Of course I don't have friends. I'm a wealthy, powerful man from an even wealthier, more powerful family. Most everyone who wants to get close to me wants something in exchange, and quite frankly, all I really give a fuck about is work. So yes, I have to look elsewhere for entertainment."

"And that's what I am. Your entertainment."

Finally, he looks directly at me. "Was that unclear in our negotiated terms?"

"Well…" I'd supposed all our interactions would be sexual, but he never actually stated as such. He'd specifically said he wanted to get to know me. I'd taken that to mean in one way only.

It's strange how it feels more of a sacrifice to give him my company than to give him a blow job.

"I guess I made assumptions." I try to be vague about what I'd assumed.

His lip curls up on one side. "I did tell you that today you'd be clothed."

I hate that he knows exactly what my assumptions had been, despite their obviousness. Or maybe I just hate that he made it a point to mention them.

Brooding, I step away from his hand. From his warmth. "Since I'd requested evidence of your dedication to our agreement, I'd expected today would be about that. I've paid out, remember? It's your turn. Quid pro quo."

Holt's expression turns dark, and he's clearly annoyed. "Quid pro quo is not something you are in a position to demand. Might I remind you that what I have to offer you is far more than what you have to offer me in this deal. If I want to dress you up and have you accompany me to an art show in memory of my grandmother, then you should accept that as an honor and willingly comply."

A chill runs down my spine, but I can't say that's rooted in fear. Not exactly.

Whatever it's rooted in, part of me feels compelled to lower my eyes and say, *yes, Mr. Sebastian.* Another part of me wants to slap him in the face, never mind that he's the boss of all bosses, and that we're in public.

I somehow manage to ignore both compulsions, and instead I laugh.

Which surprises him into a wary smile. "I don't believe I said anything funny."

"It's funny," I insist. "All of it. I promise." That I've entered into a sexual agreement with a man who just wants my company? Downright hysterical. "Come on. Next piece. At this rate, we'll be here all day."

This time his smile is genuine. "My thoughts exactly."

The next few photos are more of the same thing. The artist has skill and a good eye, if not the most original concept. Holt and I exchange critiques at each piece, but quickly, I understand why he finds this whole thing boring, and soon I'm having a hard time caring enough to mention the art at all.

"What do you mean you're required to be here?" I ask when we've made it through what I estimate to be only half of Sendari's exhibit. Several times already, Holt has been stopped and photographed—many times with me at his side—which I assume he will use as the proof that he attended today, since I've yet to see any one of his family members checking in on him. "Is your grandfather Irving that much of a hard-ass?"

Honestly, I don't know much about the man's temperament, though his accomplishments are plenty. The ninety-six-year-old was the founder of the Sebastian Empire, building both an industrial corporation and a media conglomerate under one umbrella before the government broke up the company in the eighties. Irving remained CEO of the industrial branch for another twenty years and a board advisor for the media company, eventually retiring and leaving both businesses in the hands of his five sons.

It would make sense if the guy was an asshole. Probably where Holt got it from. It's likely genetic.

"Actually, no." He surprises me with his answer. "Grandpa Irving is kind of a teddy bear now that he's retired. It's the uncles that are the hard-asses."

I urge him on with a questioning look.

He takes a breath, as though what he's going to try to sum up for me is a rather lengthy history. "Grandpa retired, but he still owns everything, which means his sons are constantly scrambling to win his favor. All of them want to be his favorite. All of them hope they'll be the one who gets handed the most power when he dies."

I follow his line of thinking. "Attending this event is a way of gaining his affection?"

"Dad seems to believe so. My uncle Reynard seems to believe the same."

"So he requires you to be here as an extension of himself."

He nods before he answers. "It's not a verbal requirement. It's more assumed. We know we'll be in the doghouse if we don't attend. I'm sure I'll face some sort of punishment for being late. Left out of Dad's next thank-you speech or cut out of the next family press event or ignored on my birthday." He considers for a beat. "Now that I think about it, I'm not sure any of those things are really a punishment."

I have a sudden certainty that I understand him profoundly. "You need him to prove his love. Doesn't matter what it's worth. You can't help yourself." Much the way I keep needing Michael to prove his love, despite him being clear that his love isn't worth what I want it to be.

"My father doesn't love," he says coldly. "I don't expect him to prove something he's incapable of. That's not what I'm after."

"Then what is it you're after?"

"Reason, I suppose. Incentive."

"Same thing. Whatever you disguise it as, it's always love."

Holt turns his attention back to the art, and I have the distinct impression I've said something wrong.

I should let it go and not care, but sometimes I push too far, and that's what I do now. "I wasn't trying to pry. I'm saying I get it. That's all."

He acts as though he hasn't heard me. "This photo I find fascinating."

I look at the image hanging in front of us. It's one of the only pictures with people in it—a lone woman in a swimsuit against the side of an Olympic size pool. It wouldn't be that extraordinary if it weren't for the expression on her face. Her eyes are sad, and she's got the slightest frown on her lips.

"She should be happy the pool's empty," I say. "Crowded pools are the worst, especially if you're training, which, considering the type of suit she's wearing and the muscle tone in her body, she probably is."

Holt shakes his head. "She wants to win." Then he looks at me. "You can't win if you're the only one in the race."

His interpretation is correct. I know it as soon as he says it aloud. I'm also pretty sure he's telling me something about himself, about his need to gain his father's love, but I'm not quite sure what it is.

Or maybe he's telling me something about his father's need to win. About his own need to win. How his father and uncles pit themselves against each other because that's the only thing that motivates them to be better, and being better—being best—is the only purpose that has been instilled in them.

He surprises me again when he returns to our conversation. "What about you, Brystin? What is it you understand? Are you trying to win your father's love?"

I shake my head vehemently. "My father was never around. Too busy being an addict."

"So that's why you're married to Michael—daddy issues."

"I don't have daddy issues."

He glares at me like I'm being purposely obtuse.

"I don't know how many times I have to tell you not to try to examine my relationship with my husband. It's none of your business, and whatever you think about it, it's wrong." More accurately, whatever he thinks is too close to right for my comfort.

"Doth the lady protest too much?" But he drops the subject and presents me with another as he steers me toward a new wall of photos. "Boring, boring, boring. All of this is boring."

"How about you be bored by yourself for a moment? I need to visit the ladies' restroom."

"Need help? I'm happy to accompany you."

This was more in line with what I thought he had in mind for me. I somehow feel more grounded with this topic. "I'm not blowing you in the ladies' restroom, Holt."

"That hadn't been what I was suggesting, but now that you've put it in my head—"

I'm already stepping away. "I'll return soon." I let a smile play on my lips as soon as I'm facing away from him.

It stays there as I make my way toward the bathroom, only vanishing when I collide into a hard body suddenly in my path. "Oh, I'm so—" I look up at the obstacle and my stomach drops. "Michael. What are you doing here?"

He's dressed less formally than Holt, wearing an everyday business suit, which is why I hadn't expected he was coming into this city for anything other than work when he'd left this morning.

Based on his expression, he's equally surprised to see me. "I should be asking you the same thing." He glances down the length of my gown. "This is new."

Being here with Holt feels wrong. Feels secret, especially now that I realize that Michael might have told Holt where

I was today, but Holt didn't tell Michael his plans to bring me to this event.

But of course those feelings are ridiculous. This thing with Holt isn't a clandestine affair.

"Just got it." I force myself to turn and look toward Holt who is currently wrapped up in a conversation with someone I recognize from one of SNC's New York stations. "Not purchased by me, though."

Michael follows my gaze. "Ah, I see." But the wrinkle in his brow says he doesn't see entirely. "Did he invite you here for any specific reason?"

Some juvenile part of me wants to run with that, let Michael think something different about my relationship with our boss. I've longed for him to be jealous over me for years, and that longing is hard to put to rest.

But again, I force myself to be mature and transparent. "It wasn't presented as an invitation. It's not going to be a one-time thing."

He seems to understand immediately, gleaning the full picture with only a rough sketch. "I realize that. Now." He pauses before he says more, scrutinizing me with new eyes. "And you're still okay with this?"

I'm even more irritated about the question now than when he's asked it before, particularly because of how little he's told me about his meetings with Holt this week. He could have told me he was coming to this event today. He could have invited me himself. If he didn't know that Holt meant to have me come with him, then Michael should have at least asked.

So instead of answering his question, I redirect. "How are negotiations going, anyway?"

"Good," he says quickly. Too quickly. "Stuck on minor details, is all. Format, airtime, vacation days. Those sort of things."

Almost identical to what Holt had said, which should be validating. Unless they're both following a script.

Which is stupid.

I'm being stupid.

"Anyway," he says, as though he's said enough for me to be satisfied. "I thought it wouldn't hurt to stop by today, show my support. Show we're committed to the Sebastian family."

Show *he's* committed to the Sebastian family, he means. There is no *we* when he shows up on his own, and not for the first time as of late, I start to wonder if our partnership ranks after his own self-interest in priority.

He's such a foundation in my life. I don't want to doubt him. The mere thought of not being able to trust him makes the ground feel loose under my feet.

I shake off my reservations. "I was just headed to the…" I point at the ladies' restroom. "If you'll excuse me, I want to get in before the line gets long again."

"Sure, sure." He bends down to kiss me, and instead of feeling butterflies over his rare display of affection, I move my mouth at the last minute, so that his kiss doesn't land on my lips. "Okay," he says when he's upright again. As though the refusal of his kiss is very not okay.

"Sorry. I just. Really have to go, is all." I hurry toward the bathroom, and when I glance back it's not to look at Michael, but to look at Holt.

His eyes are already locked on me, almost like they were waiting for mine to seek his out. His expression is unreadable, as it often is, but the tick of his jaw seems to say that he not only saw me with Michael, but also that he's very unhappy about it.

And here come the butterflies I was expecting. Only they're here for the wrong man.

CHAPTER **THIRTEEN**

BRYSTIN

I'm washing my hands when my phone buzzes with a text. After the way Holt looked at me with Michael, I suspect it's from him.

Send me a picture of your pussy.

That was not the message I was expecting.

I ignore my stupid stomach flip and type in my response.

Not a chance.

You're not wearing panties. It should be easy.

I almost ask if this has to do with Michael, then change my mind, sure that jealousy is not in Holt's nature.

But you owe me, remember?

I remembered YOU owe ME. I bought you a dress.

A dress that I didn't ask for, to wear to an event I hadn't planned to attend. Before I can mention those facts, he's texted again.

Plus, today I've given you buzz.

My hand hesitates above the screen. Was that what this was all about? A chance to get my name circulating again before announcing I'm the anchor of a new show? It could help my success seem less out of the blue.

Actually, a very good move, strategy wise.

I tell myself that's the reason I go back into the stall to send the requested pic, but the truth is, I want to send it to Holt. It's barely anything compared to what I've agreed I would do for him, and there's something exciting about the idea of getting him hot. We're not in a relationship—not like that—but this flirting feels like foreplay. It will make the rest that happens feel more natural.

As if any of this is natural.

As though I'm not already looking forward to more.

I sigh as I hike up my dress, ready to take the shot, when Holt sends another text.

Give me some real art. Something that shows me what I've purchased. Spread your lips. I want to see everything.

Just like that, I'm wet.

I sit on the toilet, legs wide, and pull my lips apart with

my fingers. It's embarrassingly porno, and I have to try several takes before I'm happy with it. I examine it. My skin is glistening with moisture. He'll know he did that to me. I shouldn't give this to him. This is so not a good idea.

I'm waiting…

Before I can think too hard about it, I curse under my breath and reply to his last text with the pic.

For some reason, I'm smiling when I leave the stall.

I have to search a bit to find Holt again in the gallery. His phone isn't in hand, and I tell myself it's for the best that he saves the looking for later. When I sidle up next to him, he acts as though his text never happened. He doesn't even look my way before picking up the conversation, as though I never left his side. "This would be more effective if it were in color."

I step forward to study the image, an abandoned roadside market. There are moldy eggplants or zucchini in one of the boxes, along with various berries, and he's right—color would help define the produce.

Behind me, Holt goes on. "Color was definitely the right choice for this. A wonderful shade of pink. And all bare. The best art I've seen all day."

I suspect he's moved on to the next image, but when I look ahead, I find it's also in black and white.

Which is when I realize what he must be looking at.

Oh my God.

Sure enough, when I turn to face him, he has his phone in his hand and his arm held out where anyone walking by could see the blown-up image of my pussy on his screen.

"Oh my God!" I try to pull his arm down, but he moves his cell to his other hand and holds that up instead.

"I hadn't expected all bare, to tell you the truth. A little bit of bush seemed more your style. Is this for Michael?"

"Oh my God, stop!" Unlike him, I keep my voice down to a low hiss. I'm blushing so hard I can feel the heat from my head to my feet. "There are people here."

He continues as if I haven't said anything at all. "Look at you, already glistening." He strokes the image, drawing his finger down between my folds.

As though he's really touching me there, I shiver.

Holt puts a hand at my back and moves in closer so we're looking at the picture together. "Not all pussies are pretty, Brystin. You should be proud. This one is a very pretty pussy." His mouth is near my ear, his breath hot on my skin, and finally he's talking soft. "Want to know what I'm planning to do to this pussy?"

I mean to say uh-uh, but it comes out more like a two syllable, "Mmm."

"First, I'll trace the beautiful lines of your lips with my finger. All the way to that tight asshole—thank you very much, for including that in the shot. Then I'll take that pink little bud." He rubs the screen over my clit. "I'll suck it into my mouth, like a juicy berry. Do you think you'll squirt all over the place, when I do that? Will I have to clean it all up with my tongue?"

I'm paralyzed with lust. The crowd has disappeared, a dull murmur in the background. My breaths feel short and erratic. I think I'm supposed to speak, but I can't find my voice.

"Answer me, Brystin. When I play with this pussy, will I

have to lap up a mess? Will I get my beard wet? Will I be wearing your cunt on my face when I'm done?"

The word falls out of my mouth without effort. "Yes."

"Yes, I will. I know I will because I'll be awfully good to this pussy, and a good pussy cries when it's happy."

I wonder if he knows my pussy is crying now.

"I can smell you. You greedy little girl. Smell how much you want my tongue on you."

"When?" It's what I mean, but not what I mean to say.

Too late. I've spoken, and I sound eager, and I can't take it back.

"When is a very good question, Ms. Shaw." A text message pops on the screen from Adly over the top of the image.

> Grandpa's getting tired of being here and Dad's about to blow.

"Not right now, I'm afraid." Holt doesn't sound nearly as disappointed as I feel. "Right now, we've got to get upstairs."

He watches me as he puts his phone in his jacket pocket. "Don't worry. I'm not done with it. I'll make it my screensaver."

I didn't think it was possible to blush harder.

Bastard that he is, Holt doesn't pretend not to notice. "Red looks good on you. But you might want to drop it a shade before meeting the good guy. Luckily, you have four flights of stairs to try to calm down."

I have much I want to say. I'd particularly enjoy telling him off for his immature antics, but I'm obviously culpable, perhaps even more than he is because I'm the one who sent him the image.

So instead of saying anything, I end up quietly spiraling.

What the fuck have I gotten myself into? And why does he have this effect on me?

As though he knows what I'm thinking, he coaxes me down while guiding me to the stairs. "I asked you to send it, Brystin. Trust me, we wouldn't be walking up these stairs together if you'd disobeyed. You were a good girl."

He must think I'm a dog.

I must *be* a dog because those words do inexplicably crazy things to my insides. All for a little bit of fucking praise. Maybe I do have issues. Not necessarily daddy issues, but kinky billionaire issues.

I'm still in my head as we wordlessly climb up the stairs. Holt directs me with his hand at my back, and when we're more than halfway up, he breaks the silence. "I hope you're about done with your pouting."

I snap my head toward him, ready with a bitchy retort, but then I realize something. "People are whispering about us."

"They are."

It's the buzz he said he'd given me. I feel it more now since the stairs are such a focal point. I wonder if this is what it's like for him all the time—people always pointing and murmuring whenever he's around. This is the type of celebrity status I've always longed for, but I have a bad feeling the talk is about Holt's hand on my back rather than about my credits in journalism. "Aren't you worried about tomorrow's headlines?"

"What about them?"

"What they'll say? About us?"

He gives a smug smile. "You seem to be forgetting, Brystin—I make the headlines. Nothing is newsworthy unless I say it is."

It's a small comfort considering I'm someone who seeks for truth in the industry.

But if I was above using Holt Sebastian's power for my benefit, I suppose I wouldn't be here at all.

Adly finds us as soon as we make it through security on the top floor. "Oh, thank fuck." She hugs her brother in a way that seems more out of formality than affection, though I have no reason to believe they don't genuinely care for each other. "Hunter and his lackey, Ax, have had Grandpa's ear all afternoon, following him around like little puppies. It's so desperate, I almost feel sorry for them."

"Any idea what they're saying?"

She shakes her head. "Most of what I know is what Reynard's saying. He's been gloating, talking about Hunter like he's nine instead of thirty-nine. 'Isn't it dear how Hunter's taken to Grandpa. He's a miniature Irving, if I ever saw one.'" She makes a gagging gesture, then quickly looks around to be sure she hasn't been seen.

Thankfully, the security check-in at the top of the stairs seems to partly be meant to keep out the press. While I've spotted a photographer, I'm fairly sure she's one hired by the family, considering the kinds of pictures she's taking. Most everyone else seems to have similar facial features—Sebastian facial features, to be precise. We've definitely arrived at the VIP party. The large open space is flanked by two bars and caterers are passing out dessert trays.

"Hunter's a vampire. He's not trying to emulate Grandpa, he's trying to suck the last life out of him."

"Preaching to the choir, bro, and also…" She steps back from their private conversation and addresses me, as if she's just noticed my presence, but is really not that surprised by it. "You look divine. Mirabelle's? She's the best, even on short notice."

I step back so she can further admire the dress. Then when she makes the twirl symbol with her finger, I turn around. I guess I perform for all Sebastians, not just the one.

"I'm actually jealous. I know I'm too short for something so ethereal, but why hasn't she fixed me up in something as grand as this?"

I glance at Holt, wondering if I should give him credit. He gives nothing away, so I don't either. "My first time shopping there," I say. "Definitely won't be my last." If I get a raise anytime soon, that is.

Adly nods, but I have a feeling she's moved on to assess something else about me other than the dress. When she speaks again, it's to her brother. "I was worried when you skipped out on lunch, but this was a good decision."

I'm not sure if she means me as the good decision, but Holt doesn't give her a chance to provide any more context clues, which I think might be on purpose. "Where's Grandpa now?"

She nods to the center of the room. "I texted you when he started talking about a nap." Adly turns to me to explain. "The man's ninety-six. Still spry as any of his sons except that he absolutely won't miss his daily nap."

"Which means he's leaving soon, and I should say hello

before he does." I expect Holt to do so on his own, but he surprises me by offering his arm. "Shall we?"

"Oh, me? You want me to go with you?"

"I thought you might like to meet him."

Yes. I would. Very much.

It just hadn't occurred to me that I might get to meet the man today, and faced with the opportunity, I'm suddenly nervous. "I don't know. I don't want to interrupt family time."

He seems bored with my reluctance. "For fuck's sake."

Once again, his hand finds my back, and he directs me toward the gathering at the center of the room. His pace is quick, and I have to almost skip to match his long stride, so by the time we reach our destination, I'm as breathless from the journey as I am from the prospect of meeting a legend.

Thankfully, there is a crowd around Irving Sebastian, and even though Holt pushes his way to the front of the circle, I imagine I'll have a minute to get myself together while conversation wraps up.

Except I'm wrong.

"There you are, Holt." Irving talks over the man at his side who does not look like he has a family resemblance. "I was beginning to think I wasn't going to see you today. Though, if this breathtaking lady is the reason you've been preoccupied, I should let you get back to her."

Goddammit, I'm blushing again.

"Sorry, Grandpa." Holt leans in to hug the nonagenarian. "I was caught up in the show. I wasn't familiar with Anita Sendari's work until today. Incredible eye. Nice choice."

Irving waves a dismissive hand. "Henry picked her this

year. An admirable artist, but your grandmother would have complained after the first three pieces. Don't tell Anita Sendari."

It's pretty much what Holt had said, and never mind that I know very little about the rest of the Sebastians, it seems more likely that Holt is the miniature Irving, especially being the CEO of SNC at such a young age.

"She's getting a scholarship for being chosen. She should be happy enough with that."

I follow the sound of the voice to see Hunter, the Sebastian I'd met at the award show who had reduced my career to local journalism. While Holt has yet to acknowledge him, I feel a very definite wall of tension between the cousins.

"There's more to life than money, Hunter," Irving says, not unkindly. "But there's also more to life than acclaim. Hopefully the woman has other things to fill her." He turns his attention back to Holt. "Was there anything you enjoyed about the exhibition?"

"The church images were particularly haunting, and the empty images of Times Square."

Irving nods, agreeing. "The Times Square pics got me in the gut. Never seen anything like that. Wonder how she got the place cleared out like that." We've yet to be introduced, when he focuses his attention on me. "How about you, Holt's young lady? You can learn a lot about a person by the art that attracts them. Which did you like?"

My mouth feels like a desert. It's dry and empty, and I have no idea how to respond. On the one hand, it feels critical to explain that I am not Holt's young lady, especially since I'm a married woman. On the other hand, how the hell am I supposed to correct Irving fucking Sebastian?

In a rare show of character, Holt comes to my rescue. "This is Brystin Shaw, Grandpa. She's one of SNC's anchors."

Irving looks to his grandson as if he's been rudely interrupted. "She's one of our anchors—fantastic. Where else would you meet someone? Doesn't mean she can't have an opinion on art." He takes my hand in his. "Tell me, Brystin Shaw, what did you like?"

Despite his age, the man seems outwardly gruff, but with his hand in mine, I'm suddenly certain that he's got a cinnamon roll inside. I lose all desire to correct him about my relationship with his grandson. "The swimming pool," I say. "Definitely the swimming pool."

"Truly lonely. Can't win if there's no competition." He squeezes my hand, and I'm so sure it was the right thing to say, that I say more.

"Though, there's more to life than winning."

"There is more to life than winning. Do you hear this, boys? This woman knows what she's talking about."

Holt puts his arm on my back again, like it belongs there. "Brystin is going to be the next star of SNC, Grandpa. I have something special planned for her."

I feel the negativity roll off Hunter and the man standing next to him—the one that I'm pretty sure isn't family. Ax, maybe?

Irving must feel it too, but all he has to do is toss a glare in the men's direction, and both seem to withdraw.

He directs his attention back to me. "She's already something special, Holt. Try not to fuck that up in the process of whatever you have planned."

Despite the warning words, I can't help but think he's

given his blessing. Especially considering how agitated Hunter and Ax are with the declaration.

"Thank you, Grandpa. I'll keep that in mind." Holt gives the man another hug, longer this time, and even though it's quiet, I hear what he says while they're embracing. "Happy Birthday to our lady. I miss her, and I know you do too."

"We all do," Irving says after they've come apart. "Nice to meet you, Ms. Shaw. Can't wait to see your face on the screen. Now I need a nap."

If it wasn't clear that talking with Irving was the climax of the day's event, there's no doubt when Holt leads me from his grandfather straight to a hidden elevator.

Wish I'd known about this option earlier. Would have been a whole lot nicer than dealing with all the whispers as we'd climbed the stairs, but I resist saying as such since I'm pretty sure that Holt wasn't bothered by the talk.

Besides, once we're alone—and in an elevator, no less—all the heat and foreplay from the day comes rushing back through me, as though my libido is on some sort of switch. A switch that Holt controls with just a look. The kind of look that he gives me as we ascend to the lower level.

The kind of look that says, *I've seen you without your panties on.*

I swallow, excited to find out what happens next. Afraid I'm not ready for it. In an attempt to distract myself, I let my thoughts settle back on the scene with Irving, and something suddenly clicks in place. "That was a power play."

Holt raises a brow. "A power play?"

It wasn't a denial, and somehow that makes me more

confident. "Everyone fighting for your grandfather's approval—you wanted his approval of me. Didn't you?"

He doesn't answer. Instead, he pulls out his phone, and my heart rate spikes, thinking he might be ready to go back to discussing my pussy pic.

But all he does is type out a text then pockets it again.

Then the door opens on the first floor. No elevator emergency this time, which should be a good thing, except that now he's escorting me out of the elevator and down a back hallway that leads out of the gallery.

Then, silently, he takes me through another hallway that ends in the parking garage, where his car is waiting. Upon sight of us, the driver gets out of the car, which I suppose is to let Holt in his place.

Until he opens the back door, and waits.

I'm about to ask what the plan is when Holt finally talks. "Hunter." He pauses, and I think he's going to explain who he is.

But since I already know, I help him out. "I know who he is. Your cousin, right?"

"Cousin. Yes. I prefer that." He doesn't try to clear up the confusion he's created. "He believes he'd be better at my job than I am."

I consider that. "Does that matter?" I try to remember what I know about how his position was passed to him. "Your father named you as his successor after his heart attack. Could you be kicked out?"

"If Hunter convinces enough of the board to oust me, then yes, it's possible."

"Is it likely?" My stomach feels twisted in knots about the potential of Holt losing his job. For no other reason than that I think he cares about it. I don't have a lot of evidence of the fact, but since he went against his inner circle to report the story with King-Kincaid, I think it has to be true. He has to care about the job more than the people around him, anyway.

He mistakes my genuine concern for him as something else. "Don't worry, Ms. Shaw. We'll get your contract signed, and then you'll have the job no matter who's at the helm."

"That's not what I meant."

He gestures for me to get into the car, ignoring my attempt to correct his assumption. "Get in."

I don't budge. "I wasn't thinking about myself, Holt. Really, I wasn't."

He doesn't say anything for several seconds. "I think, if I continue to make decisions that are good for SNC, that my job is probably safe. Hunter is a nuisance. Nothing more."

I think he means to comfort me, but I feel even more agitated.

Against my better interest, I put voice to the agitation. "Hiring me might not be the best decision, Holt."

A flash of surprise crosses his features, which he quickly schools. "You're not getting out of our agreement." I open my mouth to say it isn't about that, but he puts a finger on my lips, sending sparks through my body. "The agreement stands. Come on. Get in."

Somewhat dazed, I slide into the back seat.

As soon as I do, the driver gets behind the wheel. That's when I realize that Holt isn't getting in with me.

"The agreement stands, but I'm being dismissed. Got it." I don't mean to sound snippy.

Or I do mean to sound snippy.

Because I'm riled up and confused. I'm worried about the position he's putting himself in for my sake, but I'm not willing to give up a shot at my own show. I'm also suffering from a huge case of blue clit. My pussy has been teased and taunted all day, and I won't deny that it was looking forward to being petted.

Of course Holt's reaction is to smile, that fucker. "Dismissed for now. Not forever."

"Whatever." I cross my arms over myself, trying my best to dismiss him right back.

"Next time." His subtext oozes with promise. He leans on the open door, talking to me over the top of it, his voice so low it vibrates between my legs. "For what it's worth, Brystin, I appreciate the enthusiasm."

I can't help myself—I look at him, ready to scold him for assuming I have any sort of enthusiasm about anything he has to offer.

In other words, ready to lie.

But he's giving me that look again, the one that says we have a secret. The one that says he wants to have more secrets with me in the near future. "Besides, now I know you're looking forward to next time as much as I am."

"As much as you are?" God, I'm so needy.

He smirks. "Goodbye, Ms. Shaw."

He doesn't give me a chance to say anything in return. Just shuts the door, and lets his driver take me away.

CHAPTER FOURTEEN

BRYSTIN

My phone buzzes, but I ignore it, too caught up in arguing with the assistant producer at this week's *New Jersey Now* table meeting. "The segment on email scams isn't big enough to be a feature. It needs more meat."

"Which is why we should combine it with the piece on the retirement homes," Jen argues.

I'm not usually at odds with her suggestions, but I'm restless at the moment. It's been three weeks since the art show, and I haven't seen or heard from Holt since. Michael insists the contracts are done and being printed up, and I'm excited, if that's true, but with no contact with Holt, I have doubts.

And that means I'm doubling down on stances I would have usually been less rigid about. "I don't care if seniors are the victims of most email scams. The retirement fraud is a completely unrelated issue."

"They wouldn't be unrelated if—" Jen pauses when my phone buzzes yet again. When she sees I'm not picking it up, she goes on. "If we approached it with the right angle. I suggest taking that interview with the woman at Fall Hills—"

Michael interrupts with a sharp, "Brystin!"

I swing my head in his direction. "What?"

"Your phone."

"Sorry." I let out a sigh and reach for the damn thing. I should have turned it off when the meeting started, but I've been expecting a phone call from a source that I don't want to miss. Quickly, I scan my texts, figuring I probably had a rant from Zully about one of her rich bitch clients, and am surprised to find the messages are from another rich bitch —Holt.

Where are you? I'm sending someone.

Answer me, Brystin.

My driver is on his way to Jersey. YOU BETTER BE READY

My heart rate doubles, and not because of the shouty capitals, but because *he texted me.*

"Everything okay?" Michael's obviously eager to keep the meeting running.

"Uh…yeah…give me a second." I swallow down the excitement and frantically type out a reply so that Holt doesn't show up at my apartment when I'm not there.

Can't. Work.

His reply is practically instant.

Fuck work

The butterflies are starting to settle down, and now I'm irritated. No contact for three weeks and then a demand that I drop everything for him?

Some of us have to earn our living

I'll take care of you

Goosebumps race up my arms, and I can't even describe what happens to my insides after reading that message.

"Brystin?"

I look up to see it's not just Michael waiting for my attention, but the entire team. I must have missed part of the conversation. "Can you repeat that?"

"I said we'd go with the retirement homes and asked if you could provide us with a list of alternate suggestions for making the email scam segment a full show later on." It doesn't matter that we're married—Michael treats me as harshly as anyone in the production room, and right now his tone is short and irritated.

"Yes. Sure. By when?" I bring the phone under the table so that I can type without Michael seeing.

Work first. You'll have to wait.

Then I turn my phone on silent and throw it in the shoulder bag at my feet. Too bad if Holt's not happy. I can't sacrifice the commitment I give to a job that I already have for a vague promise of a job that I don't.

Thirty minutes later, we only have half of today's talking points worked out when there's a knock on the production room door. Everyone at the station knows these meetings are not to be interrupted, so it's strange, but Jen stands up and quietly slides out into the hall and the rest of us resume our planning.

But less than thirty seconds later, Jen opens the door and calls for Michael. "You should come out here." Then she looks at me. "You might want to come too, Brystin."

I have that bowling ball in my stomach kind of dread. Like I'm sure someone's been hurt, but who? I don't have any close living relatives, and Zully probably has her brother listed as her emergency contact. Michael's got a brother in Boston and a mother in Germany. Maybe something happened to one of them.

I grab my bag in case we have to go straight to the hospital or the airport, and follow Michael into the hall where Jen is standing with Harold, the station manager, and two security guards.

"What's going on?" Michael is less snippy with Harold, probably because he's a man and essentially his boss. "Did something happen?"

Harold glances at me then back to Michael, as though he's afraid to say whatever he has to say. And Harold is not usually the kind of guy who pulls punches.

"What is it?" A new kind of dread creeps down my spine.

"I'm sorry to tell you this way, Brystin, but you're being terminated. Effective immediately."

"What?" Michael and I respond in unison.

"There has to be some mistake," Michael says, and I actually think he's about to fight for me. Which is totally uncharacteristic. "Who's behind this? You?"

It's a natural assumption since Harold is in charge here, but I did basically blow off the CEO of the entire company. "Holt," I say.

"I don't know who sent down the order exactly, but it comes from the top." Harold is more nervous than I've ever seen him. "I'm to have you turn in your badge and escort you out."

Michael goes ballistic. "We have two hours until airtime! How are we supposed to replace one of our lead hosts that quickly?"

"I'll get on the phone and call Suri." Jen doesn't wait for anyone to approve the idea before heading back into the production room to get her cell. It's the right move. The show must go on.

Michael on the other hand is not done arguing. "Unacceptable. There has to be cause. You can't fire her out of the blue."

I don't disagree. In fact, I'm pretty livid at the moment, but I also know enough now about Holt Sebastian to realize that standing here debating what he can and can't get away with is absolutely not productive.

I put my hand on Michael's bicep to get his attention. "You aren't going to change his mind. You need to focus on reworking the show."

"I do have to follow orders," Harold says, as if I'd been talking about *his* mind. "I hope you understand, I did push back, but this is my own job on the line."

"I'll find out what this is about," I tell Michael. "Maybe it means…?" We haven't been allowed to mention our prospective deal with the main SNC network, but he doesn't need me to spell it out for it to be clearer.

"It fucking better mean that. And you better tell him this is no way to run a news program. I'll take care of your things." He jerks open the door to the production room. "All right, everyone, get ready to pivot." The door slams shut before he says anything else.

"I truly am sorry," Harold says again.

"It's not your fault." I know better than anyone how hard it is to stand up to the likes of Holt Sebastian. I reach in my bag and find my badge and grab my cell at the same time.

"Can I say goodbye first?" I ask before handing the badge over to Harold.

"I'm afraid we were instructed to have you escorted out immediately."

Of course they were. After relinquishing my bag, I look at my missed texts.

There's only one.

I never wait.

I hate so much that it's apparently true. That he can just snap his fingers and have everything go his way.

It's one thing to have butterflies and chemistry, but fucking with my career—my reputation—that's a hard no. There are so many curse-laden texts I want to send to him right now.

But this is a battle best saved for face to face. So I save my anger for later and send back a less dramatic reply.

Tell your driver I'll be outside in five.

I look around the studio and say a silent goodbye to the job that began my career as an anchor. A job that I've very much nurtured and treasured. A job that has become a huge part of me.

Then I let the security guards escort me off the premises.

A LITTLE MORE THAN an hour later, the driver turns into the private parking garage at the Sebastian Center. I'm dropped off at the same door that had led to the gallery, but Holt isn't there. Instead, a man I've never met before is waiting for me, dressed in a suit and tie.

"Pleasure to meet you, Brystin," he says. "I'm André, Mr. Sebastian's personal assistant."

"The pleasure is mine." I put on a smile for the greeting, though it is truly forced. The ride into the city should have given me time to calm down. Instead, it worked me up even more, especially after the stop-and-go traffic we encountered at the last bit of the trip—fucking rush hour. As I watched the clock on my phone, all I could think was, *I'm supposed to be on air.*

By the time I got out of the car, I'm ready to blow. And now I find out the motherfucker isn't even here to meet me? "I know you're doing your job and all, André, but I really was expecting Holt to be here."

"If you'll follow me, I'll take you directly to him."

"Oh." Of course he will. "Thank you." It's almost anti-climactic considering how badly I want to explode on someone. My fuse will have to last a few more minutes.

I follow André inside. This time, instead of taking the route to the gallery, we turn down a hallway that leads to a private bank of elevators. A code is required to access them, which André quickly types in, and then gestures for me to go in before him.

At least his staff has manners. Can't say that about the assHolt in charge.

I don't notice the uncontrollable tapping of my foot until André asks about it. "Do elevators make you nervous?"

"No, not really."

"Men with the last name Sebastian, then?" There's a smile in his tone, and I know he's trying to make me feel at ease.

"One man with the last name Sebastian," I admit. "And nervous is not the word I'd use to describe how he makes me feel."

"Understood," he says, but he can't understand. Because I don't understand, not truly. I understand that I'm currently pissed as all get out, but underneath that there is a swarm of bees in my stomach, buzzing and stinging my insides with anticipation. Three weeks without seeing Holt, and I am not able to articulate how off-balance I felt until he messaged.

Fuck him for that.

For waiting, for keeping me in the dark. For making me want him and then stretching out the longing over too many minutes to keep count.

I might be more mad about that than being fired, but I don't want to analyze that right now. I can't.

We stop on the twenty-first floor, which means nothing to me since I'm not that familiar with the Sebastian Center's layout, but if André is taking me to Holt's office, I'm surprised it's not on a higher floor.

But when we step off the elevator, all I see is one long hallway and a set of double doors at the end. Heavy double doors. The kind that prevent noise from getting through. Definitely not the kind of doors that lead to executive offices.

And yet, that's exactly where André takes me. After entering another code into another keypad, he opens the doors, and he sends me in. "Mr. Sebastian will meet you inside."

Alone, I hope.

So I can tell him off. Not for any other reason.

My heels click on the hard floor as I walk in. There's a fresh paint smell to the air. It's dark, but there are lights on the other side of the room. Immediately, I recognize that I'm in a studio. Camera equipment is circled around a center stage. The ceiling is high. Long beams hang low with lights attached. The producer's window is seen on the wall beyond the cameras. In the middle of it all is a sleek, modernly designed news desk with a huge multi-paneled screen behind it.

The entire scene isn't new to me. Even at SNC, it looks pretty much like what we have back at News 9. I wouldn't be impressed with any of it except that the screen displays a red, black, and gold logo with the words *Our Nation Now.*

My hand flies to my mouth. This isn't just any studio.

This is *my* studio.

Our Nation Now is *my* show. My national show.

"I hope you like the color scheme we came up with. It's too late to change it, if you don't."

I turn around to find Holt. He must have been waiting in the shadows because the doors haven't opened since they closed behind me. Part of me wants to tease him about that, considering that this afternoon he said he waits for no one.

Part of me still wants to scream at him for getting me fired.

The last part of me wants to hug him.

The last part wins out.

I drop my purse and phone to the ground, not caring about potential damage, and rush to him, throwing my arms around him, whether he wants it or not.

His body stiffens in surprise at the contact, but it's only for a quick second. After that, he hugs me back, his body enveloping me in a warm cocoon.

"Thank you," I whisper into his suit jacket. I swear I feel his lips brush against my hair.

Probably, I'm imagining it.

Imagining it because I've been dreaming about being in his arms like this for the last week. Being in his arms and feeling like I belong there.

Which I don't.

Remembering that pulls me out of the fantasy, and I jerk back quickly.

Then I push him hard with my palms. "You asshole!"

He doesn't budge even with as much force as I used. "What the fuck was that for?"

"You had me fired."

"I got you a better job. In case the name of the show isn't obvious, this is your new gig, Brystin." He has the audacity to sound like I'm out of line.

"I get that, and I'm grateful. Truly. You can't know how grateful." I push him again. "But you can't do that!"

"I…think I can. I obviously did."

"It's not just about the job—it's about my reputation." I'm emotional as I speak, both because of how passionately I feel about making him understand I don't accept what he did today, and also because this surprise is so ridiculously fulfilling. "Rumors will circulate. People will wonder how I could get fired and then get a job here. You and I might know the truth, but countless other people won't. And I left them without an anchor! On the day of the show. That's so fucking unprofessional, and I hate being seen that way. I hate it, Holt. And I hate how I can be so mad at you for doing that to me, for exercising your power like that, and be simultaneously so happy that you used your power to give me my dream. I seriously don't know if I want to slug you or get down on my knees."

He waits a beat before responding. "Complicated feelings you have there."

I dab at an errant tear. "Well, it's a complicated situation."

"Personally, I'd prefer you get down on your knees."

"Would you, now?" My pulse quickens at the thought.

But he's teased and stretched the foreplay so long now that I don't even know if he means it. I'm near convinced he gets off on lording his power over me more than from sexual favors.

If I never get to hold that cock of his in my hands…

I dismiss the thought and turn around to look at the logo again. *My* logo.

And the desk—*my* desk.

I walk past the cameras and onto the set. When I get to the desk I trail my hand along the smooth surface as I travel its length then circle around to the chair behind it. *My* chair.

"It's arched so that we can put more chairs behind it. It will be a similar roundtable format to *New Jersey Now,* but I thought the reveal was more dramatic with just the one."

"Uh, yeah." I smile then let it disappear, needing to take a deep breath before climbing into the dramatically placed solo chair. "Wow."

Holt moves next to the main camera, as if to see what the audience will see. "You look good there."

"Like I deserve to be here?" The question escapes before I have a chance to rein it in. He doesn't need to know how this whole arrangement has fed into my insecurities.

"You've always *deserved* to be there."

I hear a *but* coming. "But I haven't *earned* it," I say, guessing.

His smile is slow to appear. Slow and sharp like he's the big bad wolf. "You haven't earned it *yet.*"

Heat rushes through me as I recognize the lust in his tone. Lust that matches the darkening of his eyes. "I think this counts as some pretty compelling evidence."

So that's why he's been MIA. "You were waiting for the studio to be constructed."

Fuck me, why did I say that out loud?

"Before I reached out again?" He nods. "Felt…necessary."

"Necessary?"

"I wasn't sure I could spend another minute with you without tearing all your clothes off."

The butterflies have migrated lower. I can feel their wings vibrating in unholy parts of my body.

"Also why I couldn't accompany you home that day." His eyes are already undressing me.

I shiver, feeling completely bare. "I…uh." I let out a breath. "Should we go somewhere?"

He shakes his head. "Why would we do that?"

"You know, so I can…earn this chair."

"Seems appropriate that you earn it right where you are. Since this is where the magic will happen." He unbuttons his jacket, getting comfortable. "No one's coming in here."

That only addresses one of my concerns. A dozen other protests sit on the edge of my tongue, though I can't seem to voice them. Can't seem to even articulate them in my mind.

And before he utters a single command, I already know that I'm going to obey.

CHAPTER **FIFTEEN**

BRYSTIN

"Take off your clothes," Holt says. "All of them."

Slowly, I stand up and start unbuttoning my blouse, my heart thudding in my chest. We might be alone in a secure room, but it's big and empty and feels like a public space. Once my shirt is open, my nerves get the best of me.

"You're sure no one can come in here?"

Holt looks annoyed with the question. "Do you trust me?"

That's a loaded question because before today, I didn't trust him at all. Even seeing the studio, I'm wary. The show hasn't been announced. I haven't signed any paperwork. He could still give this concept to another anchor.

But—and here's what's confusing—my distrust is sort of a turn-on. It makes it riskier. I could give him my body and gain nothing at all from it, and that gets my adrenaline pumping. It's like putting that hundred-dollar bill down on the roulette table and feeling that thrill shiver down my spine as the wheel spins.

That thrill shivers down my spine now, and I give him the slightest smile. "No," I say honestly. "I don't." Then I toss my blouse down on the desk and unhook my bra, letting my breasts spill out like I'm presenting a gift.

He returns my smile with one of his own. "Good girl."

I'm not sure if he means that I'm good because I don't trust him or because I kept undressing anyway, but like the other times he's said it to me, it makes my cheeks heat and my chest lift.

"Keep going," he says, and unlike the last time that he had me naked in front of him, this time he studies my body as well as my face. I feel when his eyes latch onto my breasts. His gaze feels like love bites along my skin, and my nipples stand up like they're auditioning for a spot on the show.

My skirt is next. I unzip it and shimmy out of it, letting it fall to my feet. I'm about to kick off my Louboutins when he interrupts. "Keep the heels on."

So I remove my panties awkwardly, pulling them over one shoe and then the other. Standing behind the high desk, he can't see anything below my waist, and I start to walk around in front when he stops me again.

"Climb on and sit facing me. Legs spread. Heels on the desk."

A rush of arousal coats my vaginal walls. His request is utterly lewd and demeans a space that represents the potential height of my career. It occurs to me that this might ruin all of it for me. That *he* might ruin all of it, which is probably a thought I should have had earlier in the game.

Zully herself had suggested I might not like making it to the top if I didn't do it the honest way.

But if we're talking honesty, I honestly want to be naked for this man. I honestly want to be spread out in front of him. I honestly want his eyes on my pussy, want him to see the glisten on my lips, want him to know what he's done to me.

And so I climb onto the chair and place a knee on the desk. My breasts swing as I crawl across the three feet of white laminate. I position myself somewhat near the edge, my legs spread, heels anchored at my sides so the famous red soles face him, my hands planted on either side of my ass for support. My face heats as I realize how exposed I am, but I try my best to keep my head high in the awkward position. Try to seem like I'm completely in control, like I'm a woman who has her own network television program. Like this moment is my victory, not my shame.

Holt nods as though he's pleased. "Very nice." It's said so quietly, I'm not even sure he meant for me to hear it. He takes a couple of steps in my direction, which makes my breath stutter, but he stops when he's still ten feet away. He rubs a hand over the thick bulge in his pants, and I know with all my heart that if this is another episode of him jacking off while I remain untouched–while he remains untouchable—that I will die. Absolutely die.

"Now what?" I prod, hoping it will incite him to move this further.

"Patience." He pulls his cell out of his pocket. His attention lowers to the screen, and oh my God, I've never felt so demeaned. I'm sitting here with my cunt out, and he's going to make a call?

But after he swipes and clicks, he points the phone at me, his eyes remaining on the screen. "Now play with yourself."

I don't move.

"Brystin?"

"I heard you. What are you doing?"

His eyes float back to mine. "Watching."

"What are you doing with your phone?" It's a stupid question because it's an obvious answer.

"Obviously, I'd love to capture you like this with one of these studio cameras, but that's a lot of work and the security on my phone is better. So we'll have to settle for this. It will match my screen saver." He winks. Actually winks.

My stomach clenches with dread, as another wave of lust rolls through my lower regions. This could end terribly. It was one thing to send him a faceless image of my pussy. This is me fully exposed, on top of my soon-to-be anchor desk, with my face very much attached. If this image got out, it could ruin my career forever.

Since I didn't jump up and cover myself the second his phone came out, I've already potentially fucked myself over. I've already risked too much.

And yet I'm still unbearably turned on.

"I can see those wheels turning, Brystin. See those doubts in your pretty blue eyes. I can promise this is just for me. It probably won't lessen your concerns since you don't trust me. But I can tell you that it very much heightens my enjoyment to know how agonizing this must be for you. And before you think of backing out…I should point out that you still haven't signed a contract."

I remember now that I hate him.

Remember that he's as brutal as he is beautiful.

The realization should kill every bit of lust within me, but it doesn't.

What kind of person am I to want this? What kind of person am I to feel so turned on that my hand settles between my legs without my mind making the decision to do so?

"Just like that," Holt coaxes, and once again, his encouragement is fuel to my desire. "Show me what you're willing to do for this job. Show me what you're willing to give up."

My reputation.

My sanity.

My pride.

Still, my manicured finger swipes over my swollen clit without reservation, and it takes all my effort not to increase the pressure and give myself more.

"You're holding back," he says, because of course he notices. "I want to see you let go."

I increase the speed, hoping that will convince him I'm giving him what he's asked for.

It doesn't. "Not good enough. Is that really how you want to be touched, Brystin? Show me how you want me to touch you."

The image that sparks brings me so close to coming, I have to still my hand for a second and stifle a moan.

"So that's the trick." He rubs his free hand up and down over his erection again. "You want me to touch you."

I can't help it—this time the moan escapes my lips.

His grin widens, and the big bad wolf comes out again. "I can't touch you until you show me how, Brystin. You want me to casually rub your clit like that and nothing else?"

"No." The word rushes out as if he's yanked it with a chain.

"You'd want my fingers inside you too, wouldn't you, little vixen?"

"Please?" My voice is meek and breathy.

"Show me."

Without hesitation, I sit up straighter and bring my other hand around to push a finger into my dripping hole. Slowly, I pull it out and push in again.

"Fuck, you're so wet." He moves closer, aiming the phone at my pussy. "Another finger."

I add a second, increasing the pressure on my clit with my other hand. My eyes are pinned on the way he moves his own hand over his cock. I can practically see the ridges through the material of his pants because he's so hard. It can't be comfortable. And, God, I want to see him. Want to touch him as much as I want him to touch me.

"Three fingers," he demands, as though he knows I'm close.

"I want to see you first."

He chuckles. "You aren't in a position to negotiate right now, Ms. Shaw."

"I'm not negotiating. I'm telling you what I want, and I'm pretty sure you want it too."

He hisses out a curse I can't quite hear. But he lowers the phone and begins undoing his belt. "Three fingers, Brystin. My fingers are thick and long, and I'm rough when I fuck. Even with my hand. Show me you'll be able to take it."

I add another finger, and instantly, I come. Probably

from his words more than anything. My hands freeze, my vision dances with flashes of light, and my back arches as I let out a stuttering cry.

"Jesus, you're beautiful when you come." He still hasn't finished undoing his pants, but he crosses to me in three long strides, pointing the phone at my face as he does.

When he's right in front of me, he unzips his pants and pulls his briefs down just far enough to let his erection out, then he pulls my moisture-coated fingers from my cunt and places them around his cock.

His very hard, very thick cock.

Um, *damn.*

"Like what you feel?"

To be truthful, I'm scared of what I feel at the moment, but I'm pretty sure those aren't the kind of feelings he's talking about.

"Yes," I gasp. Actually, though, I'm scared of what I feel in my hand as well. I had not realized exactly how hard and how thick he is. Almost too big. It's a terrifying cock, and I'm torn between feeling relieved that intercourse isn't part of the deal and frustrated that I'll never get to feel it moving inside of me.

But then I'm distracted from that thought when he replaces the fingers I'd had inside of me with his own, pointing the phone down to capture the erotic scene. "This is how I'd fuck you, Brystin. With my cock. Can you imagine it?"

My body shivers with the thought as his three long fingers reach a depth that my own were incapable of reaching. He isn't slow with his strokes the way I was, either.

He's fast and rough, and I'm already starting to feel another orgasm approaching.

If it were his cock instead…

I pump the length of him, matching his speed, imagining it inside me instead of his hand. "Oh God, oh God."

"You feel like heaven too," he whispers. "Velvety and drenched."

I almost change my mind right there and beg for him to fuck me. For real. Beg for him to impale me with the weapon in my hand.

I manage to keep the plea inside, but just barely. Even unsaid, the thought occurred. A wish planted like a little seed in fertile ground, and I have a terrible feeling it's bound to grow.

I don't have the bandwidth to hold the realization. I'm light-headed from the approaching climax, madly pumping him with the furious tempo he's set, and still massaging my clit. All that while trying to keep myself in an upright position.

When I can't manage to hold myself up any longer—I really need to work on strengthening my core—I pull my hand from my clit and set it down on the desk to brace myself. I'm so close to my second orgasm anyway, and don't need the extra stimulation. Besides, right now I'd rather be focused on him.

Apparently, Holt doesn't find this decision acceptable. "Did I say you could stop?"

"You said to show you how." I don't want to admit I have weak abs. "I figured it was your turn."

He tosses his phone down on the desk next to me, without bothering to pause the video, and with his hand now free, his arm bolts forward and his fingers clasp around my neck, putting just enough pressure on my windpipe that my breathing feels threatened. "Rub your clit, Brystin. I want to feel you come all over my hand."

Holy fuck.

He keeps his chokehold on me even after my hand returns to finish the job it started, and I wonder if he knows that he's helping hold me up or if he thinks it's as hot to strangle me as I think it is. So hot that it only takes a few swirls of my finger over my sensitive bundle of nerves before I'm spiraling into an orgasm that's twice as powerful as the last.

I throw my head back as the pleasure seizes me. My hand drops from his cock and my cunt clenches tightly around Holt's fingers, slowing him down, but he pushes through, fucking me until he's wrenched out every last drop of my climax.

Then he scoops the moisture leaking from my pussy and brings it to his cock. He jacks himself quickly and within seconds, he's grunting out his own climax, shooting his cum onto my pussy.

I swear I could almost come again just from watching that.

We stay like that while we recover. We're still both breathing erratically when he runs two fingers up my seam, mixing my fluid with his. I watch him, entranced, while my emotions swirl into confusion. I'm unmoored. This wasn't supposed to be for me. The job was my reward. So why am I so into this?

I move my eyes up to his face to find he's watching me, and I'm so sure he can see what I'm feeling that I put voice to it. Whisper, actually, but it counts. "Does it ruin this for you if I like it?"

His gaze softens, but his expression remains serious. "No," he whispers back. "It definitely does not."

We stare at each other like that for who knows how long. I can feel each beat of my heart like it's marking the seconds that pass, but I'm too dazed to count, and I think if someone doesn't say something soon, that I'll end up kissing him.

And somehow I know that if I kiss him, that will be the end of me.

Something intense is happening in his features as well, but finally—thankfully—he breaks the connection, returning his gaze to the fingers stroking my pussy lips. Dragging our fluids down, he smears some onto the top of the desk. "So you'll never forget what you were willing to do to make this desk yours."

Then he picks up his phone and hits stop on the recording. "And this is so I'll never forget."

I don't need a reminder, thank you. This is a memory I'm never forgetting.

As Holt zips himself back up, a cramp hits the back of my thigh, and I stretch out one leg, then the other. "Wow. I'm a mess."

"Hang on." He looks around, as if there will magically be a hand towel sitting nearby. When he doesn't find what he's looking for, he takes off his very expensive Armani suit jacket, and uses the inside lining to clean me up.

"Oh God. You're going to ruin your jacket."

"To the contrary. I may never send this suit to the cleaners again." His eyes gleam like the devil when he brings the messed-up jacket to his nose to inhale. "Smells like you. Like us."

I shiver at the word *us*. There isn't an *us*, but the way he says it almost makes me forget the fact.

He misinterprets my reaction. "You should get dressed."

He helps me down from the desk. I collect my clothes while he puts on the cum-streaked jacket. There's the usual post-awkwardness that occurs after sex with someone new, and I do my best to avoid looking at him while I'm dressing.

Of course every time I glance at him, he's watching me, as though he's not feeling awkward at all. When I'm no longer naked, he gestures for me to come to him.

For some reason, I'm nervous as I take the steps toward him. Shouldn't I be more relaxed now? Shouldn't he be less intimidating now that I know what he looks like when he comes?

When I'm standing in front of him, he cups my face with one hand, and my stomach flip flops.

But instead of kissing me, he rubs his thumb under my eye. Smudged mascara, I'm guessing, and this gesture is worse than if he'd let me walk out looking freshly fucked. I can't explain why. It would just be easier if he didn't care. If he let this remain transactional, and nothing else. So that I can remember that I'm a married woman with no interest in any relationship that provokes feelings.

"You never told me,"—he moves to my other eye—"if you shave for *him*."

Him.

Michael.

I'm already thinking of my husband, so I don't flinch at

the mention, but I wonder if Holt needed reminding of Michael too.

More likely, it's his usual way of interfering in things that aren't his business. It isn't the first time he's poked me about my marriage, wanting in doors I've kept closed.

I stiffen, making sure those doors are locked tight.

But they're not, and the confession slips out. "He doesn't like hair in his mouth."

I swear Holt's jaw ticks before he puts on a smug smile. "What a baby."

Against my better judgment, I let out a laugh. It's a bad idea, but I start to ask what he prefers when I'm interrupted by the sound of a door opening and the sound of shoes walking across the cement floor.

I jump back from Holt. "I thought you said no one was coming in here," I hiss before turning my back so I can try to put myself together before I have to face someone. Without a mirror.

Yeah, right.

"I thought it was good enough odds that no one would." I can hear the shrug in his voice.

"Ah, sorry, Mr. Sebastian." A voice speaks behind me. "I didn't realize you were here. Just checking up to make sure the room was secured."

"I've got it," Holt says. Then quieter for only me to hear, "The security guard."

I hear the footsteps retreat, but a blush runs down to my toes when I consider what could have happened if his timing had been worse. I spin back to face Holt. "What if he'd come in five minutes earlier?"

"Then I'd be paying out a huge silence fee and reminding my employee about his strict NDA."

I scowl, not convinced that would fix anything. Sure, SNC could take him to court, but if someone leaked information about Brystin Shaw involved in lewd acts with the CEO, it would spread like wildfire. No amount of money paid could undo that damage.

"I could always have him killed, if you'd prefer."

I feel my eyes widen. I wouldn't put murder past the Sebastians.

But then I realize that Holt's suppressing a laugh.

"AssHolt." Then I allow a brief smile of my own.

"I don't think it's the best policy to use such vile words when talking about your new boss." His tone says he understands the irony of the statement, considering the vile things he was just doing with his employee.

It also brings the spotlight back to where we started today—my new job. He holds his hand toward me. "Welcome to SNC, Ms. Shaw. I'm glad to have you on board."

"Glad to be here." I accept the handshake, his touch doing strange things to my insides, even after everything else we've done in the last half hour. "Really glad."

"How about we go upstairs to Panache, and I'll fill you in on the details?"

"Okay," I say, even though spending any more time with Holt Sebastian seems like a very bad idea on top of a slew of very bad ideas.

But he's officially my boss now, which means I can't really say no.

It also means this is probably the last of the sexual favors.

The game will be boring for him without having the job to lord over me. He'll likely move on to another woman he can play "power" with. An unattached woman. A woman who will be willing to give him more. Willing to give him everything.

And over a sure-to-be expensive dinner, I'll try very hard not to let the thought of that eventuality disappoint me.

CHAPTER
SIXTEEN
BRYSTIN

"What about hair and makeup?" Holt and I have been talking for almost four hours about the show and the terms included in my contract, and it's only now, when we're just fifteen minutes from my apartment, that I think to bring up Zully.

I don't think I'm really a terrible friend. There has just been so much to go over.

"The network has a team of artists you can choose from." Holt's knees are angled toward mine and he's sitting closer than necessary, especially in such a roomy limo, but we aren't touching.

If I turned slightly…

It's been a distraction for the entire ride, one I'm proud to say I've managed for the most part because the pull toward him is strong. It was easier at the restaurant, when we sat across from each other and the conversation was too packed with information to be swayed toward the chemistry between us.

Now, as we're finally almost talked out, it's harder. I am very aware of his damn knee.

Trying to keep my focus, I force my eyes to stay forward. "Would I be able to bring someone of my own?"

"And have the network pay for it?"

"Yes. Zuleika Amari—I tried to introduce you to her on your grandmother's birthday—you probably don't remember."

"The day you first called me an assHolt. How could I forget?"

"Likely not the last." My grin fades, and I turn serious. "I've known her for years. She's very good at what she does. I've been hoping to bring her on as my personal makeup artist. I couldn't make it happen at *New Jersey Now,* since they didn't have the budget."

"Isn't your husband in charge of the budget?"

"Well. Yeah." My gaze drifts out the window thinking about Michael. He's an unwanted guest showing up at my dinner party, and I feel selfish for wanting him gone. "With Zully and Michael—it's personal. They aren't really fond of each other."

"Really?" As with everything that involves me and Michael, Holt perks up. "I got the impression you and Zully are close."

I shrug. "Some people just don't jibe."

"Maybe Zully doesn't think Michael's the right man for you."

My throat tightens. How the fuck did he hit it on the nose like that?

Then I remember Holt likes to stir the pot. He didn't hit anything on the nose. He's guessing, trying to rile me.

I smile and turn my head back toward him. "Zully wouldn't think anyone was right for me. She's loyal, and that's a hell of a good quality in an employee."

His responding smile is paired with a knowing glare, as though he sees right through me. "Am I to understand that you're going over your producer's head on this?"

"I suppose I am. Can we add it to the deal?"

"I'm sure something can be worked out." His subtext is clear, and my lower regions clench at the prospect of "earning" something else from the billionaire.

It's then that I feel the brush of his leg against mine.

And because I'm a glutton, I press into it, pretending it's a natural lean as the car turns a corner. "I appreciate it."

"I'm sure you'll show me just how much."

I have to turn back to the window to hide my smile.

We ride in silence for several minutes. It's the first time all evening we've had any sort of break in the conversation. He hadn't even been planning to accompany me home, except that when he put me in the car, we couldn't stop talking long enough for him to shut the door. In the end, he decided to drive with me so we could tie up any loose ends.

Through all of it, we've been nothing but professional, though there was a lengthy discussion about the wine Holt chose for dinner, one of his favorites. But there have been no references to the incident in the studio. No mention of sexual favors. Everything on the up and up, as if this job was given to me truly on merit.

The reminder that it wasn't should make my stomach curl.

Instead, I'm trying to decide if there's enough time to get on my knees and thank him properly for the opportunity he's given me. Would he even want it? After the remark he just made about working something out, now would be a logical time to demand payment.

But he doesn't.

Before I make a fool of myself, I remember that we aren't having an affair, and that he's my boss, and that this exchange of favors is dirty and indecent, and that I cannot be the one to initiate any of it.

The draw to him, though, is so undeniable that I have to divert my attention by focusing on other things he's done to piss me off. "I still can't believe you fired me."

"I needed you in the city. It couldn't be helped."

"Do you really believe that, or is that what you think I want to hear?"

He glances down at our connected knees then drags his gaze up my body, lingering on my lips before landing on my eyes. "I don't believe in telling people what they want to hear."

I let out a short laugh. "Ever?"

"Never."

"What if what they want to hear is the truth? Do you lie just to be a dick?"

He studies me while he considers, and my pulse picks up for no reason that I can explain. "No one really wants to hear the truth," he says.

I start to tell him that I do and pause with my chin dropped, words about to tumble out, because I realize that what I actually want to hear is that he needed me in the city for personal reasons, not business reasons.

And I want him to say that he picks on Michael because *he* thinks I'd be better off without him.

And I don't even want to think about what I wish the truth was behind our relationship.

If he's not going to say those things, there's no reason he should say anything at all.

I can't find a way to honestly refute him.

"See?"

"Yeah, I see."

What I don't see is why I feel so confused about him. I might be having fun, but that doesn't change the fact that Holt has used his power to coerce me into a sexual liaison. I have to keep my head straight about that. This isn't anything more. I can't let it venture into anything else.

Purposefully, I move my knee away from his. The tingle lingers for several seconds after disconnecting, and I fight against the urge to rub my joint and make it better.

Thankfully, perhaps, the car turns onto my street and slows in front of my building.

But as soon as it stops, Holt issues an order to the driver. "Circle the block a few times, Emilio. I'm going to walk her up."

"You don't have to do that." I'd rather he didn't.

I think.

Holt doesn't respond in words, but he climbs out of the back seat with me, and follows me into the building. He checks out the environment, nodding at the doorman and scrutinizing the security desk.

While we wait for the elevator, I try once again to dismiss him. "I make the trip up alone all the time."

Holt's eyes narrow. "You usually arrive home alone?"

There he goes again. Always digging about Michael. "I'm an independent woman, Holt. So yes."

"The man must not realize how dangerous elevators are. What if you were stuck in one with some depraved stranger? Who knows what could happen?"

The callback to our meeting at the Sebastian Center on the night of the awards makes my inner thighs buzz and my head cloud. I don't have a comeback, and when the doors open, his hand presses soft and ghost-like at the base of my spine, nudging me in with him.

He drops it as soon as we're inside, and I decide I'm thankful. But now I'm too busy obsessing over the fact that he knew which floor was mine without asking to be thinking about anything else. He'd only know that if he went looking for the information. Why would he care?

Again, the difference between what I want to hear and the truth is likely very stark.

We don't speak again until we're exiting on my floor. "Will you move to the city?" Holt asks.

"Not right away. Michael has an apartment there already that we can use if we get tired of the commute."

"*Michael* has an apartment?" There's a knowing in his tone, and I'm sure that nothing I say now can dissuade Holt from thinking my husband has a fuckpad. Which, technically, he does. I just don't like to think about it.

I make the correction, despite its usefulness, keeping my eyes straight ahead. "*We* have an apartment. He's the only one who uses it."

Holt nods. "I have a place, if you need one."

"Thank you." Why does the prospect of earning that make me so aroused?

And now we're at my apartment, and I want to feel relieved, but my pussy feels electrified and empty. I'm all of a sudden imagining ways I could sneak Holt to my bedroom, the same way I snuck my high-school boyfriend past my mother.

"Is he…?" Holt asks, as though he knows what I'm thinking.

"Home? Yes. I think he is." I avoid the use of my husband's name in an attempt to lessen the impact of his nearness. "He hasn't messaged me otherwise."

Not that I've been paying attention to my phone. I have new appreciation for how well Michael keeps his trysts from me. He's always so good at keeping boundaries. He's fairly aloof, but he answers my calls and texts, even when I'm pretty sure he's with one of his side pieces.

As I pull my key out of my purse, I wonder if he's ever stood in this hallway with one of them, the air crackling with energy, wishing I wasn't inside. There are several nights that he comes home after I've gone to bed. I suppose I'm not entirely certain he hasn't snuck someone in then.

This line of thinking is unproductive, obviously. I'm not inviting Holt inside. I wouldn't even if I knew Michael wasn't home. *That's not what we are.* I'll tell myself that until I get it through my thick skull. I'll make it my mantra, if I have to. Chemistry or not, it doesn't mean anything.

It occurs to me that Holt with his privileged expectations and lack of boundaries might need clarification. Key in hand, I turn back to face him. "It's not a good idea to invite you inside."

"I'm only here to make sure you get inside safely."

"Okay. Thank you." My insides flutter because I'm so

unused to chivalrous gestures. "Thank you for the rest, too. Not just the job, but tonight. For taking the time to talk me through everything. I know that on-air personalities are often left out of the major decisions, and I don't have the rank or status to demand otherwise. You didn't have to be so accommodating, and I really appreciate it."

Michael had certainly kept me in the dark. In this handful of hours, Holt has brought me into the discussion more than my husband has over a period of weeks.

Holt doesn't say anything. Just nods once, and even though I highly doubt many CEOs are this hands-on with their talent, I have no sense whether this evening was business as usual or not. Part of me longs for him to say that he's only given me this kind of attention.

But then I remember the retreat at his country house, and how Jessa Jones made it sound like in-depth collaboration is routine.

For that matter, this whole arrangement might be routine for him. I am not special. I have to get that through my head.

Which will be a whole lot easier if I'm no longer in his presence.

"Well, good night."

"Good night."

He waits until I put the key in the lock, and then takes a step, presumably to leave. Instead, his hand shoots out and grabs my wrist, preventing me from turning the knob.

My eyes go down to where he's grasping me—half expecting to see actual sparks in the air—then raise to meet his. "Give me something," he says, his voice raw. "Give me something without an exchange. Give me something I don't deserve."

I open my mouth to ask what he wants, but close it before the word escapes. Something dislodges in my chest, something I can't name, and I realize I don't have to say yes. There's nothing riding on this. He won't cancel my still unsigned contract. He won't take the job away.

He wants something for free, and I have every right to say no.

I can see in his eyes that he half expects I will.

So it's of my own volition when I lean up on my toes to bring my mouth toward his. I keep my eyes open, watching him, making sure it's okay. He doesn't flinch, and so I press my lips softly on his.

As soon as our mouths make contact, it becomes something bigger. An ember turned into a roaring flame. My lips part and his tongue slips easily inside to find mine. A whimper spills from me as soon as they meet, like I've been waiting my whole life to feel this particular invasion. Aching for it, and my pussy squeezes in envy.

Within seconds, he backs me up against the door, pressing his entire body against mine so that I can feel the heavy pipe of his desire against my belly. Relinquishing my wrist, his hand tangles in my hair. My fingers clutch his suit jacket, gripping on for dear life. Trying to bring him closer. Trying to ignore the places they want to explore—the planes of his chest, the curve of his jaw, the taut flesh of his ass.

We're frenetic with our mouths, with the way our bodies lean and shift, looking for relief that can't be found without turning this scene into pornography. Soon that line is crossed. My skirt is pushed up around my waist. My leg hitches around his hips, and I feel the pressure of his cock against the throb of my clit. His hand comes under my thigh, helping with the weight of my limb, spreading me farther so that the thrust of his pelvis against mine sends bolts of pleasure throughout my body.

And I want more.

I need more.

My breasts need his palms. My hands need his skin. My pussy needs, needs, needs…

And I can't think straight. Can't bring to mind the man waiting on the other side of the door. Can't remember this is all just a sick game for Holt or that we're in a public hallway or that giving him this allowance—this gift—could change everything between us. Could blur the boundaries so much that they no longer exist. Could lead me to the familiar heartbreak of being the only one all in.

It should be those realizations that bring me to push him off of me.

Instead, it's the sound of a door opening down the hall.

Holt doesn't move quite as fast, trailing my chin with open-mouthed kisses after I've turned my face away.

"Holt," I whisper. Pleading.

His lips make it to the crook of my neck before he finally relinquishes his hold on me. Just in time to deliver a smile to my seventy-something-year-old neighbor, Mrs. Clawson. "Good evening," he says.

I drop my head, unable to acknowledge her. "She thinks I'm married," I hiss after she passes.

"You *are* married." The statement seems to be as much of a reminder for him as it is for me because he steps away as soon as it's uttered. "You're married, and your husband is behind that door."

I almost break down and tell him. Tell him that Michael never loved me, that it's mostly a business partnership. That we aren't real.

But that's not exactly true. Michael was real to me. He *is* real.

And even if he isn't, it doesn't make Holt real.

"I have to go," I say, quickly. I turn to open the door, and this time Holt doesn't stop me.

Inside, I head straight toward my bedroom, hoping to hide my swollen lips and flushed face, but my luck being what it is, Michael cuts me off before I've crossed the living room.

Pulls me into his arms, actually.

His hands settle on my hips, and he turns me as though we're dancing. Which is when I notice the soft jazz playing through the speakers mounted to the walls.

"You were right," he says excitedly. "It meant what you thought."

"What?" I have no idea what he's talking about.

"Our contracts are in my inbox, sweet girl. It's happening. We have our show."

Our show.

All evening, with Holt, it felt like *my* show. So much so that I almost forgot that Michael was a part of it, that I should be expecting a confirming conversation with him, at the very least.

I'm actually glad that we're embracing so he can't see my face when I respond. "Yeah, I know. So great!"

"You saw him?" He pulls away, and I bring my hand up

to my mouth. As casually as possible, hoping he doesn't think anything of it.

"He showed me the studio and explained all the terms and everything." *Then he kissed the breath out of me in the hallway, and now I just want to get in my bed with my vibrator and get this feeling out of my system.*

"Oh." He stares at me so hard that I'm sure I'm not doing this right.

"It's amazing. I'm irritated about the way it was handled—did everything go okay with the show?"

"Yeah, yeah. We covered it."

"Good. Good." I don't know what to say or how to extricate myself from this conversation. "You know, it's been a really exhausting day. Lots of up and down emotions. I was planning on heading to bed."

Michael reaches out to my wrist—the same wrist that is still warm from where Holt grabbed it—and pulls it down from my mouth.

He sees. I can tell. He knows what a freshly kissed Brystin looks like. "He's still…?"

I shrug like it's not a big deal. I'm not even sure it is anymore, which makes it a different kind of big deal.

For me, anyway.

Michael seems to have a different kind of reaction. His eyes go dark and hooded, and he gives me that ravenous look that I have spent years longing for. Whenever it appears, I know I'm his. Even if just for the night.

I don't think I've ever turned that look down.

I consider for a moment letting it happen, letting him pull me back into his arms. Letting him relieve that ache between my legs. It wouldn't be the first time a wife thought of someone else while fucking her husband. It's kind of one of the benefits of marriage—being able to safely use a partner to fulfill desires without having to explain the source.

And one of the benefits of an open marriage is that I can fuck around with Holt and can still come home and fuck Michael without damaging our relationship.

But it's not me. It's never been me.

"I can't." I speak before he makes the move I know he's about to make. "Not while this is going on with…" It feels strange to say Holt's name. "I can't."

"You can't? He won't let you?" It's not a mean question, but an honest request for clarification. He steps toward me. "You know it's not an issue for me." He sweeps my hair off my shoulder, and a shiver runs down my spine.

The kind of shiver that occurs when a situation feels wrong.

"I can't." I back away. "I just can't. It's confusing."

Michael stiffens, and I can tell he's trying not to be mad. "Confusing." He repeats the word like it's foreign. "Having sex with your husband is confusing."

I get it. I hear what I'm saying, and if he came to me and said no more sex because of some other woman, I'd be mad. I'd be hurt.

Not that he'd ever say that.

And if I'm honest, I've always been mad and hurt that I'm not enough for him, even though it was the arrangement I agreed to from the beginning.

I belong with Michael.

We're finally getting everything we wanted. This was why we partnered up in the first place—for our careers. For my heart. So that I could have him in whatever form I could get.

Why am I trying to fuck it up?

"I'm sorry," I say because I don't have any better words to give. "I'm just…I'm sorry."

Without waiting for his response, I escape to my bedroom. Then, after having my dream handed to me with a bow, I bury myself under my covers and cry myself to sleep.

CHAPTER
SEVENTEEN
BRYSTIN

I do my best to contain myself when I give my name to the security guard at the Sebastian Center. I've never been so eager to sign paperwork in my life. While he checks for my clearance, I pull out my phone to text Holt that I'm here.

Of course I blush as soon as I open our message thread because I'm immediately greeted by the image I sent him last night—me making good use of my pink vibrator—and the response that makes my blood hot, even now.

That's my good girl.

How his praise can get me so worked up is beyond me. More mystifying is how excited I am to see him today. It's been exactly two weeks since he showed me the studio. Two weeks since we last saw each other in person. Two weeks of my contract being finalized with my lawyer and two weeks filled with dirty, filthy sexting with Holt.

My body is aching for skin-to-skin contact with the man. I swear I'm already wet as I send him my message.

I'm here!

His response comes immediately.

Wrapping up a meeting. I'll stop by when I'm done. We can celebrate.

Hopefully "celebrate" is code for "take our clothes off and do naughty things."

I'm so carried away with fantasizing about Holt bending me over the conference table and giving me his big dick energy that it takes a second to recognize my name is being called.

When I look up, Michael's on the other side of the clearance desk, his hand on the guard's shoulder like they know each other. "She's with me."

After today, I'll likely have my own clearance card. Michael's contract was signed two days ago, so he already has his. Mine took longer since I added terms regarding Zully. And since Michael had put in his month notice to *New Jersey Now* the day after we got back from Adeline (unbeknownst to me), he's been spending his nights at his apartment the last few weeks and putting in full days at the center so our show will be ready to go live in another couple soon.

In the past, the separation would have sent me into the doldrums, but with the tension between us after my no sex declaration, the time away has been good. I haven't felt like I've been missing him at all, but seeing him right now, I have a sudden rush of fondness.

At the security guard's okay, I circle around the clearance desk to greet Michael. "Are you here for me or is this a coincidence?"

"Here for you, sweet girl." He gives that smile that has a tendency to make me weak in the knees.

I'm not sure I believe him since I'm half an hour early. "How did you know I'd be here already?"

He looks at me like I'm ridiculous. "Come on. I know you." He gestures toward the elevators with his head. "Since we have a little time, let me show you my office, then I'll walk you to the conference room."

Something funny happens in my chest, and it takes me a second to fall in step behind him. The arrangement with Holt has made it easy for me to forget the history I have with my husband. He really does know me. Really does care. I've often felt it was a one-sided relationship, but when I look at it without so much emotion attached, I remember that I actually am a significant figure in his life. He's made his profession and success his priority, but of the few people that matter to him, I'm pretty high up on the list.

And this whole next phase of our careers has been orchestrated together. We're here because we both put in the work. Together.

In the elevator, when the doors are closed, I take his hand in mine and lean my head on his shoulder. "I'm glad you're here."

"I'm glad you're here too."

We get off on the floor above the studio. Michael quickly ushers me past glass-walled conference rooms and open office space until we're in a hallway with a bunch of closed doors with gold-plated names. I recognize several names I've heard here and there. Producers and assistant producers I've looked up to in the past.

Then, finally, Michael stops in front of an open door. "Ta da."

I peer in at the space. It's not huge, but it's larger than the cramped closet he had in New Jersey. There are bookshelves along one wall, unpacked boxes along the floor and on the couch, and a window overlooking…

I run over to open the blinds and check out the view and laugh when I realize that it faces an inner courtyard housing several dumpsters. "It's a window, at least."

"Definitely an upgrade." Michael beams from the doorframe.

My heart thuds in my chest, as though this honor is also mine. Considering how much time I spent in his tiny office in New Jersey, the office might as well be ours.

"Don't do it," he says.

"Don't do what?"

"You're mentally sketching out where you're putting your things, and I'm telling you right now not to do it."

"Ah, but this spot looks made for my cute ass." I sink into the sofa to show him how well I fit in only to discover it's not as comfy as it looks. "Are we allowed to request a change of furniture?"

"Not your office," he says with a grin. "You negotiated your own office. You can request whatever furniture you want there."

I fake pout. Or half fake a pout. I really am thrilled about my own space, but I've been told it's more dressing room than workroom, and some of my favorite career moments have been brainstorming with Michael over takeout in his tiny office. While this change is for the better, I'll miss the best parts of before. One of the better parts of our show was our chemistry. What if we lose that now?

Since he really does know me, he comes close to reading my thoughts. "It's different, but we aren't," he says. "We're the soul of this thing, and this new structure isn't going to change what we bring to the table."

But he's wrong—Holt has already changed us. I feel it in my bones. Even if…even *when* Holt gets tired of this game between us, the way I feel about Michael will never be the same.

Which is probably for the best, since it puts us on a more even playing field. Good for character growth, but I'm feeling sentimental at the moment.

I stand and cross to him for a hug. He's generally very anti-PDA in work environments, but he allows it without fuss, wrapping his arms so tightly around me that I think he might have missed me too.

He speaks quietly in my ear. "We did it." Okay, maybe he's just overwhelmed by our achievement, and I'm still romanticizing his actions more than I should.

I make sure I'm the one to pull away first, just so I can feel like I really have made Michael progress.

But now we're staring at each other, grins so wide and gazes so intense that I'm sure that he's either about to kiss me or this is about to get awkward.

I don't want either. So I quickly try to change the trajectory of this interaction. Reaching out to his door, I pull it back to read his name on the gold plate.

Except it doesn't say Michael Endlich.

It says Jessa Jones.

"They're scheduled to put mine up tomorrow," he tells me. "In case you're planning to be here to Instagram it."

He really does know me so well. "You took over Jessa's office? I mean, despite the dumpster view, this is the kind of leftovers I'd totally gobble. Maybe she now looks over the parking garage entrance."

Michael gives a brief laugh but quickly grows solemn. "No, she's uh…didn't you hear?"

I'm instantly wary. "Hear…what?"

"Her show got canceled. She's out of here."

My stomach feels like it's carrying a cannonball. "She got canceled?"

"I think the last one was supposed to air the day before we go live, but rumor is she was upset about the way it was all handled and her lawyer got her out of her obligation early. It's really too bad. I was looking forward to working with her again. I know you really looked up to her."

The pieces start forming a picture in my mind. The conversation I'd overheard with Adly and Steele about Jessa leaving the retreat. The way Jessa had torn out of Holt's driveway. That all happened the day after I'd met with him in his room. When he'd agreed to "get to know me" and give me a show. "He canceled her show for us."

Michael shrugged. "More likely they were already planning to cancel her, and we showed up at the right time."

My gut says he's wrong. My gut says that if I hadn't walked into Holt's room that night, if I hadn't let him open my dress and jerk off to my naked body, then Jessa Jones—a journalist who has worked her whole life to be where she is—would still have this office.

I think I'm going to be sick.

"You're looking pale, Brystin. Is the excitement getting to you?"

I swallow hard. "I think so. Getting nervous. I should probably get to the conference room."

What I want to do is get a minute to call Holt because this was not what I'd wanted. This success already feels tainted because of what I've given in exchange. Crawling over the back of someone I truly admire is not something I can stomach.

But it's not a call I want to make in front of Michael, and he insists on walking me to the room where I'm supposed to meet the contract manager. It's on another floor and takes us ten minutes to get there so we arrive right at two on the dot.

"This is where I leave you." Surprisingly, Michael pulls me into a hug at the door. A very friendly hug. The kind of hug husbands give wives. "Let's make time for each other this weekend, okay?"

A warning bell rings in my head, telling me that time for each other might very well mean sex, even after I've drawn boundary lines, but I'm too wrapped up in the Jessa Jones drama to worry about it at the moment. "I'll call," I tell him.

When he withdraws from the embrace, I'm met by André and a serious-looking woman wearing wire-rimmed glasses along with a bored-looking brunette who I'm guessing is her assistant.

"Good to see you again," André says. "Mr. Sebastian

said he'll be down shortly. He asked that I make sure that Claudia found you and that you were offered refreshments."

"Nothing for me, thanks. But—sorry, Claudia, one minute—I really need to speak to Holt. Er, Mr. Sebastian. Before I can proceed."

"Is there something wrong with the current contract?" Claudia opens the file folder in her hand before I answer. "Would you like to make sure it's the correct draft?"

She ushers me into the room as she talks, her assistant tagging along behind us, and André, as though he's confident I'm being cared for, disappears.

For fuck's sake.

"No, the draft is fine. I'm sure." I take the contract from her outstretched hand anyway, glancing over it to see if it includes all of the last additions and changes. "It's not the contract itself. It's the contract as a whole."

"As a whole?"

"I'm really not sure I can sign."

"What do you mean you can't sign?" Holt's voice booms from behind us. He arrived too quickly to have been summoned by André. He must have already been on his way.

When I turn to look at him, I'm so struck by the sight of him in work mode. His presence fills the doorway—fills the room—and while I've seen plenty of men in well-fitting suits, Holt's tailored designer outfit looks like it just came off the runway. He's the sharpest man in the building, I bet. The sharpest man in the city.

And less than fifteen minutes ago, I was hoping that I could get him out of that suit.

Now, I'm so upset, I can barely see him through all the red. "You canceled Jessa Jones for our show?"

Holt's jaw twitches, and his body seems to stiffen. "Claudia, can we have the room, please?"

"Yes, absolutely. But there's supposed to be a witness—"

Holt cuts her off. "Leave the room. Now."

Claudia and her assistant exit as fast as if they've heard a fire alarm, shutting the door behind them.

I pick up where I left off without skipping a beat. "That's why she was yelling at you in the driveway. You told her that day, didn't you? I didn't want this."

"It doesn't matter what you want."

"No, it does. Because I would never have agreed to do this"—I wave a finger back and forth between us in lieu of a definition of what *this* is—"if I'd known it was going to be at Jessa's expense."

Holt narrows his eyes. "What did you think was going to happen? That I'd magically have a spot that was unfilled? Something had to go to make room for your little idea. Why not Jessa?"

His belittlement adds fuel to the fire. "The only other woman with her own show? That doesn't make sense at all. She's a legend. She's one of your highest rated anchors."

"Her contract was at an end."

"That is the worst reason you could possibly give." I feel like screaming. My voice is definitely raised. "Did she know it was because of me?"

"Everyone will realize you're her replacement when you air."

No. No, this can't be happening. This can't be the price I paid.

One of the most exhilarating parts of my job is the camaraderie I've been able to form with other women in the field. There are so few of us.

And now, one of the greatest female anchors of all time will consider me her nemesis. Probably assumes that I've manipulated my way into her job like a modern-day Eve Harrington, using my wiles and scheming to get her canned.

Fuck, I *did* manipulate my way into her job.

I just had no idea this was the cost.

"Undo it. Bring her back."

He scoffs. "She's not coming back, even if I beg. Trust me."

The parting must have been uglier than I first thought. Why wouldn't it have been? She thought she had a secure job. She was a star.

"I don't want it." I toss the unsigned contract on the table. "Not like this."

"But spreading your legs was acceptable."

My fists clench at my side. "No. That was…wrong too. But at least no one was hurt."

"Hurt? This is the news, baby. Network news. Not some competition for lead journalist on a high-school paper. You get here by being the best, by outthinking the best, outplaying the best, out-fucking the best. It's a compliment that I took notice, and it's a bigger compliment that I believed that you could fill her shoes."

"What, because I have perkier tits? What a compliment." My voice sounds tight, like I'm fighting tears. I'm not, but I'm pretty fucking worked up.

"Honestly, she probably got her first big break the same

way."

I stare at him, unable to process that this was the same man who, only a couple of weeks ago, stood in front of me and asked for something without an exchange. As though this is the only language he understands.

It should make me feel sorry for him, but all I can feel right now is disgust. "You better get on your knees and beg Jessa then, because I'm not signing that contract."

He shakes his head. "You're acting like a child. All your time with a man old enough to be your father, you must have learned how to get your way with tantrums. That's not going to work here, Brystin."

"I'm not throwing a tantrum. I'm doing what's right."

"It's too late to walk away."

"As long as I haven't signed, it's not too late."

He quickly strides toward me, stopping inches in front of my face. With a strong finger—I've personally experienced its strength—he taps onto the wood conference table. "Sign. The fucking. Contract."

I cross my arms over my chest so that he won't see what his nearness does to me. *Traitorous body.* "I won't do it."

Somewhere in my brain there is a rational resistance. A voice reminding me that the damage is already done and that this isn't the kind of opportunity you turn down and expect to ever be offered again. Saying no would be the end of my career. Legitimately the end.

But how can I ever look myself in the mirror if I don't turn it down? I can't take a job that I know full well was stolen from another woman.

"You'd do that to Michael?" Holt's question causes the cannonball in my stomach to drop.

Michael will lose the show if I don't sign.

Okay, now I feel like I could cry. "He can produce Jessa's show."

"You're okay getting another producer fired, but not an anchor? Jessa's producer is award-winning. Probably worth more to the network than Jessa. Oh, and she's a woman."

No, I'm not okay with any of it. Why hadn't I thought this through? Why hadn't I bothered to ask how the station would make room?

"Then you can find another show for Michael." I'm begging now. And because I know how dealing with Holt works, I start to unbutton my shirt. "Is this what will convince you? Should I get down on my knees?"

I start to kneel, but he yanks me to my feet. "There are fucking cameras," he whispers.

It's the first chip I have to bargain with. "Maybe someone needs to know how you negotiate."

"No one who watches those feeds can do anything to hurt me. I'm looking out for you."

"Thank you. So appreciated." The words drown in sarcasm. I definitely don't feel grateful or appreciative. I most certainly don't feel like I'm being looked out for. "Then take me somewhere private, Holt. Let me earn Michael his show."

He drops my arm so he can slam his palm on the table. "You're not fucking earning anything for Michael. He's baggage, as far as I'm concerned. The draw of this deal is you."

My muscles quiver with rage. After all he said to me before—acting as though I was the take-it-or-leave-it part of the package, telling me that Michael had the job no matter what, that I had to put out to be considered…

It's a brutal betrayal.

He must read my thoughts on my face. "Don't give me that look. You've had fun."

"Fuck you."

"You wouldn't let me, remember?"

I'm barely listening to him. He's toxic and pathetic. Another privileged white boy playing with real people like they're toys. I can't believe I fell for any of it.

I can't believe I told Michael that I needed space for such a waste of a human.

I reach over to gather the contract pages. What I want to do is tear them up and throw the pieces in his face.

But Holt is right—it's a tough road to the top. Tougher for women. I have no doubt I'll be blacklisted if I back out now. I might have time in my life to rebuild, but Michael's twenty years my senior.

So I won't walk out.

I reach over to pull the pen out of his jacket pocket. Then I find the dotted line, and I sign my name. "I'm sure you can manage faking a witness. The world bends to you, it seems." I toss the pen on the table over the signed pages. "And the exchange between us? It's done. I got the job. I have nothing else I need to earn. Don't bother reaching out. I won't come."

I plan to push by him, making a dramatic exit, but the celebratory smirk on his face freezes in my tracks.

"Actually"—he scoops the contract into his hands—"if you recall in section four, letter D, you are required to promote the show in any way that the network sees fit."

"Promote the show, yes. Not get off the CEO."

"So you will show up when I say come, starting this Friday night. You'll accompany me to the SNC opera event. And you'll wear what I tell you to wear. And you'll suck my cock in the coatroom if I tell you to suck my cock in the coatroom. This contract was negotiated, but believe me, it's still in favor of the network. You have very little recourse if I decide to move your show to three a.m. on the weekend or reduce your on-screen time to only thirty minutes a month."

No, no, no. This is not happening. I am not chained to Holt Sebastian's whims for the length of my contract.

"I'll tell my story," I say. "I'll #metoo your ass. Harvey Weinstein went down. You think you're safe?"

He laughs.

"You think that's funny?"

He considers a minute, his lips pursed tight. "Did you know my mother died by suicide?"

Monster that he is, I'm human, and my chest pricks at the awful admission. "Suicide? I thought…" I wrack my brain to remember what I'd learned about Sonya from the internet. She'd died when Holt was young. Not even ten years old. "I read she died of a brain aneurysm."

"I assure you it was suicide. You want to know why you didn't know that?"

I shake my head, tentatively, already aware of where this is heading.

"Because Sebastians make the news, Brystin. And this contract?" He holds it up like it's a trophy. "This contract means I own you."

CHAPTER EIGHTEEN
HOLT

She's late.

I restrain myself from looking at my watch because if I know how late Brystin is exactly, I might blow a gasket. I'd feel like I had a lot more control if she'd simply accepted the ride from the driver I sent. Instead, she texted last minute that she'd be providing her own transportation. I couldn't even insist since she said she wasn't home and refused to tell me her location.

Honestly, I won't be surprised if she doesn't show up at all. I'm certain if she does show up that she won't have followed the instructions I gave regarding her attire, or rather, her accessories. I'm already prepared to be angry about that.

It isn't hard when I've been angry for the last day and a half, since I saw her at the Sebastian Center in Michael's arms. I'd thought I'd be late, but I was so eager to see her,that I rushed my meeting and went down to the conference room right on time, only to see her clinging to that asshole husband of hers like there is still something meaningful between them. As if there were ever something meaningful between them, which I highly doubt.

I don't usually care about who the women I fuck are with when they aren't with me. I'm not looking for love, and I suit up every time, so I'm not worried about catching anything. Since I have no interest in romance, I generally choose my fucks based on mood and who's available, rarely seeing any one woman more than once in a month.

This thing with Brystin is supposed to be more of the same. Casual fun that doesn't get in the way of my one and only priority—bringing SNC back to the top of the news networks.

But she's been more of a distraction than I'd expected. Pulling my interest. Making me care about who she sees when she's not with me. Who she's sleeping with. I knew she was married, but considering how often Michael steps out—which is a well-known secret among producers, it turns out—I was sure their marriage was more of a business partnership than a love match.

But then she was in his arms, and the way he looked at her when he pulled away…the way she looked at him…

I've never felt so capable of murder, and since Hunter is my half-brother, that's saying something.

I'd been so irrationally heated that I'd sent André ahead to introduce Brystin to Claudia. Then I'd started down the hallway after Michael, completely intent on firing him without cause or punching him in the face—I hadn't quite decided.

Good thing André came after me to tell me Brystin was refusing to sign or I'd be dealing with covering up my bad behavior today. Unfortunately for Brystin, I carried that anger into that conference room. She fueled it even more with her righteousness and naiveté. I've already put everything on the line for her—my career, my reputation—and now she develops a conscience? Not to mention what walking out would do to her own career and reputation.

I might have been able to calm down and talk reasonably with her if she hadn't cared more about what happened to that douche of a husband of hers than she cared about herself. I had no choice but to be the bad guy. I won't feel guilty about it.

Except she's mad now, and obviously pushing my buttons. On one hand, it's for the best. We were getting too cozy, exchanging texts every night. I let my guard down. Forgot to keep my eye on the goal line. It's better if she's mad. Maybe even more fun.

On the other hand, tonight is a big night for *Our Nation Now*, and if she blows it with her obstinance, I swear to fucking God—

"Hey, handsome."

I pause my anxious pacing outside the Irving Sebastian Concert Hall and turn to see who's addressing me. Frankly, if it's not Brystin, I don't care, but this is a night when I'm in the public eye—when am I not, as of late?—and so I put on a welcoming smile and greet… "Greta. Didn't expect to see you tonight. What a surprise."

The rail thin ex-model is one of the kinkier women I've had in my bed, and one of the few natural blondes. Not like Brystin whose roots give her away. I keep hoping she grows a strip on her pussy like I asked, so I can know for sure. I fantasize about running my tongue along the proof. I'm practically a caveman every time I think about it.

But I shouldn't be thinking this much about Brystin. Especially when there is a more than fine substitute standing in front of me.

I lean in and plant a kiss on the side of Greta's mouth—not so conspicuous that it will attract paparazzi attention, but appropriate for someone I get naked with on the regular.

"Mm, you smell good. As always." She casually puts her hand on my lapel, as if she's dusting off a speck of lint that I know is not there. "I just got back from Saint Tropez a couple of days ago. Marcus stayed in France for work, so my bed is lonely. In case that interests you."

"I'm interested." Interests me quite a lot. I fully expect Brystin to be difficult tonight—if she ever shows up—and she'll likely have me hard and aching the whole time. Only because it's been way too many days with my hand. The day at the studio was the last time anyone other than myself had touched my cock, and I desperately need a release in a warm body.

I desperately need to stop imagining that warm body having Brystin's face.

One night with Greta should have me back on my game, and I'll forget all about the high maintenance diva I just signed. "I'm waiting for someone right now. Business. Late night okay for you?"

"Text when you're on your way," she purrs.

"I will." I totally intend to, and in fact, long after she's left to find her seat in the theater, I'm planning what positions I'll fuck her in when I glance up at the staircase that leads to the main doors and realize that Greta is not the cure I'm looking for. Realize that she'll never be. No one can substitute for the dazzling woman standing on the top step, glaring down at me.

Fuck, mad and late as all get out, Brystin Shaw is still the most magnificent creature I've ever laid eyes on. She's perfect, her blonde hair left simple and straight, her makeup natural with a peach lip that I know will look amazing smeared on my dick. Even the scowl on her face doesn't take away from her stunning beauty.

How the hell could her husband ever take his eyes from her?

Personally, I can't move my gaze as she walks gallantly down the steps in her three-inch heels. I know the exact height since I'm the one who sent the shoes, along with the black velvet, floral embroidered gown from Altuzarra and the pink Prada shrug draped over one shoulder. As I'd intended, she is completely on brand, presenting both elegance and allure along with a side of bombshell. I'd been uncertain whether or not she'd go along with my outfit request, after the pushback she gave me last time. I'm idiotically smug knowing that she did.

If she donned the clothes I sent, did she follow the rest of my instructions?

The question is easily answered by a press of the remote control hidden in my left pocket. Her expression doesn't falter. Her body doesn't flinch.

Goddammit, I knew she was going to be trouble.

I meet her at the bottom of the stairs, hooking my arm

around hers so that I can easily steer her toward the gender-neutral bathrooms. "You're late."

"You're lucky I came at all." She's pouting, but that didn't stop goosebumps from sprouting along her delicate skin as soon as I touched her.

It does something to me to know that I affect her, despite how she feels about me. I'm a man who has known I was powerful my entire life, and yet I've never felt the impact of that privilege until wielding it over Brystin Shaw.

I swear, I'm half hard, and tonight's games haven't even begun.

"Where are you taking me?" she asks when she realizes we aren't headed toward the theater. "Isn't the opera about to start?"

"Already started," I confirm. "We should be sitting in our box right now, but first we have to deal with your disobedience."

She tenses in my grasp, but doesn't try to fight me as I push open the bathroom door. With one hand flipping the lock, I use my hip to pin her against the wall and my other hand to gather her dress up around her waist.

My cock jumps at the sight. "Well, at least you followed instructions about no panties."

"I didn't want panty lines," she says, but the dress isn't that tight.

"Right. Of course." I run my fingers down the skin above her folds, feeling a light strip of stubble. Either she hasn't gotten around to removing the hair after yesterday's argument, or she's not really as upset with me as she's pretending to be.

But she was upset enough to ignore the other request I'd

made when I'd had the outfit delivered. I confirm the fact when my fingers find their way into her quite wet pussy. "There's nothing here, Brystin."

"I wasn't going to wear your fucking toy thing. I'm here to promote the show. Not to be your entertainment."

"You're here for both." I reach into my right pocket and pull out a flexible silicone vibrator, identical to the one she's supposed to be wearing. "Fortunately, I didn't have faith in your ability to follow directions, so I brought a spare."

"I am not wearing that." But she spreads her legs further apart and lets out a small moan when I press one end of the toy inside her pussy.

I adjust the other end so it will press against her clit. Then I bring my wet fingers to my mouth and simultaneously hit the button on the remote. Her body shudders as the vibrator massages her tight bundle of nerves, and her eyes darken as she watches with rapt attention as I lick my fingers clean. "I knew you'd taste like honey. And with the remote in my hands, I expect there will be plenty more of the sweet stuff to come. Pun intended."

I don't know if she wants to kiss me or murder me. Either way, I love the spark of passion in her focused stare.

She pushes me, but not with enough strength to actually move me. "You're depraved."

"Not any more depraved than you, my honeybee." I turn the remote off and toss the duplicate in the trash so I don't mix the two up. Then I step back of my own accord, giving her room to adjust her dress. "Oh, and you'll want to be careful not to come too hard. It would be quite an impact on your brand if your pussy dropped that toy out during our red carpet interview after the show."

Her eyes narrow. "You wouldn't dare."

"Wouldn't I?" I push out of the bathroom without giving her a chance to respond. While what happens remains to be seen, I do intend to treat her well tonight.

I wonder how often Michael Endlich can say the same.

CHAPTER **NINETEEN**

HOLT

Brystin is right—I am an asshole.

The annual opera night at Irving Sebastian Concert Hall is an event meant to bring in high price donors for the right to free press. Growing up, the date was always circled on the nanny's calendar, and my father expected us to show up clean and respectable because "free press is our bread and butter" and this was the one night every year that the "Sebastians make a clear stand for democracy."

I'm not sure it's true that this is the only night we make a stand, but the point is, this event is sacrosanct.

And I spent the entire two hours of Madame Butterfly's performance playing Take Her to the Edge with Brystin Shaw and the Lelo toy I put inside her. It's my new favorite game. She was legitimately weeping during the death scene, and I'm fairly certain she had no idea what was going on.

Now we're making our way to the red carpet for photos and interviews, and of course I've been stopped a thousand times. I have to hide my smirk every time someone casually asks her if she enjoyed the show. She's a practiced journalist and can keep a straight face, but her décolletage turns a beautiful shade of raspberry—the same shade she turns when she gets close to orgasm—and all sorts of dirty thoughts fill my head. Mostly thoughts about how pretty the shade of cream cum would look added to the palette.

"Stop enjoying this," she hisses after we untangle ourselves from the latest encounter.

"Not a chance." I spy my assistant waiting for us at the press line, and I direct Brystin toward him, sliding my hand against her upper back rather than her lower so I can feel the soft warmth of her skin.

She starts when I first make contact, but relaxes into my touch quickly. I'm sure she doesn't realize she does this consciously. Her body already recognizes me as friend even if her mind doesn't, and I don't envy the conflict it must stir in her.

Not that I know anything about that kind of battle.

"Good evening, Ms. Shaw," André greets us when we're at his side. To me he gives instruction. "I have you queued for next. Remember to mention your father and the other members of the family. Make every effort to sound like the official spokesman of the night. Hunter has yet to go through the line, and we both know he'll try to take that honor for himself."

I roll my eyes at the reminders. It's his job, and he's good at it, but I hate being told what to do, even if I told him to tell me.

I'm also wary of Hunter's presence. I'd prefer he spoke to the press ahead of me so that I can massage any disparaging remark he makes. "Any chance I can put my walk off a little longer?"

He looks at his watch. "It's getting late as it is. Reporters are getting antsy."

"You need to get ahead of it," Brystin speaks up, as though she's been invited into the conversation.

I stare at her for a moment, wanting to tell her to butt out, but looking at her I recognize two things—she's honestly trying to help, and she's right.

André's silence means he agrees.

"Then let's get in there."

He turns to the reporters closest to the front of the line, telling them to wrap up the interview they're currently conducting with the show's director and the man who plays Pinkerton.

When André turns back to us, he focuses on Brystin. "Enjoy the show?"

Unfortunately, I'm tapped on the shoulder just then by the hall's security guard, but not before I catch Brystin's scowl in my direction. "Theater's locked up," the guard informs me.

The festivities outside the theater will continue for another hour at least, but the hall is always a priority in lockup, mostly so that guests won't sneak in and destroy the set, though the only trespassers that have ever been caught were couples looking for an unusual place to fuck.

"You've checked every door?" I ask, wanting to be certain it's secure.

"Twice. Lights out too."

I thank him and let him go on his way, in time for André to indicate it's our turn to walk. "Holt Sebastian coming through," he calls to the crowd.

All eyes immediately shift toward me, cameras pointed in my direction. I put my hand again at Brystin's back, and this time she gets so tense she doesn't move.

"Come on," I whisper.

"Not me! I thought this was just you."

"You're my date. So it's both of us."

Admittedly, I've been shit at explaining anything to her tonight. She was so grateful the evening I showed her the studio, when I let her in on all the plans about the show, when I talked to her like she had a say in the production. I don't generally have those sorts of conversations with our stars. It's not my job to interact with programming on this level in general.

That right there is reason enough not to do it again.

But the real reason I've kept her in the dark has nothing to do with practicalities. I do enjoy keeping her on her toes, but that isn't the reason either. Quite simply put, I'm still mad at her. Mad about a commitment she made to a fuck-twat way before I ever came into the picture.

And now I have to hope that she's as good on her feet as I know she is, otherwise not prepping her could end in disaster for both of us.

"I can't go out in front of cameras as your date." Before I can try to ease her mind, she voices her true concern. "I don't trust you with that remote control in your pocket."

"Fuck, Brystin, we don't have time for this." I attempt to nudge her forward.

"Hand over the remote."

No way. I'm not done playing with her, and I know if I hand it over, I'll never see it again. "We're walking the carpet together, Brystin, right the fuck now. This is not a debate."

"I don't trust you," she whisper-repeats.

She has every reason not to trust me, but I'm not sending her toward orgasm in front of the media. Believe it or not, I know when to draw the line. Usually when it's my own ass on the plate, and it is very much so right now.

Not that she needs to know that. Let her be scared I'll use it. It will keep her on her toes. "I'm not giving you the remote."

Everyone is still very much focused on us. A few people are starting to whisper. André looks ready to jump into action, an excuse for the delay likely on the tip of his tongue.

I don't need my assistant to fix this problem. "Just chatting about whether or not she left her opera glasses in the theater," I announce to the line of press. I turn to Brystin and speak loud enough for everyone to hear. "They'll still be waiting for us when we're done here."

For half a second, I'm afraid she isn't going to play along.

But then she smiles radiantly. "They were a gift from my husband. Wouldn't want to lose them."

Of course she has to mention *him*.

"Go ahead, Holt. You're the one they want to speak to." She steps aside so I can pass, and now she's beaten me at my own game.

Well, almost beaten me.

I go ahead and pass her, but I take her hand in mine to

tug her along, and yes, also it's a big fuck you to that husband of hers. A bold declaration too, but I can deal with that later.

With her hand in mine, I answer the questions from the press, making sure to deliver a good sound bite to the most prominent reporters. "As most of you know, this event is very close to my father's heart. He doesn't do too many of these evening things since his heart attack, but I assure you he's as fully supportive as always, and on behalf of him and the rest of my family—several of my siblings and cousins are here tonight—SNC is matching any donations up to twenty-five million dollars given to the Freedom of the Press Foundation before midnight."

As planned, I stay on point, neglecting to introduce Brystin until she's asked after, as though she's an afterthought when, in reality, I orchestrated this whole event around her. "Beautiful girl on your arm tonight, Holt. You usually attend these events solo."

The question even comes from a non-affiliate station. I couldn't have asked for a more perfect segue. "Ah, yes. I'm thrilled to introduce you to Brystin Shaw. Not a date—as she already mentioned, this fine woman is already married, but she's with me tonight in support of this very important cause, and, you know, I'm going to let the cat out of the bag a couple of days early—Brystin is the host of SNC's new show, *Our Nation Now,* debuting in a little over two weeks. We're privileged and lucky to have her at the network, and I know America is going to really connect with Brystin's in-depth perspective on the present state of the country on the micro-level."

She's surprised about the announcement, but she

doesn't show it. Easily, and with the innate skill that I knew she possessed, Brystin steps into the spotlight and speaks informatively about both the show and her thoughts on protecting press freedoms.

She's brilliant.

Very much the star I've always believed she could be.

Fifteen minutes later, we're through the press line, and *Our Nation Now* has been announced to the world, and Brystin has had a chance to prove she's worth the hype *before* the hype.

All in all, a good day's work.

André confirms everything has gone as it should on the back end. "I've contacted Sarah and told her the press releases are ready to go. She's setting up interviews for next week with you and Brystin. I'll have that schedule to you by morning. The first commercial spot is airing at the next break on tonight's schedule. And I haven't seen Hunter in the last ten minutes. There's a chance he missed the announcement altogether."

Doubtful.

"He'll find out when he's on the carpet, if he doesn't know before." There's no way he won't be questioned about this programming bomb drop, especially since SNC hasn't aired a new show since I've taken the helm.

But I've done what I can for now.

Hunter is not who I want to be thinking about for the rest of the evening.

"Thank you, André. We'll be heading out now. Keep me updated by text."

"Should I call your car for you?"

"I'll take care of it." I don't tell him that heading out doesn't mean we're leaving the building.

"All right then. Have a good night." He nods to Brystin. "Ms. Shaw." Then he's bustling off to do whatever it is he does when he's making sure my world continues to run smoothly.

Brystin hasn't spoken a word to me since we stepped off the carpet. I study her now, trying to read into the stare she's giving, but it's not an expression of hers that I recognize yet, and I fucking hate that I have to ask. "What?"

"This was all for me," she says. "This whole night—it was about announcing the show. You were a dick about it, but it was for me."

"What?" I'm taken aback by that perspective. I mean, it was all for her show, but it's not like I don't have skin in the game. It's not like I did something out of generosity.

But she thinks that I have, and now I'm torn about how to respond. It's been fun having her mad at me, and yet the way she's looking at me now feels…nice.

Or useful, anyway.

"Hold that thought." I leave her to cross the few feet over to the bar where I get a newly opened bottle of Caymus Cabernet, Special Selection. Not necessarily what I would have chosen, but it's nice enough.

When I return to Brystin, she's typing something into her phone—texting someone, considering how long she's at it.

And just like that, the momentary lift of my rage is gone, and it's back full blown.

"It's him, isn't it?" I ask, knowing full well it is.

She looks up as if I'm grandma and she's been caught

with her hand in the cookie jar. "Just…I was telling him…" She puts the phone back into her clutch and shakes her head. "I can tell him later."

Why wouldn't she want to tell her husband and producer that his show has just been announced, two days ahead of schedule? I should have given him the heads-up myself. Or André should have, on my behalf.

I shouldn't have left it to Brystin, and I'm as pissed at myself about it as I am at her for including him in this moment. "Does he know you're here tonight? With me?"

She nods, tentatively, as though she's afraid it's the wrong answer.

I shouldn't ask, but the next question unfurls from my tongue like a damn flag on Memorial Day. "Does he know *why* you're with me?"

She answers immediately. "I tell him everything."

I already know her well enough to have discovered her tell—a quick blink of her eyes before she spouts a lie, like she just did now.

A rush of self-righteousness flows through me like someone injected it into my vein. It's stupid, really. She doesn't tell him everything, so what? It's not like I get the point instead since she tried to lie to me about it.

I step closer to her, not caring that the action seems predatory or that we're still very much in the public eye. "So he thinks you're with me tonight for PR?"

She swallows.

"Or he thinks you're here to…please me?"

Very slightly, her head bobs. "Yes. That."

Interesting. After the incident with the contract signing yesterday, I considered that she might have told Michael that there wouldn't be any more sexual favors exchanged. I thought he might even go as far as to intervene.

Honestly, I don't give a fuck what he thinks we're doing or whether he thinks I'm allowed—consent is up to Brystin, as it always has been, despite what I said about owning her.

Mostly.

But if she didn't tell him that she was done with me, that's a good sign she doesn't think she's done either. Which makes it that much easier to say what I say next. "Wouldn't want to make a liar out of you."

She swallows again, but her eyes darken, and fight it all she wants to, she can't ignore the electricity between us.

After the orgasms I denied her all night, I'm not sure she's primed to even try.

"In five seconds, I'm going to head toward the stage door. Count to ten after I leave, then come after me. If anyone asks, we're looking for your opera glasses." It's her choice now to follow.

But I know she'll make the right choice, and not just because I'm cocky, but because I know she needs this as much as I do.

I step even closer and lean down to whisper intimately in her ear. "Don't even think about removing that toy before you get there, and when you do, Brystin? You damn well better be ready to come."

Without monitoring her reaction, I head to the private hall that leads to the stage. I key in my code then leave the door slightly ajar for Brystin. It's at least a hundred feet before I reach the door to backstage, and I feel the torture of Eurydice, wanting to look behind to see if my Persephone is following.

But I'm a Sebastian, and as I've been told my entire life, I have strength that other men don't possess—though it hardly feels like it with this woman—and somehow, I manage to keep my eyes where they belong, and eventually I push the double doors open onto the pitch black of backstage.

By the time I've switched all the breakers on to bring up the lights, including those in the house, I hear the click of her footsteps on the masonite.

She walks past me, passing under the set's constructed cherry blossom tree, all the way to the skirt of the stage. I watch her momentarily, admiring how she carries herself as she gazes out on a sea of empty seats. Even here, even when it's just us, she exudes a presence that deserves to be in the spotlight.

I set the wine bottle down on the steps of the minka façade and approach her carefully. It's so quiet, there's no way she doesn't hear me. "It feels like there are hundreds of eyes watching, doesn't it? Even when we're alone."

"It makes me nervous." She shivers, and I wonder if my nearness isn't the real cause. "I don't know how the performers do it every night."

"More people see you on TV than there are seats out there."

"I like to think I'm talking only to the cameraman. Don't ruin the illusion." She's silent for a beat, then something shifts in her, and she seems even more nervous when she turns to face me. "Why are we here, Holt?"

Nervous or excited. Perhaps a combo of both because she knows exactly why I've brought her here. "I want it to feel like we have an audience when I fill your throat with my cock."

Her eyes darken and there is no mistaking the hitch in her breath. "I don't know why you think I'm still playing that game with you."

"I don't know why you still think it's a game." I take a menacing step toward her. Then I sit on the faux stone stool where Suzuki sat during Butterfly's performance of *Un bel di vedremo*.

She frowns, apparently disapproving, and I half expect her to scold me.

Instead, she stays on topic. "You've announced the show now. Canceling it would do more to your reputation at this point than it would to mine."

"When have I given you any indication that I care about my reputation?"

"There has to be something you care about."

"I care about getting you off and making you feel morally uncomfortable about it when you do."

Pink extends across her collarbone, and I'm officially at full mast. I'm definitely painting a white necklace on that sunset skin.

I also don't miss the hint of a smile before it disappears. "That can't be all you care about."

She's right, of course. I can't care what most people think of me—a good deal of them hate me just because of my name, just because of my bank account.

But I do care what my father thinks.

What Irving thinks.

I care about holding my position at SNC.

I can't bear the prospect of being the only Sebastian who

fails.

Lately, though, I've had trouble staying focused on my priorities. I wake up with this fucking woman on my mind, and a smile to go with it, until I remember that she legally belongs to someone else.

Which should be a plus, as far as I'm concerned.

I generally prefer married women. Happily married women, to be precise. Women who will never leave their husbands. Their wants from me are clear—sexual attention and to be showered with the gifts of the Sebastian name. They don't want babies. They don't want vows. They don't care if I disappear for weeks or fuck another woman in between, and I am more than happy to send them back to their husbands when they start crying about commitment and devotion. Sebastians don't care about love. We have money, and no matter what the adages say, enough of it, and you can fill any hole.

This obsession with Brystin and her marriage is simply self-sabotage. That's what my million-dollar life coach would say. Something to blame when I don't succeed with my vision for SNC. An illusory distraction.

But damn, does it feel fucking real.

"Why are you with Michael Endlich?"

She's clearly taken aback, stammering her response. "Where did…? What kind of…? Who asks that? We're married. I'm with him because, you know. I love him."

It took a long time to get to those last three words.

And when I hear them, my gut goes as hard as the fists in my lap and the pulsing erection in my pants.

I don't fail to notice she only mentioned that she loves him—not the other way around. "You love him, and it's cool that he fucks around? I'm sure you know he does. There's no way you don't."

Any other married woman I've fucked would take this conversation in stride. They'd probably be the one to bring it up.

With Brystin, I can't help being cruel. I want to be cruel, even. I want her to feel the same pierce of disappointment that I feel every time I remember she said "I do" to a shallow fuck of a man.

As suspected, she gets defensive, pulling her shrug around her. "Who says we don't have an open marriage?"

"An open marriage where he gets to fuck and you don't? You did say that intercourse would be cheating."

Her lips purse, and her eyes blink rapidly. There's a falsehood buried in there somewhere. I'm just not sure which part is the lie. "I don't want to talk about this with you."

I lean forward. "How about I give you options? Continue the conversation or get down on your knees."

Obviously, the choice is a ruse. I'll get everything I want, in the end. I always do.

Expecting a longer debate, I'm surprised when she immediately falls to her knees. My dick jumps in anticipation, and I give her a proud grin. "That's my good girl."

I reward her with a high buzz from the toy pressing against her clit. She jolts as soon as I turn it on, confirming it's still in place. "Very, very good girl."

After considering the idea of making her crawl to me—a sight which would probably have me jizzing in my pants—I stand and cross to her, more intent on living out this particular fantasy center stage.

As soon as I reach her, I shove one hand in her hair and pull her neck back so she's forced to peer up at me. "Take a good look at my face, Brystin. I want you to remember whose cock you're sucking, in case it might be confusing."

Her plump peach lips open, but I interrupt whatever she's intent on saying with another buzz from the toy, and all that comes from her lips is a whimper.

"Don't worry—I'll make sure you come too, honeybee." I release her hair and draw my hand down the side of her face before pushing my thumb into the lush warmth of her mouth. On cue, she sucks. "You're going to have to do better than that if you want to taste my cock."

This time, she sucks with more enthusiasm, and with another line of praise. She likes this, I realize. Being told she's good. That she's pretty. That she's mine.

Michael probably doesn't tell her enough.

Has her so starving for it that what I dole out incrementally feels like a feast.

Fuck Michael. I don't want him here right now, while she's mine.

"Take my cock out, then put your hands on your thighs, open your mouth, and stick out your tongue."

She scrambles to do so, almost eagerly. When she puts her hands on her thighs, she's such the perfect image of a model sub that I almost laugh out loud in pure joy. *How the hell did I get so lucky to find her?*

Not luck, persistence. I scoured the local stations across the nation looking for her. I just never imagined she'd turn out to be such a fucking dream.

With my hand at the back of her skull to hold her head in place, I bounce my tip on her tongue, getting harder at the sight of her saliva mixing with the pre-cum on my crown.

Mother. Fucking. Dream.

"You can suck me now." It's a demand, not a suggestion.

Appropriately, she responds as such, wrapping her lips around my cock and running her tongue along the base of my length. She bobs her head over me, taking me shallow with the first few returns, then deep enough that I touch the back of her throat.

I reward her with an erratic low pulse on her clit that has her shifting on her haunches.

Simultaneously, she reverts to the shallow bobs. "I need you to concentrate, Brystin. If you get too distracted with your own pleasure, I'll have to take over. I should tell you now—I expect you to deepthroat."

Her eyes widen, possibly in trepidation, but she doesn't make any attempt to struggle. Instead, she resumes the deep plunges that aren't quite my preference but feel damn near ecstasy all the same. I hit the remote, giving her another unexpected buzz that makes her hum and sends sharp tingles down the back of my spine.

"Fuck. Your mouth." I'm afraid I'm going to come too soon, come down her throat instead of on her skin like I'm dying to.

And still, as close as I am to what I know will be a mind-blowing release, my head goes back to that same sabotaging loop. "Is this how you suck Michael?"

She can't answer without stopping, and I don't want her to stop.

I tighten the hand at the back of her head so she knows I intend this to be a monologue. Instead, I study her eyes for the answer. There's guilt there that I can't quite interpret. "He's softer, isn't he? Lets you use your hands, makes you do all the work?"

I can imagine him stretched out and passive, her head between his thighs, and feel intensely murderous.

The next buzz I send to her is the strongest yet. Meant to punish, not reward, and sure enough, her bob stutters as her muscles tighten.

I use her "drop in concentration" as an excuse to push her head forward, until her nose touches my pelvis and she gurgles as my cock slides down her throat.

"Bet he doesn't try to get you off at the same time." Jesus, I know I'm a jealous monster, deciding her husband is trash in bed simply because I want him to be. "Will you tell him about this? Since you tell him everything. Will you tell him how I made you come while you took my cock like a professional?"

I release her, giving her a moment to breathe, but this time I want an answer. "Shake your head, yes or no—will he know about this?"

She stares at me with those wide eyes for several seconds before shaking her head.

It should be a victory. That this moment is ours and not his, should be a relief.

It's not.

I want him to know. I want him to suffer from the same jealous monster I suffer from. After setting the remote on a pattern that will likely get her where she needs to go, I pull my phone from my pocket and take a picture. Her mascara is smeared and her chin is dripping with saliva, and she's so dirty and gorgeous, I know I'll jerk off to this image for weeks.

"Should I send it to him?"

She tries to pull out of my grip, voicing a clear "no" despite her mouth being full.

Whether it's to spare his feelings or her dignity, I'm not sure, but either way, I take it as concern for him, and it jars me from any sense of courtesy, any sense of kindness.

Holding her in place with a handful of hair, I take over completely, thrusting in and out of her mouth at the tempo I like. She struggles not to choke, but she's twisting and writhing at the same time, and I know it must be confusing to her body and brain to be so turned on and so victimized at once.

It's confusing to me too—wanting to hurt her, wanting to please her. Wanting her to only want me.

Phone still in hand, I find Michael's name in my contacts and hit CALL, pushing the speaker button as soon as it starts to ring. Her eyes shine with terror when she realizes. Strangely she doesn't try to pull away, doesn't try to fight.

"Holt?"

I still haven't decided what I'll say. I want to tell him in vivid detail what I'm doing to his wife, how I'm debasing her, how I'm pleasing her. How I'm doing it on a stage, how I wouldn't care if there were a million people watching.

"I'm with your wife." I watch Brystin gaze pleadingly as I continue to abuse her, as she continues to squirm from the ruthless pulse of the vibrator. Can he identify the gagging sounds of a blow job through the line? Does he recognize the whimper in the back of her throat? Does he care?

A soft laughter sounds in the background, and I realize that he's with a woman.

Realize it at the same time as Brystin does. Her eyes close for a brief second, and when they open again, the pleas are gone. Like she's closed a door inside her, shutting off the part of her heart that belongs to him.

I know from experience it doesn't work like that. Emotions seep through the cracks. She'll still feel what she doesn't want to feel.

I'm not sure it will spare her any pain, but I make a decision. "We announced the show. Ads start tonight. Thought you should have a heads-up. Enjoy your night."

Without waiting for a response, I hit END and drop the phone to the stage so I can put my hands on either side of her face and thrust in and out of her mouth at high speed. It takes maybe thirty seconds before Brystin comes, her body jerking as I use the fuck out of her throat.

I pull out and jerk my hand up and down my length, letting her finish her orgasm without having to worry about mine. She's just coming down when I hit my peak. Cum spurts out in white ropes along her collarbone, painting a design even more erotic than my fantasies had conjured.

I'm still admiring my art, my cock still semi-hard in my hand, when Brystin rises to her feet and presses her mouth to mine.

It's not as filthy of a kiss as the one we'd had last time. Not as desperate. Not as long. It's brief but sloppy and full of intensity. Full of something that feels kind.

"I didn't deserve that," I say when she steps away.

"I guess you'll have to owe me."

I've been handed more than I deserve my entire life, and

yet these gifts from her, these kisses, are what I find unfathomable. And it strikes me—with my cum still dripping down her chest and Michael's name still staring up from the screen of my phone—if she's so good to men who treat her cruelly, how much more good would she be to a man who treated her nice?

CHAPTER
TWENTY
BRYSTIN

I wake up thinking about Holt. Before I even open my eyes, I let my mind replay the events of last night. I'd been wary about attending the event after his brutal display of power. Firing Jessa Jones had been bad enough. Declaring that he owned me was something else entirely.

The biggest problem with the declaration is how it didn't make me feel entirely upset. I've never been claimed like that before. Michael's married to me, and he doesn't even wear a ring to claim me. I thought I didn't mind. He's always said, *We know what we are to each other,* but now here's Holt, saying things that unite us in ways I've never felt with the man I thought I belonged with.

And I did sign the contract with Holt.

So in the end, it was easy to convince myself that I had no choice but to be wherever he told me to be. I really had thought he'd made me go just so he could exercise more of his dominance, but as soon as he'd announced the show on the carpet, I understood the ploy. He connected me with a bigger cause and gave me the opportunity to speak on its behalf. The nation was introduced to Brystin Shaw as someone who had an important opinion. It was an impressive tactic, one that benefitted me more than it could have possibly benefitted him.

After that, I was at his mercy. He could have told me to spread my legs on that stage, and I would have let him take me in any way he wanted.

I suppose the fact that he's obeyed my boundaries where sex is concerned is a sign that the man has at least some integrity.

Possibly the best part of the night was everything after the orgasms were exchanged, and considering I'd had one of the best O's of my life in front of that imaginary audience, that's really saying something. The evening could have easily ended there.

But instead of putting me in a car, he cleaned me up once again with the inside of his jacket, then wore the cum-stained clothing while he took me up to the top of Sebastian Center. It's one of the top tourist attractions in NYC, but I somehow managed to never go. I imagine it's a totally different experience being there at night and without a crowd. Romantic, almost. Holt brought a bottle of expensive wine, which we passed back and forth as we looked out over the city below us. Tipsy as all get out, I listened to him wax on about the notes and tones of the particular variety of grape, and then we spent at least an hour reminiscing about our favorite headlines from the past decade.

It was absolute news nerdom, and I couldn't have been happier.

Holt's ability to spout cultural trivia reminded me of the early days with Michael. When I used to fawn over him after a show with all the other interns. Except with Michael, I listened more than contributed. Mostly because he had years on me, and his best stories happened before I'd known anything about journalism.

But also because, although Michael is considered behind the scenes, he really does enjoy being in the spotlight.

Sometimes I feel like that's what I am for him—someone who will bring him the light.

Holt, on the other hand…he brings the light to *me*. Even at his mercurial worst, self-serving as he is, he seems to care about my best interests. And asshole that he is, he didn't mention the woman Michael was obviously with or the fact that an empty apartment was waiting for me in New Jersey. Instead, he offered me a place to sleep in the city so that—

Wait a minute…

Where the fuck did I sleep?

I sit up suddenly, my eyes frantically surveying the strange room as the later details of the night come to me in pieces. I'd been tired and intoxicated. Holt had said he had someplace I could stay. Then…had he carried me into bed?

I spot my dress draped over an armchair in the corner. I definitely don't remember getting undressed, but I am very much naked under these satin sheets. As for the rest of the room—it looks quite lived in for a guest apartment, which was what I had assumed Holt had meant when he said he had someplace. There is a stack of books with a bookmark sticking out of one on the nightstand along with a case for earbuds and a dock for charging a phone. I pull open the drawer and find more personal items—an iPad, a legal pad, Advil and allergy medicine as well as a bottle of lube.

And now that I'm paying attention…is that the sound of a shower running?

Wrapping the sheet around me, I climb out of bed and venture toward the bathroom. It's an open concept so there isn't a door before I'm standing in front of a large walk-in shower with steamed glass.

Not too steamy to recognize the chiseled figure on the other side who has one hand resting on the tile wall, the other hand jerking up and down so quickly that, even though his back is to me, I know exactly what he's doing.

I really should turn right around and pretend I never saw this.

But I can't move. At first, I'm too stunned. Then, as if sensing me, he turns his body, and now I can't move because his eyes have me pinned in place as he continues to stroke the length of his magnificent cock.

And wow.

When I say magnificent, I mean magnificent. I swear I've never seen him look so much like the royalty he is until this very moment, with his scepter in his hand, and him in his naked glory.

I'm still admiring with wide eyes when the water turns off, and the very wet—still very aroused—man walks out of the shower and grabs a towel for his hair. "Morning, honeybee. See something you like?"

I blink.

Then I get my shit together and force myself to look away. "Sorry. Sorry. I didn't realize you were here. I shouldn't be…I just didn't…I mean…"

I'm flustered, and despite not facing him, I can tell he's amused. "I really don't mind. Though I liked it better when you were actually looking."

I turn back to respond on instinct, forgetting I'll see what I'll see, or assuming perhaps that he'd throw a towel around him like a normal person. But nope. There he is, casually drying his hair while his cock stands at full salute.

I immediately turn away again. "Could you do something about that?"

"I was doing something about it. Then I realized you were here, and I thought it might be rude to continue without inviting you to join."

Why does an invitation like that make my knees weak and my insides molten lava?

"I can't do that." Though, admittedly, I'm beginning to forget what my reasons are.

"Why not? I can start the shower again and climb in with you. The water's probably still hot."

"No. Showering with you would be a bad, bad, bad idea." My body feels differently, but for the moment, my head is in charge. I glance back to see if he's covered himself yet, and it's another big nope. "And I can't look at you with…" I refuse to say *cock*. "*That* out in the open. So could you put it away so I can talk to you?"

If he puts it away, I might even remember what it is I need to say.

"It's not like you haven't seen it, Brystin."

"I haven't." It's taking all my concentration to keep from peeking again so I'm not at my best in the wording department. "I mean…yes, I've seen *it*. I haven't seen"—I wave my arm up and down in his general direction—"the full package."

"Pretty sure I had the full package down your throat just last night."

Oh God.

I shiver with the reminder and my thighs suddenly feel sticky. "The full you, I mean. Naked. With nothing on."

He chuckles, and then I hear his feet padding nearer until his breath is on my ear and the smell of his shampoo is inches from my nose. "I find you distracting when you're naked too. Even when you're trying to hide under my sheet."

I lift my head up to meet his eyes, and I swear, if he made one more move toward me, no matter how small, the sheet would drop, and I'd have my legs wrapped around his perfectly toned waist before I could remember my husband's first name.

Fortunately—I think—Holt doesn't make another move. "Let me put on some pants."

He pads past me into a huge walk-in closet, and yes, I watch his naked ass walk away. *Damn.* How is his backside just as glorious as his front?

"I know you're watching." He peers over his shoulder after he's spoken to confirm it's true.

My face gets so hot, I'm sure it looks sunburned.

At least his backside is a smidge less tempting, and I'm able to maintain eye contact as he pulls on a pair of dark jeans.

Without underwear.

God help me now.

"Better?" he asks as he approaches me again.

Honestly…not really. He's still shirtless and dripping, and I've never so desperately wanted to lick droplets off of someone's skin.

But the lust fog must have cleared somewhat because I all of a sudden remember the big fucking red flag reason I bolted out of his bed. "This is *your* apartment?"

"Uh…yes. Is there a problem?"

"When you said you had a place I could stay, I assumed you meant an *extra* place. Like a guest place. I didn't think you meant the apartment that you live in." I most certainly didn't think he meant he'd take me to his very own bed, though that's only problematic emotionally, and only for me.

He leans his arm against the doorframe of the closet. "Not to repeat myself, but is there a problem?"

I throw my head back, wanting to scream, as much from sexual frustration as anything else, but it's definitely all frustration. "I'm a married woman, Holt. And you're an A-list celebrity. I know for a fact that paparazzi camp outside your building. I can't be seen coming out of your apartment at this time of the morning, looking hungover, and"—*fuck*—"wearing last night's dress."

How am I just realizing that last bit? It gets worse the more I think about it.

"I did offer the shower," Holt says, unfazed.

I'm so frustrated, I growl. Literally growl.

Then, gathering the sheet in my arms so I don't trip, I stomp back to the bedroom, as if there will magically be answers for alternate clothing when I get there. "What time is it?"

He doesn't answer, and when I pull my phone from the

purse that's thankfully by the dress, I find it's dead. Of course.

I stomp over to the floor-to-ceiling windows and pull back the curtain to see if I can guess the time from the sun. Early, is all I make out. Seven or eight, maybe. Which feels like a pretty typical time for a walk-of-shame.

"Goddammit," I curse.

I turn around to find Holt emerging from the closet, a pair of sweatpants and a T-shirt in hand. "You can borrow these."

I'll drown in his clothes, but it's less obvious than last night's evening dress.

Then he bends to open a dresser drawer and pulls out a baseball cap. "This should help. There are miscellaneous hair ties in one of the bathroom drawers if you want to do a pony."

It's like he knows how to sneak a woman out of his apartment. I'm not sure if I'm disgusted or impressed.

Wait…did he say miscellaneous hair ties? Like left over from the various women he's had stay the night?

Definitely disgusted.

Or…if I'm honest…jealous.

I scowl as I maneuver the sheet so I can put on his sweats without showing much skin while I do. Silly, since he's already seen all of me, and the smirk he gives as he watches tells me how ridiculous I'm being.

When the pants are on, I grab the T-shirt and turn away from him before dropping the sheet.

"Believe it or not, I find your backside just as arousing as your front."

As if to prove his point, his hand is settled on the bulge in his jeans when I turn back to face him.

"You're still hard from the shower." Shit. What am I going to do about shoes? I head to my pile of clothes to see if I can get away with wearing last night's heels.

"You don't know what I was thinking about in the shower."

I hate myself for being curious enough to look in his direction.

"All right, I wasn't thinking about your backside," he admits.

I roll my eyes and sit on the floor to strap on a shoe. He probably hadn't even been thinking of me, which makes my gut twist in a way that I'm choosing to ignore.

But then he says, "I was definitely thinking about your cunt."

I pause, my nude sandal half strapped on my foot, and stare for a beat. Stare at nothing, while the cunt in question pulses, and my heart does some flip-floppy acrobatics, and the voice inside my head has to shout, *It's just sex; don't make anything out of it, you fool.*

But even if it's not something bigger, it's not *just sex*. Because it's also my career and Holt's power game, and lately, I'm thinking about his cock more than I'm thinking about Michael's, and all the complications make it hard to talk about, but that's probably exactly what we should be doing.

I lift my gaze toward him, not sure how to start.

He beats me to speaking first. "Take a deep breath, Brystin."

While I do, he bends down to help me with my other

shoe. "First step is to stop panicking. There's nothing to worry about. We got this."

"We do?" It helps to have him put himself into the situation with me as a *we*. Maybe it's complicated for him too.

"We do. There are three hundred and sixty units in this building. No one is going to know whose apartment you came out of."

Oh.

Well, we weren't on the same page there, were we? It should have been what I'd been thinking, though. Getting out of here unmade is definitely the priority. "It's too big of a coincidence. After being with you last night, being photographed with you...and you had to be extra handsy."

"Couldn't help myself." He finishes with the buckle then rubs his hand over my ankle, under the sweats, and up my calf.

Lightning sparks through my nervous system, and it takes me a second before I wake up and pull away. "Okay, well, this was a big fuckup." Ignoring his outstretched hand, I get to my feet on my own. "I guess it's a good thing you control the news because you might have to intervene."

He shrugs as if he thinks it's unnecessary.

I huff. Dramatic, but seriously, does he not understand my reputation is on the line?

Oh, right. He's never cared about his own reputation, so it's probably not a feeling he can relate to. We're from two different worlds. I need to remember that.

I grab the ball cap and put it on my head. It's me looking out for myself here, just like it's always been. "Do you know what time it is?"

"Almost half past eight. I'll call you a car."

"No! Way too obvious. My departure should not be connected to you in any way. I'll call an Uber." Then I remember my phone is dead. "Actually, I'll take a cab." I wince thinking of the price. Public transit it is. "Where's the nearest subway from here?"

The expression on his face says he has probably never ridden on the subway in his life.

"Never mind. I'll figure it out."

It's after ten when I get to my apartment, nauseous and dehydrated, in time to find Zully waiting outside my door for our weekly brunch date.

"I'm not even going to ask," she says.

"But obviously I'm going to tell you." I insert my key in the lock, preparing to catch her up on everything. "My phone died, or I would already have called you."

"I figured you hadn't seen the news yet."

I open the door for her, my brow raised as she passes by. "Uh…what news?"

"I think you better see for yourself."

I follow her to my kitchen and throw my purse on the counter as she pulls something up on her phone. My stomach has already decided whatever it is must be bad, and it's gurgling with dread when she turns the screen for me to see the headline in bold:

SNC CONTINUES HISTORY OF NEPOTISM BY GIVING PRIMETIME SHOW TO CEO'S LATEST GIRLFRIEND.

I drop the phone and just make it before throwing up in the kitchen sink.

CHAPTER
TWENTY-ONE
BRYSTIN

The headlines are more of the same as I scroll through Zully's phone. I can't find a single one that doesn't attach some sort of romantic label to me and Holt. Most neglect mentioning I'm married at all, which maybe is better, because the few that do talk about Michael go so far as to call me an outright adulterer.

The worst quote comes from Holt's cousin Hunter, the one he and André had been worried about. I read it aloud to Zully, even though she's already seen it. "'*When we elected Holt to the position of CEO, we never expected that he would hand out serious news positions to whores. The board will definitely be discussing this.*' They call me a whore. A *whore*!"

"Can people even say that anymore? Someone's going to cancel him."

I shake my head as tears collect at the corners of my eyes. "Sebastians don't get canceled."

"Everyone gets canceled. They canceled the queen before she died."

"It won't hurt him, I mean. He won't feel the impact at all."

I, on the other hand, have been branded. This is the first impression most of the nation has of me, and it can never be undone.

The tears start in earnest. And I'm not even a crier.

"Don't do that, don't do that." Zully swipes her phone from my hand, as if I might keep looking and find something worse, then rushes to grab a Kleenex box from the living room.

"All of that work, and it's all pointless." I snatch several tissues so I can dab at my eyes and blow my nose. "No one will ever take me seriously. This show is a flop before it's even started. Maybe I'm getting canceled. Literally."

I bite my lip so that I don't succumb to deeper sobs.

I think it hits me so hard because they aren't wrong. This new show comes with a significant pay increase. Isn't that what you call someone who exchanges sex for money? A whore?

"It's Holt's fault." Zully strokes my tear-wet hair off my face. "He demanded these games and then left you open to criticism. Note that he's not getting attacked."

"Uh, I think the threat from his cousin is pretty concerning." Honestly, I don't know. Hunter is one voice. I have no idea whether the rest of the board falls more to his opinions or to Holt's.

"Sure, it's concerning. He'll probably be demoted to one of the positions that report to the main CEO. What do they call those at SNC? Oh, right. CEO." She trades a wad of new tissues for my used ones and throws them in the trash. "There're like fifty CEO spots at this company, and I guarantee you, if there isn't a place for him already, they'll make up a new job. His pay won't change. He'll still have a private jet and a billion more dollars at his disposal than you have."

She's right, but that doesn't mean it won't feel like a loss to Holt.

She knows me well enough to be able to read my expression. "Stop feeling sorry for him! He's a rich white man. He's fucking fine."

"I know he's fine. But to that end, I'm a married white woman with skills and enough in savings. I'll be fine too. Besides, I knew what I was getting into when I accepted this deal. I put myself in this position."

Zully gives me a hard stare. "Oh, no, girl. We are not yet ready to move on to being okay with this. We have plenty more bitching to do before we get to that point."

"Thank God, because I'm really, really upset. A whore, Zully. Forever, if you Google Brystin Shaw, that's what's going to show up. 'Holt's whore.'"

It's even more upsetting to realize that if he were saying those words to me directly, I'd have an O right there on the spot. How can something so degrading and terrible be such a turn-on under the right circumstances? "They should go ahead and call me a bad feminist too. I'm a problem for women everywhere."

I feel another rush of tears when there's a heavy knock on the door. *Bam, bam, bam.*

"Fuck, who do you think that is?" I look at the clock. It's not yet ten thirty. Maybe Michael forgot his key, but he doesn't like to disrupt our girls' brunch so he shouldn't be home until the afternoon. We have a doorman, but it's not impossible to get by him. "Do you think the press would already be hunting me down?"

I wonder if people are trying to reach me by phone. "I really need to charge my cell."

The knock comes again. *Bam, bam, bam, bam, bam.*

"I'll see who it is and get rid of them." Zully shoos me off the barstool I'm sitting on. "You go plug in your phone."

Grateful for someone to take care of me and tell me what to do, I let her go handle the door, and I slip into my bedroom to find my charger. I consider changing my clothes while I'm here, since I'm still wearing Holt's clothes, but I only get so far as taking off the ball cap when I realize that whoever was at the door is now in my living room, talking to Zully.

And his voice is one I'd recognize now in my sleep.

Pausing to check the mirror (and then acknowledging that there is nothing that can fix how terrible I look), I rush out of my bedroom and directly into Holt's arms.

Well, Holt's arm.

One of them is carrying a drink holder, but he shifts it to the side, making space for my body, and wraps his free arm around me tightly.

"He called me a whore," I cry into his shoulder. "Did you see? It's everywhere."

I can't see with my face buried in Holt's T-shirt, but Zully must rescue the drinks because his other arm soon folds around me as well. "No one cares about his opinion."

"People respect him. He's a Sebastian."

"He's an asshole." He pauses. "AssHunter?"

I chuckle through my blubbering, which I think was his intended goal. "I'm not ready to laugh, you assHolt. I'm too upset."

His grip around me tightens. "I knew you would be. I saw the news just after you left, so I got myself together and came after you."

Wow.

Even in despair, the butterflies still like to flutter. I turn my head so that I can breathe, resting my cheek on his shoulder instead. My eyes meet Zully's.

He came after you, she mouths, excitedly.

I glare at her, afraid Holt will see her, but I'm glad she's starting to understand what this is with him.

Not that I understand it myself.

Still, I'm definitely happy he's here.

Except then something occurs to me, and I push away from his embrace. "Oh my God, what if you were followed? Did you make it worse?"

"I wasn't followed," he assures me. "And I valet parked almost a mile away at a twenty-four-hour strip club. If there's a tracker on my car, that's where they'll think I've gone."

Then he gestures to the drinks and a brown paper bag sitting on the coffee table. "I picked up some coffees and breakfast tacos down the street, in case you'd been too distracted for your regular brunch order."

"From Chico's?" Zully dives into the brown bag. "Oh yeah. Forget what I said about him before, B. This guy is…" With both hands clutching aluminum wrapped tacos, she manages to give two thumbs-up.

"...what you said about me before?" Holt shakes his

head. "Never mind. I don't want to know. Get some food, Brystin."

I'm too hyper focused to eat and hyped up with nervous energy that has me pacing the room. "What do we do, Holt? How do people know? Is this going to fuck up the show? Is my contract going to be canceled? Will you get kicked off the board? I thought you said you controlled the news. Isn't the *City Post* an SNC paper? They had Hunter's quote front and center."

"Whoa, there. That's a lot at once." He seems relatively unconcerned with getting to my questions though as he opens a coffee lid. "Two hazelnut creams, no sugar, right?"

I pause my pacing to exchange a glance with Zully. "Um...yes." I can't ever remember having coffee with him. "Do I just read like the two cream no sugar type?"

"It was your breakfast order every day at Adeline." He must notice my gaping mouth when he puts the doctored coffee in my hand. "I was curious, okay? I asked the staff."

I've been with Michael for how long, and he still sometimes forgets I prefer hazelnut.

It means nothing, it means nothing.

And this isn't the time to get all puppy dog on him anyway.

I take a sip of the coffee, and proceed with my badgering. "Do we need to release a statement? Should I be getting in touch with the PR team? Or is that something Michael should do?"

Since I haven't made a move to grab a taco, Holt unwraps one for me and puts it in my hand while I throw questions at him. Despite being too cool for school at the moment, I don't miss his flinch at Michael's name.

"Brystin, sit down. Eat your taco. While you eat, I'll tell you why everything is going to be fine."

I don't think I should trust him.

I don't know him well enough, and he has less at risk in this whole thing than I do. Logic says I should watch my own back. I should look out for my own interests. He's likely doing that for himself.

But I have a problem because I do trust him. For no reason other than that he makes me feel taken care of. He makes me feel safe.

I sit down next to Zully and start eating the taco. I take a delicious bite. "Barbacoa. Nice choice."

"I got picadillo." Zully hands it out for me to take a bite. "Good, right?"

"Oh, it is. I've never been brave enough to order that one."

"I got a variety." Holt sits across from me, watching me carefully. "You'll keep eating if I start talking?"

I nod, my mouth full of egg and meat and cheese.

"All right then. Let me go back." He puts a finger up in the air. "We don't really do anything." Another finger pops up, and so on as he counts. "They don't know anything—they're sensationalizing because Hunter made a stupid comment that he knew would be taken as fact instead of opinion. This doesn't fuck up your contract. The show is definitely not canceled. I doubt I'll get kicked off the board over this. If I interfered with every news report about me in the *City Post,* I *would* get kicked off the board. If we released a statement it would mean we consider this an issue, which we don't. I've already spoken to my cousin Scott who is in charge of the PR team, which Michael should have done, but maybe he's been too busy to see the news yet."

Without thinking, I wince at the last comment, realizing what he's implying.

Holt clears his throat. "I'm sorry. That was uncalled for."

"Eh," Zully says, her mouth full. She takes a sip of coffee to swallow it down. "I think it was called for. By the way, if you're curious, I take mine black."

I almost spit with laughter.

But I quickly sober up again. "What do you mean we don't do anything? This undermines the entire brand that I've worked so hard to build. No one will tune in."

"Everyone will tune in," he insists.

"Not for the right reasons."

"Maybe not at first. But I wouldn't have hired you if I didn't think you would prove yourself as soon as you opened that beautiful mouth."

I try very hard to ignore the palpitations happening in my heart.

"Look, Brystin. You're going to get criticized no matter what. The more successful you are, the more criticism. A lot of it, unfounded. A good deal of it legit too, but if you react to it all the same, no one knows the difference. What matters is that you continue to stay focused on your goals. The rest is noise."

"'The rest is noise,'" I repeat.

"Loud noise, sometimes, but noise all the same." He smiles, and I swear it's like he still has that toy pressed against my clit, the way my female parts light up. "Have you ever tried Googling my name?"

I have, of course. There were a lot of scandals, but

nothing I can remember off the top of my head. Which is maybe his point.

Next to me, Zully types something into her phone. "'SNC Continues History of Nepotism by Giving Primetime Show to CEO's Latest Girlfriend.' That's what comes up when I Google."

He laughs. "Well, today, yes. Next week, it will be something else. The world doesn't burn down. I've still got my job. You're still going to be America's next top journalist."

I stopped crying a while ago now, but tears of a different kind prick at my eyes.

Zully turns to me, pointing a finger in Holt's direction. "You should consider losing that other guy and hooking up with this one."

I cover my face with my hand. "Zully!"

"Just sayin'."

The worst part is that when I dare look at Holt to see his reaction, he doesn't seem at all appalled. Maybe he's ignoring her comment completely.

But then he says, "You're moving up, Brystin."

And he could very well be continuing his pep talk from before, but I'm fairly sure he intends the double meaning, and now I'm starting to wonder…if I fall for this guy—is there actually a chance he might fall for me too?

CHAPTER TWENTY-TWO

BRYSTIN

"I have one," Zully pipes up. "Hunter Sebastian made some frank comments regarding the reason you were hired for this show. Do you have a response?"

"That's a good one," Holt says. "You should come work for me."

"I already do, thank you, but I appreciate the offer."

On any other day, I'd love that they're getting along so well, but I'm too focused on myself at the moment. "Good one, like it's probably a question I'll be asked? Or good one because it was creatively asked?"

"The former, unfortunately." At least he smiles as he delivers the news. Holt's smile makes everything less daunting.

Thankfully, he's been smiling a lot this last hour as he and Zully have helped me prep for all the interviews I'm booked for leading to the show's debut while we finished breakfast. According to Holt and the PR team, our best way to get past the negative coverage is to flood the media with new headlines.

Up until now, the hardest question they've given me was *explain your relationship with Holt Sebastian,* which flustered me for a hot minute until Holt coached me to answer truthfully, but only focus on the professional aspects.

"Okay, fine." I blow the air out of my lungs, shake my arms out, and then lower my head. When I raise it again, I'm in interviewee mode. "Unfortunately, these are the kinds of comments that are made against any woman who makes headway in a man's world. It's a sad display of toxic masculinity and misogyny. If the roles had been reversed—say if Adly Sebastian were the current CEO—and she gave an undiscovered male anchor a show, no one would call that man a 'whore'—see there isn't even a male equivalent for the word—but he wouldn't be called any other names for that matter, and Adly wouldn't be accused of nepotism because men don't have to prove themselves in our culture the way that women do.

"Honestly, it's one of the reasons Holt fought to get *Our Nation Now* on the air. Because women-led news needs to be normalized, and I'm grateful I've been given the opportunity to be part of this progressive change in programming."

"Brava," Zully says, clapping her hands.

Holt, though, wears a serious expression. "Follow-up question—if SNC is so focused on women-led news programming, why did they recently part with long-term female anchor Jessa Jones?"

My stomach tightens at the reminder of how my show replaced my idol's, and I frown at the man who posed the question. "So you do the shit behavior, and I'm the one who has to answer for it?"

"You're my employee, and that's your job."

I refrain from rolling my eyes and put on my happy interviewee face. "I'm not personally privy to Jessa Jones's contract details nor her reasons for leaving SNC. You'd have to ask someone who gets paid a lot more than me."

Holt is not amused. "You'd have to ask Jessa Jones directly," he suggests instead. "You might even mention that she's taken a job at SHE as a producer and part-time anchor, which could be considered a promotion."

"She has?" SHE is a fledgling news network with a mission to deliver progressive and balanced coverage with transparency in all their decisions. While it's also owned by a man, there are more women than men on the executive team, and the company has announced publicly that their salaries are commensurate.

It's actually exactly the kind of place I'd like to work one day. When I'm older and nearing retirement. "Was that the real reason Jessa left SNC? Because she wanted to?"

Holt gives a slight shrug. "You'd have to ask Jessa Jones directly."

"Ha ha." I try not to give him the satisfaction of smiling, but I can't resist when Zully bursts out laughing for real.

"It wasn't that funny," I insist.

"What can I say? I like the guy." She stands, pulling her hair with both hands to tighten her high pony. "It's been fun, but since we did your nails yesterday, B, I booked a full face job for noon. Which means I need to leave, like, now."

Holt waggles his brows suggestively. "Full face job sounds like a euphemism."

"I'm sure it would sound that way to you, Mr. I'd Like to Get To Know You Biblically Before You're Hired. Should I be flattered or offended that I didn't get the same proposal?"

"Oh my God, Zully. I told you all that in confidence." My face is so hot that I don't really dare to look at Holt, but I brave it anyway. "Sorry about…her."

As always, he seems unaffected. As though he couldn't care less that I told my best friend that he offered me a job in exchange for sexual favors.

Ignoring me, he addresses her directly. "Brystin signed up for double duty in your place."

She gives me a faux scowl. "Fucking Brystin. I could have handled him."

"Are you suggesting we revisit your contract?"

I know Holt's teasing, but my chest tightens with jealousy all the same. Clearly, she needs to go.

"Okay, this is getting weird." I stand up so that I can escort her from the apartment.

Well, that and chide her quietly at the door. "I can't believe you said that out loud!"

"Oh, please. He already knows I know everything. He's perceptive and so obviously into you. It's not a detail he would have missed."

"So obviously into me?"

"He asked his staff how you take your coffee, Brystin. And he's fucking here, unlike Mr. Endlich."

"Because Michael knows you're here."

"Holt knew I was here too, and he still came running. Also, unlike the douche you call a husband, this guy seems to actually see you as a person instead of as a coattail to ride to the top."

It's my turn to say, "Oh, please. If anything, I'm the one riding Michael's coattails."

"I love you, but you really need to get a reality check." She hugs me quickly then opens the door, but pauses when she's halfway over the threshold. "Also, also—Holt was always going to give you that job. You've said that. Have you asked yourself why he decided to play this game with you instead?"

"Because he's a rich dick." But even as I give her the standard answer I've given myself, I realize there might be more to it. There's been chemistry from moment one. On both sides. "Clearly, he wanted to get in my panties all along."

"But just as clearly, you wanted to get into his boxer briefs—and do not correct me if that's not what he wears, because a girl needs to be able to dream."

I can't help myself. "Well, today, I believe he's commando…"

She closes her eyes and throws her head back like she's enjoying the best dessert. "On that note, I'm leaving."

"Bye!"

"Don't be good."

I close the door before she can offer any more nuggets of Zully wisdom that will threaten the carefully crafted belief system I've set up regarding the men in my life.

Men in my life.

Like I ever thought there'd be anyone besides Michael.

I let out a sigh and let go of Zully's fantasy. Whatever is going on with me and Holt, I'm smart enough to know it's a passing phase. He's never had a serious girlfriend, according to the internet, but he's been seen with many different women over the years. He's obviously a player, and I'm just one of his many plays.

I suppose I should enjoy it while it lasts.

With that thought, I head back to the living room, only to find it's empty. "Holt?" I cross to my bedroom, sure I'll find him snooping through my lingerie or browsing through my books in search of a diary. Whatever he thinks will make me the most uncomfortable, since that seems to be his kink. Him being in there at all is embarrassing since my bed is still unmade from two days ago, and I have bras hanging on my bedpost.

But when I peek in my room, I realize he's not there either.

Ah, fuck.

I take off for Michael's bedroom, and sure enough…

"Was this a special occasion?" Holt is holding the one picture Michael has in his room of us together.

"The day he was recognized as producer of the year. It was a New Jersey only award." I rarely invade Michael's space, so I feel antsy with Holt in here. "Can you put it back now?"

He puts it down, but only so he can examine the other items on Michael's dresser. A few images from other important days in his career. Various trophies he's acquired over the years. Holt scans over them quickly, then spins to take in the rest of the room. "There isn't a wedding picture anywhere."

"We didn't have a photographer." I know how it

sounds, and I try to make it sound...*less*...like it does. "We had a small ceremony at City Hall."

"City Hall?" He sounds disgusted.

"We didn't want to make a big production. We're not into those sorts of symbolic gestures. It's a waste of money. What matters is our commitment to each other."

"Do you really mean 'we' or is that really a 'he'?"

I don't know how to answer. In the past, I would have sworn I was on board with all of that too, but honestly? I was so into him, I would have taken whatever parts of himself that he was willing to give.

And that's exactly what I did. Took the pieces. Hoped I could give more in exchange and call us whole.

It's not a topic I should try to analyze when Holt's around, so I sweep those thoughts from my mind. "We shouldn't be in here, Holt."

He ignores me, and sits on the end of the perfectly made bed. "Has he ever made you come in this bed?"

I shake my head because I don't want to do this with him, but before I can say that, he assumes the shake is an answer to his question.

"He hasn't? Has he even ever fucked you in here?"

I know better than to answer.

Why am I so bad at being smart when I'm with this guy? "We've never had sex on that bed."

"Really." It's not a question. More of a processing statement. "Do you not fuck at all?"

"Come on," I say, because most people assume I'm a trophy wife, and isn't sex part of the job requirement? And because I can't bring myself to tell Holt that I have sex with my husband.

Or that I *had* sex with my husband, pretty regularly until Holt came around.

"So you fuck. Just not in here." He takes that in, adds these new pieces to whatever picture he's already formed regarding my marriage. "Your bed is the copulation bed, then."

"Holt, this conversation is…" *Strange, bad, uncomfortable, too revealing.*

He stands up suddenly. "Come here."

"Why?"

"Just come here."

Reluctantly, I trudge toward him. As soon as I'm next to him, he pushes me toward the mattress. "I have to make you come on this bed."

I pull away. "What? No!"

"Yes. I have to."

"You don't have to do anything of the sort." Though, admittedly—traitorously—my lady bits are slick with the thought.

"I do. I can't not make you come on this bed. It's all I'm going to think about until I do." Again, he pushes me toward the mattress. "Up here. On all fours. I'm going to make you come real good. I promise."

I don't know why, but I allow him to direct me into place.

Okay, I *do* know why—because Holt gives really good orgasms, and like his cousin said, I'm kind of Holt's whore. Which sounds really fucking hot at the moment, despite how fucking ugly it felt an hour ago when I first read it.

"Spread your legs and back up a little." When my knees are near the edge of the bed, he praises me, and then reaches around my waist to undo the drawstring of his sweats. They're so loose, he easily pulls them down to gather at my knees, exposing my pussy for him.

"You're already wet." He slides a finger down my seam. "It's the praise, isn't it? You like when I call you a good girl?"

"I..." Why is it so hard to admit?

Without warning, his hand smacks across my ass. "You like it a little mean, too. So easy to please, my honeybee. You'll take the sweet, you'll take the sting, won't you?"

Yes. I'll take whatever you give.

My modus operandi. To my detriment and my delight.

And then I can't be bothered with examining what I'm into any further because Holt's tongue is suddenly on my clit, I'm moaning into the mattress, and I'm no longer capable of functional thought.

He's aggressive immediately, sucking and nipping then licking down my slit so he can tongue-fuck my hole before returning to my clit. It's a form of feasting I've never experienced, and I always considered Michael good at cunnilingus. Apparently there was room for improvement, and within a handful of minutes, Holt has put every pussy-eating experience I've ever had to shame.

"Ah, fuck." I wrap my fingers into the bedspread, stars already forming behind my eyelids.

Holt responds with another slap on my ass, and the sounds that follow—a zipping and then skin against skin—tells me that he's jerking himself off at the same time.

God. I can't even see him and yet...

Why is it so hot?

My orgasm comes much too fast and borderline too

strong. The world goes black, and I'm lost. Spinning in an ecstasy that should be illegal, or at the very least, ethically wrong. To be sure, it might actually *be* wrong. The same factors that have my toes curling and my body shaking are the same ones that will keep me up tonight in confusion—we're in my husband's bed; he's not my husband; he makes me feel too good in comparison.

Is it the wrongness that makes my body react so right?

If Michael weren't in the picture, if it were just Holt and me, would the attraction still exist for either of us? Would the orgasms be this good? Would he still "come for me"?

I'm sweating and dizzy as I start to find my place in the world again, as if that's possible, since I'm pretty sure my world will never be the same. Even after the mind-blowing O, I'm unsatiated, wishing and wanting for more.

Which is why I don't fight when Holt is no longer kneeling, but instead standing behind me, his swollen cock sliding against my slick folds.

"I could do it," he says. "I could fuck you right now. Get it over for both of us."

I don't breathe. The decision is too difficult in my current state. My brain is too unbalanced with lust to make an honest choice.

It's also too dazed to put a stop to him.

So I make the decision not to decide. I leave it up to him.

He pulls back and slides his cock against my folds again, letting his crown nudge my sensitive clit, which sends another skittering of shivers through my body.

"Fuck." It's almost indiscernible. A curse spoken so quietly, I'm not sure I was meant to hear, and this time when he pulls back, he returns with his head notched at my hole.

"Just the tip." He pushes in, just an inch before retreating. "The virtuous girls I dated in high school played this game. Just the tip, and it won't count."

His thick crown pokes in again, and it's all I can do not to thrust my hips backward in invitation. In acceptance.

"Just the tip," he repeats. "That's what I'd promise, and then when I got them in this position, I'd push all the way in, virginity be fucking damned." His palm rubs my haunch. "That's who I am, Brystin. Don't trust me. I could fuck you now, and you'd let me. Don't say you wouldn't."

I open my mouth, not sure what response is waiting on my tongue.

"Don't. Say. A thing." He sounds like it's taking every effort for him to speak, and I want so much to please him that I swallow the words in my mouth. "If you say no, I still might do it. If you say yes, I don't want the guilt of knowing I changed your mind."

My last orgasm is still fresh in my limbs, and yet I've never felt so empty. Like I've been carved out and hollowed, and Holt's cock is my only chance of feeling filled. And I know it's just sex. I know it doesn't last. It's a momentary need, and as soon as he puts his dick away, that emptiness won't seem so bulging.

But it will still be there.

I will still be empty, and I'll keep chasing a way to fill that hole. I'll keep chasing career accolades and Michael's love and neither will ever, ever be enough.

Could it be different with Holt? Could he love me back and be…more?

It's too big of a question, and I'm cum drunk and a fool, and I need Holt inside me right the fuck now.

"Please?" I beg. "Please."

"Ah, fuck. Brystin."

I'm a thousand percent sure that the next thing I'll feel is the thrust of his cock, filling me up to the hilt.

But right before he drives in, there's a sound from the other room.

We both freeze. Which means Holt heard it too.

I strain my ears. And then... "Brystin? Are you here?"

"Fuck!" I repeat the word over and over as I scramble to my feet, pulling up Holt's sweats and tying them as fast as I can while he puts his very erect cock inside his pants. "Fuck, fuck, fuck, fuck, fuck."

Hurriedly, I smooth out the covers as best as I can. "In here!" I call out, then pull Holt over to the dresser so that when Michael shows up in the doorframe of his room, it looks believable when I say, "I was just showing Holt your Dupont award."

On cue, Holt picks up the metal bar to inspect the engraving. "Lighter than I thought it would be." He returns it to its spot. "It's cute."

I want to slug him for the passive-aggressive show of male superiority, reducing a respected journalism award to "cute," while simultaneously praying that my husband doesn't have a habit of glancing down at men's crotches because commando Holt means that he currently has a tent in his jeans.

"I didn't expect you to be here, Holt. Where's Zully?" Michael looks from me to Holt. Back to me. He's not an idiot. If I had any decency, I wouldn't push the façade.

I'm pretty sure all my decency flew out the window the minute I laid eyes on Holt Sebastian, and so I cross to Michael and give him a peck on the cheek, even though I rarely greet him this way normally. "Zully had an appointment. Holt came by after he saw the news today. You saw it?"

"Quite a scandal to wake up to," Holt says, as unfazed as ever.

His expression is hard and unreadable as he again looks from me to Holt. "That's why I came home early. You weren't answering your texts. I knew you'd be worried."

See, Zully? Michael came for me too.

Somehow it doesn't feel the same.

"My phone's charging. I haven't looked at it all morning. Holt has been coaching me for my interviews. And he talked to PR. They don't think it's going to be an issue." I'm smiling too much and too wide, and I don't know what to do with my hands, and I'm keenly aware that I'm still wearing Holt's clothes and that there's a faint smell of sex in the air.

But Holt acts as though he's the king of innocence. "Not worried about the publicity at all," he confirms. "Scott agrees that we shouldn't address it head-on, but I've prepped Brystin's responses, and I've sent someone to pay the doorman at your Manhattan apartment to say he saw her there last night as well as leaving with you this morning."

Well, I hadn't been aware of that.

And now, Michael knows I didn't spend last night in my own bed.

Holt doesn't know we have a completely open marriage

or that the "no intercourse" rule is just mine. He has his suspicions, but I've never validated them, and if he was wrong, this information could be a bomb drop to my relationship with Michael.

It might be a bomb drop regardless.

I should be more worried about it. Should be mad at Holt. Should be concerned about Michael's reaction. Should be, at this very moment, mentally preparing my defense.

But the only thing I'm thinking about as Holt shakes Michael's hand, and passes close enough for him to likely get a whiff of pussy breath, is how soon I can be alone with Holt again.

And when I am, how long it will be before my rule is officially broken.

CHAPTER
TWENTY-THREE
HOLT

"God, finally. Where have you been? Steele already left, and I'm already drunk." Adly is the most mature of me and my siblings most of the time, but whenever she gets a little intoxicated, she lets loose and I'm reminded of the chubby cheeked wild child that got in as much trouble as her two older brothers, if not more.

Honestly, I think she should let her guard down more often. But not necessarily when I'm around. She can be a lot of fun, and I can be a lot protective, which doesn't make a good time for either of us.

She's on her own tonight, though. My attention is elsewhere.

I sit down on the stool next to her and nod to the bartender before I respond. "I'm sorry. It's been a day."

Hopefully, that's a sufficient recap of the last twenty-four hours. Despite assuring Brystin that the news leaked this morning was nothing to be concerned about, I've spent the ten hours since I left her house, doing cleanup. It's not like I lied to her. *There is no bad publicity* is a motto I firmly live by, but that doesn't mean that I could let Hunter's comment to the press ride.

First, I called an emergency meeting of the board where I vehemently recommended he be removed since his actions could be seen as a plot to undermine the company. I knew it was futile. Half of the members, including my father, couldn't be there on such short notice. Hunter didn't even feel threatened enough to show up.

Nevertheless, it felt productive.

The same way it felt productive to yell at the managing editors of the *City Post,* telling them that if they ever again published the word *whore,* or any other salacious comment about Brystin Shaw, they would immediately be fired, no matter who said it.

Again, futile. The news is the news, and if it's a Sebastian who made the remark, it's going to be front page. If I stepped in and prevented that from happening, it would be the board calling an emergency meeting about me.

In the end, I did get my employees to agree that they would be more careful about quoting derogatory comments about women in general, which felt like a win, and on my way to meet Adly at the club, Hunter's father, Reynard, called to let me know that he didn't approve of Hunter's actions and would see to it that he worked more to support the family's interests.

That doesn't mean Reynard and I are on friendly terms, by any means, but it does feel like I might finally get some reprieve from Hunter's constant attacks. Though, I might fuck that possibility if I go through with my plans tonight.

But you know what? It will be worth it.

"Want to tell me about it?" Adly asks out of habit, but her sloppy mannerisms say she's in no state for a serious conversation. She doesn't even give me a chance to answer before distracting herself with another topic. "It can't be worse than Dad's news. I'm seriously disturbed. It's going to be so fucking weird."

Great. I don't have the energy for whatever this is.

Thankfully, the bartender sets a glass of something red in front of me like a gift from the gods. "What is it?" I ask as I bring it up to my nose. Not that I don't trust Denim. He always works Saturday nights at Spice, and knows what I like.

"La Playa Estate Merlot, 2019. One of the best Chilean wines I've tasted in a long time. I discovered it a couple of weeks ago, and made sure to save a bottle for you."

"It smells like suede." It's a unique bouquet for sure. I'm pretty sure I also detect berries and a mossy scent. The first swallow is smooth, while flavors of cherries, stewed plums, and spices tantalize my tongue. "Very nice."

It really is an excellent wine, but even now, the taste of Brystin's cunt permeates. It's a flavor that has been branded into my neural pathways. One that I swear will be the measure for any other flavor that touches my palate for the rest of my life. It's distracting, to say the least.

Let's not even mention how my dick feels after the sample it got today. It's a miracle that I was able to stop. Even after I heard Michael's voice, I was tempted to push all the way in and fuck her like she deserved. Fuck her right there in front of him on his prissy-ass bed.

Yeah, I really need this drink.

Denim gives me a hand gesture to say he's got me and then leaves to attend to other customers, which leaves me attending to Adly, who is practically clawing at my jacket to get my attention. "Do you think we'll have to be in the ceremony? What are we even supposed to call her?"

I stare at my sister, wishing I could ignore whatever this is, but I'm getting the sense that I can't. "What the fuck are you talking about, Ad?"

"Oh my God!" She throws her hands up in the air in frustration, or more like she's about to strangle me. "You and Steele never read the goddamn sibling text thread. It's maddening. I'm talking to the void in there. Do you think I want to repeat myself every—"

"Adly," I cut her off sharply. "I don't fucking care about this right now. I have other shit. So get to the point, or leave it for another time."

There's no way she can leave it. "Dad," she says. As if I hadn't already gathered that part. "He's getting married."

Whoa.

That is…

I don't even know how to process this. "No, he's not. He can't be. What do you mean he's getting married? Did he tell you that? He's not dating anyone."

"I know. That's what I said. He called me this morning, super early because the time diff and everything, because he wanted to tell me. He said, he's old enough 'to know' and that Giulia is the real deal, and he's, like, 'over the moon.'" She leans in close to enunciate her point, so close, I can smell the lemon drop martinis on her breath. "He literally said he was over the moon, Holt. I don't know who he is anymore. It's almost like I should be happy for him, but..." She shrugs.

I shake my head, unable to put the words she's saying into a proper shape. "He's been in Italy for that business deal for...what? Three weeks? And now he's telling you he's getting married? It's a joke, Ad. He's pranking you."

Odd because he's never been the pranking type, but it's easier to believe that than the idea that something massive happened to him, and he didn't bother to call me.

"He's not pranking. It's for real. He's gaga over her. He sent me a pic, but I don't have my phone, obviously. I'll send it to you later."

"You have a picture? Why didn't he tell me or Steele?"

Again, she shrugs. "Probably knew you were busy with all that Hunter shit."

I roll my eyes. Fucking selfish Adly. If she knew about the 'Hunter shit,' she already knew what kind of day I was having, and she expects me to have room to focus on this bullshit?

I'm too annoyed now to continue the conversation. Turning away from Adly, I take a big swallow of my wine.

The dismissal only prompts her to get in my face again. "He's in love, Holt." She sings the word *love*, drawing it out over a couple of notes. "It's almost adorable."

She knows exactly the words to draw me back. "No. He can't possibly love her. He does *not* love her. She's probably got big tits and a warm cunt."

"Holt," she says, cringing. "You're so—"

I cut her off. "She's a trophy wife, if anything. He's bored. He isn't running the company and now he's fucking bored." That's got to be it. Hundreds of women have lined up to be Dad's second wife over the years, trying to get their nails into his money. Why else would he suddenly be interested? "A thousand bucks says it's off before he even gets back in the country."

"Maybe." Adly doesn't seem to agree.

I see in her eyes exactly when she gets in my brain. "No, no, no, Holt. You can't try to pay her off. Let Dad have this. You can't—"

But I don't hear the end of that sentence because the voice behind me is louder. "Holt, you made it."

I turn around to my cousin Reid, and with him is his brother Alex. Both are Reynard's younger sons, and while they're both monster dicks, I actually get along with Reid quite well.

"I wouldn't miss your birthday party." I slap him on the back as we hug. "If it were me, I would have chosen to celebrate somewhere other than where I work, but you know. Spice is fine enough."

"Fuck you." He smiles, though, knowing I'm joking because let's be honest—I would totally have my birthday party at SNC. Reid is just as dedicated to the club.

It's one of the reasons we get along so well. He cares about the actual work and not just trying to climb the Sebastian status ladder like so many of our kin. So much so, he basically took himself out of the running for any top positions at the two main companies our family owns—the news network and the industrial corporation—and somehow bargained with his father to get a loan against his trust fund so he could buy and manage his own private club.

Sure the club is located at the Sebastian Center, but for

our family standards, it's really as close to doing his own thing as anyone gets.

"Thirty-three," I say. "You're as old as Adly now. Can you handle your liquor any better than she can?"

"Ha ha." She turns toward Reid. "He's upset 'cause Dad is getting married."

"No, I'm not." I mean, I might be, but I have other things weighing heavier on my mind.

"He's still standing, anyway. For now. We'll see how he feels when the shots kick in." It's maybe the friendliest thing Alex has said to me in a while. Most of the time he doesn't talk to me at all since he's usually hanging out with Hunter.

Reid dismisses the idea that he's anywhere near inebriated. "Shots are for teenagers. I'm fine." He's certainly thinking clearly enough to pick up on Adly's comment. "Uncle Sam's getting married?"

Adly jumps on the chance to discuss today's tea. "Right? It's crazy. We've never even met her."

Reid looks to me for my take.

I put my hand up, not interested in delving into that with my cousins. "Just rumors at the moment. I'll keep you posted."

Then, because I'm also selfish and also a monster dick, I focus my attention on the real reason I came tonight. "Hunter here?"

"Yeah, he's…" Reid stops himself, then narrows his eyes in my direction. "What do you need Hunter for?"

I guess I could have been less obvious.

My lack of a response confirms any suspicions he has. "There's a rule, Holt."

Oh, yes. The rule.

Instituted by Grandpa Irving years ago. *When you're in the Sebastian Center, you're on the side of the Sebastians.*

In other words, this is neutral territory, and for the most part, every one of us behave when we're on this sacred block of Manhattan. Sure, we snark and jab at each other, but we don't do or say anything that will cause real harm. Not here. It's one of the reasons most family events are planned on the property. Any other locale has the opportunity to bring drama.

I've followed the rule to a T until now. Tonight, I'm making an exception. "Hunter should have thought about the rule before he issued a public attack last night at the concert hall."

"It wasn't a direct attack," Reid says.

"It was sure the fuck close enough," Alex pipes in, which is surprising since he's usually team Hunter.

"See? Even Alex agrees. So have you seen him?" I cast my gaze across the crowd, trying to see if I can spot him myself.

"It's my fucking birthday, man," Reid protests. "In *my* club. Can't you find him on his own turf?"

I could, but the other benefit about going after Hunter here means that whatever happens won't get out to the press. Reid has a strict phone check-in policy at the front door. It allows celebrities of all types to be assured privacy, which makes this one of the hottest clubs for the elite.

We all know that, so there's no point in explaining.

There's also no point in expecting Hunter's *real* brothers to turn on him. "Don't worry about it. I'll find him on my own."

"If you're looking for Hunter"—Adly suddenly tunes into the conversation—"he's with Ax. Playing pool."

"You made your way around the club earlier?" I'm curious how she knows that.

She looks confused for a moment, the alcohol affecting her cognition, perhaps. "He's always with Ax."

That doesn't explain how she knows they're in the pool room, but I don't really care about the answer because as soon as I turn toward the pool tables, I spot Hunter and his best bud Ax racking up.

Bingo.

Without excusing myself, I head toward the pair, my eyes pinned on my adversary the whole time. I'm only a few strides from them when Ax finally notices me.

"Hey, boss," he says, dripping with disrespect.

God, I wish I could fire his ass.

Hunter looks up. "Holt."

Just in time to see my fist coming toward him before it makes contact with his face.

"Fuck!" His hand immediately comes up to cover his jaw. "Fuck you, fucking Holt."

"No, fuck you. Deserved." I shake my fist out, trying to hide how painful the punch was on my end, which isn't too hard because the satisfaction definitely outweighs the physical pain.

Not surprising, Adly, Reid, and Alex followed me over. Reid handles the crowd that is starting to gather while Alex jumps in to make sure that Hunter doesn't throw back. Ax puts a hand out in my direction, as though that would stop me if I wanted to land another punch.

Adly, on the other hand, looks as smug as I feel. "Take that," she shouts, as if she's the one who threw the hit.

Hunter moves his jaw back and forth, testing it. Unfortunately, it doesn't seem broken, but there is blood when he spits. "If you broke my tooth…"

"You'll what? Whine to the press again? You got a problem with me, you address it with me." Because that's really the issue. None of this has to do with SNC or the CEO position. It definitely doesn't have anything to do with Brystin. It has to do with me and Hunter, and what we are to each other. The secret relationship our family has kept from the world.

"Proved my point, though," he says. "That she's your girlfriend."

"Girlfriend was not the word you used, Hunter." It's the second time Alex has taken the opposing side tonight, and I have to wonder if he's finally seeing what a douche our brother is or if he just has enough morals to know he crossed a line.

"He thinks whores *are* girlfriends," Adly says, like a tough guy. "Since he pays all of the women he's seen with."

"Stay out of it, little girl." Ax leers at Adly, and now I might punch *him*.

"Hey, hey." Reid steps in between us. "No more swinging or I'm barring all of you for life."

Since I can't punch, I point my finger at Ax instead. "Watch your fucking mouth, Morgan. I'm still your boss. I can make your life miserable." Then I turn the point to Hunter. "Don't you ever fucking say anything about Brystin again. Or I swear to God, I'll kill you with my bare hands."

He smiles, like I've walked into his trap, and I probably

have. He thinks he knows my Achilles' heel now, and of course, he does. "Looks like Holt has feelings after all."

Adly laughs. "Only thing he'll ever love is his job. If you knew anything about him, you'd know that, you, you, twat...scum."

"Twatscum?" Ax sneers. "Nice one, Adly."

Words might be hard to access in her inebriated state, but she's right about me. Love is not in my cards. I won't allow it. I've seen the damage it does. More importantly, I've seen how it is never enough.

Hunter ignores our sister, though, his eyes still pinned on me like I'm a target. "She's a married woman," he says, goading me on.

But I prepped myself while I was prepping Brystin, and I have the right comeback waiting. "She's not my girlfriend, you piece of filth. She's a *person*. An innocent person who doesn't need to be caught in our crossfire."

"Sure, sure. An innocent person who has never sucked your cock."

I'm so close to tearing into him right now. The only thing stopping me is knowing that's what he wants. "You want my job, Hunter? Then go after it like every other Sebastian who wants the position. Prove yourself. Prove you can do better. Your obsession with me makes you appear unhinged. Bringing your fight to the media makes you look desperate. These pathetic strikes at the people around me make you look soft. The board might kick me out one day, but they'll never put a weak, desperate dumpster fire like you in my place."

I can tell my words hit because he looks like he's about to make a run at me until Reid turns to face him, blocking his pathway. "He's not wrong. Derogatory shit like that looks worse for you than for him. Misogyny isn't in anymore."

Surprisingly, there's a light of understanding behind his eyes. A recognition that he may have made a mistake. Gone too far. I hadn't thought it was possible for him to be so self-aware.

I take advantage of the recognition, and tie it in a bow. "This is done now, Hunter. You pull this kind of shit again, I'll take it to Grandpa Irving. You know he won't stand for it, and how will you possibly destroy me if you're kicked out of the fold? This is done."

The adrenaline is coursing through my veins, which means I need to get out of here before I pick another fight, so I turn to leave, but can't stop myself from throwing another dig at Ax. "Look at my sister again like you're undressing her, and I'll personally remove your eyes."

Thank you, she mouths as I pass by. Then shouts after me, "I can fight my own battles, you know."

That's Adly. Proudly feisty, privately gracious.

No one comes after me. Probably everyone's glad I'm leaving before I cause more chaos. Since I've already broken the rules, I pull out my phone before I've hit the club exit. I hold it in my hand, my thumb hovering over Brystin's number. She's the only one I want to talk to right now. The only one I ever want to talk to, these days.

But if I call her…then what?

She's married. She's not mine. I can't tell her about tonight. That I protected her name like she belongs to me because she doesn't. It doesn't matter that she likes the games we've been playing because I forced her into them. It doesn't matter that I can make her come better than that piece of shit because he's the one who gets her pussy.

Eye on the prize, Holt.

I hired Brystin because she's good for SNC, and I want to earn this job. I want to prove myself. I want the board to know I was the right choice. I want my father to be proud. That's the goal. The fun with her was an added benefit, but now it's taking too much of my attention. What I said to Hunter should be said to myself—this is done now.

This has to be done.

CHAPTER TWENTY-FOUR

BRYSTIN

"...Then when that dick kept refuting you with national policies, and how the president is trying to make these mandates, but you shut him down like a badass. 'We're specifically talking about local policies, Doug. This show is only about local policy. Please don't bring up the national government again.' I swear people cheered in the viewing room." Zully finally takes a breath. "And we get to do this again tomorrow. This job is fucking A-mazing, B."

She's talked nonstop since we left the production floor, recapping every moment of the debut episode of *Our Nation Now*. She's in fangirl mode, and I appreciate it more than she can know because I barely remember anything that happened. "Is that really what I said?"

"Damn straight you did! Like I said—total badass."

The whole thing is a blur to me. I went on autopilot and let my instinct guide me. Adrenaline is still coursing through me, and my body is shaking and my mind is dazed as we follow the rest of the crew to Panache for the celebratory reception. The one conscious thought I have plays on a loop in my mind. *I fucking just hosted my first national news show. I fucking did it.*

Pinch me, because is this really my life?

I vaguely note the Closed for Private Event sign as we walk through the lobby of the restaurant, and then we're rounding the corner to the main room, and applause erupts.

"Oh wow." My throat feels tight. This is not how I imagined this would feel. It's different…and better. Harder to process than I'd expected. Impossible to actually be in the moment because I'm too buzzed to absorb the emotions.

At my side, Zully squeezes my hand then lets me go so Michael and I can embrace.

"We did it, sweet girl." He pulls back to kiss me on the lips, but it's the kind of kiss I'd exchange with any producer. No passion or romance involved. Just excitement and celebration.

Nevertheless, another round of applause breaks out, like someone's just announced the bride. I suppose that's natural when the creative duo in the spotlight are also married, but it feels untrue when I'm scanning the room for the only person I want to see right now, and dying a little inside because he's yet to appear.

And it's not like I can go looking for him. I'm quickly inundated with congratulatory praise from people I know and even more people I don't know. Important people. People whose names I need to remember. People who had a big part in making this happen. Axle Morgan, the head of programming. Scott Sebastian, the head of public integrity.

Adly Sebastian, the head of HR. Then so many more Sebastians with titles I can't keep straight.

So many Sebastians that aren't Holt.

Almost an hour goes by before I first see him, but he's across the room, deeply wrapped up in a conversation with someone I don't know, and the stream of people wanting to talk to me still hasn't died down. I don't see him again until Michael's assistant hushes the room to announce that the early viewing numbers surpassed what we'd expected, and then it's like I have to go through all the rounds again so people can congratulate me for and comment on this specific achievement as well.

Two hours later, my heels are pinching, I haven't managed to eat more than two bites, and Holt has yet to talk to me, though we've exchanged a couple of glances, always from across the room.

"He's avoiding me," I whisper to Zully when she comes to refresh my champagne. At a natural volume I refuse the refill. "I've barely eaten. I better not."

"He's not avoiding you. He's busy doing his job like you're busy doing your job."

I glance toward Holt who is talking to Michael now. Across the room, of course. The conversation appears involved, and as I've finally had a break from my own circus, I'm sure I could easily join them without Holt running away.

But I don't want to see Holt with my husband. I want him to myself. I want him away from this room and this crowd, and I want things from him that I shouldn't want.

It's the most intense this longing for him has been. Maybe because I haven't seen him for more than five minutes in the last two-plus weeks since he came to my house. I wanted to believe I hadn't seen him because of the grueling media promotion schedule he had me on in preparation for tonight's debut, but now that we've been in the same room for two hours, I know it's not that. "He's definitely avoiding me, Zul. I think he's done."

She raises one of her perfectly penciled thick brown eyebrows. "Every time I look his way, he's staring at you. He is not done."

But that's just our chemistry. We have no control over that. I feel that same tug to look for him. It's not even conscious, how my head turns in his direction. It's an instinct.

The ability to *act* on that instinct, however, *is* in our control, and I know in my heart that he's purposely staying away. And I know why, too. Because after the last time we were together—when I almost gave him everything, when he almost took it all—I don't think it's possible for us to not be different with each other.

We got too close, and he's being the responsible adult about it.

Why don't I have that same impulse?

"He's done." I'm sure of it, and my throat tightens again, like it did when we first walked into the reception, but this time the threatening tears are not happy.

"Don't do that." Zully reaches for a passing tray, grabbing a napkin, which she dabs under my eyes. "Waterproof mascara only goes so far."

I shrug, afraid speaking might bring on a flood.

She purses those enviably plump lips. "Then don't let

him be done." Like it's that easy, and to be fair, it probably *is* easy for her, no-nonsense rebel that she is.

I wonder what it would be like to be her as I watch Holt wrap up with Michael. Believing I deserved what I wanted. Having the courage to unabashedly pursue my dreams.

Then I remember that my national news show just debuted because I went after it like I was Zuleika Amari. I do have the courage. It's been proven, and so when I see Holt slip into a private dining room in a section of the restaurant we aren't using, I hand Zully my empty champagne glass and follow after.

It's not a direct path. I'm stopped no less than three times, but I've lost my patience, and instead of nodding and smiling, I excuse myself from each encounter. At the dining room, I cast a quick glance over my shoulder to make sure no one is paying attention, then push through the double doors, quickly shutting them behind me.

It's dark, but light slips in around the curtains on the glass doors behind me and reflects in the mirror on the other side of the room. It's enough for me to be able to make out Holt's figure, a few yards in front of me, just standing there.

He's so committed to not talking to me that he's hiding in a dark room by himself. I'd laugh if it didn't hurt. I almost turn around and leave, but force myself to confront him, if it can be called a confrontation when I can barely make out his face. "You're avoiding me."

"No, I'm not." Before I can argue, he takes a couple of steps toward me, and I can see his features better. See that he's sincere. "I'm waiting for you."

Time bends then. The seconds that bring me from where

I am to where he is pass without me noticing them. One moment I'm standing on my own, the next, I'm in his arms, my lips seeking his like it's the only source of oxygen. I think it must be the same for him, because his mouth crashes against mine, desperate and greedy, his teeth clashing against mine in his haste to consume me.

"One time," I say, breathlessly, when he finally lets me up for air.

"One time," he agrees. He pushes me backward until I'm against the wall. "One time, and it's out of our system."

"That's all we need. One time." The lie feels believable when his hands are on me. One time, and we can close the door on this desire. One time, and I can go back to living for my career. Living for whatever it was that I lived for before Holt.

"One time," he repeats, the final syllable turning into a moan as I stroke my palm over the thick outline of his cock. He reciprocates, shoving his hand down my pants and past the band of my panties, quickly finding my clit and applying just the right pressure with his thumb to make me pant like a bitch in heat. His fingers crawl lower, sliding into my wet pussy like a magnetic key. Like he can't resist putting them inside me, even if he wanted to, and once inside, they curl perfectly to rub against a magic spot that has my knees buckling.

"This is mine," he says, and I know it's just sex talk, but I love it. Love being claimed by his hand and his mouth, even if the claim expires after this one momentary time. "This belongs to me."

I whimper as his tongue slips past my lips, mimicking the ministrations of his fingers. Showing me what he's planning to do to me with his cock. Making me so desperate with anticipation that all I can do is cling onto the lapels of his jacket and beg. "Please, Holt. Please take what's yours."

"You think I need your permission?" He leans in to bite my upper lip, and I reach for his belt, only to have my hands shoved away. His gaze is hooded and challenging when it meets mine, but I'm impatient and so full of want, and so I reach for him again.

This time he grabs my wrists and draws them over my head, pinning them to the wall with one hand. My pussy feels instantly empty. Emptier than it had before he fingered me, and I let out a cry of frustration. "Please." Tears form in the corners of my eyes.

He answers with another punishing kiss, this time rocking his hips against mine as our lips dance together. I can feel the whole length of him against my lower belly. So close to where I want him, but an inch too far away, even when I rise up on my tiptoes.

I don't realize he's as frustrated as I am until he releases my hands with a growl, and then immediately unbuckles my pants and pulls them down, along with my thong, maneuvering both over my shoes so that, below my waist, I'm naked, except for my heels.

It feels a bit strange to be fully clothed otherwise, complete with my two chunky necklaces and my hair still in a chignon, but I don't care enough to undress any further. My focus is singularly on Holt's cock. On getting it inside of me as fast as possible.

Without discussion, he hands me a condom from his jacket pocket, and I rip through the wrapper with my teeth while he lowers his pants. I have every intention of putting it on for him, but as soon as his cock springs out, all thick and milky at its head, I'm distracted by its size.

I've fantasized about having that monster inside of me on more than one occasion, but since I never truly believed it would happen, I'm only now understanding what's about to happen. What I'm about to feel. "That's… a lot."

"You're just now realizing this?" Holt smirks then snatches the condom from my hand and rolls it down his very proud cock. Then he pushes my chin up with his knuckles, forcing my eyes from his prize appendage to his. "It will fit. I promise."

"Could you maybe hurry up and prove it?"

He chuckles as he brings his hands under my thighs and lifts me, using the wall as a brace against my back. I wrap my legs around him automatically, and shiver when I feel his ridge slide against my seam. He tilts his pelvis back, and I'm about to help him notch the tip up to my hole, but he doesn't seem to need the help, because next thing I know, he drives forward and thrusts inside.

"Oh my God." Tiny fireworks explode across my nervous system. Almost like a mini orgasm, from one thrust. One very snug thrust. He's enormous, filling me so tightly, I have to take a breath to help him wiggle the rest of the way in.

"Jesus, Brystin, you're so fucking tight around me." His words are tortured, like he's as affected as I am. Like it's taking all his strength to hold still and let me stretch around him.

I'm not even sure he's all the way seated before he gives up trying. "Goddammit," he says, and then he's thrusting in again, again, again, ramming into me with an energy I haven't seen in a partner for years.

"This fucking cunt," he says as he plows into me. "This beautiful fucking cunt…I thought I could resist it, but it owns me. Fucking owns me."

I tighten my legs around him, feeling like I'm the one owned. In my head, I tell him that, but I don't have the ability to say the words out loud. A string of incomprehensible syllables leaks from my mouth, instead, blending with the *slap, slap, slap* of our thighs. I'm vaguely aware that I'm not being that quiet, that there is a whole restaurant full of people—important people, people I know, my husband—outside the room, that the doors next to us are very much unlocked.

Still, I can't keep the pleasure to myself. Every nerve ending is lit. My whole body is a tingling mass of sensation, and euphoria has taken over my brain space. Even the bite of Holt's fingers digging into my thighs to hold me up feels pleasurable, though I'm sure there will be bruises later. Bruises I know that I'll stand before my mirror trying to capture with a photograph so I can have a souvenir.

It's soon—too soon—before my pussy is clenching and impeding Holt's tempo. "Don't you dare slow me down," he orders. "If you're going to try to push me out, then you don't get to come, Brystin. Not until I say you can."

"I don't think I can stop," I say. Or try to say. It comes out as a series of ahs and moans.

"Brystin." His warning is sharp and through gritted teeth, but it's my orgasm controlling me now, and it rolls over me with tsunami force, paralyzing me momentarily before sending waves of bliss through my torso and limbs until I'm a trembling leaf in a storm.

Cursing, Holt waits until my body lets him in again, then stabs into me with a frenetic speed, chasing his own orgasm, which comes soon afterward, but not so soon that I'm not recovered enough to watch his features as he does. His face tenses up, his color seeming to darken, even in the weak light. Then his mouth parts and a groan that might be the most erotic sound I've ever heard escapes.

Afterward, he barely takes a second to catch his breath before dropping my legs to the ground, cuffing my throat with his hand, and kissing me mercilessly. His mouth slows as my heart rate settles, as though he's timing it with my pulse under his palm, and when it doesn't feel like I've just run a race anymore, he slowly pulls back, leaning his forehead against mine.

We stand like that, wordlessly breathing in tandem, and I wait for the shame to descend. For the moment that I feel inclined to mutter excuses and apologies and scurry to dress and depart.

It doesn't come.

Finally, I dare to speak. "By one time we meant like one set of times, right?"

Holt is already nodding his head as he bends to get my pants. "We're going to my office now because I most definitely have to fuck you again."

CHAPTER
TWENTY-FIVE
HOLT

As soon as we walk into my office, I know this is the wrong place to bring her. I spend so much time here, it's more of a second home than Adeline is. One time to fuck her—one session of times—and this fifteen hundred square foot room will be marked with her. How will I ever be able to be productive again with her permeating the space?

But taking her to my penthouse is an even worse idea. Not just because of the paparazzi that might see us entering together or her leaving in the morning, but because it's my one safe spot. A place where I can be without the world, and its conflicts. It was a stupid enough choice to bring her there when she was drunk. I barely slept that night, watching her. Memorizing every twitch of her sleeping form. Placing ghost kisses on the features of her face.

My home is already haunted enough.

Now I'm bringing the ghost to my office as well.

I should have taken her somewhere else. Somewhere still in the building so there's no worry about being caught together. There are plenty of places that will be private at this time of night. The studio. Ax's office. Michael's.

I leave the lights off and consider more suitable locations while she looks over the dimly lit space. There's a lot to see, even in the dark, since so much light enters through the bare windows—a large seating area with two couches, two armchairs, and a coffee table; a table that seats six; an executive desk that is completely clear of anything on the surface; a second desk with my computer; several bookcases; a media wall; a pool table; the mini kitchen; a private bathroom with a shower and jacuzzi.

I'm prepared for one of the typical remarks I get when introducing someone to this space: *This is bigger than my apartment.*

A person could live here if there were a bed.

Want a roommate?

But she doesn't say anything of the sort, heading instead for the wall of glass behind my work desk. "This view… how do you get any work done?"

"It's distracting, I admit." Our building is taller than many around us, and my office is on the highest floor that isn't reserved for tourism. It's an incredible vantage point, but I'm not talking about the same view as she is. My view is of her, standing in the exact spot that I've stood in many a night as I plotted and schemed and worked out strategies for the company. It's always been a good place to think.

Now looking at her in that spot, my chest tightens, and I don't know what's going on inside me, but I'm pretty sure I'm fucked.

So there's no point in leaving. She's already marked this place. Even after she's gone, she'll always be here.

Besides, I'm already hard again, and my dick is in command. I've already crossed to her by the time she turns away from the view, and I meet her lips with mine, kissing her as ravenously as I did downstairs in the restaurant. How can I still be this hungry for her?

It's the pressure, probably. How much I've been working. I haven't made time for fucking anyone in weeks, and I usually schedule it in as regularly as my visits to the executive gym. Brystin and her show have consumed so much of my work life, it's only natural that she's spilled into my recreational life as well.

Tonight will do the trick. Fuck her brains out. Fuck her on all the furniture. Fuck her so hard that she walks into her apartment limping and has to make up excuses to the dickwad she calls a husband. Fuck her so good she'll be out of my system, but she'll never be able to forget.

I kiss her with that intention now, my tongue wrestling with hers while I push her backward until her ass meets my executive desk. Almost frantically, I begin to strip her clothes off, removing her jacket first, then the shell underneath and her bra, pausing our kiss when I need to pull her shirt over her head and breaking it completely when her tits are exposed so I can step back and admire them properly.

Immediately, her arms cross to cover them, but she catches herself, and drops them down nervously at her side. "This would feel more fair if you were undressed too."

I shake my head. "I own you, remember? There is no fair."

She cocks her head, as though annoyed, but then I palm

both breasts, and her annoyance dissolves into a soft sigh of pleasure. They're teardrop shaped and on the smaller side but are firm and perfectly fit my hands. I experiment with my touch, brushing my thumbs lightly over her nipples then squeezing her tits like stress balls, discovering that the rough makes her melt but the soft drives her wild. Such a honeybee with her love of both the sweet and the sting.

I bend to put one in my mouth and pull down her pants at the same time. She doesn't have her thong anymore—I pocketed that after the last round—so she's in nothing but her heels when they're gone. Her nipple is bright red and swollen when I'm done with it, and I have half a mind to make the other one match, but her cunt is bare now, and I need to taste. Need to watch her writhe on my desk while she comes all over my tongue.

As soon as I fall to my knees, she tries to stop me. "No. I want you."

"You're about to get me." My tongue anyway. She'll have to be more specific if she wants something else, and even then, it will be when I decide. "Lean back and spread yourself out, baby, so I can see what's mine."

She fakes a pout but she does as I say. Leaning back on her elbows, her torso fills the width of my desk, and when she props the heels of her shoes on the surface edge, I have to blink because fuck she looks good. "Look at you. Showing off your pussy to the city like you expect them to worship it."

She giggles, but it's tight with tension and need. Suddenly, she starts to sit up, her gaze searching the windows. "No one can actually see me, can they?"

We're way too high up, and with the lights off, it's next

to impossible. But like the theater, it feels like we're being watched, and even cautious as she is, I don't want to rid her of the fantasy. "Doesn't matter who sees. It matters who makes you come."

She's about to argue, but I cut her off with a single swipe of my tongue across her clit, which seems to make her forget what she was fussing about. I linger on the next swipe, burying my face into her skin. It's then I realize the landing strip of hair where she was previously bare. I run my finger over it, and then my tongue. This was for me. She grew this for me.

I don't bring attention to it, afraid to attach too much meaning to a simple choice in grooming style. But before I go back in to eat my fill, I give her a warning. "This pussy has been my torment for weeks. I'm not planning to be nice. Hold on to my hair if you need to. Scream my name when you see stars."

Then I put my hands under her thighs to spread her wider and eat her like the starving man I am. I could feed on her until morning. If my cock wasn't in charge, I actually might. She tastes so sweet. The best a pussy has ever tasted, and I'm quite fond of the taste in general. She comes easily and is squirming on my tongue, screaming my name in no time.

After her second orgasm, she attempts words. "Please, no. I can't. I want you."

I consider torturing her longer, but my cock is angry from neglect so I make my way back to my feet.

"Want what? These?" I stick three fingers inside her, making sure she's ready for me. We moved a little too fast the first time, and I'm worried she won't last the night if I'm too rough.

"No, not your fingers." But she moans as I stroke against a tender spot.

Her cunt is dripping and eager, and I'm already undoing my pants, but I taunt her anyway. "Want my tongue again?"

"No, Holt. I want your cock."

My cock falls out like an escaped prisoner, fat and straining. I'm convinced it isn't possible to be any more hard until her eyes land between my legs, heavy and lust-filled, and my cock swells with pride.

"Say it again. Tell me what you want my cock to do to you." I rub the tip across her opening, finding a strange kind of satisfaction in the excruciating effort it takes not to plow right into her.

"Fill me up," she pants, then shakes her head, as if realizing I'll want her to be more precise. "I want your cock to fill my pussy up, Holt. I want it to fill me up so good it hurts."

Goddamn she's a devil. Asking me to fuck her rough. Making me wonder—if I break it do I get to keep it?

I punish myself a little longer, pushing in bare while I look for a condom. It's agony pulling out to wrap up, but I'm usually a boy scout where protection is concerned, and I've already crossed the line of acceptable behavior.

Once I'm sheathed, it's no holds barred. With my back to the night skyline, I fuck into her at a grueling pace, loving the way her tits bounce and our thighs slap. She wraps her legs around me, and the bite of her heels in my ass adds to the pleasure. I will myself not to come yet, but at this speed, I don't have the best odds.

Then I catch sight of my cock sliding into her, and I have to slow down to watch it again and again and again. Watch how I come out gleaming with her juice. Watch how I disappear into her to the hilt. Wonder if I've already disappeared into her completely.

The question makes strange things happen in my chest. An unfamiliar pinching. A feeling that I've worked hard in my life to avoid.

Only way I know how to deal with it is to pound it out.

Perhaps in a different position this time.

I pull out of her and sink back into my desk chair. She sits up, her makeup running, her hair falling out of her chignon. I love messing her up so much that I almost consider taking her to the shower, just so that I can mess her up again.

But then I'd have to strip, and while I'm dying to be skin-to-skin with her, it's too much. I know I'll lose whatever control I have left. I don't want to think about what would happen then.

"Where did you go?" she asks, and I'm not sure if she means mentally or physically. Maybe both. Her lips look even more swollen when she turns them down like that. "Do you need a break?"

"Fuck no." Because I'm a smug motherfucker, I automatically assume that's what she's used to with her husband. I'm tempted to ask, but decide I'd rather not invite him in here. Instead, I pat my thigh. "Come bounce on my cock, honeybee."

She bites that puffy bottom lip of hers and smiles at the same time. "Okay."

Reaching out a hand, I help her to my lap, positioning her so her back is to my chest. She slides easily onto me, and I let her explore for a while, trying different angles as she bobs up and down while I play with her clit. It's not too long before she finds a spot that seems to light her up, and soon she's tightening with another orgasm.

I consider that my cue to take over. Spinning around so the chair faces the windows, I grip my fingers into her hips and drive into her, eliciting a steady hum of pleasure from her mouth. "This view, Brystin? You know what it represents?" It's hard to talk at this tempo, and my voice sounds raw and gravelly. "This view represents power. That's what you traded this sweet little cunt for. You wanted what this view could give you, and I wanted this cunt. I'm pretty sure I got the better end of the deal."

Wrapping my arms around her waist so we don't become disconnected, I stand up with her and bend her over so she has to reach her hands out and place her palms against the window to support herself. She moves the way I want her to, and I try to keep thinking of her like she's a toy. A plaything. Nothing more.

But I'm at war with myself. Because as much as I want this to be greedy and contractual, I know without a doubt that it's gone beyond that, and I want her to admit it. "But you wanted this too, didn't you? Not just the job. Not just the power. Your pussy has been begging for my cock. Hasn't it?"

"Mm," she says.

It's not good enough. "Say it, Brystin. Tell me you've

been begging for my cock. Tell me you've been dreaming about it. Tell me you'd trade everything else I've given you just to have this moment right now."

She doesn't hesitate. "I wanted this, Holt. I risked everything for this."

"Good girl." It's not exactly the same, but I gather it's more true, even in the midst of sex, when any words spoken should be off-limits from scrutiny. The truth of it is intoxicating, or the illusion of truth, anyway, and it takes everything in me not to draw more of the same from her lips. In the state she's in, I think I could get her to say almost anything.

But more truths like this would be dangerous.

And I don't want to wonder if they're lies.

With a growl, I spank her haunch, and then dig my fingers into her hips. My pants fall from my knees to my ankles, and I ram into her with all that I have left, chasing my own climax to the finish line. Chasing it like my sanity depends on it.

And I'll do it again. And again. All night long, until I've fucked her on every surface in my office. Until she can't come another time. Until she's worn out and used, and then I'll send her back to her prick of a husband, and I'll go back to fucking uninteresting married women, and this time —*this time,* on my mother's grave—this is done.

CHAPTER **TWENTY-SIX**

BRYSTIN

My lips are raw and my legs are Jell-O as we make our way through the parking garage to Holt's car. It's still dark outside, but I'm trying not to guess the time, knowing I'll panic when I see it. I have to be at the studio by ten in the morning, and this is a job where I need my brain to be alert and functioning. Not to mention Zully will kill me if I have deep bags under my eyes.

I'm sure Holt has to be to work even earlier. "I really can take a cab." I don't want to part from him yet but feel guilty at the same time.

He looks at me like I'm being ridiculous. "I'm driving you."

When he opens the door for me, I have to remind myself not to make anything of it. It's hard enough not to turn the sex into something meaningful. The borderline romantic gestures are a whole other ballgame. If I'm not careful, I'll have cupid arrows in my eyes every time I look at him, and I'm really trying to build my professional reputation here.

Once the car is started, he has me enter the address into his GPS as he maneuvers out of the garage. It's impossible not to see the time since it's displayed right there on the dashboard—a quarter to five. I visibly wince.

Thankfully, Michael and I have been staying at the Manhattan apartment this week, so it's only a fifteen-minute commute each way instead of a full hour plus, but still. I can't help but do the math in my head. *Home by five. I'm a mess, but I can take a shower when I wake up. I should be able to get four hours if I grab something to go for breakfast.*

Even though he's driving, Holt must catch my eyes on the clock. "I should have gotten you home earlier."

"No, you shouldn't have." I'm prepared to be miserable today, but it will be worth it. This night has been a kind of incredible I could never describe, and I wouldn't exchange it for the world. Especially since we've promised one time only.

Keeping my eyes on the road before us, I feel his gaze on my profile. "Yeah, you're right," he says after a beat. "We didn't make it to the worktable as it is."

"Or the pool table."

"We fucked on the pool table," he says. "I distinctly remember your heel getting stuck in the pocket while I was eating you out."

"Yeah, but you didn't come. It doesn't count."

"You stained the felt. It counts."

After everything we did tonight, and all the ways we fucked, I thought he couldn't make me blush anymore.

Apparently, I was wrong. "I stained the felt? Oh my God. You're joking, right?"

"I most definitely am not joking."

"That's…oh God…" I know how many important people go through his office on a daily basis. More blood rushes to my cheeks. "Is it going to be a bitch to replace?"

"Oh, I'm not replacing it. I'm not letting the cleaners touch it either. That's a historic landmark." He grins as he glances at me, but I'm pretty sure he's serious.

"I am mortified."

"That's too bad because I'm fucking proud." He reaches over to put his hand on my thigh, and even though I'm exhausted and satiated, tingles run up my spine.

Different kinds of tingles than I've spent the last several hours feeling. Tingles that are less directed toward my pussy and more directed to my heart.

Ah, fuck. I think I'm in trouble.

He doesn't let his hand linger, which is probably for the best, but it feels like a deliberate severing of connection since he removes it with a clearing of his throat. Like the hand had been a mistake that he's now realized.

An all too familiar ache replaces the warmth of his palm. This is how it's always been with Michael. He's wary, his every touch guarded. As though I'm a fragile thing to be careful around. Don't want to be too effusive or affectionate with Brystin. Don't want her to think there's more between us. Don't want to lead her on.

My thoughts spiral from there as we drive in silence. Until I can't stand it, and I need to hurt myself before Holt does. "How many women are you fucking?"

I study him while I wait for a response, so I see the

tensing of his jaw and the twitch of his eye. I watch his lips draw tight as he decides his reply. "You mean like how many men are you fucking?"

I'm immediately ashamed. Because, of course, he thinks there's Michael. And since I have someone else, do I really have a right to ask about Holt? If I were braver I'd say what I really meant. That I'm not ready to be done with him. That I don't know what's going on between us. That I'd be willing to reexamine my marriage if he thought for a second that he wasn't ready to be done with me too.

But I have love PTSD, and so I stay in the safe lane. "I'm sorry. That's none of my business. I shouldn't have asked."

His features relax ever so slightly, but he's quiet for almost a full minute. "It's not so much that you shouldn't have asked. It's that there's another question that matters more."

"What question is that?"

"How many women am I romantically inclined toward. That's the question you should be asking."

There's a ringing in my ears, and my heart thunders in my chest. A strange storm of elation starts to build inside me. Could we actually be on the same page?

But then he goes on. "The answer is none." He swivels his head in my direction, looks me in the eye. "I don't have romantic relationships, Brystin. It's just sex and a good time. So it doesn't matter how many people I fuck. Because no one's special."

I turn my head toward the road, unable to hold his gaze. Otherwise, he might see how watery my eyes suddenly are, and wouldn't that be stupid to cry? When I asked the question in the first place. When I knew I was opening myself up for hurt.

But this stings more than any answer I'd been expecting. It's an echo of too many previous relationships. Men who've thought I was perfectly fine to fuck, but little else. Men who've been clear that they don't want more, and yet I can't help but give every part of myself and still feel shredded when they refuse to take it.

I'd started out so good with Holt. Putting intercourse off-limits, then as soon as he breaks me down, he's already worried I'll become attached?

No. We've already said one time. This speech wasn't necessary. "Why are you telling me this?" I force myself to look at him. "Have I given you any indication that I need to know that I'm not special or are you just particularly fond of being cruel?"

He doesn't answer, because he's more in control of himself than I am. Because he's so uninvested that nothing's driving him to be out of control. He just chews on his bottom lip and gives a slight nod of his head. As if he's thinking, *yep, here she goes with the emotions.*

And because I am who I am, and because I'll always wish there was something bigger, something real behind the callous front, I let myself consider for a second that he's protecting his own emotions. Maybe he's afraid of getting hurt. I'm the one with—for all intents and purposes, though not literally—a ring on my finger, and we've basically said this is all there will be between us.

What if he's as neck deep into this as I am?

But that's the same sort of optimistic thinking that has trapped me in a loveless marriage. I can't *what if* about Holt.

Only way to keep my heart is to take everything at face value.

Luckily, the next intersection is half a block from my stop. "I'll get out here." I take advantage of the red light so that I don't have to spend another minute trapped in this painful awkwardness.

"Come on, don't be like that. I'm not letting you—"

But I'm already out of the car. "I had a good time, Holt. Thanks for the ride." I manage not to slam the door, then hustle down the street to our apartment, pretending I don't notice Holt driving slow enough to keep pace with me or him idling when I stop to put in the door code.

Fuck him for that. For caring enough to be sure I'm safe.

In the lobby, I wave at the doorman as I quickly bolt past, hoping he doesn't have a chance to take in my freshly fucked appearance before I make it to the elevator. I will myself not to cry before I make it to my floor, and somehow manage.

Outside our apartment—*Michael's* apartment, since I'll never feel like his fuckpad is mine—I gather myself before walking in, then shut the door as quietly as possible, so as not to wake him.

As soon as I turn around, I realize the attempt was in vain because he's sitting in the living room, a single lamp on, and a book in his lap. No reading glasses, though, so I know he's only been pretending to be reading.

Great. He waited up for me. Just great.

"You're awake." I'm not in a space to have anything more remarkable to say.

He's careful with his response, but his tapping foot says he's not happy. "You disappear without a word from the party and stay out all night without answering your phone. You think I could sleep?"

"So now you know how it feels." I regret going there as soon as the words are out of my mouth. I'm too exhausted to make good decisions, it seems. "Forget I said that. Sorry I kept you waiting. I'm obviously fine. I'll be better about communicating in the future."

Hoping that's good enough, and that we can save any further discussion aka lecturing for later, I turn toward the room I've been using as mine.

"No, hold on." Michael stops me before I can get very far. He waits until I pivot back to face him. "Is our"—he pauses, searching—"arrangement not working for you anymore?"

Oh my God, I want to scream. It never worked for me. Is this not something he already understood?

At the same time, I perk up. Even though I couldn't care less, at the moment, who he's fucking. Habit, perhaps. "You'd be willing to go closed marriage?"

He shrugs one shoulder, as if he wasn't once adamant that he'd only get married if we kept it open. "If it bothers you that much…we should definitely revisit."

Irony is fun, isn't it?

I've waited my whole marriage for this. Fantasized since we first got together that one day he'd say, *Brystin, you are enough. I don't need anyone but you.* I should be doing fucking cartwheels.

But I'm not dumb. I'm a fool, but not dumb. This isn't about me. It's about him. He hated waiting for me. Hated the thought of me with Holt. That's what's bringing on this sudden change of heart.

It's a nice twist of karma that I might relish when I'm feeling less wrapped up in another man. But unfortunately, I'm still the same fool I was when I married him. Just a fool for another man.

"It doesn't matter," I say. "This is done."

"What do you mean, this is done?"

"This. Me, coming in at five in the morning. Leaving parties without a word. All of it." I don't say Holt's name, but he's still very present in the subtext. "We have our show, and it's a hit. The rest of it is done."

"Okay," he says. "If that's what you want, sweet girl."

As if any of it has ever been up to me.

As if what I want has ever mattered to anyone.

CHAPTER
TWENTY-SEVEN
BRYSTIN

I step in the elevator after Michael, and fidget with my necklace while he pushes the button for the penthouse. "Why are we supposed to go to this dinner again?"

It's the billionth time I've asked, and I already know the answer, but I'm trying to focus on something other than the fact that I'm about to see Holt for the first time since he stuck his dick in me. Multiple times. Eleven and a half days with no contact, knowing he was in the same building as I was, wondering if the memory of my scent haunted him the way the memory of his has haunted me.

"I know you hate getting into it with the politicians," Michael explains, patiently, "but if you want the work you do to affect real change, then the big ones should know the face that goes with the name. Not only will the governor be here, but at least one of our senators, and several statesmen."

He leaves out that this was Holt's idea, which has been

the norm this week. We've both stayed away from his name, like…well, the way we would have if our show had been picked up the way shows typically do. We would barely mention the CEO of the company. He's too high above us. He has several people under him that deal with the day-to-day programming so that Michael and I rarely have to deal with Holt face-to-face.

Michael reaches out to grab my hand, something he's done a lot more since he suggested we reevaluate our arrangement, though he's never brought it up again. "Don't be nervous. You've got this."

These are the kinds of moments with him that swept me away in the first place. I try hard to remember what that used to feel like, and can almost feel the beginning of a spark in the center of my chest.

"You look incredible, by the way, if I haven't told you yet. This dress new?"

Just like that, the spark turns into a flame, but it's not burning for Michael. My mind goes back to yesterday in my dressing room, when André arrived with the box from Bergdorf Goodman. I opened it to find a chic black dress with large cutouts on either side. Sexy, but sophisticated. Completely my brand.

Along with it came a handwritten note that I've read an embarrassing amount of times. *Wear this on Saturday. - H*

"He gets you," Zully had said. Which led to a maelstrom of emotions because if he gets me, why can't I "get" him? Why is it always these men wanting to dress me up and build up my confidence then get me on my knees and praise me for my commitment to them, all while telling me I'll never own their hearts?

I almost hadn't worn the dress, out of spite.

But here I am. Fool of the century. "Bergdorf Goodman," I answer Michael, omitting that it was from Holt.

And then I don't have to say any more because the elevator is opening into the foyer of Arthur Sebastian's penthouse.

We're greeted first by a waiter who hands us each a champagne glass and encourages us forward where we're then met by a woman maybe twenty years my senior, with brown eyes and dark blonde hair that might have been a light shade of auburn naturally.

"Welcome to my home." She shakes Michael's hand first. "I'm Arthur's wife, Evangeline, and I'm delighted to have you."

Michael tells her his name and then turns to introduce me, but Evangeline cuts him off. "Oh, I know who this is. *Our Nation Now* has become a nightly staple." She leans forward, lowering her voice. "Which is saying something, because Arthur rarely watches anything on SNC, please do not quote me on that."

Back at her original volume, she continues to compliment me for several minutes, despite the elevator door opening at least twice behind us to deposit more guests in her foyer. "I know I should let you go mingle." She likely feels the pressure of neglecting her latest arrivals. "But Arthur's really going to want to meet you."

She turns to scan the room, and naturally, I scan it with her. The penthouse occupies several floors—I count three different landings on the staircase—but the main room is open concept with ceilings that extend to the very top. White linen-clothed table rounds have been placed strategically so that there is plenty of walking room around them. I can only imagine what the space normally looks like with furniture in place, or where the furniture is being stored for this occasion, but from the antique frames and gilded details on the remaining décor, I'm guessing the place is spectacularly traditional in style.

Since we've arrived fashionably late, many guests are already here, socializing in various bunches of three or four. A hundred people total, says a quick eyeball estimate. I can't fathom the cost of an apartment in the city that can accommodate this many people, but I guess that's why this night is being hosted by one of the Sebastian billionaires.

Speaking of which…

"There he is," Evangeline says, locating her husband. Vaguely, I register her saying something about having to meet him later because he seems to be immersed in a conversation with the mayor, and then something that makes Michael laugh and then there is another couple standing with us and more introductions happening.

I'm barely aware of any of it, because it wasn't Arthur I spotted. Honestly, I'm not sure I could ID him on my own, but I can identify his nephew. Quite easily. Naked, if I had to.

And there Holt is, center of the room with a willowy brunette on his arm.

Not just any brunette. When he moves so I can see her face, I realize she's Jisella, a supermodel famous enough to go by one single name. Beautiful enough to make any ounce of beauty I've ever possessed seem like everyday plain.

My gut pulls with jealousy. I'm about to throw back the

full glass of champagne when Holt's eyes meet mine. He holds the stare, his gaze a lightning rod, sending a hundred thousand megawatts through my body and igniting a fire between my legs. Every second that passes, I feel more and more inflamed, like I'll incinerate completely right here in front of everyone, and that motherfucker has the audacity to raise the side of his lip into a smile.

"Oh, damn," Michael says quietly at my side. "Is that that Victoria's Secret model with Holt?"

Way to rub it in.

"Pretty sure it is." Lucky him, he's about to meet her because next thing I know, Holt is heading in our direction, bringing his model/date with him.

"Glad to see you both made it. Michael, Brystin." Smoothly, without introducing us to his companion, Holt takes the champagne out of my hand and gives it to Michael, who is still holding a glass of his own. "You won't mind taking care of this, will you? I need to steal her."

And like that, Holt abandons his bombshell date with my husband, and guides me away from them with his hot hand at my lower back, his long fingers connecting with the bare skin at the cutout on one side of my dress. My body is a traitor, wanting to press into his touch despite my head yelling to *step away from the assHolt*. My chest tightens, trying to protect my fragile heart, and still, I'm pretty sure that if he's taking me to find the nearest bedroom, I won't put up a fight.

But Holt steers us toward the crowd, rather than away. With his free hand, he waves at someone who looks slightly familiar across the room—a state senator, I think—and seems to gesture that we're headed that way.

So it's all about work then. Which is good, since I don't seem to have a functioning survival instinct. I'm pissed at myself for not feeling more relieved.

Then, with his eyes still pinned on our destination, he moves his mouth near my ear. "You wore it. I knew it would look stunning."

The low timbre of his voice, the volume just above a whisper, sends as much of a thrill through my system as the words themselves.

I refuse to let him see their effect on me. "It's perfect. Thank you," I say coldly.

"You're welcome." One of the most common phrases in the English language, and he makes it sound like sin.

He makes no effort to continue the conversation, but I swear I feel the same anxious energy rolling off of him that's rolling off of me. I should let it be. Act like I'm immune to the force field surrounding us.

"I thought you didn't bring dates to these things." Oh, for fuck's sake. Why am I like this?

He chuckles with smug satisfaction. "Jealous?"

I pause our gait to turn to him. "Of someone else who isn't special to you?"

His smile tightens into pursed lips, and I feel him battling an impulse to say something.

Before he can speak, we're interrupted by the flash of a bulb. The hired photographer taking candids, fortunately not of us, but of a trio nearby.

The distraction silences whatever Holt had been about to say. No surprise, he's better at keeping his mouth shut than I am. Probably because he doesn't care if I'm wounded —I don't matter enough to him for that. Instead, he returns his hand to my back and directs me to the waiting politician. "Senator, I have someone you should meet."

The next hour is more of the same. Holt escorting me around the room until I've met everyone he deems important, me pretending that it's just another part of my job and that I'm not queasy and heartsick inside. Shockingly, I'm good enough at what I do to turn on the charm. It helps that several of the people I meet already know who I am, have already tuned in to the show. It's the most surreal experience to be validated in my career while simultaneously battling tumultuous emotions.

Will this be how it is from now on? Will I never get to enjoy the fruits of my success because I'll always have this history with Holt?

I try not to think about it too much, and when dinner is announced, I gratefully excuse myself from Holt's arm to go sit with Michael, who has already found our place cards.

"How did it go?" he asks, and I wonder for half a second if he understands my inner turmoil. But then he adds, "The governor seems to have been truly beguiled. I've never been so proud to call you my wife."

"Have you ever been proud to call me your wife?" It comes out so fast, I don't have time to stop it. Perhaps it's something that needs saying, but this isn't the time, and I know that.

Fortunately, Michael doesn't detect the snark in my tone and seems to take it as a need for reassurance. "I've had faith in you longer than you've had faith in yourself. Yes. I've always been proud of you."

When it served him, anyway.

"But especially now," he says louder, cupping my cheek

with his hand, in an unusual display of affection. "You are my queen, sweet girl."

I don't realize the words and gesture aren't meant only for me, until I turn to discover that the person who sat down at my other side is Holt. His not-so-subtle attempt to claim me with praise is both patronizing and demeaning, but I'm too thrown off by Holt's reappearance to care.

And with him is Jisella, of course, because she's his date, even if he's barely given her the time of day since we've arrived.

I suppose that most of the women he's with understand that he will never give them his full attention. I should have known too, but stupid me, I threw away the memo.

"Oh, you're sitting with us. Awesome. Wow." I take a large sip of my wine, praying Holt doesn't burst into some diatribe about the particular variety of grape in this specific bottle because I just decided I'm going to do my best to pretend he doesn't exist, and that's harder when he's talking directly to me.

He picks up the place card next to me and shows that it says his name. "I suppose Evangeline wanted to be sure we got to dine with people we felt comfortable around."

Hahaha. I feel anything but comfortable at the moment.

"That's nice," I say, then bite into my salad to discourage a continuance of the conversation.

The meal progresses with no relief in tension, though I'm not sure anyone notices it besides me. It's Michael who introduces me to Jisella, whom he seems to have chatted up for almost the entirety of the time Holt was escorting me around the room. They even have inside jokes already, which is so Michael whenever he meets a pretty woman. Especially a woman from his own home country.

Holt doesn't seem to be bothered by it, and is relatively quiet for most of the meal. Every now and again, I swear I feel him looking at my profile, but when I turn my head, he's always staring elsewhere. He doesn't talk about the wine, and while that's a blessing, I'm also stupidly disappointed. It's embarrassing how much I enjoy hearing him go on about his passion. How much I love hearing him say anything, actually. Like I'm a silly teenager with a crush instead of a grown married woman.

What the fuck is wrong with me?

I am here with Michael.

When he puts his arm on the back of my chair, I sit straighter. He's marking his territory, but fine. I am his territory, aren't I? I should be happy about that. It's what I always wanted, wasn't it?

I pay little attention to the conversation around me, until halfway through the meal.

"I can't keep them all straight." Jisella's accent is slightly thicker than Michael's. "There's Arty and then your father. Is he the oldest? He's getting married," she says as an aside to everyone who is listening.

"We'll see about that," Holt says, quickly.

If I cared—which I most certainly do not—I would ask why he seems so defensive about it.

But I don't care, and it's probably rude to ask, and anyway, I'm more interested in proving that I know more about Holt's family than Jisella. "Henry is the oldest. Then Reynard. They both run Sebastian Industrial. Then it's Samuel—Holt's father—and August who both ran SNC until Samuel's heart attack. Then Holt took over. I'm not sure why it didn't go to August."

Think I'm not special? Think again.

I'm such a child.

For the first time since dinner started, Holt perks up. I know exactly when he sees Michael's hand on the back of my chair, because his eyes narrow and his features darken. "The board voted me in," he says. "After much campaigning on my father's part."

"Oh, that's right." Jisella looks as if she's trying to see it all in her head. "And then Arty's the baby of the family."

"A very well-off baby," Michael remarks. "Is he working?"

Jisella launches into explaining how Arthur has become devoted to lobbying, mostly in the best interest of both of the companies because, although they aren't all under the same umbrella, all the brothers have shares in both. It's surprising how much she knows about all of it, and how detailed she gets. It's somewhat disgusting, in my unspoken opinion, how much money plays into what laws get passed, but that's not my business, and frankly it's hard to think at all because in the middle of her speech, I feel a hand slip through the side cutout of my dress, over my stomach, and down.

And it's not coming from the side my husband's sitting on.

The dress doesn't allow me to wear panties, which I'm beginning to think was Holt's plan all along, but there's an easy way to shut this down. Press my thighs together. That's all.

Instead, I slowly ease my legs further apart.

It's like I'm an addict. Or a glutton for shame.

Or I just know how good it will feel when Holt's finger reaches the hidden bud of nerves. When he presses against my clit with the expertise he somehow managed to achieve in such a short time of knowing me, it's all I can do not to audibly sigh in relief.

I don't know how this can possibly end. There's no way I can try to hide an orgasm from six strangers, one who is my husband and is familiar with my O face. But I lift my hips up, an invitation for Holt to travel lower.

Which he does.

My breaths get quicker. I smile and nod my head as if I'm listening. Bring my napkin to my mouth to hide the need to bite my lower lip as pleasure builds and builds. As I feel it start to get away from me.

Then Michael places his hand on my thigh, surprising me and jolting me to my senses. I drop my fork, and it clatters noisily on my plate. Holt pulls his hand away, but it still feels like the whole room is looking at me. Like the whole room saw.

"Sorry." I glance at Holt, in time to see him lick my pussy juice from his finger.

My cheeks redden, out of proportion to the perceived faux pas because no one except Holt knows the real reason I'm blushing. Another dirty secret we share. Another taboo intimacy. Another reason to feel there is something special between us.

No one's special.

I jump to my feet, so fast I almost knock over my wine. "I'm sorry. I'm a mess right now." I force a short laugh. "Excuse me."

"Bathroom's down that hall, first door on the left." Michael assumes that's what I need.

I nod and head in that direction, needing to be alone. Needing to be anywhere that Holt isn't. Needing it so badly, I practically run.

The bathroom door is closed when I approach it. Before I can even consider knocking on it, Holt's threadbare voice comes from behind me. "Keep walking. Two more doors. On the right."

We're pretty much alone in this hallway. It's as fine a place as any to say this has to stop, but I'm driven by something stronger than reason when I'm with Holt, and I don't hesitate at all. Just continue until I'm opening the door he indicated and walking into what appears to be a mudroom of sorts, with a bench for storage and hooks for coats, and under cabinet lights that turn on when I enter.

Holt is on my heels. I hear the click of the door shutting, and when I turn around, I collide into him, my lips finding his for an instantly frenzied kiss.

I give into it for the smallest of moments, wrapping my fingers into his suit jacket, feeling the want in my belly and the clench of my pussy as his mouth bosses mine. I want him. It's a lie to try to tell myself otherwise. I want him, and it hurts to want him because even when I have him, I don't have him.

I never have him.

The thought cuts through the lust haze, and I break off the kiss, and back away. "What are you doing, Holt?"

He looks at me with disbelief. "What are *you* doing?"

"Reacting naturally to your very inappropriate actions."

He chuckles. "In here or out there? Because that kiss felt very much initiated by you."

"In *here* started out *there,* which was very much initiated by *you.*"

He takes a step toward me. "So it's my fault my fingers were drenched."

"What was between my legs was none of your business."

"Then you shouldn't have spread your legs for me like a greedy little slut." His next two steps are quick, and then he's got me in his hold, my arms pinned behind me at the base of my spine. He spins me around and walks me backward until I'm against the door as he talks. "I could smell your arousal all through dinner, Brystin. I *reacted naturally.*"

I shake my head, unable to look him in the eye. He's manipulating me, but this is on both of us. I had my rules for a reason. What did I expect would happen when we broke them?

Who am I kidding? This thing between us was already out of control before that. "Let me go," I whisper, meaning as much metaphorically as literally.

He doesn't budge. "Tell me you need to be fucked."

"You don't know what I need."

Leaning forward, he presses his forehead against mine. "Tell me the truth, honeybee. I heard you all night, charming those men, telling them that truth was essential. So tell me the truth. Tell me you need to be fucked."

I could turn the demand back on him. *Tell me the truth, Holt. Tell me that I mean something to you.*

But I'm not sure that I'm not just hopelessly romantic. He doesn't know my true relationship with Michael because I haven't told him. Because the truth is embarrassing, but also incomprehensible. Who could grasp why I'm so loyal for so little in return?

Yet, part of me feels like he does know, at some level, and if he does, and if he can still treat me like this, then I'm not just a hopeless romantic—I'm delusional.

And I still want him.

"Why are you doing this?" I ask, stalling the inevitable.

He brings his mouth to my chin, ghosts his lips along my jawline. "I can make it better, Brystin. As soon as you say it. Let me make it better."

I open my mouth, and let the plea escape. "I need you to fuck me."

Because that's all I dare ask for. Because that's all I dare believe I'm worth.

"Yeah, you do. I need that too." Instantly, his hands are on me, cupping my breasts as I undo his pants. He moves me toward the bench, turning me to face it when we get there. "Put your foot up."

He helps me gather my skirt around my waist, then comes up behind me, nudging his cock inside me with hardly any warning. He's big, but I'm so wet, he slides in easily. All the way, and for a brief beat in time, I feel the relief of him. The relief of having such a heavy want met. It's euphoric, and he only just got inside.

But then he's pumping, fast and frantic, and the relief is forgotten as another need starts to build, one more pressing and urgent and heavy. I'm all hushed moans and swallowed whimpers while Holt speaks dirty at my ear.

"Your cunt is so greedy. Eating my cock up like you're a

starving woman. Like you're a hungry little cum slut. Is that what you are, Brystin? Tell me you're my cum slut."

"I'm a cum slut." I'm surprised at how turned on saying it makes me. Almost as turned on as it is to hear it.

"No. You're *my* cum slut. Say it."

"I'm your cum slut."

"Yes. Yes." He feels harder all of a sudden, bigger. "Say you live for this cock inside you. That you can't stop thinking about it. That you get yourself off every night thinking about how empty you are without it. Say that I'm the one who owns your pussy, Brystin. Say it."

I close my eyes, and lights form against the back of my lids. Words aren't possible anymore, but they're all true. All the things he wants to hear—every word honest.

He does get me.

He gets me, and brutally takes advantage of me.

And I let him.

And I love it.

I can't help the cry that rips from my throat when my orgasm smacks through me. Holt claps his hand over my mouth to silence me, then a few rapid pumps, and he joins me, collapsing against me.

The feel of him pressed at my back, our breaths in tandem…this is the moment that never lasts long enough. I'd stretch this part forever, the part where I feel warm and held and wanted. It's my favorite part of sex when it's happening.

But then it passes—it always passes—and when I can think rationally again, I'm disgusted. With myself more than him. Disgusted that I'd still fall back into his arms if he invited me to.

Which means I need to get out of here. Now.

As soon as I'm able to move, I push him away, but he quickly pulls me back to him, so I can face him this time. He cups both sides of my face, staring at me like I could be his world.

And that's what sex does to men. Makes them think they're in love for half a minute.

It also never lasts.

I pretend for the moment that it's real, and I let him kiss me. Slowly, this time. So slowly that I can feel each individual slice to my heart as he stabs the knife in over and over. Finally, he pulls away, and sighs.

"Your cum is running down my leg," I say.

"Fuck. We didn't use a condom. I'm…fuck. Are you—?"

"I'm on birth control." So it's fine, but it's more proof that we're out of control with each other. I let out a quiet *argh*.

"What? Is there something else? Are you okay?"

I wave my hand dismissively. This isn't the time or place to get into the discussion we need to be having. "We need to get back out there. Mich—" I stop myself. "We have people waiting for us."

"We do. Okay. I'll wait to follow." He steps away, giving me room to get past him. "Stop in the bathroom on your way. Your eye's…" He makes a gesture that implies my makeup has smudged.

"All right."

I start past, but he stops me again. "Jisella is my uncle Arty's mistress. She wanted to be here to meet that YouTube celebrity that was here, and somehow I got roped into being her date so it wouldn't look suspicious to his wife."

"...uh, what?" I take that in. "But Evangeline is so…perfect."

"Men are pigs. What can I say?"

"Well, truer words…" The more important point is not lost on me—that Holt wasn't here with anyone. It shouldn't matter, but it does, and I almost tell him the truth about Michael, that he doesn't love me, but even if that does matter, it's not the time.

So I keep my mouth shut, and make it to the door before he stops me again. "But, um, Brystin? Don't clean up *everything*. I like knowing my cum is running down your leg."

So help me, I do too.

CHAPTER TWENTY-EIGHT

HOLT

"Then you're saying that viewer numbers show the publicity from these tabloids has had no negative effect on ratings?" I'm careful how I word the statement, not wanting to influence how Scott answers. I already know the answer.

"I'm actually saying that the publicity seems to have had a positive effect." He leans over the table to point at the graph in front of me. "Here's where we debuted. We expected *Our Nation Now* to come in at this number of viewers." He points to a number then points to a higher number. "This is the actual viewership we had."

"Right. We performed better than expected. That happens."

"That's what I thought until this latest scandal in the media. Those came out on Sunday and Monday. Look at the ratings for Monday night. They jumped by thirty percent and stayed there last night as well." Scott sits back again, letting the data speak the story for itself.

"And there's nothing else that can account for the jump? No increase in ad spend or any planned publicity that contributed?"

Scott shakes his head. "She had that *Good Morning America* interview the week before and didn't see these kinds of results. They're tuning in to find out more about the woman involved with Holt Sebastian."

I pretend that I'm surprised, even though I'm not. All publicity is good publicity, and all that. It all works toward the end goal.

My cousin, however, tends to prefer publicity that's controllable. "I'm not even sure these numbers are sustainable, Holt. How do you keep this kind of reaction up?"

"You mean you think they'll drop after the scandal dies down?"

"Possible. Probable, even, that she can win the audience over with her charm. But some people will be turned off when they realize it's not all gossip. Her show is the real deal. She's not a sensationalist."

I mull that over.

The latest scandal he's talking about are the reports that followed after the dinner at Uncle Art's house. While the major news didn't carry the story this time, and neither did any SNC reporter, there were several popular social media sites that did, most of them repeating the earlier claims that Brystin must be my lover. No mention of the horrible word that Hunter had used, thankfully, but one site does say she was seen leaving the dinner with me hot on her heels.

After the way we'd left things Saturday night, I'd thought there might be a possibility she'd reach out. Then Scott brought these latest articles to my attention, and I was sure she would.

Three and a half days later, I haven't heard a word. This should be a good thing. She's a temptation I can't explain. She should be out of my system, or at least an attraction that I can put out of mind when she's out of sight.

But that's not what she is.

I crave her. Like the taste of a sweet Bordeaux. I could drink a case of her and still want more. It's not a feeling I've ever experienced, and instead of getting better when I'm away from her, it seems to get worse.

It's made a bitch out of trying to concentrate. I shouldn't have her on my brain when making vital decisions for the company. I shouldn't be so wrapped up in one SNC anchor. It's not my job to be wrapped up in anchors at all. Her show was supposed to be one part of a greater vision for our future. It wasn't supposed to be the center of my world.

Yet, here I am. Calling impromptu meetings with my head of PR so he can give me the lowdown on every word spoken about Brystin across all forms of media when normally I'd wait for a report at the end of the quarter. "What happens if we play into the scandals?"

His answer won't change my plans, but I'm curious.

He raises an eyebrow, letting me know exactly what he thinks about that idea, but he considers all the same. "From a pure business perspective, it isn't any different than other forms of stunt publicity, which works as often as it backfires. But you're selling the news here, Holt. Not a gossip network. I don't see how it benefits you in the long run. Not to mention what it might do to her reputation."

My ribs tighten at his last remark, but I force myself to breathe past it. "But for the short run, it can move numbers?"

Scott closes the folder in front of him, sits back and crosses his arms over his chest. "Will it look impressive for the board review at the end of the quarter? Yes. Reynard and Hunter won't have much of a leg to stand on if they're still trying to boot you with these kinds of results—"

"—perfect." I stand up, having heard all I needed.

"—but, you're going to have to follow up with another stunt the following quarter, Holt." He raises his voice to chase after me as I head toward my desk. "Is that what the Holt era is going to look like? Stunt after stunt? First the bringing down of King-Kincaid, then this? How long can you keep this up?"

That's the problem with working with family members —they aren't afraid to cut the bullshit and deliver real talk. Even worse when they are both pragmatic and ethical, qualities that are often hard to find in my family tree.

I pick up the water bottle from my desk and take a long swig, wishing it were later in the day and that it was something stronger. Something with a sweet taste that went directly to my veins.

With a sigh, I slump into my desk chair. "I don't know, Scott. As long as possible? Until I come up with something better? This is what I know how to do. Get people's attention."

He crosses a leg over the opposite knee and taps a pen against the table. "Get people's attention? Or get Uncle Sam's attention?"

"Jesus, Scott. Hit below the belt, why don't you?" I run

my hand through my hair. "Just because you're the one of us who doesn't have daddy issues—"

"Fuck that. I've had my battles with Henry. I'd still be working for SIC instead of the news corp, if that wasn't the case, and you know it."

"I know, I know. My apologies." His father went so far as to tell him who he had to marry if he wanted a place on the board at the Sebastian Industrial Company. At least my father doesn't care about my love life. "Maybe we should all follow your lead and cross over to parts of the business that our fathers didn't run before us."

"And let Hunter have your job? Bad idea."

"You're worried about sensationalism and stunt publicity now…" I laugh, but it dies quickly. Scott's right. I haven't formed a long-term vision for SNC, and my current growth tactics are unsustainable. My father would have been content with slow and steady headway. Why do I feel the need to prove I can do better?

"Speaking of dads…" There's the slightest hint of tentativeness in Scott's tone, and I'm instantly sure I know what he's going to say.

I groan.

"Samuel's really getting married?"

"Supposedly." I spin my chair to face him. "How does everyone even know? There hasn't been an official announcement. He's yet to tell me."

"You haven't talked to him?"

I give a one-shoulder shrug. "He's extended his visit for the next few weeks. I told him I'll talk to him when he gets back. Hopefully, whatever this is burns out in the meantime."

"You're such an asshole."

"AssHolt," I correct. "I've been told."

He laughs. "Good one. Seriously, though. Let him be happy."

"Okay, you think you've found someone you want to spend your life with and that's great and all for you, but don't bring that shit into my office."

Suddenly, I'm thinking about Brystin, which makes sense considering how many places I fucked her in this very room, except I'm not thinking about the sex. I'm remembering her face when I showed up at her apartment after the first scandal broke out. How she looked up at me with those pale blue eyes. *"You came for me."*

Something in me wanted to promise her I'd come for her every time. Every motherfucking time.

But she's not mine to make promises to, and it was bullshit anyway because three days have passed since the latest scandal, and here's Scott worried about her reputation, and the only effort I've made is to try to forget she exists.

"Last words," Scott says. "Wait until you find your someone. It'll turn your world upside down, and cousin, I'm here for it."

"Oh, fuck off." My phone buzzes with a call from my secretary. She rarely interrupts me, unless it's important, usually sending everything to my assistant first. I put the phone on speaker. "What's up, Bette?"

"Sorry to bother you. Ms. Shaw burst past me, insisting to see you. André is talking to her in the hall."

On cue, I hear loud voices in the hall, hers floating to me like honey incense. It's embarrassing how my dick is half hard just from the sound, and the strange pinch in my chest is annoying as hell, but I'm so the opposite of bothered by her presence. "Tell André to go ahead and send her in."

"I'll get out of your hair." Scott stands, but he's still gathering his materials when she bursts in half a minute later, and I swear to God the earth moves under my feet at the sight of her.

The chaos she brings to my system is confusing, and I try to tuck it away under cold stoicism. "Hello, Brystin. Usually people make appointments when they want—"

She cuts me off, storming toward my desk with her phone displayed toward me. "Have you seen this?"

It's the social media site that had caught me chasing after her, so yes. I've seen it. Considering how worked up she is, I'm guessing she's only now discovered it. "Actually, Scott and I were just discussing it."

She follows my gaze and startles to find my cousin. "Oh. Hi, Scott. I didn't realize you were with anyone." She collects herself quickly. "But perfect. You're both here. What are we going to do?"

"Nothing," I state, matter-of-factly. "We aren't concerned about it."

"Not concerned? How can you be *not concerned*? This can't be good for the show."

"Actually…Scott? Would you like to tell Brystin what you were telling me?"

Scott throws me a look, and I know he's thinking about her reputation and the harm these sorts of continued rumors might have for her in the long run.

But his job is to protect the network, not Brystin Shaw. "Ratings have gone up by thirty percent since the latest round of gossip. It's not hurting the show at all." He pulls out the graphs for her, and she studies them with a gaping mouth.

Such a beautiful fucking mouth.

"But these viewers aren't coming for the news. They're coming for the scandal." She addresses Scott directly, instead of me, which makes me feel strangely jealous. "They'll drop off eventually."

"Most likely," he agrees. "I doubt we'll lose any viewership over it, though. Maybe we'll eventually net zero, but it probably won't be noticeable since you're in the growth phase anyway. Best to ignore it and let the rumors die down. You didn't even notice them yourself until today, I'm guessing?"

"I've been doing my best to avoid social media, after last time, but Michael got tagged, and he brought it to my attention." She hurries through her explanation, seeming to still be concerned about repercussions. "But the things they're insinuating…"

She takes a beat and then turns her focus to me.

The things they're insinuating are true. She won't say it in front of Scott.

"I've got this, Scott. Thanks for pulling everything together on such short notice. Let me know if anything changes."

He agrees and gives some sort of farewell that I'm not paying attention to because Brystin is in orbit, and I can feel the pull of her gravity like she's the moon, and I'm the tide. She has me drowning already, and once Scott leaves, we'll be alone, and I'm claiming not responsible for my actions when it's just the two of us.

I'm fucking thrilled.

Brystin doesn't seem to share my excitement. As soon as the door shuts, she's in my face, and not in a good way. "These aren't rumors, Holt."

"I'm aware of what the truth is."

"They're calling me a cheater and a homewrecker, which is terribly sexist, considering it's you who is essentially the homewrecker in this situation. Everyone just assumes. Michael has sympathy tweets pouring in, as though he's being mistreated in this whole thing. No one understands the real deal."

As usual, the mere mention of Michael riles me. "What is the real deal, exactly, Brystin?"

"I mean…" Her chest rises and falls, her eyes locked with mine. Internally, I dare her to say it. Dare her to tell me that her marriage is a scam.

"What, Brystin? What is it you mean?"

If she'd just admit it, then…

I don't know what then. It's not something I can even think about until she does.

But she swallows, and when she speaks again her fight is back. "The real deal is that you offered me a job that I wanted in exchange for sex. That's the real deal, Holt."

She has every right to turn this back on me. Nothing she's said is a lie. But it feels like a threat, and even more, it feels like a dismissal of everything we've shared together. "Are you saying you want to make that accusation publicly? And before you answer, remember whose reputation usually suffers in situations like this."

It's a low blow, and she takes it as such, her eyes misting as she tries to shake off tears. "No, Holt. I'm not suggesting I take it public. I put myself in this position, and I acknowledge that. I guess I thought that you would give a shit, but fuck me for expecting anything from someone who doesn't have any meaningful relationships."

She turns to leave the room, and that thrill I had at her arrival is completely turned into panic.

I jump out of my seat and follow after her, catching her with an arm around her waist. "Don't leave." My voice sounds foreign and full of need, and I'm grateful that she's facing away and can't see my face, which probably shows more of the same. Pulling her against me, her back to my chest, the smell of her hair intoxicates me, and collectively we sigh together.

"Why are you doing this?" she asks, the same question she asked on Saturday night.

Fuck if I know. I don't have the words for the reason behind my compulsion, so I answer with a question instead. "What do you need from me?"

She pauses, and I sense she's going through a list, trying to pick the answer she thinks is best. "Stop giving the press something to comment on," she says finally.

I wish I could know what the other choices were that she bypassed for this one.

"If you mean stop with the publicity events, I can't do that, Brystin. This show is too important." But I know that isn't what she means, and again, I'm glad we aren't face-to-face. Glad that she can't see that what I really mean is that *she's* important. That I can't bear to give up the opportunities to be with her, as selfish as that is.

She nods, her hair tickling my jaw. "The publicity events are fine, Holt. As long as they're really warranted. But you can't parade me around on your arm like I'm yours. And we can't disappear to..."

"I'm not the only one who can't keep my hands to myself."

"I know. I'm going to be better. I have to be."

She's trying to sever this thing between us, and part of me is grateful that she's strong enough to make the attempt, but a bigger part of me feels like I'm losing a limb, and I feel desperate to hold on. I can't help but believe that there's something I could say that would make all of this better, but I don't know what it is, and besides, she's right.

This is the right thing to do. For her, for me. For the company.

I bury my face in her neck. "I don't know how not to want you."

Her chest rises sharply as her breath hitches. When she speaks again, her voice trembles. "But you don't want me, Holt. You're just a spoiled boy who thinks he wants what he can't have."

That's what it is. That has to be what it is. Spoiled, privileged, billionaire boy. It's a slap in the face because she sees me so clearly. It's a knife in the gut because I think there's more truth to it than that, but if she can't find it, I don't think I can either.

I loosen my hold around her, and take a step back, clearing my voice. "I'll have Bette send over a calendar of events. André will continue to deliver you personally selected clothing. I guarantee that everything on the schedule is warranted, Brystin, but beyond that no promises. What happens when we're together happens. Is that clear?"

Her body tenses, her spine growing taller, but she doesn't refute. "It's clear," she says, then leaves my office without looking back.

The thing is that I'm spoiled for a good reason—because I have enough money and enough power not to have to deny myself anything at all.

CHAPTER
TWENTY-NINE
BRYSTIN

I hold my phone against my shoulder with my chin. "Maybe he doesn't think it's fair," Zully says, as I climb out of the car Holt sent for me. "You're expected to work five days at a high stress job, and then you have to go spend your weekends doing publicity? Maybe he thinks it's too much."

It's a lot, but it's not beyond expectation. Not when I'm a nobody, and I'm trying to build my reputation. "You know that's not the reason Michael's upset about the PR schedule. And since when do you defend him?"

I pause to get my bearings. It's my first time at the North Shore Yacht Club, and I'm not sure where I need to be. All Holt said was to meet on the deck, so I'm guessing it's around the back?

"I'm not defending him. I'm trying to think of why he might be throwing a fit besides the obvious reasons. If you start believing he's jealous, next thing you'll be happy-dancing that it proves he has feelings, and a month later when he's neglecting you again, I'm bringing you tea while you sob in my bed."

The accurate depiction of many past episodes makes me cringe. "Believe it or not, his jealousy doesn't make me feel anything but annoyed."

"Because you're all up in your feels for Holt?"

I lower my head, as though passersby around me might hear her, though of course they don't. "I don't want to talk about it."

It doesn't matter if I don't want to talk about it—she already knows. I've spent many a Sunday morning the past six weeks relating the details from whatever event Holt had required me to attend the night prior:

The charity showing of Hadestown where he fingered me in the dark during the second act.

The book festival at the Javits Center where I blew him in a bathroom stall.

The Summer Fun parade in Brooklyn where we were almost late because we were doing sixty-nine in the back of his limo.

The SNC VIP Fourth of July party where he fucked me in a hidden corner on the rooftop while fireworks filled the night sky.

I can't even blame all of it on Holt. Every time, like the night at his uncle's, I've encouraged it. Spread my legs. Opened my thighs. Got on my knees. Once, when it seemed he was trying to keep his hands off me, I actually begged.

"You don't have to talk about it for it to be true."

I push through the door of the main building. Spotting a bar and a deck behind it, I head in that direction. "We can't keep our hands off each other. That's all," I lie. "It's physical. Like all of Michael's side relationships."

"I know you are not trying to convince me this means nothing to you. Don't forget I know you."

"I'm not trying to convince you. I'm trying to convince me."

"Did it ever work when you said that about Michael?"

The reminder that I'm in the same exact situation with Holt as I was with my husband is a knife that I have repeatedly stabbed in my gut for the last several weeks. "What am I supposed to do, Zully?"

"Stop giving them part of you, B. Figure out who you want to be with, and make them take it all."

As though it's that easy to cut off either of them. "Michael wants more of me than Holt does."

"Are you really sure about that?"

I am, and I'm not. Holt said I wasn't special to him, but he doesn't act that way when he's with me. The way he looks at me, the tender way he touches me even after we've fucked rough, I keep thinking there's a part of him that might want something more between us. I don't know how to bring it out of him, though. I don't know if he knows how to bring it out of himself.

In the end, it isn't something I should be exploring. "My marriage is open to sex with other people, not emotions," I tell Zully as I step onto the outside patio.

"Well, I've been telling you all along, your marriage is bullshit, so that's how I feel about that."

"Thank you, Zully, for clearing that up and, as always,

mocking the important choices I've made in my life." It's more biting than I intend, with bitterness better directed at myself, but I'm in a mood now and not in a place to act with such self-awareness.

Especially now that I have to put on my professional face because I've just spotted Adly. Or been spotted by her, rather. "Love you, Zully, but I have to go."

I click off my phone and slip it into my purse then make my way over to Holt's sister, who is alone at a standing table, waving me over like I'm supposed to be meeting her, and hell, maybe I am. Holt wasn't very forthcoming about tonight's event, and the simple black sleeveless number he provided for the occasion didn't help with any clues. As far as I know, this could be another whole Sebastian shebang, as many of them tend to be.

"Are you here for…?" Adly asks when I make it to her.

Not wanting to sound clueless, I simply say, "Holt asked me to meet him here."

Her eyes go wide before breaking into the most genuine smile I've ever seen her give. "I knew it. I knew it." Without warning, she wraps me into a hug. "I'm sorry, I'm just so happy for him. For you. For both of you."

"Uh…" Whatever she thinks is happening, I'm pretty sure she has the wrong idea. I'm going to need to have some more information, but now her attention is on flagging down the waiter for her check.

As I wait for her return focus, I scan the marina around us for details. I figure tonight's event is either in the clubhouse or on one of the boats, and sure enough, I see Holt's brother, Steele, with a beautiful dark-haired woman on his arm. And is that Samuel Sebastian escorting a woman onto that yacht?

When I turn back to Adly, she's handing the waiter her card. "I had a feeling," she says to me, "but I know better than anyone not to believe what you read in the media, so I wrote it off as wishful thinking. But then when Holt punched Hunter over you—"

I blink, utterly confused. "Holt punched Hunter…over *me*?" I'm trying not to get ahead of myself, but I'm glad I have the table to hold on to because my knees suddenly feel weak.

"Oh, you didn't know? After that shitty, shitty thing he said about you. I mean, between you and me, my brother's always been a bit of a fuck face, but that was a low blow."

Actually, *now* I'm utterly confused. "*Holt* is a fuck face?"

"No, Hunter." She must have meant cousin and accidentally said brother. The two and a half empty cocktail glasses in front of her and the extra effusiveness suggest she might be a bit tipsy, and I'm too eager to hear what else she has to say, so I don't stop to clarify. "He was the oldest when…" She shakes her head. "Anyway, it's not you. It's definitely him. He and Holt are always bumping heads, and usually Holt is the bigger man and lets all his antics roll off his back—I mean, he doesn't really let it roll off his back. The pressure does get to him, but where Hunter is concerned, he usually can keep his cool. But then Hunter said that shit about you, and next thing you know, Holt is seeking him out at Spice and then slugging him in the jaw. It was a highlight of my life. I wish I'd recorded it. You know—Reid might have caught it on a security cam. I'll make a note for myself to ask."

She halts her rambling to pick up her phone and dictates into the microphone. "Ask Reid if he has footage of Holt hitting Hunter. Point being, I knew it then. Holt would never have bothered with Hunter if he wasn't into you."

She doesn't put her phone back down, so it takes me a second to realize that she's talking to me again. "Uh… what? I'm sorry. I'm not following."

She giggles. "No, my fault, sorry. Truly sorry. I'm nervous about this whole thing tonight, and so I accidentally drank more than I should, and I know I'm a mess. Daddy's not going to be happy, or you know what? Maybe he will be happy because apparently he's found the love of his life, and he's been on cloud nine since, and all I can think about is what if she's like some Cinderella stepmom, and she hates me? I know. I'm a full-grown woman. It shouldn't matter. But it does matter. You don't know how Dad keeps us all jumping like circus monkeys. More hours on my psych's sofa, I suppose. SNC pays for my insurance, and you better believe I use it for my mental health, because Daddy definitely deserves the bill. Oh, there's Chase, my date." She waves to someone behind me, just as the waiter brings her card back.

I look over my shoulder to see a tall, athletic man waving back.

"Want to walk down to the boat with us, or are you going to wait for Holt?" Adly asks as she signs the receipt.

I glance toward the boat that Samuel and Steele got on. No one else seems to be boarding it. How small is this event, exactly?

My stomach starts to sink as dread settles over me. "I

think I'll wait." Really, I think I need to leave, but I don't say that to her.

"Sure thing. But in case I don't get another chance to say it..." She takes a breath. "I didn't realize that you were into Holt back then, but since you're here for him...I'm just really happy for him. He doesn't let people in, you know. Especially not women, and he's taking this hard, so I'm glad you're here for him."

She reaches over to squeeze my hand. Hopefully she doesn't notice how clammy it is. "I'll see you on the boat." With that, she leaves to join her date.

Holy fuck.

I try to process everything Adly revealed. Try to decide what to do next. Her half-drunk gin and tonic sits before me, and I finish it off quickly, but I don't give it time to enter my bloodstream before I push myself into gear and walk back into the yacht club and out toward the parking lot.

I'm staring at my phone, opening the Lyft app when I hear my name being called. Looking up, I see Holt getting out of the back seat of a car. He signals to the driver to wait when he sees my expression. "What's wrong?"

I wait until I'm closer to ask, knowing very well that there are always onlookers. "What the fuck is this tonight?" When his jaw tightens, I clarify my question. "Why does Adly think I'm your date, and why do I only see members of your immediate family here?"

For the first time since I've known him, Holt seems speechless. He runs a hand through his hair, searching for something—words, maybe—in the horizon before looking back at me with empty eyes.

"I can't be your date to a family affair, Holt." I'm astonished as I say it because the truth is, there is a part of me that very much wants to be Holt's date. To be someone that he cares enough about to bring into his inner fold.

But the other part of me knows this is too far. "What the fuck is wrong with you?"

"I can explain."

"Then explain."

"It's..." He swipes his hand down his chin this time, and I've never seen him so on edge. "Just come with me. I'll explain it all after."

"No." It's sharper than I planned. "No, no. I am not getting on that boat. I'm sorry. That's a family thing, and I am not..." Not qualified. Not available. Not...I'm not sure how to finish. "I am not... Why?"

That's the real question, the one pleading to be answered.

"I...." He grabs my arm. "Come on, Brystin. I need you."

Those are magic words where I'm concerned. Usually. He needs me? Then better believe I'm here for him.

Substitute any name from my past for that he/him, and it would be a true statement.

But Zully's advice from earlier is still fresh in my ear—*stop giving them part of you*—and I force myself to stand my ground. "For what, Holt?" When he lets a beat pass, I push on. "You demand honesty from me while you hide behind your position? Tell me the truth for once."

I feel his resistance as he looks from the waiting car to me to the marina back to me. His posture slumps when he makes his decision. "My father's getting married. Uh. He's introducing us to his fiancée tonight, and I'm..." He rolls his shoulders back. "I can't do it alone, Brystin."

"So you want me to be your distraction?" I let out a half laugh, backing away. "No. No."

"It's not like that."

"Then what is it like?" I've been his toy since day one, his personal plaything. Thinking back now, how so many of the events he's had me at were family related, maybe that's what it's all been about. An attempt to disengage from a toxic family environment. Is that why he *needs* me tonight? "Why is this even a big deal, Holt? Your dad's getting married. So what?"

"Because he isn't supposed to be able to love anyone again. Okay?" His voice is raw, and for the first time since I've known him, there's a vulnerability that makes my heart trip.

I'm gentler when I step toward him. "Are you afraid it ruins what he had with your mother?"

"No. It's. I..." He swallows, looking at his expensive shoes as he shakes his head. "I always thought he couldn't. Couldn't love anyone but her. Was incapable. But if he loves Giulia—" He turns his head in the direction of the yacht. "If he really does, then..."

"Then what?"

When he shifts his gaze back toward me, his expression is devastating. "Then why couldn't he love me?"

"Oh, Holt." My eyes prick with tears, and my chest tightens, but I know he isn't looking for my pity right now. He already told me what he needs—me.

"Get in the car," I tell him, a little surprised at my own boldness. "I'll get in with you."

He opens the door without hesitation, letting me get in first before sliding in next to me. "Where are we going?"

"I don't know, but we're not getting on that boat." Tonight, Holt needs to be with someone who loves him.

Detrimental to my heart as it may be, I'm ready to admit to myself that's me.

CHAPTER THIRTY

BRYSTIN

"Confession..." I pause, wondering if I have the nerve to go big and talk emotions.

Nope. I'm chicken, and I choose something minorly embarrassing instead. "The night you took me to the roof of the Sebastian Center was my first time ever at the top."

Holt raises a stunned brow. "You're kidding me."

I shake my head, pulling my feet underneath me. We're sitting together on Holt's living room couch, the space between us mere inches, and have been here like this for the better part of three hours. Just...talking.

Mostly mundane shit, at first. How he found his apartment and why he chose the art and furniture pieces that he did. I'd been in and out so fast last time that I hadn't taken the time to notice. He has a very contemporary taste, and though he had a designer for Adeline, I see his influence on the country home now based on his choices for the three thousand square foot space here.

Then Holt introduced me to the best biryani delivery in the city, which he, of course, paired with a pinot noir that made the taste of the chicken and rice explode in my mouth.

After that, he gave me a very thorough, very sexy lesson on wine tasting, which loosened our tongues a bit, and our conversation got a little more personal, but we've managed to skirt the most meaningful topics.

Unlike other times we've talked, though, I don't sense a wall between us. The door is open wide in both directions, and I have little doubt that one of us will eventually cross the threshold, but I also don't feel like there's any rush. Just a summer storm of anticipation gathering in my belly, and each minute that passes by, I'm more and more excited for the rain.

"Okay, I have to hear how you have lived in the city for over ten years and yet managed to bypass one of the top five tourist attractions." The hunger in Holt's eyes isn't just about lust. He's eaten every word I've had to say with a voracious appetite, and I'm starting to think I've never had anyone truly desire me before now.

While I feel as greedy for him, it's a transforming feeling to also be on the other side of it for once.

"Well, I told you I grew up in Missouri, and we never came to New York for vacation. Then when I moved out here for college, I was too broke to do the touristy shit." I mean to leave it at that for a second, but then decide to tell him all of it. "Wait, that's not exactly true. My mom and I came once when I was fifteen over summer break, and we saw some of the sights then."

"Let me guess—you did the Empire instead."

"No way. I was already in love with journalism so I insisted on coming to the Sebastian Center. We had every intention of riding to the top, but my mother has a fear of small spaces. She knew what it meant to me, and she really wanted to try to ride the elevator. She stood in the line and made it for a decent while before she had a panic attack. Security came and they rushed an emergency team. It was so embarrassing, and in the end, we had to go back to the hotel."

He grazes his knuckle against my bare shoulder, back and forth, sending goose pimples scattering down my arms. "Were you disappointed?"

I shrug. "We did the studio tour. That's what I really cared about. I probably still have the scrapbook somewhere in our storage unit."

Our.

It's one of the few plural pronouns referring to me and Michael that I've used tonight. I hold my breath, hoping it doesn't kill the mood.

If Holt noticed, he doesn't show it. "Let's see…you were fifteen, and it was summer, so I was nineteen. I interned every break for my father starting at seventeen. I would have been in the building."

"That's…weird." That I could have known him first. Before Michael. But I don't want to explain that's where my head went. "Weird to think about. You know? That we were both there at the same time and didn't know it."

"Your mom could have left you with me."

"Would we have made it up here or would you have had other plans for me?" I ask with intended innuendo.

"You were fifteen. That would have been illegal." He can't hide his smile.

"Other plans then." I laugh. "I could have knocked out losing my virginity a whole year earlier."

He shakes his head as if the thoughts going through his mind are too much to handle. "Let's not even… You can't fathom the ways I would have corrupted you."

Another laugh. "I think I can, actually."

My eyes lock on his, and although I love the carnal ideas I see there, I'm not ready to give up the intimacy we're sharing in words.

Fortunately, it seems he isn't either. "Was it just you and your mother by then?"

Oh, wow. We're going there now. To the real stuff. "It was always just me and my mother. Even when my father was still living with us, I never knew him as not a junkie."

"Is he still…?"

I say the word he politely avoided. "Alive? No. Died in a mugging when I was twenty. *A mugging*. I'd been certain he'd die of an overdose, but nope. A mugging. It was probably over drugs."

He withdraws his knuckle, giving me space that I don't need. "I'm sorry."

"Don't be. I'd lost him long before that. His death was closure." I shift, stretching my legs out and propping my bare feet on the edge of the ottoman. "My mother was finally able to let him go. Married a nice Protestant man and now she lives a happy suburban life. At least that's what the Christmas cards say."

"You aren't close?"

"Not really. The only thing we ever had in common was how much we stupidly loved my father." I look out through his floor-to-ceiling windows at the city sky, unwilling to watch his reaction. He's suggested that I have daddy issues in the past, and now I've basically confirmed the fact.

Except it's not my father that instilled the patterns that I seem to retrace over and over again, and for some reason, I find it worth acknowledging. "You know, she was my only role model where love was concerned. She treasured whatever scraps she got. She gave and gave and gave until she was a scrap herself."

Summoning my courage, I dare to look at him. "I think I'm doing better than she did, considering."

I'm surprised how much I want his validation. From his expression, I see he's contemplating giving it, but I can also tell that, if he does, it will be a lie.

I reach out to his forearm, forgetting the effect physical contact with him has on me until electricity flashes up my limb, even though we've been casually touching off and on all evening. "Don't respond to that. I know you have your opinions about me…"

"Don't think you know my opinions, Brystin." He places his hand over mine. It's firm and gentle all at once. My gaze drifts to where we're connected. I turn my hand so our palms kiss, and he laces his fingers through mine.

It's basic touch considering all the ways we've been physical, but I feel dizzy and out of breath. My fight or flight response yells at me to run, even though I'm usually a freeze kind of a girl. Apparently, my instincts know this is turning into something bigger. Am I ready for it?

Hyperaware of my every move, Holt notices my panic. "You okay?"

"I'm…" I take a deep breath. I'm okay, but vulnerable, and in need of a distraction.

So I do what I do best and turn the tables so I'm the one asking the questions, knowing this will send us into the territory we've been cautiously working toward all night. "What about you? How did your parents fuck you up?"

"Isn't it obvious?" He gives a genuine laugh, something he does so rarely, it's hard not to feel like it's a gift.

"Obvious is in the eye of the beholder." I don't know what the fuck I'm saying. I'm buzzed—from him, not the alcohol—and I feel like I'm walking a tightrope toward him. He let me onto the platform in the parking lot, giving me a path to get inside his head—inside his heart—but I'm afraid of falling before I reach him. I'm trying to tread carefully. "I guess I'd like to hear it from your perspective."

"Well, let's see." He lets go of my hand so he can fidget, smoothing out an invisible wrinkle on his pant leg with his palm. "My father, as you know, is a strong-headed ruler of the western world. Until his heart attack a couple of years ago, anyway. He's impossible to live up to, and yet his approval requires that I do. I know I never will, but I haven't figured out how to stop trying so I think that's probably the bulk of my fuckedupness, as you may have guessed by now."

He takes a beat, and I think this will be as far as he dares go, only to discover I'm wrong. "But then, of course, there's my mother. Who actually did die from an overdose—on purpose—not that I can talk about it truthfully with pretty much anyone, which means I probably have a lot of mental shit to deal with. Especially because my father worshiped her. She was his only weakness, if you ask him. He loved her to the point that it crippled him.

"And that was confusing for me, because I hated her."

His bluntness startles and moves me. "Hated her for killing herself?"

"Before that too. She had fo—" He takes a breath. "She had children who loved her. And it wasn't enough."

I'm quiet, knowing there's no way my response will adequately express how much I'm feeling for him. Another beat passes where I try to figure out what he needs most to hear me say. "You know she was probably suffering from a mental health condition."

I swear I feel him resist an eye roll. "I realize that. I know it's unfounded."

Yeah, Brystin. I'd eye roll too. Do you hear yourself?

"I don't mean that. I just..." I pivot to face him and try again. "It helps sometimes for me to remember that my father wasn't capable of choosing me. Maybe your mother wasn't either."

"Maybe I'm more fucked up than you are because realizing that doesn't help." He takes my hand again, squeezes it. Lets me know I didn't say anything wrong, and that he wants me to understand. "I still hate her. Even when she was alive, she wasn't there. Not mentally or emotionally. Her heart was always with...him."

"Him? Your father?"

"Hunter," he says, purposefully.

"Your cousin?" As soon as I say it, I remember Adly's slip at the yacht club, and I start to wonder if I missed something.

"I see your brain going. What do you know about Hunter? I'm sure your inquisitive mind has looked him up."

I researched him the day after the awards. He hadn't been on my radar and then he'd been nasty that night, so of course I needed to know more. "He's a year older than you. Reynard's son, who comes right before your father in birth order. He has two half-brothers—"

"Yeah, okay," Holt says, with a strange chuckle. "Go on."

"Reid and Alex. Both younger. And a stepmom."

"Nelani is his second stepmom."

"Right, because he divorced Reid and Alex's mom—"

"—Pavla."

"Right." Then I remember the odd thing about Hunter's biography. Pavla had married Reynard when Hunter was two. Nowhere on the internet could I find a mention of Hunter's mother. I hadn't been interested enough at the time, but now I realize why the information had been hidden, why Adly made the remark she did. Why Holt's mother was absent. "You and Hunter have the same mom?"

Holt gives the slightest of nods, as if he's still unsure he wants to share this secret. "I've never told anyone that."

Warmth flutters up my spine. A day ago, it would have felt dangerous to feel honored where Holt is concerned, but now I feel privileged. Special. It's the most vulnerable I've ever seen him, and I wonder if he's ever been this vulnerable with anyone else.

I could dwell on that for hours, but there's also the bomb that just exploded. "Wait—your mother had an affair with Reynard—*had a baby with him*—and no one knows about it?"

His half smile is panty-melting. "It's just one of our many dirty little secrets."

"So…" I have so many questions. I don't know where to start. I turn to face him, pulling my feet underneath me again. "Was it actually an affair? Were your parents already together? How did Hunter end up with Reynard instead of your mom?"

Holt takes a breath, and it seems he's going to shut the whole conversation down, feeling that he's already said too much. Part of me wants to give him permission to stay silent, but another part of me believes he needs to say these words he's never said and get them off his chest.

I wait quietly, and after a beat, I'm rewarded.

"It's a taboo topic in our household, so what I know is what I've worked out on my own. Before my mom and dad got together, she was with Reynard. She got pregnant. They broke up? Reynard, being a Sebastian, was able to get full custody. And he's the worst, Brystin. You think any of the rest of us are bad…we look like angels in comparison to that man. He must have denied her any contact with him. So…I think my father must have felt sorry for her? Or he already loved her. I don't know. But I'm pretty sure the only reason she married him was so that she could have whatever contact she could get with her son."

"Oh." It's a punch in the gut. That poor woman, and I sure as hell know what it feels like to be Samuel if his love was as one-sided as Holt seems to believe it was.

But my sympathy at the moment is all for Holt, unloved by his father, believing he was always an afterthought for his mother. "She was put in a terrible position," I say, as if that might make it better. I want to touch him, stroke his face. Ease his pain with touch, but I'm afraid of being too invasive so I squeeze the hand that's still wrapped around mine. "An impossible position, Holt. I know that doesn't—"

He cuts me off, seeming not to want my platitudes. "She should have focused on the kids she had. We were *there*. Instead, she pined over Hunter. Talked about him all the time. Stared at his pictures, looking for her own traits in his features. It's impossible"—he enunciates the word, the same one I'd used—"for me not to hate them both."

It hits me so hard, this grief that he carries, that I have to bite my lip so that I don't cry. The heated interactions he's had with his cousin—*holy shit, his secret brother*—make sense now, and I have no words. No words to console him. No words to address this pain.

But the more I study him, the more I'm not sure that's what he wants. He's explaining to me. That's all. Telling me his secrets.

He brings my hand up to his mouth and brushes a kiss across my knuckles. "He was my role model, Brystin," he says, echoing what I said to him earlier. "He taught me that love will die and to never let anyone in."

My heart feels like it's shrinking as disappointment sinks in. All of this work tonight, all this opening up only to get to this excuse?

I refuse to let the door close without pushing back. "But now he's letting someone in."

He nods, considering. "And now I'm letting someone in."

Every muscle in my body releases as I realize he wasn't shutting a door at all.

I swallow, afraid to let elation in until I'm certain. "Are you?"

Another nod, slow but sure. Then his own caution steps in. "You and Michael...?"

I can't shake my head fast enough. "There's nothing, Holt. I wanted him, but he never wanted me. Our marriage isn't anything. We aren't...real. We've never been real."

Relief spreads like sunrise on his features. He leans toward me and reaches his hand out to stroke my cheek. "Is *this*...real? Are *we*…real?"

A dam of emotion breaks inside me, and I know if I don't kiss him soon, I'll cry, and it hits me how cruel Michael has been all these years, able to sit on this side of the same kind of plea I've given to him, feeling nothing. Thinking instead that there was an emotion to be played and used. I don't think I could ever do that to a human who looked at me with as much vulnerability as Holt has looking at me now.

But maybe it's not fair to judge Michael because I'm not in his position. I feel so much for Holt. And it's so genuine that I practically burst when I tell him. "So fucking real, Holt. So fucking real."

We come together tentatively, our lips brushing once, twice, three times before clutching together in a static kiss. As frenzied as we've been every time before, this time we're deliberate, exploring as though we're new to each other. As though we're new to making love, and perhaps we both are because everything about this feels different than any other time I've been with a man, despite how infatuated I believed I was.

Once, years ago, Zully said to me that love was different when it was reciprocated, and I bottled up and didn't speak to her for days, though I'm not sure she realized it. I was certain that she couldn't know how I felt, how I loved enough to make up for what was lacking on the other side.

Now, as Holt kisses down my neck, as he undresses me with gentle hands and learns the religion of my body with the reverence of a zealot, I see how true Zully's statement was. So true that I don't need to hear the words from Holt's lips to know that what we're both feeling is love. It might even be a long time before either of us are familiar enough with the emotion to be capable of expressing it in words.

For now, we express it like this, with his tongue along the hollow of my neck, with his palms splayed across my belly, with his fingers feathering the skin at my hips, with his mouth between my thighs.

Perhaps the greatest tell that this time is different is that, when I go for the buttons on Holt's shirt, for once he doesn't stop me. Except for the time I caught him in the shower, I've never seen him undressed. I even wondered once or twice if he was hiding some childhood scar or some imperfection beneath the layers of clothes he kept between us, but now in his naked magnitude, I discover he is physically flawless. Toned where a fit man should be toned. Groomed where a man of class should be groomed. Hard where a virile man should be hard.

I touch as much of him as his patience allows, skating my lips over taut biceps and firm forearms. Dancing my fingers over the plane of his torso. Finding him adorably ticklish behind his knees. Discovering how sensitive he is at the spot between the backdoor and his balls.

By the time he picks me up and carries me to his room, I feel like an advanced scholar in the language of Holt Sebastian, only to realize I've barely begun my studies when he lays me on his bed and teases me to orgasm several times before sliding into me with the hottest, hardest cock I've ever had inside me.

Only then does the Holt I know make an appearance, talking dirty as he rolls so I'm on top. "Such a wet hole when it's happy, isn't it? Able to take as much as my cock will give, such a greedy little cunt." He abuses my sensitive clit with the pad of one finger and pinches my nipple with the other until I squeak out in pleasure/pain. "Bounce on me, baby. Show me you know what to do with a cock that wants to treat you so right."

His tolerance for leaving me in control only lasts so long, though, and soon his fingers are gripping into my hips, lifting and lowering me to meet the rapid thrust of his pelvis. His cock at that angle sends blinding sparks across my vision, and I collapse against his chest with a jagged moan.

"Oh, no. You aren't done until you're filled with my cum." He rolls us again and takes my mouth with a passionate kiss while he brutishly beats into me, and I think about his words while I drive my nails down his back, while another orgasm threatens to twist through my exhausted body. Think about how I could never be filled with him. Think about how there would always be room inside of me for more. How I could never just take the pieces, because until I had all of him, I could never consider myself whole.

How easy it is to love someone completely.

How easy it is to be loved completely in return.

Afterward, in the dark, when our skin is soaked with sweat, our bodies coiled around each other, we flit around the heavy sentiments in fragmented phrases.

"I've never," he says.

"I know. Me too."

"It's not what I thought." He strokes a strand of damp hair out of my face. "You?"

"It is, and it isn't."

He nods, and I'm sure he understands.

"We can't…" Lose this. Let each other go.

"We won't," he promises.

"We have to—"

He cuts me off with a finger to my lips. "We'll figure it out, honeybee."

"We will?"

"We will."

I fall asleep believing him.

CHAPTER
THIRTY-ONE
BRYSTIN

Leaning forward on the barstool, I put my elbows on the kitchen island and prop my chin on my hands, watching Holt as he gathers ingredients to make the one and only thing he says he can cook—scrambled eggs with "stuff" added. "While you cook…we should talk about the elephant in the room."

Big of me to bring it up, honestly. Or maybe self-sabotage. I shouldn't be allowed to feel this good. Shouldn't be allowed to feel this happy.

Holt looks down at the bulge in his boxer briefs. "That's awfully generous, Brystin, but I like to think a python is a more appropriate metaphor."

I've giggled so much in the last twelve hours, it's embarrassing. But teenage humor deserves teenage giggles, so I sound off another round. "It's too pretty to be a python."

"Pretty?" He chokes, and I'm lucky he doesn't throw the egg in his hand at me. He does use it to point in my direction. "Never, never, never refer to a man's jewels as pretty."

"Then never, never, never refer to them as jewels." I return his smirk with one of my own. "You walked into that one."

"I did. I did. Truly." He turns back to the pan, giving me a glorious view of his backside. He's wearing nothing but his boxer briefs, and holy mother of all…either God's a woman or he's gay because Holt's ass is divine. His entire figure, actually. I spent the better part of the night exploring it, and I still can't get enough.

"Seriously, though, can he be hit by a train?"

I'm so focused on the display that I've forgotten what we were talking about. "Hm?"

"Or have a heart attack while in some sordid position." He peers over his shoulder—his perfectly sculpted shoulder. "I'm sorry about what you'd have to deal with in that case, but it would be worth it to see that fetid piece of shit have to endure the scandal."

Oh, yes. Michael.

For once, I don't feel obliged to defend him. "Then you'd want him to survive the heart attack?"

Holt considers. "Yes, but just long enough to go through the scandal. Then he can get hit by the train." He turns around completely, spatula in hand. "I'm only going to say this once, and I'll deny it if you ever try to say I said it, but I could probably arrange something like that. No questions asked."

I manage to only gape for a few seconds. There's no way I would ever advocate murder, especially not for Michael, who doesn't deserve anything so vicious, but it does give me new insight into Holt's life. I already get that billionaire life is akin to royalty—a lifestyle unimaginable by most, including me. Still, for something like that to come out of his mouth with such frank ease is jarring.

The suggestion also makes me feel more tingly than it should. "I really don't think that's necessary."

"But I'd do it for you. If you wanted me to." His smile is genuine, and the butterflies that have taken residence in my stomach decide to put on a rave. It's borderline too intense, and Holt turns it down by a swift turn to humor. "Okay, let's be real here—it would be for me."

I laugh. Half-heartedly, though, because what I really need to do is somehow harder. "I should leave him."

"Uh, no shit you should leave him." This time when Holt turns, he brings the frying pan with him. "I told you my family secrets, and now I have to keep you. You're mine. Sorry, Michael."

"Do you want to keep me?" I ask as he scrapes eggs onto the plate in front of me.

He pauses to stare at me. "If you have to ask that, I'm not doing a good enough job of staking my claim. I'm letting you wear my T-shirt—which is distracting, by the way, though slightly less distracting than you naked. You think I let anyone else wear my things? You think I make breakfast for all the married women who stay over?"

I think the answer is supposed to be obvious, but we've never talked about his love life. "I don't know…do you?"

"No. No, Brystin. I do not." He finishes scraping the rest of the eggs onto his plate, then picks up his fork before squarely looking me in the eye. "Not only do I not make them breakfast, I also don't let them stay over. I don't even bring women here."

"Never?"

"Well…not never. But mostly never." He takes a bite of the eggs. "I told you I didn't really believe in that relationship stuff, and women get ideas when you bring them to your home. Even the married ones."

And yet he brought me here weeks ago. When I get a chance, I need to covertly ask the internet if a person can die from swoon.

Though, now I'm focused on another detail. "You date a lot of married women?"

We've been no holds barred since last night, revealing every little thing the other wanted to know with no hesitation. With this question, however, he seems reluctant. "Yeah," he says finally. "I suppose I do."

"You like the challenge? You want to possess what other men possess?" I'm trying to be journalistic about it. Asking the questions without attaching emotion.

"I don't know that I ever really thought about the husbands much. Though, it does make it…hotter." He doesn't have to remind me how many times my marital status added to the sexual tension. "Mostly, I think it felt safer. The married women I hook up with have already given their hearts to someone else. It's less likely they're going to try to push them on me."

I nod while I take a bite, trying to understand. Thinking I do a good job of succeeding.

"Now you—" Holt puts his fork up in the air like a pause button while he swallows from his juice glass. "I've never not been aware that you were unavailable. It's the first time I've cared. Cared in confusing ways. Like, fuck your commitment to fidelity—as soon as you said it was off-limits, I wanted in your pussy. Well, I wanted in before that, but I wouldn't have been so obsessed."

"You were obsessed?" I'm grinning like a fool. "Also, these eggs are really good."

"Don't sound so amazed. They're fucking eggs." Another sip of his juice. "And yes. Obsessed. At the same time, I felt constant guilt about trying to tempt you to cheat on your husband. I, um. Don't feel so guilty about it right at the moment, though, so, uh. Don't go thinking I'm a nice guy or anything."

I duck my head, feeling like a not nice guy myself. "Michael and I have an open marriage."

"Then why…?" He studies me for a second. "You made that a hard limit because you didn't want to fuck me?"

"I always wanted to…*fuck* you. I just—"

"I have to interrupt and tell you that it's such an incredible turn-on to hear you say the word *fuck*, particularly when you're talking about fucking me, so feel free to say it often."

I fight a smile. "We have an open marriage, but I've never taken advantage of it."

"...at all?"

I shake my head. "Not even a stray kiss."

"Oh." He doesn't seem so much surprised as honored.

At the risk of over stroking his ego, I admit the rest. "I haven't slept with Michael either, since…since you, really."

To his credit, he doesn't act like a cocky bastard about it. "No?"

"I can't do that. It's not how I work."

He nods, and I can see the gears in his head turning, making me die to know what's going on in there.

"So it was all Michael's idea. Of course it was. Like I said—fetid shit. I don't know how you…" He trails off, but it's not like I don't know a hundred ways he could have finished the statement.

I don't know how either. How I put up with so much, so long. I'm more than ready to move on to whoever I am after him, whoever that is. Hopefully, someone who gets to be with Holt, but even if that's not in the cards, it's time for me to be done with Michael.

After several seconds, Holt drops his fork and leans over the counter between us so we're eye to eye. "Let's get something straight right now, honeybee. I've always considered myself a modern man, but I'm going to go caveman here and lay something down for you—I can't share."

There goes my feminism because I just swooned again.

"I don't expect you to share either," he continues. "Fair's fair and all that, but mostly, I don't want anyone but you."

Oh, wow. "I think I just orgasmed."

"Is that all it takes? I've been working too hard."

I crumple up my napkin and throw it at him. "Stop it. I love how hard you work on me. It's…refreshing."

The subtle dig toward my husband sends Holt into his own version of swooning, which looks a lot like a rooster cocking around the pen. His pecs look even more pronounced as his chest swells.

"Speaking of Michael…" He puts his dishes and the pan in the sink before turning back to me. "I want you to leave him, if it matters at all what I think."

"It does." Unable to eat more, I push my plate toward him and pick up my coffee mug. "But they're two separate things—me leaving him, and me and you."

"Sure, sure." He takes my fork and finishes off the rest of my eggs. He's so comfortable in the domestic act, it's hard to believe this is all as new for him as he says. "It has nothing to do with me."

I pretend to roll my eyes.

"It's a little bit because of me, though, right?"

Damn, that smile.

"It's all because of you, you narcissist, but I'm trying to be an adult here."

He adds my plate to the sink then returns to lean against the counter. "You're being very adult right now, and I respect it. I do. I'm going to go so far as to encourage you to be adult about it, and not tell him you're leaving until you have a plan."

In just a few words, he's forced me to acknowledge how big leaving a marriage can be. There will be drama. Michael will push back. We still have to work together. Then we have to figure out the details of who gets what, who lives where. Add a relationship with Holt into the mix, and the whole thing feels a bit overwhelming.

He's right. I need to go into it with a plan. "Will you help me make one?"

"I would love to help you make one." His eyes are sparkling, but his expression is serious, and I appreciate how thoughtful he's being about this when he could be a macho jerk. "Want to have an after-breakfast fuck and then start working on it?"

I feel my cheeks get red, more because he gets me deliciously heated than out of any sort of embarrassment.

But I really am trying to be a grown-up. It's already almost ten a.m., and tomorrow I'm back at work. Supposedly back to Michael's city apartment tonight. There's a lot to work out, and not a lot of time. "Though your suggestion is awfully tempting, I need to be practical with the day. I've been spending the weekends at the New Jersey place, and I need to stop by and get some clothes for the week."

"I didn't realize you were still going back and forth."

"We aren't used to spending so much time together. Usually, he'd spend at least part of the weekend in Manhattan, so now we've just reversed it. It's been fine. It's only the weekend that I have to commute. I haven't had a reason to..." I realize I'm explaining too much. Defending the arrangement that I've hated from the beginning.

I don't want to do it anymore.

"Point is that I need to get some clothes. And then I have to figure out where I'm sleeping tonight, and—"

"Uh, here," he says, cutting me off. "What part of I'm keeping you do you not understand?"

My insides feel like warm mush. "Well, I don't have to see Michael or explain my whereabouts until I don't show up at our apartment tonight. We should have at least a few things figured out by then. Is there anything you need to do today?"

He can't help himself. "Besides you?" Then he's serious. "I have a few things for work. Maybe take me an hour, two at most. I should talk to my father at some point. Make excuses for ditching. I should work out."

I can barely move without my muscles reminding me of

every position we were in last night, and he wants to work out. I want to say not fair, but I also don't mind feeling Holt in my body, hours after he's not there. "Okay, then. You can do all that while I run to Jersey—"

"I'll come with you. I'll drive."

"You can, but." I appreciate the offer, but part of me needs a little time to process. "If we split up, we can be done with everything we need to be done with by one o'clock. Then we'll have the rest of the day to—"

"Fuck like bunnies. Okay. Sold."

"Holt!" Again, I'm giggling.

"And we'll make a plan. There's a lot we should figure out between me and you too. A lot still to, um, say."

It's almost like he just said the word that I'm pretty sure we're both feeling. "Yeah, there is."

The air feels heavy around us. Heavy in the best way.

Keeping his eyes on mine, he comes around the island to my side, and turns me so I'm facing him. "We'll talk more later, but I need you to know something right now. I wanted you since day one. Day one, Brystin."

"I think it was pretty obvious since you practically assaulted me in the elevator."

He shakes his head dismissively. "Day one was before that."

"You watched videos of me." I remember Adly had told me he'd pointed me out to her when I was up for the award. This also isn't really new.

"Would you stop guessing what I'm trying to say and let me say it?"

"Sorry." Properly chided, I zip my mouth shut.

"I came by the studio too. To watch you before we

chose the award winner." He puts his hand up to stop me in case I'm about to comment again, and frankly, I was. I hadn't realized he'd ever come by. "You didn't know. Michael didn't even know. But I watched you, and Brystin, I think I knew even then that you were going to be different. I've never been so immediately…I don't have a word for it. Charmed? Obsessed? You were—you are—the most captivating person I've ever encountered. I knew right then and there I had to have you, in whatever way you'd let me. I'm the one who stopped the elevator."

I can't help it. "You stopped the elevator?"

"Thought I would have a chance to figure out what it was about you if we had a few minutes alone. A moment like that is usually all I need to get a phone number. Make a plan to meet later. But as soon as I was sharing space with you, I knew it wasn't going to be enough. Everything that happened later, me and you and the things I pushed you into—"

I wave my hand, not caring at the moment about the manipulation tactics, though it would be something we'd have to talk about eventually.

"I was always going to give you the show. And I was always going to want more. But I would have taken whatever you would have given me, Brystin. That's how into you I was. How into you I *am*. I would have taken the scraps. From day one. Okay? From day fucking one."

I never realized how much I've needed to be wanted until now.

It takes all my strength not to let his declaration turn me into a puddle on the floor. Forget my clothes, forget the shit we have to do—I'm ready to let Holt take me right here on the kitchen counter.

But Holt's being an adult today too. "Okay, now you can go." He steps away from me, deliberately. "And don't shower—I like knowing my scent will be on you when you're in his apartment."

It's as much my apartment as it is Michael's, but I'm not about to argue.

CHAPTER
THIRTY-TWO
BRYSTIN

I'm buzzing so hard from Holt that I forget about optics. This time when I leave his apartment, I'm wearing his T-shirt and a pair of his drawstring gym shorts, which is better than leaving in last night's dress, but my visit is hard to explain away as professional in this getup.

I don't think about it until someone's calling my name. When I turn, a phone camera is pointed in my direction. Luckily, it's just a fan who wants an autograph. I'm not even sure they know this is where Holt lives, but it jostles me from my everything-is-perfect mood, and I instantly regret having conceded to using Holt's driver.

Instead of reminiscing about every exquisite moment from the night before, I spend the hour to Edison charging my phone and worrying about a new possible scandal. Scott has been coaching us to act like no one knows anything, but if I end up openly dating Holt, there will forever be speculation that he's the cause of my divorce.

Which is obviously true, but it's a truth that lacks nuance. It's a truth that will forever point at me as a greedy ladder-climbing money-grabber, and as always, Holt will remain relatively unscathed. There's probably nothing to be done about it, but it's a fact that I'll have to come to terms with, and another issue to add to the list of things that Holt and I need to discuss.

Holt's driver lucks out and finds a parking spot right in front of my building. He offers to come up and help me bring things down, but I don't need a stranger looking over my shoulder while I pack my underwear, so I tell him I'll try to be back down in thirty minutes.

I don't feel the lack of sleep hit me until I'm walking in my apartment, and I have to force myself to get busy instead of collapsing on the sofa. The suitcase I've been using to travel back and forth is still sitting in the hallway. I grab it on the way, and then head to my bedroom.

I freeze as soon as I walk in my door. "Michael. What are you doing here?"

Specifically, what is he doing in *my* bedroom, perched on my unmade bed as though he's waiting for me.

"Trying to figure out if I should worry about your whereabouts. An unmade bed means nothing where you're concerned."

I let out a stilted laugh. My lack of housekeeping skills is a frequent joke between the two of us, but it feels especially pointed today.

It's probably just that I hadn't expected to see him. And my decision to leave him informs how I behave around him, and that feels awkward since he isn't privy to the same information.

But wait a minute… "You mean you're trying to figure out if I slept here last night?" I set the suitcase on the chest at the bottom of the bed. The loss of weight in my arms doesn't lessen the guilt pressing on my shoulders.

Which is stupid, since I have every right to sleep where I want, considering the terms he set for our marriage. "It was your night in Manhattan. Why were you thinking about me?"

He smiles. "I'm always thinking about you, sweet girl."

I'm immediately annoyed. Because sure. When he's railing a different woman every weekend, he's definitely thinking of me. When he's prowling the night scenes without a wedding ring, I'm top of his mind. When he's sending me to the bedroom of SNC's CEO to "discuss" the opportunity to host the show that I helped conceive, I'm all he's thinking about.

It's bullshit. All of it.

It hadn't been clear to me before, when I thought I was in love with him, but now it's so clear I smell the stink for what it is—fetid shit, just as Holt had said.

But I'm not ready to fight with him, so I open my suitcase, hoping that the distraction will keep me civil. "I guess what I'm really asking is, why did you come by to check in the first place?"

He answers with one word. "Jared."

"The doorman?" I grab a handful of panties from my dresser drawer and drop them into the empty suitcase. Having already thrown all my dirty things in the laundry on Friday night, all I have to do today is restock.

"He texted me when he left his shift this morning. Said you never came in last night, and he was concerned."

I'm on my way to the closet, but I spin back toward him. "Hold up. Jared texted you because I didn't come home last night?" I'm practically blind with fury. "That is such a violation of privacy. Have you called the management company yet? He should be fired on the spot."

Michael sits forward. "Hey, hey, don't get so worked up. He only texted because I asked him to. No need to get anyone fired."

Um… "You, what?"

"I asked him to. Months ago. Explained I'm not always here, and that I worry about you alone."

"Oh, hell no." So many thoughts cross my mind at once, it's hard to decide which one to follow first. "First of all, you aren't always here because you're fucking other women. Did you tell that to Jared, too? The reasons for your absentia? Second of all, per the agreement that allows you to fuck these other women, I'm also permitted to fuck other men. So it seems there might be plenty of nights that I either don't sleep here, or I don't sleep here alone. Was that what you really wanted to know from Jared? Whether I'm fucking other people?"

Whether or not I'm fucking Holt, more likely. He's been consumed with our relationship, wanting it to be over. Threatened, perhaps, by Holt's money and status. He never seemed to care who I was sleeping with before.

"No. Don't be ridiculous. I am…just…aware…that you…" Whatever he's trying to say, he's attempting to say it carefully.

It hits me where he's going, and I jump in to finish for him. "That I usually don't take advantage of our open marriage. Uh-huh. I see."

He never cared who I was sleeping with because he knew I wasn't sleeping with anyone.

It occurs to me that the woman I was would have found sentimentality in this. Would have thought it was endearing to look out for me while he was preoccupied and that it meant something that he knew me so well as to know that I wouldn't have been similarly preoccupied.

I am not that woman anymore. "Did you ever intend for me to take advantage of our open marriage?"

"Come on, Brystin. Whatever you're thinking—"

"What I'm thinking is that you set up this arrangement knowing full well that I wouldn't sleep with another man. I mean until you sent me to use sex to get the host spot on this show, which you probably didn't think I would go through with, did you?"

"It's not like you're suggesting. Sex was never important to you."

"Are you kidding me? You're going with men just like sex more so instead of assuming the traditional unfaithful husband role, you came up with this deal, knowing you'd get your cake and get to eat it too?"

He stands, probably not enjoying being yelled at from someone standing over him. "I'm not talking about men and women, Brystin. I'm talking about you and me."

Now his height towers over me, and once upon a time, that might have made me cower.

Today, my spine is ramrod straight. "You know what, Michael? There is no you and me. I'm done with this. With all of this. I want a divorce."

Holt was being smart when he suggested I have a plan, but saying the words, getting them off my chest like this feels liberating in a way that I never imagined. And it has nothing to do with Holt. It's about finally freeing myself from the awful contorted positions I put myself in, in order to have this man. This man who took more and more space until I was so curled in on myself that I could hardly breathe.

Right here, right now, my lungs have more room to expand than they have in years.

Despite the power I feel flowing through my veins, Michael rolls his eyes like I'm nothing more than a nuisance. A bug to be squashed. "You're being over dramatic. A divorce? Did you not get what I promised out of this relationship? Look where you are. Look where you were."

I huff. "I'm where I am now because of my talent. You told me that. Remember?"

"Oh, is that why you're where you are."

"Okay, I'm where I am because I fucked the CEO. Many times, in fact. Not because I fucked you." Knowing it will piss him off, I turn my back on him and open my closet. I'm usually thoughtful about my weekly wardrobe, but I want to get out of here, so I grab a handful of items at random.

"Is this because of him? You think you'll make a happy home with the billionaire who can have any woman in the world he wants. That sounds realistic, Brystin. I thought you were smarter than that."

I know he's trying to hurt me. Remembering how important it was for me to keep Holt out of it, I ignore his goading and give him an honest answer. "It's because I don't love you anymore, Michael. The reason many a marriage falls apart."

"We were never about love."

"No." I drop my clothes, hangers and all, into the suitcase. "*You* were never about love. I tried to love you enough for both of us. Now it's run out, and I'm leaving."

I turn back to the closet, hearing him mutter something about dumb bitch under his breath.

It stings, but my eyes don't prick. Instead, it fuels my rage. Pretending to deliberate, I stay turned away longer this time, trying not to let the adrenaline get the best of me.

"It was all his idea, you know," Michael says, behind me.

I refuse to engage.

He continues on his own. "Holt's. The whole charade. He said he needed a show with ratings, that's all he cared about. Ratings that would astound the board. He didn't care what our idea was really, but he needed it to be you—a woman who was young and attractive. It helped that you were white and blonde. Someone the press would want to gossip about. 'Perfect ingredients,' he said. All that was left was to create the scandal."

I pretend I'm not listening. Except I am, and my heart is thumping a million beats an hour in my chest while my stomach is slowly descending.

"He thought it was best you weren't aware that it was all a PR scam. Neither of us were sure you'd be a good enough actress. Holt said he'd take care of making it look like you're having an affair."

He's lying. He has to be. Trying to manipulate me as always.

"I didn't think he was actually going to convince you to

fuck him. He's better at his job than I thought. Or you're more willing to spread your legs than I realized."

I spin to find him standing over my suitcase. "Fuck you." When he turns to face me, I realize he's holding a pair of my panties.

A chill runs down my back. I step forward and swipe them out of his hand. "You're pathetic, right now, Michael. This...this...story of yours. You think I'm going to come running back to you if you demonize him?"

"I'm trying to protect you! Don't you see what you've fallen for? He's using you, Brystin."

"*He's* using me? *You* used me, Michael. You just admitted it. That the only reason we got this show was because of me. Isn't that what you just said? You used your young, attractive wife to land you the job of a lifetime. And somehow you think you should get credit because it wasn't your idea? You were just the one who thought you had the right to sign me up for it."

I pause to swallow back emotion. "Well, you got the job. But you don't have me anymore. We are done."

He's quiet for a beat, seemingly kicking himself for revealing that I've absolutely carried him to this position. Finally, he says, "Then you believe me about Holt."

I blink back tears.

Because he's right—if I believe this part, I have to believe it all. Have to believe that Holt lied when he said he always wanted me. Or rather, that his speech earlier wasn't about love. It was about how he wanted me only for his show. For his ratings. Have to believe that he used me exactly the way Michael says he did.

I'm not taking Michael's word for it.

And I'm not standing here listening to another word he says. Slamming my suitcase shut, I point to the door of my room. "This is my space. Get out."

He doesn't move. In fact, he settles in, a challenging sneer on his face. He knows I can't make him budge if he doesn't want to. "You know, I've thought a lot about the two of you together. Imagining what he does to you."

Refusing to listen to this, I start past him. He grabs me by the wrist. "Was he rough with you? You can't convince me he's gentle. I didn't realize you had to be forced to be into it. Did he even let you come?"

"Let me go." My teeth are gritted, but his eyes are dark, and when his grip tightens, I'm certain he's going to do something terrible.

It's either the worst thing in the world to say or a shot at getting out of this. "And not only did he let me come, but he could also go all night. I haven't had a reason to be so tired in a decade."

I imagine he wouldn't want to show what little his dick can do in comparison to Holt's. Luckily I'm right, and he lets me go.

Abandoning my suitcase, I tear out of the apartment. I'll figure out what to do about my stuff later. Right now, I'm glad to be away from him.

And now I need to talk to Holt.

CHAPTER
THIRTY-THREE
HOLT

I love you.

Why couldn't I say it? It's three simple syllables.

After finishing the shit I needed to do for the office, I hit my home gym, and all I've been able to think about as I've done my AMRAP workout is how I feel like I spent all night talking to Brystin—well, talking and fucking—and somehow couldn't manage to say the most important words on my chest.

I'm not scared. Fuck that shit. I refuse to be scared.

Maybe it's that invisible ring still on her finger. Or maybe it's that I'm worried I'll scare *her*. It's also possible that I'm worried I don't have enough experience with the emotion. What if I'm wrong? What if it goes away? What if she doesn't say it back?

Fine, I'm fucking scared. Terrified out of my mind. From what I've gathered, that piece of shit husband of hers could never bring himself to say it, so I'm still doing better than he is.

I'm also plainly aware that there are other things I should tell her about our arrangement. I need to clear the air, let her know that I used her too, and the only excuse I have for it is that I wanted to succeed. Frankly, I'm surprised Michael hasn't told her already.

But she came into this wanting the same thing for herself. I guess the difference is that she was always honest about it, and I wasn't. If she feels at all the way I feel about her, she'll understand. I definitely think it needs explaining before I give her my heart.

Scratch that—before I tell her she already owns it. I always wondered how anyone could want to do that. Make themselves vulnerable by giving away such a vital part of their being. I didn't realize that being owned by someone else was a sort of freedom. This is the most tied I've ever been to a woman, and yet I feel like I could fly.

Imagine how I'll feel when I'm married to her.

My incredibly domestic fantasies are interrupted by a phone call. Sweating, I pause my workout music to check the caller ID and answer instantly when I see her name on the screen. "You couldn't go ninety minutes without hearing my voice, could you? Well, I'm good and sweaty right now. If you want me to get you there too, we can have a little phone sex."

I know something's wrong when she doesn't laugh. She's been giggling at every stupid joke of mine since last night, but this time she doesn't even acknowledge my comment. "Why did you greenlight our show?" she asks, out of left field.

A bad feeling crawls like a bug up my spine, but I tell myself I'm being paranoid. "Because it was a good idea. Or do you mean why did I give you the host spot, because I can remind you when you get back here. Are you on your way?"

"You didn't need someone bringing you an idea like that. You have whole teams of people with ideas. Especially if you weren't sure that you were going to give me the host spot. You could have brainstormed something in house. Given the spot to Jessa Jones."

She's talking fast and her voice is pitched higher than usual. If I had to guess, she's trying to hide that she's upset.

If she's upset and these are the questions she's asking…

"Brystin, where are you? Come back to my place, and we can talk about this."

"Talk about what exactly? Is there something that you need to tell me?"

I run my hand through my damp hair and start pacing the length of the gym. "I have lots of things to tell you, but you obviously have something specific you want me to say. Did something happen? Did you…?" She couldn't have, could she? "Did you talk to Michael?"

There's a pause, like she's trying to decide what to reveal. That silence tells me everything—she knows.

"Look, Brystin, whatever he said, that's only one part of it."

"He was at the apartment," she explains, sounding more like the woman I spent the night with. The woman who wants me to know all the things about her life. "He wasn't supposed to be, but he was, and he was awful, Holt. He basically admitted that our marriage arrangement was only ever supposed to be for him, and I'm sick about this part, he was having the doorman keep tabs on me."

"Fuck. Are you kidding me?" I'm already heading to my bedroom closet to change. I don't care if I'm sweaty and gross—I'll go after that motherfucker right now if she gives me the okay.

"He was…I don't know. Maybe I should give him credit. He was being honest for once." There's a dig at me in there, I'm sure of it. "Anyway, one thing led to another, and I told him."

My heart is thundering in my chest. I already see how the rest of the conversation went down. She told him about me, or that she was leaving him, or something to that effect, and he got vicious in return and threw me under the bus.

Part of me is ready to deny. It will be my word against his. He can't verify any of the conversations we had that night in my library.

But Michael has a talent for getting her to believe in him.

More importantly, she needs to know. "He told you that I planned to create a scandal, didn't he? To promote the show."

I hear the hitch in her breath, as if she'd prayed it was a lie, and I've dashed her hopes. "Did you?"

I want so badly to defend myself, but I know she's looking for honesty. "Yes. I did."

A muffled sob slips into my ear, and I'm slayed right in the heart.

"I did, Brystin, and that's true, but it's not the whole truth, okay?" Now I'm pacing my closet, and I feel like a wild cat in a cage. "It's only part of it. Come home, and I'll tell you everything. Where are you?"

"I don't..." She trails off and follows up with a sniffle. "I'm in the car. We just left. I don't even have my things."

"Fuck your things. We'll get them later. Just come home, and I'll explain."

"I don't know, Holt. I don't know."

Anger surges through me. Anger at Michael for fucking me in the ass when he was even more ruthless than I was. Anger at myself for not being straight up in the first place. Anger at the goddamn board and my fucking father who've pressured me and pressured me to make this network something, by whatever means possible.

"Look, Brystin." I'm terrible at apologies and even worse at admitting I'm wrong, but I know they're what's called for. "I wanted the best chance possible for a hit show. I knew I needed a hit concept, and a fresh, hard-hitting anchor, and I should have trusted that was enough—and I do trust that it will be enough. Once the viewers are there, they're going to stay. They've *been* staying. But you have to get them there in the first place, and—"

She cuts me off. "That's what marketing is for! And time. It takes time and word of mouth—"

"I know, I know. Believe me, I know, but I didn't feel like I had time."

"Why? Because you wanted to impress your father?"

It stings that she's willing to throw that back on me so fast after I shared it with her, but it's fair, and so I take it. "It's not just about him, but yes, he's a lot of it. But the board won't keep me in this position if I don't provide results, Brystin."

"So you used me."

Of course that's how she feels.

Why wouldn't she? It's the truth. "I did. I did use you. But I didn't *know* you. And it benefits you too, baby. My success is your success."

"Benefitted me? You could have ruined me!"

"I wouldn't let that happen. Never." Though, it wasn't something I really had any control of, and it's a lie to say otherwise.

"Everything you said this morning—about wanting me from day one—"

"All true," I insist. "Every word of it. I swear on my mother's grave."

"Right. But you wanted me for *ratings*."

"No!" I shake my head, even though she can't see me. "I mean, yes, but I wanted you, too. In my bed. In my life. It was two birds, one stone."

"So strategic in how you deal with your desires." She moves the phone away from her mouth so the next part sounds muffled. "I'm such a fool. Always such a fool."

"Don't do that." I stop my pacing, so frustrated I think I could shred the Armani suit in front of me. "Don't blame any of this on you. You are talented and beautiful, and I coveted those things about you, both professionally and personally, I admit it. And I'm sorry. I'm so fucking sorry I didn't tell you yet, but the truth is, I would never have taken a chance on you any other way, and then you, you, you…" I have so much I want to say that the words get stuck in my throat. "You turned my world upside down, Brystin. You changed my priorities. Don't you see that? You changed me. Can you believe in change?"

"I want to."

"Then do. It's the truth. Believe *me*."

"I just...do you see why you're asking too much? After everything you know about me?"

The problem is that I do see it. She's been burned, and now she's afraid of the fire, and I'm a fucking inferno to her right now.

I can't help but think this would be a better conversation had face-to-face. "Baby, let's talk about this when you're here. No more half truths. I'll tell you anything you want to know. I'll make everything right."

"I don't think I can."

Panic shoots through me like a line of cocaine. "What do you mean you can't? You're already on your way—"

But then I hear her talking to the driver, telling him to drop her off at the next corner.

"Brystin, don't do this. I deserve a chance to talk to you about this."

"It doesn't matter what you say, Holt. Don't you see? I don't know how to trust you."

"No, no, no. Don't say that. I'm the same person you spent last night with, Brystin. The same person."

"How do I believe you?"

"You tell me." I'm desperate. "Tell me what I need to do, and I'll do it."

"I don't know what you can do," she says, and I hear a car door slam. Hear the sounds of traffic around her. "I have to get my head around this first. I'm sorry."

I try convincing her not to hang up for several seconds before I realize she's already gone.

"Fuck!" Needing to throw something, I pick up a random shoe and spike it hard, narrowly missing the full-length mirror.

Thankfully.

Not that I believe in superstition, but I need all the luck I can get right now.

Actually, what I need to do is think. Because like hell is this over. I'm not letting her get away from me. If she needs space or time, fine, but not until we've talked this over in person. Not until I've had a chance to say everything I need to say.

So what do I have to do to make that happen?

Phone still in hand, I dial the number of the guy who was driving her car. "Hey, it's me." He starts to tell me that Brystin got out of the car, but I cut him off. "Yeah, yeah, I know. I need you to, uh..." I take a beat. The guy's on my payroll, and he'll do whatever I ask, but for once, instead of using my power however I see fit, I want to be sure I'm doing the right thing.

"I need you to follow her," I say, finally. Which maybe is still an abuse of power, but at least I took a second to consider it, and that's progress. "She's upset. And I'm worried about her. So if you could follow her and make sure she gets wherever she's going, and then let me know where she's at." If she goes back to that apartment, and if Michael is still there, I might have to consider bringing a gun when I show up.

As predicted, the driver agrees.

While I wait for his call, I jump in the shower and get dressed so I'll be ready to go. I'm so eager to hear from him that I answer my next call without checking my ID. "Yeah."

"So you're not dead, then."

"Dad?" *Fuck.* I pinch the bridge of my nose. "I was actually just going to call you."

"Then I saved you the trouble, didn't I?"

Interestingly, the person who taught me not to apologize or admit I'm wrong is the man on the other end of this call. He believes that apologies make men look weak, and I know I'm caught between a rock and a hard place here—as always with him—because he will either want me to stand up for my choice to not come and then belittle me for my priorities, or he'll want me to grovel for missing the dinner last night, and then berate me for it.

It's a lose-lose, so instead of trying to hold out like I usually do and deflect any accusation of wrongdoing, I cut to the chase. "I'm sorry I didn't show last night. Something came—"

He cuts me off. "Fine, fine. I'm sure you have your reasons. Listen, I'm calling about something Steele was telling me last night."

I'm still too focused on Brystin to be able to truly appreciate my surprise. "Okay. Go on."

"He mentioned your cockamamie plan to get ratings for this new show of yours. Some sort of media scandal."

Ah, shit.

I'm going to fucking murder my brother.

And then I'm going to fire his fucking ass.

That is, if I'm not fired first. My father's never been into shock marketing. He prefers more conservative methods to get ahead. "I know, Dad. It was a mis—"

He goes on as if I haven't said anything. "I thought it was quite arrogant of you to believe anyone would care enough about who you're dating to tune in until I saw the ratings. Remarkable. The taste of viewers has declined over the years, but it appears you know how to take advantage of the fact."

Uh...what?

"Are you...giving me a compliment?" I can't remember the last time he said anything that was even remotely like approving.

"I'm saying you might have been the right one for the job. Keep it up, and the board will be convinced as well."

He hangs up then. Without a goodbye because Samuel Sebastian is too important to waste words on formalities, even with his children. Especially with his children.

And I stand in my living room, staring at my phone in awe.

Receiving praise from the man gives the oddest hit of dopamine. It's unsustainable, and barely pleasurable, but it sure makes me crave more. I read once that humans aren't programmed to be happy; that instead they're programmed for survival.

My annoying-ass lizard brain must think praise from Samuel Sebastian is necessary for my survival because I want to hear it again as much as I want to have Brystin back in my arms.

By the time the text comes through from the driver five minutes later, I have a surefire plan to get both.

CHAPTER THIRTY-FOUR

BRYSTIN

"Is it me? Do I have a big sign on my forehead that says, 'easily used'? Am I just a big fat sucker for toxic men who love their careers more than people?"

Zully strokes my hair as we lie in her bed, my head in her lap, which has been surprisingly soothing. I was a big snotty mess when I arrived at her door, and now the only signs of my tearfest are swollen eyes and an occasional hiccup.

"Of course it's not you," she says, which is a lie.

"I'm already in a bad place, Zul. Just give it to me straight."

Her hand pauses mid-stroke, and I swear I can hear her thinking.

I turn my head so I can peer up at her face. "You're taking too long to answer. Is it that bad? It's that bad, isn't it? I'm hopeless."

"You're not hopeless. You're big-hearted. Does that make you a target? Maybe. Do I think you're doomed to a life of toxic relationships?" She tilts her head back and forth as she considers. "I might have had a different answer a couple of weeks before. But after hearing what went down with Michael, it sounds like you've finally grown some balls."

I sit up. "I really did feel like a badass."

"Obviously."

"I think it was the first time I've ever left an argument with him without feeling whittled down."

"See? It's a massive step forward." She gives me a cautious smile. "As for Holt, I'm not so sure I'm ready to lump him in the same category of toxicity."

At the sound of his name, I have to twist my lips in order to stem any new tears. Officially telling my husband I'm leaving him has my feelings all in a knot, but the true source of my heartache right at the moment is Holt.

I try to access the same strength I found in the confrontation with Michael. "It's a big red flag, though."

"Sure it is. He played you, and that's gross as all get out. But I've seen you together. He's into you. He's into you in a way that asshat never was, and I think that should count for something."

"So you think I should just forgive him?"

"No. No. That's setting a precedent that you don't want to set. But maybe wait and see what happens next. Make him work for you. Make him grovel." She considers for a beat. "Yeah, make him really grovel. Make him get that big fat billionaire checkbook out and buy you stuff."

I laugh for the first time since I arrived, and it feels

foreign, like I haven't laughed in ages, even though my stomach still hurts from all the giggling I did last night.

Or maybe it hurts from the sex.

Whichever, it's a reminder of how recently I was happy, and how quickly my world turned upside down.

Zully latches on to my amusement and attempts to draw it out. "He can buy me stuff, too."

"You? Why do you deserve anything?" I tease.

She doesn't have a chance to answer before a knock sounds from the front door. We exchange glances. Zully doesn't have a doorman, but there's an intercom system, and visitors have to be buzzed in.

"It's probably Ashish." She stands, talking to me as she walks out of the bedroom. "He's been popping over lately, every time he gets a fill up on his weed."

"Zully, do not tell me you're leading that boy on just so you can get drugs." Her neighbor has an obvious crush on her.

She pops her head back in the room. "Not *just* drugs. I'm using him for sex too." With that bomb drop, she disappears to address the visitor, as another round of knocks starts, more insistent this time.

I collapse back on the bed with a sigh, knowing I need to start thinking about what I want to do with Holt for real. It's not like I can put it off since I work with him. It's possible he's already tried calling me, but I've turned my phone off, mostly because I don't want to have to deal with Michael.

And fuck, I have to deal with him too. I need to meet with a lawyer, make some preliminary separation arrange—

My thoughts stop cold when one of the voices outside the bedroom registers as Holt's.

I sit up, propping myself on my elbows just as Zully appears in the doorframe. "Apparently, he gave someone a hundred dollars to let him in," she explains. "That computer techie with the dog, I bet. I told him if he wanted to see you, he should be paying *me*."

She holds up a stack of bills and fans them out, all Benjamin Franklins.

"You ratted me out for a thousand bucks?" It's play mad, though, because my insides went to mush as soon as I heard his voice, and I'm working very hard not to bolt out of the room in search of him.

"I would have paid more." Holt peers over Zully's five-foot-two frame, and dammit, the man is my kryptonite. I'm not even standing, and I'm weak in the knees.

Zully puts her hand on her hip in not-so-mock rage. "You can't tell me that after we've already bargained."

"I actually can, and I just did." Before she puts up more of a fuss, he reaches in his pocket and pulls out another few bills. "But you can have these as well, if you'll give us the room for a bit."

She snatches the cash from his hand, then looks at me. "Up to you, B." To Holt, she adds, "I'm keeping the money no matter what she says, btw."

My head is warning me to be cautious, but everything it's saying is in vain. I'm helpless to my heart, and my heart is a magnet, and Holt is iron pulling me to him. I'm already standing when I answer. "It's fine."

At the same time, Holt says, "She's okay with it."

Dammit, why is his attempt to answer for me so maddening and heart melting at the same time?

"All righty, then." Zully backs out of the way so he can come in. "Don't break anything."

When he's stepped past her, she mouths in my direction something that I'm guessing is like *make him grovel,* based on the accompanying hand gesture of hands clasped together and the pleading look on her face.

I respond with an expression that says *get the fuck out of here, ho.*

Then she's gone, the door is shut, and it's just the two of us.

I take a step toward him. "How did you find me? Did Zully text you behind my back?"

"Had you followed." He takes a step toward me.

"Sounds right." At least, he was honest.

Next thing I know, my mouth is on his, and his hand is down my shorts. *His* shorts, because of course I'm still wearing his clothes, and oh my God, he really learned how to get me there last night, because I'm already halfway to an orgasm.

"Fuck, you're so wet." He removes his hand only to pull the shorts all the way down while I grapple with the buckle on his khakis.

"Need you." I 'm so desperate I'm incapable of full sentences. "Inside. Now."

"Yes, yes. I know."

Somehow we migrate backwards until the curved metal of Zully's bed frame is pressing into my back. Cock out, Holt lifts my left thigh and hitches it against his hip. His other hand finds my throat, and he holds me there as he slides in.

God, he feels so…right.

Not just physically, but metaphysically. The idea of him is right, in a way that me and Michael never were. Us together feels natural, like every other thing that pairs in nature. Magnets and iron. Clownfish and anemones. Oysters and pearls. Everything else is just noise, isn't it?

Or it's just sex. Really good sex.

But sex has never been like this with anyone else. Not even with Michael in the beginning, when it was especially clear that was all there was between us. Or am I misremembering? Rewriting my past with the knowledge of the present.

It's too big of an idea to explore while I'm getting railed against my best friend's footboard.

"You feel so good, Brystin," Holt says, his voice gravelly. "Fuck, you feel so good. But this is a punishment."

For running away, I'm guessing. I suppose it's deserved, though I wouldn't quite call this a punishment.

Then he slaps his free hand against my hip—several times—and tightens the pressure on my windpipe, and okay. I see. My breaths are ragged, and my skin is stinging, and somewhere in my head I'm conscious that the smacks are likely loud enough to be heard in the next room, but all I can think is *yes, punish me.*

But then I remember I'm the one who's supposed to be mad at *him*. "What about your punishment?"

He shakes his head, dismissing the question. Then he speeds up his thrusts and moves his hand from my hip to my clit, where he massages me with precise strokes that instantly take me to orgasm.

When I cry out, unable to control myself, Holt stops thrusting and pushes my face into his chest, letting his shirt absorb my sounds. I cling to him, shaking as the pleasure spreads through my limbs. Adrenaline fires in my brain, and the headache I've had for the past two hours disappears like magic.

As soon as I'm through it, Holt pulls out and steps back. "It was *my* punishment," he says.

It takes me a second to understand, and when I do, I'm annoyed.

I close the gap between us and wrap my hand around his sex-coated cock and pump up and down quickly. "You don't get to choose your own punishment, assHolt."

Though, he'd done a good job at getting himself right to the edge, because it's only a few pumps before he starts the low grunting sound he makes when he's about to come. Suddenly mindful that I don't want to deal with evidence of this encounter, I fall to my knees and wrap my lips around him, just in time to swallow.

I peer up at him as he unloads, marveling at how magnificent he looks like this, feeling quite humbled to be someone who gets to see this side of him. It makes me feel as warm and funny as any orgasm does.

But then he finishes, and it hits me that here I am on my knees. Again. For another man who doesn't deserve it.

I fall back against the footboard, muttering to myself as I pull the shorts back on. "How do I let this happen?"

Holt zips up his pants and joins me on the floor. "I think this thing between me and you is bigger than us both."

"You feel out of control too?"

He nods as he reaches his arm out around me.

I let him pull me into his chest. "This doesn't change anything, Holt."

"It wasn't supposed to. But we both know the sexual tension is distracting. Now we can talk with it out of the way. Better hurry though, cuz you know how fast it builds again."

I chuckle into his shirt.

Despite saying we needed to talk, we're quiet for several minutes. I'm still getting my head together after the orgasm, and I assume he is as well. In the silence, I can hear his heart thudding. I swear I can hear it calling to be mine. Zully says I should make him give me stuff, but that's the only thing I want. Would he ever truly give it to me?

After a while, I pull away, too lulled by the intimacy of being held to be able to have any sort of meaningful conversation. "I think I need a little space between us."

I stand and climb on the bed, resting my back against the headboard.

Holt stands as well, then comes to kneel on the floor beside me. "Is this far enough?"

"It's fine." He looks good on his knees, for a change, honestly. "Look, Holt—"

"Brystin," he says, and I'm not quite sure if he's cutting me off or if he started talking at the same time I did, but he's the one who goes on talking. "I know it's not enough to say I fucked up or to tell you that I love you—which I do."

My stupid fucking heart does a cartwheel.

"I know you need me to prove it to you."

I bite my lip, not trusting myself to speak, and nod.

"I'm going to prove it to you, then. Okay? You ready?"

A laugh slips out. That fucker.

"I'm ready." And I mean, really ready. Ready like I've been waiting my whole life for someone to prove they loved me in the way I need to be loved. In the way I love in return.

He lifts up one leg so now he's only on one knee. "Marry me."

I sit forward, sure I heard wrong. "What?"

"Marry me."

"I'm…" I'm overwhelmed, is what I am. "I'm still married! We just… You and I barely…" The excuses are all there, and I mean each and every one of them, but it's so hard to voice them when my heart is running in the other direction, ready to shout to all the world that Holt Sebastian wants to marry me. Like, for *real* marry me.

"I know," Holt says, as though he can truly read my unfinished thoughts. "I know it's fast, and it's crazy, but I also know it's right, and I mean it, and we don't have to make anything official right away. We can take our time until we get to the church."

He wants to get married in a church!

"But this proves it, Brystin. Proves that you changed me. I was never going to marry anyone. Ever. I was never going to fall in love, and you've. You've changed everything for me."

"Holt…" I don't know what to say. It's so fast, and so sudden, and I feel like I'm on one of those amusement rides that jerks back and forth, giving you whiplash. "I'm…"

"Think about it." He's back on both knees now, and he takes my hand between his. "It makes sense. *We* make sense. It's the perfect solution. And can you imagine the ratings?"

"The ratings?" Just like that, I'm ejected from the ride, and tumbling to a hard fall. "The show ratings?"

"People were so into it when they thought we were dating…" He seems to realize he's made a wrong turn. "That's not why I want to marry you. It's not. Just an added benefit, which will be a win for both of us because we'll have time to focus on you and me when I don't have my father breathing down my neck."

Stunned, I pull my hand away. "What? No."

Shit, did I really just say that?

"No?" he asks.

It appears I really did say that. "Yeah, no." I scramble around him so I can get off the bed, needing some distance. "No. No. No, I'm not doing this. Again. No."

"No," Holt repeats, his tone dejected.

But fuck him, he doesn't get to be dejected. This is madness. This is fucked-up insanity. I'm the one wronged, and he wants me to coddle him, when his solution is just more of the same?

No.

"No," I say again, with as much might and strength as I've ever had. "I will not marry you, Holt. Not like this. To solve a problem? Without a ring?" He tries to interject, but I mow right over them. "I've done that before. That's not what marriage is supposed to be. That's not what love is supposed to be.

"And yes, I heard you. The ratings are a bonus, but you shouldn't be thinking about ratings at all when you're planning the rest of your life. And I'm sorry if this stings, but all of this is selfish. Have you ever given up something for someone else? Have you ever truly sacrificed? That's what love is, Holt. Real love. I know because I haven't had real love before, and what you're offering looks like a carbon copy of what I already have. I. Want. Something. Different. I *deserve* something different."

"Okay, okay. You're right." To his credit, Holt stays on the floor, sitting now. Doesn't try to usurp this one moment of power that I've finally stumbled into. "It doesn't mean I don't want to marry you, but you're right. It's not the right time, and it was shitty to think I could use it for personal gain. But I mean it when I say I love you, and I need you in my life, so tell me what I can do to prove that. Tell me what I can say that will have you walking out the door with me when I leave."

"I don't know." I shrug. "I think that's the point of proving it, Holt. It needs to be authentic, and that means I can't tell you what it is."

He stares at me with shadowed eyes, trying to figure me out when I'm not even sure if I've figured out myself. "You're saying this can't be solved tonight. You need time."

"I don't need time, necessarily. I need…" I turn away from him, and rub my eyes, hoping if he isn't there to distract me, I'll have a better chance at seeing what I need. It's all been laid out for me for so long by Michael, I haven't had to think about it on my own, and all those plans were centered around career. Around the career Michael wanted me to have, and me too, but for me, it was always more important that I earned it. Then Holt came along, and offered me the sky, but at a price I shouldn't have had to pay, and how can that kind of start not taint our future?

How can he ever hope to prove anything to me when I'm still as tangled up in our wrongs as he is?

Then it hits me.

I lower my hands from my face, but I can't turn back to face him. "I can't host the show anymore."

He lets out a laugh of disbelief. "You don't mean that."

"No, I really do." I take a deep breath and turn around. "It's poisoned. All of it."

"It's not, Brystin. Don't do this. You're overreacting. You deserve the show."

"I do deserve the show. Just like I deserve love. But right now, I don't believe any of it's genuine. How can I? Michael used me to get the show. You used me to get your ratings. You claim to love me—I need something I can believe, Holt. This isn't it."

"Please, honeybee. Please, don't do this." He leans forward so he's on his knees again, and he truly looks like he's pleading.

He looks so desperate, I'm almost shattered.

Tears threaten, but I will myself to be strong. If he can love me after this, if he can still want me after I've taken something big from him…

It's not my reason for doing this, but it would be an added benefit.

Oh, the irony.

"It's done. I quit. I'm not going back there."

"Is it Michael? Is that it? I'll have him fired."

I'm not even tempted, though it would be nice to see the rug get pulled from under his feet, especially when Michael definitely didn't deserve it.

"It's not just him. It's you too. And it's me." The more I

think about it, the more I talk it out, the more convinced I am that this is what I want. "It's not real, Holt. I'm a joke. You made me a joke. People are tuning in to see what it is you see in me, waiting for me to fail, and I know you say they'll stay, but no, they won't. The people looking for gossip aren't going to be interested in what I have to say about the nation's problems. Not unless I change my messaging format, and that's not what I want. This isn't who I want to be. I didn't work this hard, to get here."

I see when he finally gets that I'm serious.

He stands, his business face on. "You can't quit without notice, Brystin. You have a contract. Who will go on tomorrow night? Everyone will be inconvenienced."

I throw my head back with a laugh. "You didn't care about *New Jersey Now* when you got me fired, and the crew had to scramble. Somehow the show went on."

"You've made your point. I get it. You want to get even, but let's be real here."

"It's not about getting even, Holt." My voice rises with frustration. "I can't be there anymore. I won't do it. I won't."

My words hang in the air, and I watch Holt's emotions wrestling on his features. Each time compassion cuts through the dark of his eyes, his jaw tightens, the line of his mouth straightens.

"You have a contract," he repeats, eventually, seemingly unable to separate the man from the CEO.

"You have the ability to override it. Don't say that you don't."

His expression is hard now. "Give me one reason why I should."

It's not the route I wanted to go, but I pull out my ace. "Because I was offered the job in exchange for sexual favors."

Holt might never face the consequences of a sexual assault charge, but I'm certain the accusation could get me out of my contract.

"You wouldn't." He's steel now, so hard that I can barely see the man I'm in love with through the façade, and I'm not sure that he doesn't mean it as a threat.

How did we get to this?

We're so far from the two people we were when he walked in the room. Dying to narrow the distance between us, I cross to him and place my palms on his arms. "I won't need to, Holt. Because you'll let me go. Because you love me."

He hesitates for the briefest moment before giving in and wrapping his arms around me and leaning his forehead on mine. "Will this prove it to you? Will you believe me if I let you do this?"

"It's a start."

He closes his eyes tight, and shakes his head back and forth against mine.

When he opens them again, he grips my shoulders and bends down until we're eye to eye. "This is crazy, Brystin. You want me to let you make the worst career move of your life to prove I love you? It's really fucking hard to believe that's what love looks like."

"Love is messy like that sometimes. Sometimes it looks like a man marrying a woman just so she can be near her kid. Sometimes it looks like a man supporting a woman's decision, whether he thinks it's right or not, because she *knows* it's what she needs."

Pain shoots across his face. "Fuck, Brystin. You're killing me." He crashes his mouth against mine, and it's the sweetest, most brutal kiss I've had in my life. "It's career suicide," he says when he breaks away. "What will you do?"

"It's not career suicide. I can go back to local."

"It's the wrong direction."

"I'll figure it out, Holt."

"Can I figure it out with you?"

I think about it for longer than I need to. "I need to figure this out by myself. And you have some things to figure out too. Your job, for example. What you're going to do next to get real ratings."

"What to do to prove you belong with me."

I wipe a stray tear from my eye. "You still want me after this?"

"Oh, honeybee." He kisses me again, softly. "I want you even more."

"Then you'll figure it out."

I almost believe he really will. Maybe he was right when he said I needed time, because only time will tell.

We hold each other for long minutes.

Then he lets me go in pieces. First, our torsos part. The space grows between our lips. He drops his arms to hang them awkwardly at his sides. Finally, he tears his eyes from mine.

My heart, he takes with him.

And it takes everything in me not to run after him when he leaves.

CHAPTER THIRTY-FIVE

BRYSTIN

The next several days are spent untangling my life from Michael's. Or beginning to, anyway.

I meet with a lawyer on Tuesday to start the separation process.

Wednesday morning, Michael and I have a cordial conversation via telephone about division of property. He'll keep the apartment in the city, of course. I'll get the one in Edison. We arrange a time for him to get movers to pack up his stuff when I'm not there. He sends an Uber with the few items I have in Manhattan. It's only enough to fill two boxes.

It's an allegory of how our life together has always been—he takes all the space while I make myself small to be in his world.

I imagine I'll eventually sell my Edison unit—it all depends on where I find a job—but wherever I end up living, I plan to occupy every square inch.

Our finances are harder to agree on. Without a job, I will need to depend on Michael and on savings. He, on the other hand, is under the impression that Holt will be my new sugar daddy, which is frankly none of his business, but even if we end up together, I want to deserve my keep. Maybe some people view alimony as no different than being put up by a man, but I earned that money. I'm responsible for Michael's success as much as he is, and I'm not giving away what's mine.

For the time, he gives me the checking account with a lump sum to tide me over, and he takes control of the savings.

We don't say a word about my departure from the show.

I spend the rest of Wednesday getting my resumé together and talking to a headhunter who says my job outlook all depends on what recommendations I get from my previous employer, but I'm not ready to ask Michael or Holt for any favors so I leave that on my to-do for another day.

Thursday morning, Zully has breakfast with me before she heads into the city. She's been kept on to do hair and makeup for the anchor who has temporarily filled my spot —a filler who's been a regular at the network for years. Zully makes her out to be a monster, but I know she's just trying to bolster my spirits. I've met Megan before and seen her work. She's always been both kind and professional. Frankly, she's probably more entitled to the job than I am.

When Zully's gone, I almost break down and text Holt.

That night, Holt texts me.

I'm missing you.

It's late, and the timing fits so many of our nighttime sexting sessions, so I respond with the obvious.

What part of me?

All of you, Brystin. All of you.

It takes me several minutes to catch my breath. When I do, it takes another several minutes to compose a response. Before I settle on the right direction, he sends another.

But if you send me a picture of your fingers in your pussy, I'll make it worth your while.

You already have a pussy pic.

Not one with a landing strip. *wink emoji*

Two orgasms later, I sleep better than I have in days.

Friday, my strength leaves me, and I spend the day in bed with my phone off and a tub of ice cream. And a bag of Ruffles. And a medium gluten-free margherita pizza.

Saturday night—or Sunday morning, I guess, since my phone says it's twenty minutes after midnight—I show up at Holt's apartment. The doorman has to call before he can let me up, so Holt's not surprised when he opens the door to find me standing there.

"I'm not here to talk." I set the terms straight up front. It's the most selfish I've ever been in a relationship, taking what I need for me. Making demands.

He doesn't ask questions, and he doesn't argue, and when he wakes to find me dressing at five in the morning, he gets up to make me a travel mug of coffee and calls me a car.

Later that day, he sends another text.

I'm still going to figure out how to prove it.

I don't tell him that he's, little by little, already proving it.

Monday, I put on my big-girl panties and go to the Sebastian Center to deal with exit paperwork that Holt insists I can only sign in person.

Just kidding—I don't wear panties at all because I take it for the booty call that it is, and after I put my signature on the dotted line, he bends me over the worktable that we never got to the last time we fucked in his office.

After that, we text on the regular. Sometimes it's dirty. Sometimes it's mundane commentary on our day. Sometimes we veer into emotional sentiments, but we both steer clear of talking future plans. It's like we've both accepted that this is a season in limbo. A season of transition. A season meant to get our shit together alone before we can work on getting our shit together together.

Thursday, Zully comes over again for breakfast, and this time she seems like she isn't lying when she says I'm looking better. I fill her in on everything, as I always do, including the texts and the booty calls and the movie Holt and I watched together over the phone last night.

"What the hell are you doing?" Her tone is more of curiosity than judgment.

"Honestly? I think we're dating."

We're still laughing when my phone rings. It's an unfamiliar number so I send it to voicemail, then play it afterward on speaker.

Hi, Brystin. This is Jessa Jones. We met earlier this year at Adeline. I was wondering if we could grab lunch.

TWO DAYS LATER, I take the train to Brooklyn to meet with Jessa at one of her favorite spots for brunch.

Have you told Holt?

Seeing Zully's text on my screen stirs my guilt. I turn my phone over, wanting to ignore the question so that I can ignore the answer, because of course I haven't told him, and of course that makes me feel like shit.

When I don't text back, though, she calls. And since I always arrive early when I'm nervous, I don't have anything else to do but answer.

"Your lack of response is all the answer I need. Are you afraid he'll be mad?"

"I don't know." More like I worry he'll feel betrayed. "I don't know the details of their parting, but I think it was not good. I'm sure that's why she wants to meet up with me, right? She probably realizes I'm not on the show anymore, and she probably thinks I'll trash talk with her."

"Then trash talk. Get it out of your system. Use her to spew all the shit so you can move on."

"But if I use her to trash talk, what do I need you for?"

The bell on the small café door jingles, and I look up to see Jessa walking in. "She's here. Gotta go."

I hang up and tuck my phone away, then wave at Jessa so she sees me. Always awkward at these sorts of interactions, I don't know if I should stand or not, which is so stupid. If I were on the job, I'd be able to handle the whole exchange with grace.

Then just pretend you're on the job, doofus.

The change of mind frame helps, and I stand to greet her with a casual but professional hug.

"Brystin, it's so good to see you," she says, sitting down. "I enjoyed our time together so much that weekend in April. I really should have met up with you before, but well, you've been busy, haven't you?"

She's so good at the lead-in, reminding me why she's always been one of my idols. It's surreal to think that a woman like her wants to know about me, but I give her the PG-rated lowdown, leaving out most everything personal. When she asks why I left, I tell her it wasn't the right fit in the end, and she leaves it at that.

Aware that she actually might have a bone to pick with me, I address that early on. "I want to say, Jessa, I'm sincerely sorry if I stole your spot at SNC. I would never have taken a job if I'd known it was at your expense."

"Please tell me that isn't true."

I'm not sure how to respond, so I don't.

"I'm sorry, that wasn't clear. I'll try again—you're a woman in a man's world, Brystin. Every job will come at another woman's expense. You have to look out for you in this business. No one else. It's cutthroat, but you can make friends elsewhere."

"Okay." I'm mentally taking notes, wondering if I could ever be that hard. Wondering if I ever *want* to be that hard. "Is it worth it? I mean, I'm sure it is. It would just be nice if it didn't have to be women against women all the time, you know?"

Her smile is one I recognize. It's the one she offers every time an interviewee walks in to her next question. "Funny you say that..."

We're interrupted by the arrival of the waiter.

Once our orders are placed, and we've received our bloody Marys, I expect her to pick up where she left off. "By the way, I didn't exactly get canceled because of you," she says instead. "My contract was up for renewal, but I didn't want to sign."

"What?" I know Holt had alluded to Jessa leaving on her own terms, but I've never been quite able to wrap my mind around it.

"I went to Adeline that weekend hoping that I could get Holt to agree to letting me move into a producer position. I heard he was kicking around bringing on some fresh talent, and when we met, I figured it was you. I apologize if this seems stalkerish, but I did a little digging on the internet when I was alone later that night—"

"—as any good reporter would do—"

"Exactly—and what I saw was incredible. A little unpolished, but the raw talent was there. The spark that can't be taught. The rest, I know, will come with time and guidance. So I went to Holt, and said I wanted to produce whatever he was putting together for you."

"Oh my God, are you serious?" I'm beside myself. Jessa Jones wanted to produce *me*?

I try to imagine for a second how it would be to work under someone like her rather than someone like Michael. There's such a prevalence of men in producer positions that I've never thought about the possibility of working with a woman.

Well, and I haven't pictured myself working with anyone besides Michael in years.

"It would have been amazing, wouldn't it?" she says. "We would have turned that show into gold."

I can see it. It could have been something special.

But I don't have the show anymore, and of course, the producer position went to Michael. For the first time, I see how my partnership with my soon-to-be ex backfired. The intent had been that he could use his experience to take me into whatever new jobs he was offered. I've always believed he was limiting himself with me as his ball and chain. I never realized he was *my* ball and the chain.

I wonder if Holt ever even considered hiring me without Michael. Did Jessa ever have a chance? "I saw you arguing with Holt the day you left Adeline—was it about the show?"

"Yes and no. It was me throwing a tantrum, really. I told him that putting a talent like you under an out-of-touch misogynist like Michael Endlich was a crime. I meant it, but I only said it out loud because I was disappointed to not get the job." She seems to remember my relationship with the man she's dissing. "Sorry. I know he's your husband."

"Soon-to-be ex." I'm surprised how liberating it is to say out loud.

She lifts her bloody Mary in a toast. "Good for you."

"Wait a minute—you said the same thing when you found out I was married to him."

"Yeah, but this time I mean it." She winks. "Anyway, it all worked out for the best. For me, at least. I took a position at SHE. You familiar with it?"

I am. "It's a platform like Netflix, only all the programming is for women."

"Programming for and *by* women. Nearly every person in a decision-making position is female or non-binary."

"It's owned by Bob Peterson, though, isn't it?" I don't know much about the man except that he's frequently on the richest people in New York lists.

"Yes, that is a downside. So far he's remained really hands-off, so I'm hopeful."

"Well, congratulations. That's really great. But what are you doing there? They don't have any news programming."

"Not true. They have one show that walks the line between talk show and news show, which is a start. It's a daily program. There are three women who rotate the host position. Two of them are really happy about the arrangement. It allows for them to have time with their families."

"What about the third woman?"

"The third woman is me. I'm just filling in right now until this other host gets back from her maternity leave in another few months. What I've really been tasked to do for the network is to conceive of and produce a news show from scratch. Something like what Jon Stewart is doing on Apple. Well-rounded news with topics that affect women in particular. Not so sure on the concept yet. The vision is still in the works."

"That sounds…incredible." As someone who's currently jobless, I'm more than a little jealous.

"Does that mean you'll take the host position?"

I practically spit alcohol-spiked tomato juice all over the table and have to cough for several seconds before I can speak. "You want…me?"

"I just told you that I wanted to produce you. I thought it was obvious where I was going this whole time."

"No, no. It's a delightful surprise." I let it sink in. "And yes! I'm yours. I don't even need to hear more, but you know, you can go ahead and tell me."

She does just that, explaining that she'd like for us to come up with the exact concept together. The pay isn't anything like what SNC paid, but it's more than I made at *New Jersey Now*. Most importantly, it's a job. One I've earned all on my own merit.

"I'm also hoping you'll take my temp spot on the other show in the meantime," she says after we've spent the whole meal discussing details and ideas. "I want to get your face in front of viewers as soon as possible, and it's good to have a place for people who loved you on *Our Nation Now* to tune in before they forget they loved you."

I love how blunt she is, never sugarcoating anything. It's refreshing compared to the way Michael talked to me, which was always patronizing or overly flattering. "Sure. That's good thinking."

"Thank God, I'm done with the in-front-of-camera life."

"Really? May I ask why?"

"Honestly? I'm tired of covering the gray in my hair." She laughs. "And I've done that. I need something new. I'm ready to mentor."

"I'm ready to be mentored." Really mentored, for once.

We talk for another two hours. It's comfortable and inspiring and exciting—a lot like many of my conversations with Holt, but also totally different. I can't remember a time in my career that I've had another woman who can talk at my level.

By the time we leave, I can't remember why I ever thought a show on a network as big as SNC was the best place for me. That was Michael's dream, I realize. I'm still figuring out what *my* dream is, but I know I'm finally on the right track.

"Jessa." I catch her before we part in different directions outside the café. "Can I ask how you got my number?"

I know the most likely answer, but I want to hear how it came about.

"Holt called me," she said, confirming my suspicions. "Apologized for ever thinking that you and I weren't meant to be together."

"That was big of him," I say.

"Real big," she says, as if she knows there's something more between me and Holt, and maybe she does. She doesn't strike me as the type to believe the tabloids, but people are surprising. "I think he might be one of the good ones."

"Yeah. I think he might be too."

When I'm on the train, I text him.

I'm starting to believe.

Just wait. I'm still proving it.

Still wearing a grin, I call Zully. "Guess what? I got a job. And this time I didn't have to sleep with the producer *or* the CEO."

"Well, well. Look at you."

I am looking at me, and for the first time in a long time, I like who I see.

CHAPTER **THIRTY-SIX**

HOLT

"Here he is—fuckup number one. Most people call him Holt." My father's offensive introduction amuses no one but him, and yet all of us standing around him pretend like it was fine.

That's what you do with men like him. He's royalty, not because he's worth being worshiped, but because he's got the power to cut your head off—both literally and figuratively. We've all learned to treat him with deference, even though most of us here are related to him by blood.

The woman I'm meeting, my soon-to-be stepmother, is the only person brave enough—or possibly stupid enough—to call him out on it, her Italian accent almost making it sound like song. "Samuel, that's terrible. He's running your empire. Not everyone can do that. He obviously deserves some credit."

I'm too intrigued by what my father will say in return to

notice Giulia step toward me, and next thing I know, I'm being embraced.

"Oh. Uh. Okay."

It's weird being hugged. I can't remember the last time a woman that I wasn't fucking put her arms around me. My grandmother, maybe? Before she passed away. Years ago now. It's both invasive and relaxing, and I'm not sure what to do with it so I let it happen and then quickly retract.

"It's so good to finally meet you." She's closer in age to me than my father, but she has the mother vibe down well. Everything about her is warm—her dark eyes, her honey tone, her gentle smile, her blonde highlights.

"Sorry for missing the family dinner." This whole interaction is painful, but I think I almost sound genuine.

"Like I said, you're running an empire. We're meeting now."

It's not like I made an effort. Dad scheduled this meet and greet with the extended family at the gallery during my workday, which meant I could pop over on my lunch break. Meant I had no excuse, more like.

I give Giulia the most sincere smile I can manage. "Now we've met."

Meanwhile, my father hasn't bothered to demean her for contradicting him, which is a Samuel Sebastian miracle. He does still stand his ground. "Was running it well there for a minute, too. Then he had to go and let his ratings darling walk out on him. If the contract wasn't ironclad, you need to fire those lawyers, Holt."

"It wasn't the lawyers, Dad. I misrepresented myself. She could have sued if I didn't let her terminate without penalty." So far, I've been able to leave it at that, but I know I'm running on borrowed time.

"What does she have on you, son? You fuck around with her? Offer her a bonus under the table and get her back on the air. Problem solved."

I exchange a glance with Adly, who seems to think she knows what's going on, despite the fact that we haven't had a single conversation about Brystin in weeks. "It's more complicated than that."

"Nothing's so complicated you can't solve it with a check. You're too soft. This is not a position for a pansy."

Again, it's Giulia that comes to my rescue. "You promised me you weren't going to talk work today." She sidles up to my father, and casts her doe-eyes at him like she's weaving a spell.

"That's right, that's right. Sorry about that, darling." He kisses her on the forehead, and I exchange another glance at Adly who looks like she wants to throw up. "But we're not done discussing this, Holt. I'm going to want a full account later."

"Yep. I'm sure you will." It occurs to me that I'd thought the CEO position meant that I didn't have to account to anyone, except of course, the board. How am I still having to explain myself to my father when I'm a thirty-seven-year-old man?

He turns to say hello to my cousin Brett—one of the Lesser Sebastians, as the family calls them, since they're descended from Grandpa's sister. I look at my watch, wondering if this is a good time to make my escape.

Then I feel a soft hand on my upper arm.

"I'll have a word with him," Giulia says quietly, as though any of this is her business. "Get him to ease up on you."

"Good luck with that." I reconsider as soon as the words are out of my mouth. "I really don't need anyone fighting my battles, thank you. I'm fine."

Her smile isn't as warm now that my father isn't part of the conversation, and I imagine I'm seeing a truer version of her rather than the performative version she's worn this last hour as she's greeted one Sebastian after another. "Adly told me you'd be the hardest one to win over."

"Did she, now?" I turn to scowl in my sister's direction, only to find she's conveniently disappeared. In her place is a woman—a girl, really—who looks very much like an Irish version of Giulia.

Giulia follows my gaze. "Ah, my daughter Lina." She summons the redhead to her side. "Fresh with her master's, and soon to be working at SNC, I believe. Lina, this is Holt."

It feels strange to shake hands with a girl who can't be older than twenty-three. Stranger shaking hands with someone about to become my sister. "Soon to be working at SNC?"

Lina gives a modest shrug. "Adly said she'd try to find me something. We'll see." She turns to her mother. "Mamma, I'm going downstairs to look at the art. You'll be okay without me?"

When Lina's gone, Giulia lets out a breath. "She has her father's coloring," she says, as though that weren't obvious. "He passed only a couple of years ago, when we were still living in the States. Lina and I are still working out what our relationship is without him. He was a buffer for the two of us. I'm hoping Samuel can fill that role for her."

I choke back a laugh. "Sure, sure."

Though, already, he's been a very different man today with Giulia. Maybe she's got some magic between her legs that I don't know about.

I regret the thought immediately, not wanting to think of my father as sexual, ever, ever, ever. Still, I can't ignore the fact that she's got him wrapped around her finger, and I wonder what that might mean for our family. What might change, if anything.

Who am I kidding? Nothing will change. Not with us. The man will never be happy with his offspring, even if he's happy with his new wife. How can he be? We're all half him, and the man is impossible. Lina might actually have a chance with him since she doesn't share any of his genes.

I'm envious and hate that I am.

"Can I ask you one thing?" I'm a fool because I can't help myself.

Giulia tries to guess where I'm going. "Do I love him?"

I shake my head. "I don't give a fuck if you love him. The money, the lifestyle, the notoriety—it comes at the price of having to live with him. Honestly, it might not pay enough."

She's about to protest, but I meant it when I said I didn't care, so I tread over her. "Do you think he loves you?"

She seems taken aback by the question and isn't prepared with an answer. Glancing at him, she considers. "I do think so."

"Really? How can you tell?" I think I'm looking for

something that will tell me something about his relationship with me. As though she has some translator book to Samuel Sebastian that I've never known about.

"Hm." It only takes her a beat to come up with an answer. "He lets me control the thermostat."

My father's conversation must have wrapped up because he hears and jumps in. "The damn woman is always freezing. I'm sweating my balls off all night, and she's got it turned up to seventy-five."

Giulia waves him off. "He sacrifices his comfort for mine. Does that help?"

It isn't what I was looking for, but now I'm thinking about Brystin, and thinking about her makes everything better. "Yes, actually it does. Welcome to the family." Lowering my voice, I add, "I hope it's not as miserable an experience for you as it has been for the rest of us."

"What did he say?"

"He's happy to meet me." Giulia gives me a conspiratorial smile. "And now he has to get back to work."

Fuck. I might have to like her.

"Until next time. Dad, I'm buying you an Ooler. Google it." He's a billionaire, and he can't figure out how to regulate dueling body temperatures. It was definitely time for the man to retire.

But was I definitely the man for the job?

I walk away half thinking about that and my father and about what I'm eventually going to say to him to explain Brystin's departure, but mostly I think about how Giulia said that my father gave up his comfort for hers. If that's how love is proved, what the fuck comfort can I give up for Brystin?

I'm so in my head, I don't see Scott's wife, Tessa, until I've practically bumped into her. "Hey, stranger." She gives me a side hug. "It's been a while."

"Work." As if she needs an excuse. "Oh, and congratulations." I look down at the small bump that has taken the place of her flat stomach. "It's a ways away still, right? I didn't miss any gender reveal or shower yet?" I know nothing about how pregnancy works beyond the actual conception.

"Quite a ways. Five months still. Thank you. And we're not doing a gender reveal."

Scott sidles in next to his wife. "They're out of fashion, Holt. As your image rep, I recommend you catch up on the current PC trends and lingo."

"I appreciate the suggestion." But I give him the finger too because that's his job, not mine. If I get canceled, he'll get me out of it.

As if he knows what I'm thinking, he says, "It's really better not to get canceled in the first place."

This time I give him two middle fingers.

He ignores my inappropriate gestures and nods toward my father. "Is he still pushing you?"

Scott has been the one who's had to address the public fallout from Brystin's abrupt departure. While he's done a fantastic job, there's only so much he can say or do without delving into subjects that I have flat out said were off-limits. Dad has been to him behind my back, asking for a statement basically claiming Brystin was let go at her fault. In other words, he wants Scott to lie.

Fortunately, Scott knows he works for me now, not my dad.

"Eh." I think about how I want to answer and land on the truth. "He hasn't said it yet, but he's going to threaten to get me fired if I don't reconsider my approach."

"Do you think he'd actually go to the board?"

"Yeah. I think he would."

Tessa frowns. "Yikes."

Scott, on the other hand, shrugs. "Would it be the worst thing in the world?"

"Losing my job?" My tone says *yeah, duh,* but that reaction came automatically. Once upon a time, I couldn't imagine anything more awful.

Now I can think of other things. Losing Brystin. That would be the worst thing in the world.

"It's not too late to switch gears." Scott's gone into full work mode. "You could still put out a statement. Better yet, you could do an interview."

"And say what? Admit that I sexually harassed her and then let her out of her contract so she wouldn't sue me?" When Tessa raises an eyebrow, I add, "It's more complicated than that."

"It always is." She gives me a look that says she understands.

Scott's more shocked by the statement than his wife, or shocked that I said it out in the open anyway. "You might want to keep your volume down, and I was thinking more of a focus on the emotional component."

"Ah, admit that I'm in love with her and let people think she left because it was too complicated of a situation?"

"It's an option," he says.

It's an option that puts me in a vulnerable position in

front of the entire world. For a second, I wonder if that would prove my love to Brystin, but then realize that I'd still end up gaining from the situation with better ratings. "I don't know."

"Is Michael Endlich still harassing you about it?"

Scott had given Michael instructions on how to handle any questions, but the man still called my office no less than once a day until I agreed to see him personally. I managed to put him off for almost three weeks. "Broke down and talked to him yesterday. Turns out he just wanted reassurance that I wasn't going to fire him. Told him if he says one word that he shouldn't, I'll fire him for cause, and that will be the least of his worries."

As much as I wish I could terminate the fucker now, his contract holds.

I'm pretty sure he also wanted to know what was going on with me and his soon-to-be ex. Apparently, Brystin has kept our business to herself because she's a decent person. I, on the other hand, was very tempted to throw our relationship in his face with a tour of every place I fucked her in my office.

I kept my mouth shut in the end, which felt more gratifying than I expected. Especially when it riled him up enough to trash talk her. *She's easy to get,* he said, suggesting she was an easy lay. *Wait and see how hard she is to keep.*

I asked if he'd ever just tried loving her.

Very grown-up of me, I know. Really, I wanted to punch him in the nuts, but I didn't want to give him the satisfaction of thinking he'd gotten to me.

"That would be one good thing about getting fired." I'm

only half joking. "All contracts made under my time as CEO have the ability to be terminated." Mentally, I make a note to tell Adly to make sure he's sacked too if I'm ever canned.

"See? Always a bright side." Scott wraps an arm around Tessa's waist. It's the second time I've felt envious in half an hour.

I have the whole world at my fingertips, but money can't buy what I want most.

With that, my thoughts are back to Brystin. "Tell me something, Tess—how does a guy go about proving his love?"

She grins like she's glad to be asked. "Oh, good. I was afraid I wouldn't get a chance to follow up on that bit where you said you were in love."

"If you're going to make a deal about this, I'll take my question elsewhere." Not really, but I'm not interested in hearing all the *I'm so glad you finally*…and *didn't you say you'd never*…bullshit that usually follows these sorts of confessions.

"Not making a deal. I swear. Hm." She looks adoringly at her husband, which makes me both want to puke and also wish I was looking adoringly at Brystin. "Choose her," she says finally.

"*Choose* her?" An image of a Miss America type of pageant flashes in my head, except the women are vying to be my wife.

"Above everything else," she clarifies. "Above yourself and your job and your family and your money. Above everything."

"Ah. So simple," I say, with obvious sarcasm.

But it's all I can think about as I go on with my day. Well, that and all the other shit that I'm currently dealing with, and it all starts to form together into a potentially really good idea.

Tomorrow, I'm calling Jessa.

If I'm going down, it might as well be in flames.

CHAPTER
THIRTY-SEVEN
BRYSTIN

I turn my voicemail on speaker so I can clean out my inbox while I'm getting my face put on. It's a quick job since I can delete almost all of them within five seconds, which is how long it takes to determine that they're someone looking for the scoop on my relationship with Holt or my departure from *Our Nation Now.*

"You're still getting that many calls?" Zully still has her job at SNC, but the show airs in the evening so she can do my makeup for SHE too since the interviews I'm helping with are midday.

"The phone calls aren't as bad as the in-person badgering. Someone followed me all the way to Edison the other day, and there's someone with a camera almost every time I leave Holt's, even when I leave before dawn."

"You know, if you quit leaving before dawn, there might be less scandal to report on." Zully doesn't really care about minimizing fodder for the tabloids. It's been a month since

Holt's faux proposal, and she's annoyed that I'm still keeping him at arm's length.

Personally, the time alone has been good for me. I needed to be sure I could stand on my own, and now that I am, I'm ready to entertain something more serious. Holt has done a good job proving himself. Besides getting me the job with Jessa, he's sent flowers and chocolates and got Zully and me tickets to a sold-out Broadway hit.

I really do believe he loves me, but I'm still holding out for a grand gesture. I'm not doing another relationship where I'm not a priority, and I'm not sure yet that Holt is capable of putting me first.

"I don't know why I expected this would go away when I left SNC." I delete the last message and look up so that Zully can apply my eyeliner. "I guess I thought Holt would make it disappear."

"Maybe he's afraid you'll think he's just addressing it for publicity."

"Maybe he's not addressing it because it's better publicity to let it ride." I don't want to believe that ratings are still so important to him, but I'm not easily trusting these days.

I hear my dressing room door open behind us. I glance to the mirror and see Jessa. She's probably here to see if I'm ready, since we're nearing film time. It's a cake job, part-time, that's really more online-personality than journalist. The questions are written beforehand for me, and I just have to smile and read them off the prompter. Our interviewees are notable people in the nation, mostly women, usually people not too busy to sit down with one of the smaller streaming platforms. Presidents of big universities,

Broadway stars, state-level politicians, prominent business-people. Today will be my third interview, and I'm already so comfortable with the format, I'm not nervous anymore. Especially since none of our shows film live.

"Hey, Jess," I say. Zully lifts her pencil so I can turn my head toward my mentor. "I'm getting hounded by paparazzi. Any advice on how to deal with them?"

She doesn't even need to think about it. "Easiest way is to address the questions head-on."

"I was afraid you were going to say that." I look up again so Zully can finish my second eye. "I have no problem talking on air, but I get all itchy when the subject I'm talking about is me. Can't someone else do it for me?"

I'm kidding, but seriously. It's the one downside about not having Michael anymore. He handled my image, which came with both plusses and minuses. I suppose it's time I learned how to do it myself.

"She wants Holt to deal with it." Zully's such a freaking tattle.

"No, I don't," I say too quickly. "I mean, I do, but I don't want it to be for the wrong reasons."

"Interesting." Jessa leans her hip against the makeup counter. "What would you want him to say?"

That's a fair question that, of course, I haven't thought about. "I don't know. Whatever would take the heat off of me."

Jessa won't let me leave it at that. "Come on, you're a journalist. What questions would you ask him?"

I think while Zully puts on my lips. "I guess I'd want him to admit that he staged our 'affair' for the ratings. So I'd ask him questions that would lead to that."

"Great." Jessa stands so she's towering above me. "You have fifteen minutes to come up with those. We're rolling at two." With that, she heads toward the door.

"Uh, what?" I nudge Zully out of the way, jumping out of my chair to follow Jess into the hallway. "What are you, what are you talking about?"

"There's been a last-minute schedule change. Mary Barra is on for tomorrow. Holt Sebastian is filling her spot. As usual, we have questions already prepared, but since you have a personal connection to Holt, I'm giving you the opportunity to add some of your own." She's about to walk away again, as though this isn't a big deal when it's a capital B, Big Fucking Deal, and there's no way she doesn't know that.

"Wait, wait, wait."

She's annoyed when she turns this time, impatience written all over her face.

There are too many questions, I can't prioritize which to ask first, and I end up standing there with my mouth open.

"Are you going to be able to handle this?" she asks, with no malice. Just someone getting straight to the facts.

For half a second, I'm not sure that I will.

But then I remember how fucking strong I am. "No problem."

"Good. I'd get to writing those questions unless you're comfortable on the spot."

I'm usually very comfortable on the spot, but this is Holt. Holt, who couldn't be here coincidentally. Holt, who's trying to prove himself. "One more thing—was this him or was this you?"

"Now you're asking the right questions." Her smile is proud. "All him, baby. Make him squirm."

For all the times he's made me squirm, this feels like proper payback. I only wish I had more time to prepare.

With my mind whirring, I run back to the dressing room where Zully is waiting with a powder brush to set my makeup. "I'm interviewing Holt," I say. "That's all you're getting. Don't say anything because I'm prepping in my head."

It's obvious she's dying, but she clams her lips together and doesn't say a word until she's done. "Go."

She follows me out to the studio with her powder and brush, for when I get shiny when we're filming, which will probably happen sooner rather than later today. Straightening my jacket over my blouse and slacks, I pause as soon as I see Holt already sitting on set wearing a designer three-piece that makes him look so good, my thighs rub together.

Zully rushes past me, presumably to powder Holt, but I'm betting she's also hoping to exchange a word or two with him before I get there because she can't stand not being involved. I'm grateful, actually, because it gives me a minute to get myself together, so that when I walk out to join him, I don't look like the nervous wreck that I am inside.

"Hi," I say when I approach, not sure how to greet him. Usually I would shake the guest's hand, but that feels too formal, and a kiss would be too intimate, not to mention mess up my makeup.

Luckily, he's better at this than I am. He stands and leans in to press his cheek next to mine—half hug, half European kiss without the kiss.

"You look spectacular," he says.

At the same time, I lose all cool. "What are you doing here? This is crazy!"

"I'm proving myself, honeybee."

My insides turn to goo at the endearment, but I'm still not sure I understand what he's up to. "Okay. Want to tell me how, exactly?"

"Two minutes," the assistant director calls, and my heart rate doubles.

Holt doesn't bat an eye. "Well. This interview will only be aired on SHE. I can't stop my news teams from commenting on it when it airs tomorrow, but you have the exclusive."

"Okay, okay." In other words, SNC won't benefit from this interview. Furthermore, SHE will, especially considering how infrequently any Sebastian sits down for a one-on-one with an interviewer they don't employ.

He still might be trying to control the narrative, though, and so I ask, "Did you write the questions?"

He shakes his head. "I made some suggestions, but I left the rest to Jessa."

"One minute." The assistant director is looking at me.

"We should get to our places." I hope I don't sound as jittery as I feel. Wishing I'd had time to review the questions before I had to read them off the prompter. Praying I don't make a total fool of myself on camera.

Holt sees through me. "You're going to be great. And don't hold back. I'm here for the beating."

We take our seats across from each other on the set that's made to look like someone's living room. I had thought it pretty fancy before, but frankly, Holt makes the decór look plain.

Despite that, he looks comfortable, which is a sign of opportunity to a journalist willing to ask hard-nosed questions. The thought puts me in the right mindset, and when the slate snaps and the camera rolls, all the unease fades away, and I'm *on*.

My intro comes succinctly and naturally, and I only glance at the prompter to be sure I have a couple of my facts straight. When I welcome Holt, and with the exception that he's the hottest person I've interviewed, he's like any other guest.

Then it's on to the questions. "Tell me about the pressures of taking over a CEO position that, until a year and a half ago, was inhabited by your father since its creation. Many critics have stated that Samuel Sebastian's shoes are impossible for anyone to fill, including his own flesh and blood. Do those voices get in your head?"

I can tell from Holt's reaction that he didn't suggest this particular question. Jessa didn't pull any punches.

"Wow." He adjusts his already straight tie. "I guess we're doing this."

He takes a deep breath, and then he pours out everything. From growing up with a workaholic, perfectionist father as his idol to what it was like living with a mother who struggled with mental health to his desire for succeeding where many of his family members have predicted failure to the lengths he'd go to earn his father's praise. We volley back and forth with questions and answers, the conversation coming so instinctively, I barely have to look at the prompter for cues.

Okay, when I said everything, I didn't mean *everything*. He stops short of calling his mother's death a suicide, and he doesn't talk about Hunter at all, and I remain professional and refrain from trying to pull those secrets out of him. Even without those off-limits areas, it's apparent that some of his answers will rock the boat with the SNC board. A lot of them will piss off his father. I see the sacrifice he's making, what he's laying on the line for me, and he's already proved himself before we even get to talking about us.

When the natural opportunity arrives, I bring up my show without hesitation. "Many of our viewers know that I was employed for a brief time with SNC. Could you tell me about how the pressures of wanting to impress your father, the board, the world, how this enormous pressure led you to promote *Our Nation Now*?"

It's kinder than necessary, giving him the benefit of the doubt in the lead up. It's an approach more fitting for *Fresh Air* and Barbara Walters, and not one I usually employ, but it fits the style of this particular show, and besides, I don't really want to see Holt suffer. I just want to know he's willing.

"Good question, good question." He keeps his eyes locked with mine. "I, um. It was a risk hiring someone virtually unknown. I hope you don't mind me referring to you as such."

"No, that's appropriate."

"I recognized your talent and knew that was the direction I wanted to take SNC, bringing in a fresh perspective, but drawing viewers in is always daunting, particularly when it's something new, which is no excuse, but it sets up the situation. Anyway, I knew that if people thought we were having an affair, they'd be likely to tune in."

"So you leaned into that notion." I want to clarify his point further. "And used your position of power to force me to make appearances that would lead to these claims, and then purposefully didn't make an effort to correct reports that we were indeed together."

"That is correct."

"And did that work?"

"It did work," he says. "You pointed out, correctly, that it wasn't a tactic that would likely succeed, but we ended your involvement with the show before we could really test that out."

"Was my departure related to this false pretense that you created?" My heart feels like it's pounding out of my chest. I have no idea what he'll say, and I'm giving him the opportunity to not only expose his vulnerabilities, but possibly my own.

Maybe I trust him after all, because although I'm nervous about his answer, I'm not so scared that I didn't ask.

"It was. Yes. Definitely. You discovered what I'd done, and that didn't sit well with you, but there were other factors at play as well. I, uh, ironically, fell in love with you in the process of creating the façade. Which created an uncomfortable situation," he briefly looks directly at the camera, "as anyone can imagine," then returns his gaze to mine. "Especially since you were married, and your husband is the producer of the show. Under all those circumstances, it felt unreasonable to require you to see out your contract."

Tears prick my eyes. Zully almost always uses waterproof mascara, but I'd really rather not cry on camera. "Thank you, Holt. For sharing that."

Then, because I'm starting to lose my composure, I blurt out, "I'm in the process of getting divorced, by the way." And as long as I've started going off the interviewer rails, I might as well go all the way. "Did you really just admit to all the world that you're in love with me?"

He said it before, at Zully's house when he proposed, but I had to put everything he said that night into a box, and tuck it away deep inside me with a sign that says *do not open or risk heartbreak*.

"Yes, Brystin Shaw. I am completely and utterly in love with you, and not only will I not benefit from ratings for saying that, or for being here, I also might very well get fired and will face the wrath of my father forever, and I don't even fucking care. That's how much I love you."

And then I'm in his lap, with my arms wrapped around his neck and my mouth on his, cameras be damned, because I completely and utterly am in love with him too.

CHAPTER THIRTY-EIGHT

BRYSTIN

It's another hour before we're officially done with the interview. My makeup had to be reapplied to cover the happy tears, and Holt had lipstick everywhere, including his collar, but after we were cleaned up, we were able to do a far less emotional wrap-up.

As soon as the director calls it, I tug Holt with me to my dressing room, intending to make out with him like a teenager on prom night, only Jessa is waiting there for us.

"You know, I don't have to ask your permission to let that air as is, but we're friends, so I'm asking." She turns to Holt who is busy texting someone. "Not you. Brystin. I don't give a shit about your opinion."

He looks up from his phone and raises his hands in surrender. "No offense taken."

"Too bad. I really meant it to be offensive." She smiles, though, and I know that most of their animosity is play acting.

"I don't want special treatment," I say. "Air it as is, edit it, whatever you think is best." Jessa is amazing, and I honestly trust her, but really, the only thing I care about at the moment is getting my man alone.

"Thank you. Will do." She starts to leave, but stops in the doorway. "These walls are paper thin, by the way."

Apparently, she can read minds too.

I prepare myself to be quiet.

"No way." I swear Holt is in my brain. "I want you screaming. I already texted the driver. The car should be here by the time we get to the street."

I open my mouth to say okay, but he beats me to speaking. "If you want to leave with me, that is."

"Uh, yeah. I'm leaving with you." Did he not get the hint when I jumped in his lap and threw my arms around him? "I thought it was kind of obvious that I'm yours."

"Are you?" He closes in on me, trapping me at the makeup counter, and I'm not clairvoyant, but I can totally foresee how this will go if I don't call timeout right the fuck now.

"How about we focus on getting out of here, and then we can discuss it further." Preferably without clothes on. And then possibly again, with clothes on, so that I'm not so distracted.

"Good call."

I gather my things into my shoulder bag, and like an infatuated schoolboy, he carries it for me as we walk outside. And because he's a Sebastian, and the heavens work in his favor, the car pulls up just as we get to the curb.

Holt must have given instructions via text, because the driver doesn't ask questions, and as soon as the door is closed behind us, he hits the button to make the privacy window opaque.

Then, he's on me.

He pivots me so my back is against the door and my ass is pressed against the partition between us. Kneeling in his own seat, he undoes the snap on my slacks and lifts me so he can remove them. "These need off. Now."

"Yes, yes."

Too impatient to bother with my panties, he pushes the fabric aside and hoists my hips up, bringing my pussy to his mouth.

"Oh, fuck yes." I wrap my legs around his head and pray that it's a smooth ride because Holt is in a precarious position, and oh my God, that thing he's doing with his tongue…

Seconds later, my orgasm hits me, and now I'm praying that the divider between the front and the back of the car is soundproof because the noises coming out of my mouth are animalistic.

Holt pauses only to say one thing. "I said I want you screaming."

Then he returns to his task, adding his teeth this time and even more tongue, but it's not until he slips his thumb past the tight ring of my asshole that I really see stars.

And yes, I scream.

Mostly curse words, but I manage to personalize it with a few mentions of his name.

Only then does Holt lower my hips, resting them over the console between the seats. I watch him through a cum-colored haze as he tears off his jacket then furiously gets his belt undone and his cock out.

"I told myself I was going to eat you out until we got to my place, but I'm selfish, and I can't wait to be inside you."

"I can't wait eith—" My sentence turns into a gasp as he drives into me. With my hips lifted on the console, he hits deep. Deeper than he's ever been, and I swear he's deeper than anyone has ever been inside me. It's overwhelming, but in a good way—in the very best way—and I have to close my eyes. "Holt, it's so much. It's so, so much."

"Look at me, Brystin." His tone is so forceful, my lids pop open in surprise. "Don't you dare look away."

I level my gaze with his. I have to force my eyes to stay open as he grinds his pelvis, finding a sensitive spot inside me that feels so good, I can barely stay still through it. "Please," I beg, unable to articulate what I need.

"Take it," Holt demands. "I want you as ruined as I am."

"I am. I am. Oh God."

"Only me, right now, honeybee. I'm the one pleasing this pussy right now. Such a greedy, greedy kitty, taking all of me like a good girl."

He lifts my legs so they're on his shoulders, then increases his tempo, jackhammering into me so fast that it takes me a second to realize the car is pulling over.

Fortunately, Holt is more aware than I am right now. Without easing up, he hits the intercom button. "Keep driving," he orders.

Immediately, the car swerves back into motion.

The driver has to know what's happening back here, but I'm too lost in Holt to be embarrassed. Too lost in the pleasure. My eyes start to close again as another orgasm starts to build.

A smack on my thigh startles my eyes wide. "Look, Brystin. Watch what you do to me."

Again, I lock eyes with him, and I'm suddenly transported to that first night in his bedroom at Adeline, when I stood there naked while he pleasured himself. He kept his eyes locked on mine then, ignoring the rest of my body, and I thought it had to be the power balance that had him so turned on.

Now, I see his gaze for what it is, see that he's turned on by *me*. By *all* of me. Not just the parts of me that seem made for him, but my thoughts and my feelings. My inner workings. The independent parts of me that he can never truly own. The whole package.

This time I cry when I come. And I keep my eyes open so I can watch him be ruined right along with me.

Holt waits until we've cleaned up and our heart rates have settled before he tells the driver we're ready to go home. With the console between the seats, the car isn't made for cuddling, but we've abandoned safety for the entire ride so far, so I don't complain when Holt drags me into his lap.

He buries his face in my neck. "You good?"

"I'm real good."

His grip tightens, and I almost say it, the three words that I have yet to say, but then we're slowing down, and the car is pulling over, and it doesn't feel like the right time anymore.

In the lobby of his apartment, before we head to the elevator, Holt pulls me with him to the concierge desk. "Brystin Shaw needs full access to my apartment," he says. "Anytime she wants."

"Yes, sir." The older man's eager-to-please tone shows he knows who he's talking to, and he jumps to the task of updating the computer. "I need a copy of her ID for the files, and—"

Holt cuts him off. "Contact my assistant, André."

"Yes, sir. Of course."

I have a feeling that isn't the normal protocol, but Sebastians are above the rules. No wonder Holt is only just now learning how to play fair. It hits me then how much he's trying to change for me, when he's never had to change for anyone, and again, I almost tell him that I love him, but as nice as the concierge is, I don't really need him present for a milestone that should be private.

In the elevator, as soon as the doors close, Holt pulls me into his arms and kisses me until I'm gasping for air.

Then we're on his floor, walking into his apartment, and three steps in, I stop dead in my tracks. "Where's all your stuff?"

The entryway hutch is still here, but the art above it is gone, as is the chair and the Oriental vase.

I glance toward Holt who gives a tight-lipped shrug.

He follows behind me as I explore further. The couch is missing from the living room, and almost all the knick-knacks are gone from the built-ins. The kitchen table is gone and the china cabinet is empty. Every room I look in has been cleared of at least half its items, except for the office and the gym.

Even in his bedroom, I find the mattress is still there, but it's on the floor, and the dresser and nightstands are both gone, and all his personal items that used to be kept inside are stacked on the floor.

"Holt, what's going on? Did you get robbed?" More likely, he's moving, but this is the first I've heard about it, and an anxious pit grows in my stomach, wondering how I fit into whatever his plans are.

"No, I didn't get robbed. I made space." He shoves his hands in his pockets—nervously, perhaps? Though his tone sounds as certain as I've ever heard him.

"Space for…?"

"For you." He removes a hand to scratch behind his neck. "I know you probably need time to be independent, but I want you here, Brystin. I want you in every part of my life, and I don't want to carve out a little corner of my world and expect you to cram yourself in. You deserve more than a drawer or a closet or a room. I want you intermingled with me, whether that means bringing in your own items, or shopping together or—"

I don't need to hear more, and I can't hold back any longer. "I love you."

His eyes widen, and a smile spreads slowly. "Does that mean—?"

"It means, yes. Yes, I'll move in with you. Yes, I want to intermingle." Dammit, I'm crying again. "I don't need time to be independent, Holt. I've lived for years with a man who gave me more independence than I wanted."

I close the gap between us, and he instantly wraps his arms around my waist. As though they belong there. Which, in my opinion, they do. "I want to be wholly part of someone for a change. So, yes, I'll move in with you. I'll never leave if you let me."

"I'm definitely letting you never leave." He wipes a tear from my cheek. "Say it again."

"I love you." Oh no, the giggles are back.

"Is loving me funny?"

I shake my head. "It's so not funny that it makes me lose control of myself."

"I think I get that." He wipes another tear, then presses his forehead to mine. "I always thought falling in love would be such a brutal twist of fate, after everything I've done to avoid it my whole life. But Brystin, the brutal twist of fate is that everything people envy me for, everything I've been clinging to—my money, my lifestyle, my family. My job. All the things that I thought made me happy—they're nothing. I'll give them all up for you."

I kiss him, the kind of kiss that will lead to the bed because we are who we are, but also the kind of kiss that tells him I feel the same, and that this isn't just about sex. The sex is just a bonus.

Sure enough, I'm soon scooped off the floor and carried to the mattress, but I stop him after he unbuttons one blouse button. "Out of curiosity…I appreciate that you'll give everything up for me, but *did* you?"

He grins. "Are you worried that you might have really ruined me? That you might have to be the breadwinner of the family?"

I shrug. It would certainly be a change. For both of us.

He unbuttons another button. "You have nothing to fear." Another button. "Even if I lose the job, I still have my resumé." Another button. "And this apartment." Another. "And Adeline." He spreads the fabric apart and licks my bare skin. "And the hundred-million-dollar trust fund from my grandfather."

"So you won't be needing me to pay half the rent," I tease.

"Don't you dare even offer."

Talking is over then because Holt has other ideas for occupying my mouth—indecent ideas—and I willingly comply, still a girl who loves to be treated mean, but also a girl who, turns out, loves to be treated nice.

So I give him all of me, and he takes every bit offered, and when I fall asleep in his arms, I'm not diminished. I'm finally whole.

EPILOGUE

HOLT

Seven months later, April

Jessa sidles up next to me and Zully as we look out over the yard at the game in progress. "I didn't realize croquet could be so bloodthirsty."

"Steele's girlfriend is cutthroat," I agree. Poor Brystin. She can be so hard-nosed when it comes to her work—or arguing with me—but she doesn't have it in her to carry that aggression to the real world. Particularly if it means breaking rules or playing unfair.

It's a good thing, frankly. Or she'd still be working for SNC instead of helming her own current events show. Similar in theme to what *Our Nation Now* was supposed to be, *Real Talk* airs once a week on SHE, which gives her the opportunity to really delve into her topics, and explore all sides of issues that often get ignored in day-to-day political forums.

The show's first episode aired last night, and I might be biased, but I'm convinced it's a hit. However it fares, the viewing was an excuse to gather the crew and friends and family for a weekend at Adeline, much like our old brainstorming retreats when I was still at SNC.

"Look." Zully nudges me toward Grandpa Irving who is also watching the game from the sidelines. "He's trying to give her pointers."

I'm dubious about what Grandpa thinks is helpful, and sure enough, when I pay attention, he's leading her to hit her ball through an area that's out of legal bounds.

She can take care of herself, I know, but I can't help being protective. "Grandpa, quit trying to convince her to cheat."

Brystin looks up from the shot she was about to take. "Wait, what? Is that not part of the course?"

Grandpa shrugs, as though he's innocent, that devil. "The boundaries are vague."

"They're not *that* vague," I shout back.

"It's not going to give her any advantage to go that way anyway," Zully adds, which is what convinces Grandpa it's a losing strategy.

"Then the girl needs to stop being so soft," he says. "I've got money riding on this game."

Steele laughs from his lawn chair a few feet away. "You picked the wrong horse, Grandpa. Come on, baby! We're gonna take home the pot!"

If it comes to choosing sides between my grandfather and my brother, I'm definitely going with the former. Especially, since he's rooting for the love of my life. "Forget the hoop, honeybee. Go for her ball, and hit her out of play!"

"Who's winning?" Scott asks as he joins the watch party with his wife.

"Who cares?" Jessa zeroes in on the bundle in Tess's arms. "There's a baby in the vicinity. I can't even remember what we were talking about." She moves to hover over the two-month-old love bug. "Oh my goodness, he's adorable. What's his name?"

"Oliver," Tessa says, beaming.

It's sort of disgusting, particularly because every time I see her cooing over that damn thing, I can't help but picture Brystin cooing over a baby of our own. The caveman in me wants to throw away her birth control and make it happen now, though we've discussed and agreed that right now is the time to focus on her career.

"Ugh, he's so adorable, I want to puke." Jessa reaches for him. "Let me take that off your hands. I'm not at all sad that I didn't have children, but I'm really annoyed that I don't get to be a grandmother."

"You can be Nana to Ollie." Tess hands him over, despite the fact that she only met Jessa yesterday.

Much as I hate to be, I'm admittedly distracted by Jessa's attempts to get Oliver to smile, and next thing I know, Brystin is joining us, a defeated pout on her face. "I lost."

I slide my arm around her. "It's okay, honey. We'll poison Simone's wine later. Steele's too."

She leans into me, which makes me feel simultaneously gooey in places and hard in other places, every damn fucking time. "Why Steele? All he did was cheer her on."

"I'm sure there's some reason he deserves it." He's my brother, after all. I could easily make a list.

"Oh, hey." Jessa finally looks up from the baby to see that Brystin is here. "I meant to tell you I bumped into Michael the other day."

I cringe at the mention of his name. It's been four months since their divorce was finalized, and we've pretty much gone that long without mentioning him. He created some fun sexual tension for us in the early days, but the sex is just as hot without bringing him into our relationship.

Brystin is much more graceful at handling references to him than I am. "Really? Spill."

Jessa jumps on the chance to gossip. "He asked me out, believe it or not. I said no, obviously."

I'm an asshole, so I laugh. Michael deserves to be rejected by every woman for the rest of his life, as far as I'm concerned.

Brystin gives me a scolding nudge. "Why obviously? He's not marriage material, but he's really pretty decent in bed."

"I do not want to hear that." I wrap my arm tighter around her waist, a reminder that she's mine.

Jessa nods. "Oh, I remember, but have you seen him lately? He's losing his hair, and that man really needs to get back to the gym."

"Oh, this conversation just turned fun." I can't help it. I despise the guy. The best thing that came out of my, um, departure, as I prefer to call it, from SNC was that Adly came through and got the guy canned. "Is he still out of work?"

Brystin nudges me again. "*You're* out of work."

"By choice."

Speaking of which…

I survey the yard to find my sister. "Adly's finally alone."

Brystin pulls away from me in a not-so-subtle foreshadow of what she's about to say. "You should talk to her now."

"That's what I was thinking."

"And don't forget to mention Zully."

"I won't." Before I extricate myself from the group, I give Brystin a kiss that's probably far too intimate for public display, but I don't give a fuck what's appropriate, where Brystin is concerned.

"Oh, please," Jessa says while Scott insists we, "Get a room."

"Holt," Brystin scolds, but she loves it. She's practically glowing when I leave her to ambush my sister.

"Whatcha reading?" I ask, snagging a deck chair next to her.

"Smut," she says, without looking up from her book. Her tone suggests that she doesn't want to be bothered, and I quietly consider whether or not I should wait until I have her full attention.

She makes the decision for me when she sighs, puts down her book, and peers at me over her sunglasses. "What do you want, Holt?"

"I've decided what I want to do with my life." Besides Brystin. Repeatedly.

Adly's a supportive sister, even when I interrupt her reading, and she perks up. "Oh?"

"Bob Peterson has indicated he'd sell SHE for the right

price. I want to buy it." Without a job, I've spent the last six months focusing my entire life around Brystin, which gave me lots of time to learn more about the network. Me being me, I dug into all the available data and business reports, and I'm predicting SHE is on the verge of a big boom.

"That's a great idea," she says, but she's wary. "But do you really think you're the best person to helm a network for women?"

"No, I don't. Which is why I think you should buy it with me."

Her jaw literally drops. It shouldn't be such a surprising suggestion, particularly because she's so miserable being stuck in HR at SNC. Dad doesn't believe women should have the "real" jobs, so she has no chance of ever getting out of the role unless she leaves.

But I understand how daunting it is to walk away from the family empire. I knew I'd likely be fired when I pulled the stunt that I did, and part of me wishes I'd had the strength to resign before that happened, but I stuck it out, devoted until the very end.

She blinks behind her shades, her mind already in motion. "Co-CEOs?"

I shake my head. "You'll be CEO. I'll be Chief of Strategy. I already have a lead on a new show we could bring to the network."

She raises an eyebrow in question.

"Zully doing makeovers while she gives hairdresser style therapy. Brystin's idea, but I think it's got legs."

"Oh, it does." She's in, I can see it. She's planning the future right before my eyes. Except, "How will I afford it? I'm more than two years away from getting my trust fund."

Grandpa is a firm believer that young people aren't responsible with money, so all of our trust funds are off-limits until the ripe old age of thirty-six.

"We'll figure it out," I say. "Maybe work out a deal with Dad like Reid did with his father." It's a legitimate obstacle, and I know we'll need to chat about it a lot more, but not now because it's four o'clock, exactly. The time I instructed my staff to start serving champagne. "Later, though."

"Is it time?" she asks as I stand up. She's one of the only people who knows what this weekend's gathering is really about. "Are you nervous?"

"Not in the least. Come on."

I help her up, and together we walk to the higher deck where most everyone is already gathered. It takes a few minutes to get their attention, but when I have it, I call Brystin to my side.

"Last night, we all had the wonderful opportunity of watching the debut of *Real Talk,*" I say.

Everyone applauds, and I note Jessa's confusion, probably wondering why I didn't include her in the tribute, but this isn't about that. "That's not why I gathered everyone here this weekend, though."

Murmurs spread through the crowd as they try to figure out what I'm up to. Brystin gets it right away, and starts crying before I'm even on one knee.

As soon as I'm down, I hear gasps and a smattering of early applause as I pull the ring out of my pocket and place it on my woman's hand. "Brystin Shaw. I knew the first minute that I saw you that you were special. I tried to deny it so hard, it should have been obvious. I'm hardheaded, I guess, but I immediately loved you. I'm sorry it took me a minute to figure it out, but I know now. And when you say I do—*if* you say yes, that is—I'm never going to take my ring off because I want the whole world to know how I feel about you. Please say you'll do me the honor of becoming my wife, and I'll spend the rest of my life showing you that you're the most important thing in my world."

She's a blubbering mess, but she manages to squeak out a yes.

Then I pull her to my knee and kiss the fuck out of her, in front of everyone, I really don't give a damn who sees.

"You'll be a married woman for real this time," I promise her, quietly so just she can hear.

"Good thing," she teases. "'Cause I'm really into you, and I hear you have a thing for married women."

"No, honeybee," I say, giving her the brutal truth. "I only have a thing for *you*."

Want more Holt and Brystin? Sign up for my newsletter and you'll get instant access to a scene from their happily ever after.

Already a subscriber? Check your last or next newsletter for the link to my bonus material. Or resubscribe and the scene should be in your inbox in minutes.

Holt and Brystin have found their happy ending, but there are many more brutal billionaires in this world.

Up next—**Dirty Filthy Billionaire**

and **Brutal Secret**.

Chances are you'll see plenty of familiar characters and two more brutal alphaholes you'll hate to love.

Haven't read Tess and Scott's story yet?
Man in Charge introduces the world of the Sebastians and begins their love story.
Available in ebook, audiobook, and paperback now.

ALSO BY LAURELIN PAIGE

WONDERING WHAT TO READ NEXT? I CAN HELP!

Visit www.laurelinpaige.com for content warnings and a more detailed reading order.

Brutal Billionaires

Brutal Billionaire - a standalone (Holt Sebastian)

Dirty Filthy Billionaire - a novella (Steele Sebastian)

Brutal Secret - a standalone (Reid Sebastian)

The Dirty Universe

Dirty Duet (Donovan Kincaid)

Dirty Filthy Rich Men | Dirty Filthy Rich Love

Kincaid

Dirty Games Duet (Weston King)

Dirty Sexy Player | Dirty Sexy Games

Dirty Sweet Duet (Dylan Locke)

Sweet Liar | Sweet Fate

(Nate Sinclair) Dirty Filthy Fix (a spinoff novella)

Dirty Wild Trilogy (Cade Warren)

Wild Rebel | Wild War | Wild Heart

Man in Charge Duet

Man in Charge

Man in Love

Man for Me (a spinoff novella)

The Fixed Universe

Fixed Series (Hudson & Alayna)

Fixed on You | Found in You | Forever with You | Hudson | Fixed Forever

Found Duet (Gwen & JC) Free Me | Find Me

(Chandler & Genevieve) Chandler (a spinoff novel)

(Norma & Boyd) Falling Under You (a spinoff novella)

(Nate & Trish) Dirty Filthy Fix (a spinoff novella)

Slay Series (Celia & Edward)

Rivalry | Ruin | Revenge | Rising

(Gwen & JC) The Open Door (a spinoff novella)

(Camilla & Hendrix) Slash (a spinoff novella)

First and Last

First Touch | Last Kiss

Hollywood Standalones

One More Time

Close

Sex Symbol

Star Struck

Dating Season

Spring Fling | Summer Rebound | Fall Hard

Winter Bloom | Spring Fever | Summer Lovin

Also written with Kayti McGee under the name Laurelin McGee

Miss Match | Love Struck | MisTaken | Holiday for Hire

Written with Sierra Simone

Porn Star | Hot Cop

ABOUT LAURELIN PAIGE

With millions of books sold, Laurelin Paige is the NY Times, Wall Street Journal, and USA Today Bestselling Author of the Fixed Trilogy. She's a sucker for a good romance and gets giddy anytime there's kissing, much to the embarrassment of her three daughters. Her husband doesn't seem to complain, however. When she isn't reading or writing sexy stories, she's probably singing, watching shows like Billions and Succession or dreaming of Michael Fassbender. She's also a proud member of Mensa International though she doesn't do anything with the organization except use it as material for her bio.

www.laurelinpaige.com
laurelinpaigeauthor@gmail.com

Printed in the USA
CPSIA information can be obtained
at www.ICGtesting.com
CBHW021204190724
11674CB00005B/362